MILLEN

CHRIS NYST

First published in Australia by Aurora House
www.aurorahouse.com.au

This edition published 2022
Copyright © Chris Nyst 2022

Typesetting and e-book design: Prepress Plus | www.prepressplus.in
Cover Designer: Donika Mishineva | www.artofdonika.com

The right of Chris Nyst to be identified as Author of the Work has been asserted in accordance with the Copyright, Designs and Patents Act 1988.

ISBN number: 978-1-922697-67-7 (paperback)

 A catalogue record for this book is available from the National Library of Australia

Distributed by: Ingram Content: www.ingramcontent.com
Australia: phone +613 9765 4800 |
email lsiaustralia@ingramcontent.com
Milton Keynes UK: phone +44 (0)845 121 4567 |
email enquiries@ingramcontent.com
La Vergne, TN USA: phone +1 800 509 4156 |
email inquiry@lightningsource.com

Also by Chris Nyst

Cop This
Gone
Crook as Rookwood

Screenplays
Gettin' Square
Crooked Business

ONE

Rowdy McQuillan set his cold stubbie down gently on the flat, wooden arm of the squatters chair, slid his bum onto the canvas seat, slipped off his thongs, and rolled back comfortably. 1988 had been a real tough year, but it was all but over. Rowdy was back home again, and it felt good. Heaving his bare, gingery legs up onto the rests, he picked up the stubbie, poured a long draught of beer back into his throat, and gulped it straight down. Then he sucked in a lungful of air and breathed it out slowly. Life couldn't be sweeter.

The view from the veranda of Tom Wilson's squat little cottage on the outskirts of town was nothing too flash. Straight across the red, dusty road was a broad vacant block, sparsely dotted with tufts of grey grass and rusted-out car bodies. On either side of that was just more of the same, long-beaten little dumps like Tom's joint, all cracked paint and overgrown weeds, intermittently dotting both sides of Castle Street, all the way back to the centre of town.

Such as it was. Millengarra was no thriving hub. It wasn't much more than a fly-spot on the map of outback Queensland, with just two pubs, the town hall, a post office, cop shop and not too much more to speak of these days, all for the sake of the dwindling population of a tad under four hundred people. But Millengarra was the closest thing to home Rowdy knew, and it was still a whole lot more civilised than anything he'd seen in a long while. At least a bloke could get a cold beer in Millen. Right now, with his boots off, his arse out of the saddle, and not a single scraggy cow in sight, the view from Tom Wilson's veranda was all Rowdy needed.

He'd seen enough cattle to last him a lifetime. For the past eighteen months he'd hunted them, chased them, mustered them, driven them, yarded them, thrown them, hobbled and knackered them. But mostly he'd just plain followed them, through stinking heat and driving rain, thick, prickly mulga and dry, arid wasteland, up-hill and down dale, staring for hours on end at their bony, shit-streaked arseholes, and listening all day to their non-stop, mooed moaning, complaining about being herded to wherever they were supposed to be going. That's why drovers were called 'ringers,' Rowdy reckoned, because they spent all their days staring up the ugly ring of them cows. The view from Tom's Wilson's veranda was a definite improvement.

A distant sound took his attention, making him look up the road, into the hot-orange afternoon sunset, where a rumble of gravel and a cloud of dust was rapidly approaching. Rowdy could just make out the hazy silhouette of what looked like an old Holden ute, barrelling towards him on Castle Street, no doubt heading for town. No surprise. It was Friday afternoon after all, well after five, and the working week was all done and dusted. All the contractors, road workers, shearers, pickers, farmers and cow-cockies would be heading for town, looking to wash back the week with a couple of beers, a counter tea, and maybe a night on the town in Millen. Who could blame them?

Rowdy shaded his eyes and squinted into the sunlight. Was it anyone he knew? It looked like three people, maybe a bloke and two sheilas. But he couldn't see much looking into the sun, certainly no one he recognised at any rate, and the old ute looked pretty much the same as a thousand other farm bombs belting around the shire. He raised his hand in a perfunctory wave, just in case, then raised the bottle to his lips, tipped his head back again, and poured in another good guzzle.

'Rowdy.'

The utility had slid to a noisy stop on the gravelly road, ten metres or so past Tom Wilson's front door. When Rowdy looked up, he could see through the settling dust the shapely outline of a young woman, hanging half-way out the passenger window, waving one arm energetically in his direction.

'What are you doing in town, stranger?'

At first he hardly recognised her. Larnie Mitchell. It had been a long time, but she still looked as good as ever. With both breasts hitched up high, half-squashed against the window-frame, her skimpy blue top looked just about stretched to its limits, barely containing her perky, soft white bosom.

The very sight sparked a flood of memories and emotions that brought an embarrassed, involuntary flush to his face. He tried to disguise it as best he could with an awkward, self-conscious, toothy grin, as he pulled himself out of the chair, beer in hand, slipped on his thongs, and stepped down onto the footpath, ambling as casually as he could over to the idling car.

'G'day Larn. How're you going mate? Alright?'

'Yeah, good mate. Good.' She was looking him over, her face screwed into a familiar, knowing smirk, just like she used to do when he and his mates walked into the pub on a Friday night, in that evaluative way that always made him want to check his fly was done up. 'I heard you was out bush.'

'Yeah. Been working up Craigie Station the past year or so.' She nodded silently, in a contemplative fashion that made him feel obliged to offer a little more information. 'Done the dry season in the Top End before that. Up Nelson Downs.'

'Yeah?' She looked like she was still deliberating, trying to work out whether or not it was worth continuing the conversation.

'Hey Rowd. What's happening?'

Rowdy leaned on the car and bent forward, peering into the cabin, where he straight away recognised the smiling moon face of Jodie Lanham, all blonde hair and black roots, poking around Larnie's shoulder. And beyond her was the unmistakeable mullet of Mozzie Blane, slumped forward over the wheel, looking keen to get going wherever it was they were heading.

'Hey Jode. Moz. How're yez going, alright?'

'Yeah, good mate,' Jodie gushed cheerily, as Mozzie impatiently muttered back something more or less indecipherable, before turning his attention away to the road ahead of him. He didn't like Rowdy, never really had, and that was no secret. Fair enough, the feeling was mutual. In Rowdy's opinion, Mozzie was useless as tits on a bull.

'So how was the Top End?' Larnie was still eyeing him off with that half-smart smirk on her face.

'Yeah, not bad,' Rowdy nodded. 'Alright coin, ay. Nothing much to spend it on but.' He half-grinned, blushing awkwardly at his feeble attempt at levity, but Larnie just nodded back into the momentary silence, awaiting more information. 'So yeah,' he continued. 'It was good.'

'What are you doing back here then?' she shot back, staring him straight in the eye, the smirk now slowly disappearing. 'Had enough droving, have you?'

He had forgotten how crazy Larnie Mitchell could be, how uncomfortable she could make him feel when she wanted, and sometimes without even trying. There was something about her right now that unsettled him, more than those ruby red lips and perky white breasts; an intensity that seemed somehow sad, maybe angry, and even a little bit scary. Rowdy had known her most of his life, they were about the same age, practically grew up together, but when Larnie Mitchell looked into his eyes the way she was looking right now, he felt small, insignificant, and timid, like a scared little kid facing a stranger. What did she want from him?

'Yeah, maybe.' He was fumbling for words. 'For now, anyway, I s'pose. What about you? What you been up to?'

She was still staring blankly at him.

'Same old shit. You know Millen.'

Rowdy nodded silently in response. Yes, he knew Millen. They both did. He knew what it meant to him, and what it meant to her. She was born right there in the Millengarra Medical Centre. She grew up in town, went to the local kindy, and the state school, worked in her old man's paper-shop, chatted up the old blokes and charmed the old sheilas… She played up like a second-hand lawnmower, and generally gave cheek to everyone, especially the cockies like Rowdy McQuillan and his younger brothers, who rode into town from the outlying properties on horses and bikes, and on the tray of rusted old trucks, or packed in between hessian hay bales, stuffed in the back of their old man's ute. He remembered the games they played and the fun they had. Kids running wild through a town the size of a double-bed sheet, where everyone knew them, and nowhere was closed, or off-limits. And how things eventually changed—slowly, gradually, but surely, and permanently—how Millen itself seemed to shrink, turning from a playground into some kind of suffocating closet they'd suddenly found themselves locked in. He remembered the passions they'd hid from their parents, the secrets they'd shared, and the dreams they had whispered when no one was listening.

'Thought you'd be gone by now.'

The last of the smirk had now faded away from her face.

'Yeah, so did I.'

Larnie Mitchell was angry with him, he could see that. Disappointed he had come back to Millen, annoyed he hadn't kept going, like he promised to do, out of the country, into the city, off to the Big Smoke somewhere. She was disappointed in him. *What a joke.* At least he'd got out, if only temporarily, just to go droving, just for a while. But who was she to criticise him? Look at her, all tarted up like a two-bob trollop, still cruising around Millengarra in a beat-up old shit-heap with Mozzie the Mullet.

Jodie Lanham was no longer able to contain her natural enthusiasm, and forced her fat, smiling face around Larnie's shoulder, pushing her way into the conversation.

'We're heading down the Arms for a rumbie. You coming down?'

Larnie Mitchell sat back, looking miffed.

'Yeah, a bit later maybe. Just got into town. I told me Aunty Ada I'd drop in and say hello first.'

'Whatever,' Larnie huffed. 'Come on, Mozzie, let's go.'

Mozzie Blane wasn't waiting for a written invitation. The words were no sooner out of her mouth than the utility burst into action, spraying a new cloud of dust and gravel in every direction as Rowdy stepped back, covering his beer with one hand. As the wheels took traction, the utility rocketed off down the road, bouncing and squeaking in the general direction of the Millengarra Arms Hotel. Rowdy watched it go, waiting for the dust to settle around him, then eventually raised the bottle to his lips and sucked in another swallow. Good riddance.

What did she think, that he'd never come back? That was just stupid. Of course he'd come back. His family was here. His Aunty Ada and a couple of cousins still lived in town, his brothers were running the family property just an hour away, and his old man was up managing Castleton Station, less than two hundred clicks as the crow flies. This was his home. His whole life was here.

He'd got out, just like he always said he was going to. He'd spent three weeks in Brisbane, with hot and cold-running town water, full TV reception and the whole box and dice. He was crawling up the walls all day with nothing to do, drinking flash beer in bars where nobody knew him from Adam, chasing molls down the Valley at night, wishing every one of them was no one but Larnie, and walking the streets, hemmed in shoulder-to-shoulder like one of them miserable, moaning, bony, shit-streaked cows. The city was no place for Rowdy. The land was his life. He loved the country.

But not country towns. He'd long ago learned country towns were good for cold beer, a quick catch-up with mates, and not too much else. Stay too long in any small town and eventually it became a prison. A cloistered, mean-spirited place, where everyone knew everything about you, sometimes before you even knew it yourself. Full of gossip and lies, bad memories, and shameful secrets.

Country towns were bad news, especially for sheilas. Any sheila. They either married off quick and turned into the fat, dowdy housewives of thick-headed, ham-fisted farm-boys, or they hung around way too long, till the local dills were all telling dirty stories about them, and they became drunken old Dorries hanging out down the pub, dancing alone in front of the jukebox and flirting with the pissheads that propped up the public bar.

Larnie Mitchell was too good for that. Too good for any country town, and least of all Millengarra. She was the best-looking sort around, and funny and smart along with it, real smart; she knew everyone in town, had everyone dangling on a string. She was tough too, had plenty of ticker, could ride any horse with four legs, ride any bike, and drive any truck, car or tractor she had to. And she knew stuff, about people, and places, and things most people had hardly ever heard of. She wrote stories and poems Rowdy didn't even get half the time. But they meant plenty to her. In her head she lived in a world outside Millen, and she talked about going there, to places like Sydney and Melbourne, even joints overseas, like London and New York and Paris. Her dreams were too big, and she was too smart and too talented, for a country town anywhere. And she knew it.

Larnie Mitchell could run rings around anyone west of St George. From what Rowdy had seen of the mob down in Brisbane, probably anyone north, east or south of St George as well. He loved her for that, but sometimes he hated her for it as well. Larnie Mitchell was too good for Millen, and too good for a yokel like Rowdy McQuillan.

She needed to go. She'd talked about going so long Rowdy had had a fair gutful of it. She was the reason he took the Top End job in the first place; she was the one that convinced him if they both didn't get the hell out, they'd be worse than useless. So he did. He went a-droving, about as far out of town from Millen as a man could find himself, all the way out to the West, north to the Timor Sea, from Darwin across to the Gulf, and back down to the Big Smoke of Brisbane. He'd seen some of the stuff Australia had to offer—ocean beaches, flash beer and cold city streets. And now he'd come back. Back home to his family and friends. He was happy to be here. And he didn't need Larnie Mitchell calling him useless for doing it. Because—*guess what*—for all her big-noting talk and fancy ideas, she was still here as well, smack-bang in the middle of Millen. She never went anywhere.

Rowdy slowly eased back in his chair, still watching the red-tinted cloud gradually dissipating, all the way down the long stretch of Castle Street, down to the centre of town. Such as it was. He tipped back his head and poured in more beer, feeling every cold swallow washing away the bitter resentment caught in the back of his throat.

Larnie Mitchell was disappointed in him for being so weak, for crawling back to Millengarra, defeated. Another home-town hick with his tail tucked between his legs. *What a joke.* Who was she to talk? She'd never gone anywhere. She just talked big about what she was going to do. *Gunner Mitchell,* Rowdy reckoned she ought to be called. *Gunner go here, gunner go there.* But in the end, she never went anywhere. It was high time she did, before she turned into just another fat farmer's wife, or a barfly in front of the jukebox.

Larnie Mitchell needed to go.

•

A month later, Larnie was gone.

No one knew where, exactly. Her mates hadn't seen her, suddenly she wasn't in the pub of a weekend, she hadn't been home to her oldies' in weeks, or into the shop. Even Jodie Lanham was asking around. But no one had seen her in town. She was just gone, without saying anything to anyone, not even her mates. She'd just disappeared, into the ether.

By the time Lyall Mitchell dropped in at the station to report his only child missing, Larnie hadn't been heard from in more than ten days.

Of course, Police Constable Brian Ingles had heard plenty of talk around town long before that. In a small place like Millengarra, news travelled fast, and when one of the local kids took off, up north or down south, or off to the city somewhere, it was pretty much all people talked of. For a time, anyway. No one was ever particularly surprised, or excited. It was just something to chinwag about—through the back fence, over the phone, or down in the pub—a regular occurrence. Like in any country town, kids eventually grew up, looked around, and occasionally shot through.

Lyall Mitchell didn't seem worried when he dropped into the station. He just thought he should probably formally let the constable know what he had undoubtedly heard around and about anyway. That Larnie had shot through, and that she hadn't been heard from since.

The truth was Lyall's wife Sue had downright insisted he come down and lodge a report, because she was missing some of her jewellery, including a good drop pearl necklace her mother had left her when she passed away, and Larnie had always had her eyes on it, so Sue figured she probably snaffled it before she took off. Not that Lyall wanted any sort of stealing complaint lodged against Larnie or anything. His wife just wanted her jewellery back, and if that might help track Larnie down, that'd be good. But he definitely didn't want her charged with anything.

Constable Ingles could tell the local newsagent wasn't entirely at ease discussing such a sensitive matter with him. Could the policeman be trusted to do as Lyall was suggesting—show some common sense and discretion— or was he just as likely to go and put in a stealing complaint anyway?

Over the years, the locals had got used to having good old Bill Commerford as their local police sergeant, and they'd grown comfortable with him. Bill and his wife Faye were part of the community, and they knew how things worked in the country. But this new bloke was out from the city, not much more than a kid himself. A fresh-faced, junior constable who was still wet behind the ears, they reckoned. Could he be trusted?

Brian Ingles didn't care what the local yokels thought of him. They may not be thrilled to have him, but so what? He was none too happy himself about being stuck out in the middle of nowhere, in a one-man station back of Bourke, doing his country police service. So, as far as Brian could figure it, they were all going to have to just cop it sweet and make the best of a bad situation. He wasn't there to pander to their sensibilities; he was there to get the job done, in accordance with the law of the land and the directions of the Queensland Police Manual.

Constable Ingles recorded the detail of all items of personal property missing from the Mitchell residence, when and where they were last seen, and what, if anything, Lyall knew about Larnie having any of them in her possession at any stage. He also took a brief statement from Lyall Mitchell about his daughter's friends, her habits, movements, and living arrangements, and their most recent contact with her.

She still had a bedroom at home, where she kept most of her things, and where she was more than welcome anytime she saw fit. But Larnie was a spirited kid, with big ideas in her head, and for some reason she and her mother just naturally clashed. She was inclined to be insolent and answer back when she shouldn't. As a result, the two of them were at each other's throat the whole time.

So, over the past year or so, Larnie had started to occasionally stay out all night, stopping over at friends' places, and as time went on that happened more and more often, until eventually she was hardly ever home. She'd kept on at the newsagency though, until a couple of months back, when she and her mother had another almighty ding-dong at work, and Larnie just walked out. She hadn't been back to work since. She'd drop over home now and then, when she knew her mother was out, but other than that, so far as Lyall knew, she was just bunking down here and there with various mates around town. She told him she was getting the dole, but he still gave her a little bit of money now and then, just to help her get by.

The constable asked around town, spoke to a few of Larnie's friends, like Jodie Lanham and her mates, and the various other assorted drop-kicks they all hung around with down at the pub. He even got the police up on the Gove Peninsula to chase down Maurice Blane, who left a week or so earlier than Larnie to go work in the bauxite mines up there.

But they all said the same thing; no one had seen her, or heard anything from her, in weeks. For ages she'd been telling them all, as soon as she could she was going to hitch a ride down to Brisbane, to see if she could find a job in a shop in the city. The general consensus was she'd probably done just that. So, Brian Ingles checked with the bus companies out of St George, ran a scan on the state-wide crime indexes, requested contact updates from Social Security, and registered her on the missing persons database. Then he put her file in the cabinet and waited to hear. She'd turn up eventually. They always did.

For the next several weeks, the not-entirely-mysterious disappearance of Larnie Elizabeth Mitchell was all people talked of in the small country town of Millengarra. But then, out of the blue, they suddenly had something more serious to gossip about. Something unthinkably awful, infinitely more shocking and sinister. Something none of them would ever have thought could possibly happen in a nice little town like Millen.

TWO

Detective Senior Sergeant Dave Hocking was a very lucky man. The bullet had been fired at point blank range. It entered laterally, through the left front side of his abdomen, just under the costal margin, at a roughly fifteen degrees angle from right to left, exiting his back only centimetres from his spine. If the angle had been five degrees more acute it would have shattered his spinal column. If the entry point was three centimetres lower, it would have punctured his kidney; three centimetres higher and his liver would have been cleft in two, leading to massive blood loss, and likely death within a matter of minutes.

But none of that happened. As Dave Hocking's young GP, Dr Aaron Gill, scanned the hospital surgeon's operative notes, he quickly focused on its brief but concise summation: *The projectile missed the left lobe of the liver, and did not traverse the stomach, presumably because the patient had not eaten recently. The small bowel was not punctured. The path of the projectile was inferior to the transverse colon. The spleen was well superior and not involved.* It was all pretty clear and simple. The bullet had passed straight through him, without any major damage whatsoever.

'You're a very lucky man.'

'Yeah.' Dave Hocking's reply was not much more than a Neanderthal grunt. 'I'll be sure to grab a Casket ticket on my way to work.'

The doctor looked up from the notes, a thin smile forming on his lips. It faded quickly when he saw his patient's face. Hocking was in no joking mood, staring back with a blank, fatigued expression. It came as no surprise to his doctor; of late, Detective David Hocking had been through a pretty tough time.

'Okay,' Dr Gill announced, as cheerily as he could in current company. 'Let's get you up on the bed and have a look.'

His careful and meticulous inspection revealed pretty much what he expected in the circumstances. The laparotomy scar was well healed, the sixteen sutures removed without the slightest sign of any infection or other complication, and the patient had been left with nothing other than some minor discomfort on touch. Physically, Dave Hocking was perfectly fine.

'So how are you otherwise?'

Hocking was studying his fingers as he buttoned up his shirt, and didn't even bother to look up.

'I don't know, doc. You're the medico—you tell me.'

The young doctor nodded pensively, sat back down at his desk, and pulled out his pen.

'Overall, you look to be in pretty good shape to me.' He clicked his thumb down, and then pulled a writing pad across in front of him, preparing to put pen to paper. 'But I might just give you a certificate for a week or so sick leave.'

'Don't need it, thanks doc.'

Hocking was now on the move, a bundle of business, stuffing his shirt into his pants and buckling up his belt, looking in no mood to loiter any longer than absolutely necessary.

'Maybe not. But it won't do you any harm to take a little R and R.'

'Can't,' Hocking shot back, zipping up his fly. 'I'm due in Southport Court at ten.'

Aaron Gill looked him in the eye, laid his pen down on the desktop, then motioned to his patient to take a seat across from him, as if there was some bad news coming. As Dave Hocking tightly pulled his tie into a tidy knot around his neck and fidgeted it neatly into place, he eye-balled the doctor with a cautious mixture of bemusement and intrigue, before he eventually, reluctantly, pulled the chair out from the desk and sat down.

'You sleeping alright, Dave?'

Hocking rolled his head back and shifted uncomfortably in his chair. When he looked back at the doctor, he stared silently for several seconds, before finally responding.

'Occasionally.'

'What's that mean?'

'It means occasionally.'

David Hocking was a big, fit man, a strong, imposing figure with an iron will, and Dr Aaron Gill couldn't help reflecting, not for the first time, on how intimidating it would be for any hapless criminal to find himself in the Detective Senior Sergeant's considerable presence. But he also knew his patient's background and personal history. He could see the dark rings circling his eyes, and he was fully aware of the damaging psychological effect a traumatic, violent episode, like the shooting incident Hocking had recently been through, could potentially have on anyone.

'What's keeping you awake?'

He narrowed his eyes and stared down the doctor.

'Don't know,' he eventually said. 'The fact I can't sleep, I suppose.'

'Since the siege?'

'Yeah.'

Aaron Gill nodded silently, assessing the problem and tossing up the solution.

'Want me to organise some counselling for you?'

The patient's upper lip curled contemptuously as he snarled back at his doctor. In Hocking's opinion, counsellors, quacks and trick-cyclists were a waste of good space, nothing but highly paid mumbo-jumbologists paid to pander to hopeless sooks, and make up excuses for crooks, frauds and low-life malingerers.

'Fuck that shit.'

It was a predictable response, and the doctor just quietly nodded his acknowledgement, taking it all in his stride.

'It could help, you know. You might have a touch of PTSD.'

The detective scoffed audibly at the very suggestion.

'I'll live.'

But it wasn't as simple as that.

'How are things at home?'

The question stung him, his doctor could see that, but Hocking batted it back, straight-faced and devoid of emotion.

'Same as always.'

'Any news?'

Dave Hocking pursed his lips thoughtfully and gave a slight, barely perceptible shake of his head, staring into the empty space between them with that same blank, tired expression.

'Nuh.'

As far as Detective Sergeant Frank Vagianni could figure, the case against Holden Waldo Winchester was as tight as a drum. Winchester was an absolute flea, a known heroin addict and street-level dealer with a rap sheet as long as his arm, and Frank and the boys at the Gold Coast C. I. Branch had been glued to his clacker for months. But lately, he'd been popping up regularly on the Drug Squad's radar, and the intel was that Holden was starting to move up the rungs of the distribution ladder.

On the afternoon of the offence, the BCI boys had spotted him driving into the carpark of a South Brisbane pub, where he was observed to enter the front passenger compartment of a parked motor-vehicle they were surveilling, and have a short conversation with the driver, a male Asian person known to police and suspected of being a major distributor of imported narcotics throughout south-east Queensland. After several minutes, Winchester alighted from the vehicle, carrying what appeared to be a black or blue-coloured overnight bag, before returning to his own vehicle and departing the scene. Brisbane Police then followed him back to his residence at Burleigh Heads, on the Gold Coast, where he alighted from his vehicle, carrying what appeared to be the same overnight bag, and entered the residence.

That's where Frank came into it. Detective Senior Sergeant Dave Hocking of the Woolloongabba Criminal Investigation Branch had contacted him around 6.20 that night, to get in and make the pinch. All they needed Frank to do was get to a local JP as soon as possible and get him to issue a warrant for Winchester's house, bust in there, get hold of that overnight bag, and see what Holden had to say about its contents, and where they came from. Dave had stressed he didn't want Frank and the local coppers to blow Brisbane's cover so far as the surveillance of the Asian importer was concerned. For now, he just wanted it to look to Winchester like a chance raid by the local cops, out of the blue, and see what information he might cough up to save his own sorry skin.

Frank knew the drill. Dave Hocking was an experienced copper and a top operator, and he didn't have to spell it out to his old mate Frank. The equation was simple. No one was interested in Holden Waldo Winchester. He was small beer. Just a hopeless, fly-blown junkie running errands for the big boys, in return for a lick on the side. But he knew plenty, and he was vulnerable, like all junkies were.

Frank would go in, grab the overnight bag, which no doubt would be chock-full of goodies, then point out to Holden that, with that much heroin in his possession, and with his lamentable history of prior drug convictions, he would be looking at some serious gaol time. For starters, he'd be going straight into the Southport Watchhouse that night, and they both knew that was no fun for anyone, especially not junkies like him. He wouldn't be getting his fix tonight or tomorrow morning, and even when he could get in front of a Magistrate sometime tomorrow to ask for bail, the police would oppose his application and, with his form, including a couple of bail breaches if Frank remembered rightly, and facing a serious charge of possession of a commercial quantity of heroin, he was no living certainty of getting out on bail at all.

Of course, there were two sides to any story. So Frank would also explain to Holden that, on the other hand, if the heroin in that bag wasn't all his, if he was just holding some or all of it for someone else, and he was inclined to give them a name or two, just so they could check out his story, things could be different completely. Who knew, depending on what he could tell them, and how useful it was, there might not be any charge at all. If what he could tell them was useful enough, he might even find himself back home tonight, snug and warm in his own little beddy-byes. In fact, depending on just how helpful he wanted to be, someone might even let him souvenir a tiny taste from the overnight bag before he left, just as a nightcap to tide him over till the morning.

Holden would sing like a nightingale. No junkie could turn down an offer like that, and certainly not Holden Waldo Winchester. He'd start with some bullshit story about whose junk it was and where he got it, and then eventually, after they leaned on him a little and time slowly dragged on, with him getting more and more strung out as it did, sitting around fidgeting and scratching, waiting for his hit, he would finally come up with the truth. Then they would really start talking, until Frank eventually ended up with a useful informant, and Dave Hocking maybe even jagged himself a witness for the prosecution.

That was how it was supposed to go down, how it should have turned out. Unfortunately, that's not what happened.

Frank and his offsider, Detective Constable Brad Killen, had just left the home of Frank's good mate Mick Farr, when the bad news came over the radio. Mick ran a hire car joint just south of Surfers Paradise, and he had his JP qualifications, so he was always happy to swear out a warrant whenever

Frank needed one. So Frank and young Killen were armed-up with a warrant to enter and search Holden's house and were well on their way to go kick his door down, when the Communication Room radioed the news—an ambulance had been called to Holden's residence for a medical emergency.

The detail came through in bits and pieces as Frank and Killen sped to the scene, siren sounding and blue light activated. An unidentified female had rung through on triple-o, panicking, claiming a man had overdosed on heroin at the house. He had lost consciousness and the female didn't think he was breathing; somebody needed to get there immediately. She wouldn't give a name—his or hers— or any phone number, and she wouldn't say if there was anyone else at the residence. She screamed hysterically, hung up the phone, and had not called back. Meanwhile, an ambulance was now on its way, and uniformed police had been notified. When Frank got through to Dave, the Brisbane police were just entering the premises.

By the time Frank and Killen got to the scene, Holden was sitting bolt upright on the lounge room floor, looking around wide-eyed, like he'd just fallen asleep in front of the telly and rolled off the couch. He was surrounded by ambos, a couple of uniforms, and the Brisbane coppers, Dave Hocking and his partner Steve Leyland, who quickly filled Frank in on what had happened.

When the ambulance officers arrived, Holden was in the house alone, lying on the lounge room floor, out like a light, in serious overdose territory. So the ambos hit him with a jab of Narcan. Frank knew exactly what that meant; he had seen it done before. A quick intravenous injection of Narcan—aka Naloxone Hydrochloride—reversed the effects of a drug like morphine or heroin like flicking a light-switch. Within a matter of minutes, a comatose, zapped-out junkie with his eyes rolled back in his head and slag dribbling out of his mouth would be suddenly sitting up, bright-eyed and bushy-tailed, as if nothing had happened. In fact, the reversal effect of Narcan was so complete on an overdosed addict, most of them would then start going into instant withdrawals, as if they hadn't had a hit in days. As Frank followed Dave into the kitchen, he could already see a pained expression beginning to settle on Holden's miserable dial.

There on the kitchen table was a navy-blue sports bag, the outside of it dusted with traces of a cream-coloured powder. Frank had a pretty good idea what it was. But whatever it might be, the dust on the bag was all that was left. When the uniforms arrived at the house they found the empty sports bag on the floor in the bathroom, next to the toilet bowl, as if someone—probably the girl who rang the triple-o emergency line—had just flushed the contents straight down the dunny. Whether she did, or she jacked it all up, or took it with her, the dust was all that remained.

But it was enough to charge Holden with possession of a dangerous drug. As it turned out, once the remnants were all brushed together from inside and outside the bag, they amounted to nearly a gram of high-grade heroin. The Scenes of Crimes boys were unable to lift any usable prints from either of the two picks found on the lounge room floor, but the fact that Holden had earlier been seen in possession of a bag matching the description of the sports bag, coupled with his medical condition as diagnosed by the ambulance officers, was enough to tie him to the bag and its contents.

And just to put the connection safely beyond doubt, Detectives Vagianni and Killen recalled a quick conversation they'd managed to have with the suspect later, back at the hospital, wherein he'd admitted the bag and contents were his, and they had faithfully recorded the details of that conversation in their official police notebooks.

It wasn't much of a charge, as it turned out—not enough to convince the Magistrate to refuse Winchester bail. But, with his long history of prior criminal convictions, if he was ultimately convicted, even of the relatively minor charge of possession of a gram of heroin, he was likely to be going inside, if only for a couple of months. So the pressure was on. For a junkie like him, a couple of months without hammer would feel like a lifetime. And that meant, if Frank and Dave could jag a guilty verdict, Holden would soon be itching—literally—to do whatever deal he could with the police.

It was simple; all the detectives had to do was convince a magistrate Winchester was in possession of the smack in that bag. And so far as Frank could figure it, the case was an absolute, iron-clad, lay-down misère. For the life of him, he couldn't understand why Holden hadn't just put his hand up and pleaded guilty on day one and got it over and done with. Now, three months later, it was listed for a summary trial that day, in the Southport Magistrates Court, and Frank still couldn't work out why Winchester was insisting on defending the charge.

That was until he found out who Holden Waldo Winchester's lawyer was.

As Dave Hocking pulled into the bitumen car park at the back of the Southport Courthouse that morning, for court at ten, he could see Frankie Box standing outside the red brick police building, in a huddle with his protégé, young Bradley Killen, laying down the law in animated fashion. Detective Sergeant Francesco Vagianni—better known to his police mates as just plain Frankie Box—was the tough, nuggetty son of an Italian canefarmer, raised in North Queensland, a good, staunch, no-nonsense copper who didn't let too much rattle him. But, before he even killed the ignition, Dave could see something had got right up Frankie's nose this morning.

'G'day Box,' Hocking called, as he stepped out of the car.

Vagianni was already striding toward him, waving both hands in exasperation.

'Do you know who that little grub's got for a mouthpiece?'

'Who's that?'

'The biggest arsehole on two legs, that's who.'

•

'If it pleases Your Worship, my name is Moran, initials EC, solicitor. I appear for the defendant.'

The truth was it didn't please His Worship Arthur Oldfield—Southport's Chief Stipendiary Magistrate—one bit, and they both knew it. As far as Arthur was concerned, Edwin C Moran was a bumptious, self-opinionated upstart, and any time the young defence solicitor appeared before him in his court, Arthur invariably found himself dragged into some bothersome and time-consuming side-show. No court case was simple with Moran. He always took every point available, and argued everything up hill and down dale, all day long, until the cows came home. So no, it did not please His Worship Arthur Oldfield. But proper court procedure dictated that each party must thus announce their appearance at the commencement of proceedings; and while, in Arthur's view, Eddie Moran was perilously short on court decorum, there was no doubt he was more than up to speed with court procedure.

'Yes,' His Worship growled perfunctorily. 'What's happening with this matter this morning?'

'We're ready to go, Your Worship.'

As usual, Moran looked like an unmade bed. His hair was standing up and poking out in various directions, as if it hadn't seen a comb in weeks at least. His skinny tie was insolently askew, and his crumpled suit was crying out for a good iron. But, as always, none of that seemed to in any way diminish the young man's invariable, irritating air of smug superiority and arrogance. Without so much as Arthur's imprimatur, he had already slumped back into his chair, alongside his client at the bar-table, and was leaning forward, hunched over his notepad, furiously scribbling out his opening argument. He was ready to go.

With other lawyers, there was always at least an outside chance that, at the eleventh hour, on the day of trial, after the reality of things had finally hit home, and after careful explanation by his lawyer, the defendant would finally see the futility of his position, and good sense would ultimately prevail. Usually there'd be some sort of last-minute negotiations or discussions with the prosecutor, some attempt to find some sort of middle ground, perhaps even some agreement on a lesser charge. But not with Edwin C Moran. He was ready to go.

Dave Hocking had never seen Moran before, but already he didn't think too much of him. He was a long, tall streak of misery, all spindly arms and gangly legs, and he looked to Dave more like some sort of a punk rocker than any lawyer Dave had ever seen. All lawyers had their head stuck up their arse, of course, but even from where he was sitting alongside the police prosecutor Mick Millane at the other end of the bar table, it was obvious to Dave this bloke had absolutely massive tickets on himself. Which was exactly what Frankie Box had reckoned.

According to Frank, Eddie Moran was the youngest boy of old Digby Moran, who ran pubs in Sydney for years, and ended up in Queensland in the late '70s, running some show on the Gold Coast. Dave had met the old man when he was down in Sydney on extradition jobs a couple of times; he was a good bloke, and always looked after the coppers down there. But Dave could tell, just from looking at Eddie Moran, Digby's youngest lad was a thorough disappointment.

Frankie Box had apparently run up against him in court plenty of times, including in the McCabe kidnapping trial a few years back in Sydney, which was a big deal at the time. By all accounts Moran played up like an unregistered dog in that one and caused some real embarrassment for the coppers. Nearly six years later, Frank—and plenty of other blokes as well—were still spewing big time over it. That much was crystal clear from the tirade Frank had unleashed earlier that morning; he hated this character Moran.

But there was more. The way Frank had carried on before court earlier that morning and judging by the scrum he was packing with young Killen in the carpark when Dave first arrived, he was more than a little gun-shy of him too. And just looking at Moran from the other end of the bar-table, Dave could see why. There was something about the young lawyer that had trouble written all over him, in big, bold print.

'Very well, Sergeant,' Arthur Oldfield mumbled. 'Call your first witness.'

With that, Sergeant Mick Millane put one hand on the bar table, and propped himself up into a half-standing position.

'Your Worship, I wonder if Senior Sergeant Hocking could remain at the bar-table to assist me in the proceedings.'

It was a reasonable, and quite usual, request. While best practice dictated that all witnesses should leave and remain out of earshot of the courtroom during any hearing, things were generally more relaxed in the Magistrates' jurisdiction, particularly in Southport. Here it was quite common for an arresting officer, or another uncontroversial police officer witness, to sit beside the prosecutor throughout the proceedings, to lend him assistance, communicating instructions, organising witnesses and running whatever errands might be necessary.

'No, I object,' Moran barked from bar table, without even standing up. 'He's a witness. I want him out.'

Moran didn't say another word. He hardly even looked up from his notes. Arthur Oldfield curled his lip and stared down at him from the bench cantankerously, but the lawyer just kept scribbling notes, studiously avoiding any eye contact. Eventually, His Worship grunted something to the prosecutor, who turned apologetically to Dave Hocking.

Within minutes, Dave was sitting on a row of seats outside the courtroom, alongside Frank Vagianni, Brad Killen and Steve Leyland, feeling like a recalcitrant, cheap drunk, who had just been unceremoniously thrown out of a public bar.

As they sat there silently, waiting to be called into the fray, Vagianni leaned in close to Hocking, speaking to him sotto voce.

'We're not going with the admissions.'

Hocking turned to look at him, his face twisted incredulously.

'What?'

Vagianni bounced up from his seat, and with a flick of his head motioned out through the glass doors towards the front landing of the courthouse. They walked together to the top of the stairs, before Frank turned back to face him.

'I talked to Killen. He doesn't want to go with the admissions. He's shitting big ones.'

Vagianni was telling him his partner Killen didn't want to give evidence of the conversation they both had claimed they'd had with Holden Winchester at the hospital, in which Holden allegedly made admissions to them that the sports bag and its contents were all his. Both of them had made a very detailed—and remarkably consistent—note of the conversation in their respective police notebooks, and until this very moment there had never been a single, solitary suggestion either one of them would do otherwise than give evidence of that conversation entirely in accordance with the contents of their notebooks. Hocking could see this wasn't just about Killen. Frankie Box was looking genuinely spooked.

'Frank, the admissions are the strongest evidence we've got.'

Vagianni couldn't look him in the eye. He'd been a cop for more than fifteen years, always stood firm, shoulder to shoulder with his mates. But times had changed. He lowered his balding head slowly, looking embarrassed and ashamed. When he looked back up at Dave Hocking, his eyes were glistening with emotion.

'I don't trust this bastard, Dave.' He was talking about Moran, Dave could see that. He had known Frankie Box for the best part of ten years, and he'd never seen him take a backward step to anyone. But for some reason, this lawyer really had him rattled. *Why?* 'Moran's a loose cannon, mate, I'm telling you. If he gets any sort of a sniff, he's just as likely to go to the Inquiry.'

For eighteen months now the Commission of Inquiry headed up by the Brisbane QC Tony Fitzgerald had been filling newspapers and television screens with sensational revelations of deep-seated corruption in the Queensland Police Force, all the way from the top right down through the ranks. It had started with Queensland's worst-kept secret, the so-called 'Joke' the Licencing Branch boys had been running for as long as anyone could remember, a corrupt police protection racket that took filthy lucre from the SP bookies, pros and sly-grog merchants to keep the piss, punt and pussy on the streets. Who cared about that shit anyway? But then the Fitzgerald Inquiry started shining a torch into darker corners, lifting the carpet on police involvement in illegal drug deals, bribery, extortion, and arson, and eventually even perjury and fabricating evidence.

Of course, a few lawyers took the opportunity to slip the boot in, and the journos soon forgot how much they all liked to lay a quiet bet with their local SP now and then and get a sly drink or a root when they wanted one. But mostly all the dirt was coming from the cops themselves. From the day the former Assistant Commissioner of Police rolled over and tipped a bucketful of rotten fish-heads over all his Licencing Branch mates to save himself, the 'thin blue line' had folded like a deck of cards, with once-staunch coppers lining up, queuing in the streets to dog on each other. No one trusted anyone anymore, and everyone was looking over his shoulder. It was embarrassing.

So that was what was rattling Frankie Box.

'Sniff of what, Frank?' In times like these, some uppity, half-smart lawyer making waves could cause a lot of trouble for a copper. 'Did he make the admissions or didn't he?'

Frank looked him in the eye. They'd known each other way too long, been through too much together, to start bullshitting to each other now.

'What do you reckon?'

They both knew the answer to that question. A few months ago, it wouldn't have mattered. Dave wouldn't have even asked the question. But he could see why Frankie might be nervous now.

'Frank, we need to pin this Winchester bloke. He's the key to everything.'

'Yeah, but Killen's just a kid, mate.' He was looking Dave straight in the eye, almost pleading with him. Vagianni was a good cop, staunch as they came. Dave could see he didn't want to let the team down. But he was right; Killen was just fresh out of uniform, and who knew how he'd shape up if a drop-kick like Moran put him under any pressure in the witness box? 'He's my corroborator and he's got himself a bad case of the Hail Marys.'

It was a dangerous situation without doubt. Killen was Frank's partner, and they had gone to the hospital together. If Winchester made admissions to Frank, Killen should be able to corroborate them, and if he didn't—if he told the court he didn't hear any such admissions made—that would leave Frank's balls flapping in the wind.

But, on the other side of the ledger, if Holden Winchester walked on this charge, the police would have nothing over him, and not a snowball's chance in hell of convincing him to help them wrap a brief around the Asian heroin distributor.

'If Winchester walks, we're back to square one with the Chow.'

'Fuck the Chow.' Suddenly there was a tinge of desperation in Vagianni's gravelly voice, one that Dave had never heard before. 'It's not worth the risk, mate.' He moved in closer to his old friend, lowering his voice almost to a whisper. 'Listen, it's none of my business. Okay? You're as good a copper as I ever knew.' He hesitated, almost too embarrassed to go on. 'But everybody knows you've got Internals up your arse about that missing money.' Hocking stared straight at him, a cruel glare in his eyes. Vagianni was right again —it was none of his business. 'The thing is, mate, they've been sniffing around me too lately, trying to re-open that whole Waterworld thing.'

Dave was disappointed to hear it. Waterworld was old news, and everyone figured it was dead and buried long ago. No doubt the Fitzgerald Inquiry investigators had dug it up. A couple of years back some junior female constable had claimed Frank and a few of his detective mates had temporarily borrowed some of the proceeds of the Waterworld armed robbery from the exhibit room, to back a rank outsider that came home for them at around ten to one.

They all denied it of course, and there was no money missing, so it all died down pretty quickly. The consensus was, even if it was true, it was a pretty ballsy effort, with no harm done. But now, by the sound of things, it had all jumped up again to bite poor old Frank on the arse. He was a good little bloke, and he didn't deserve that kind of drama.

'We've got to keep our heads down Dave, both of us. That's just the way it is these days. If a prick like that Moran manages to pin us, even on a shitty little verbal of a pissant grub like Holden Winchester, we're fucked mate. It'll go straight to the Inquiry, and they'll run with it for sure.'

•

Suddenly the Winchester case wasn't looking quite as airtight as it had done. But it was still pretty good, so far as Dave Hocking could see. The police still had Holden in possession of the bag earlier in the night, they had him overdosed on heroin not much later, and they had the bag itself, with a gram of heroin in it, lying on the floor of his bathroom. The consensus was they could all be pretty confident that was more than enough to convince a hard old head like Arthur Oldfield.

Dave figured his evidence would be pretty simple, straightforward and uncontroversial. On the night in question, he was carrying out police duties with Detective Constable Steven Leyland, in relation to an unrelated matter, in the street where Winchester's residence was located. While positioned at a location approximately forty metres from the front of the residence, he saw Winchester's Toyota sedan pull into the driveway, whereupon he observed him alight from the vehicle, carrying a dark blue overnight bag, and enter the residence.

He thought nothing of it at the time. But, approximately fifteen minutes later, he was still in the same approximate position, dealing with the same unrelated matter, when an ambulance arrived at the scene, with emergency lights activated and siren sounding, and pulled into the driveway of Winchester's residence, coming to a stop behind the Toyota. He then saw two Queensland Ambulance Service officers alight from the ambulance and proceed, in an apparently urgent fashion, into the residence. At that time, it was clearly evident to him that an emergent situation was developing, so he and Leyland immediately proceeded to the residence to lend whatever assistance they could to the ambulance officers in attendance there.

When they entered, they saw the defendant lying prostate on the lounge room floor being attended to by the Queensland Ambulance Service personnel, who advised he had suffered an apparent narcotics overdose. Upon being so advised, Dave immediately radioed local police for their assistance.

And that was it. He didn't speak to the defendant. He didn't locate any drugs; he didn't even lay his eyes on them. He wasn't present when the defendant made any statement to anybody, and he couldn't provide any other evidence to advance the prosecution case in any way. Pretty simple really. Dave reckoned he'd be in an out of court in no time flat. It didn't quite work out that way.

Moran's initial foray quickly set the tone for what would follow.

'What were you doing in that street?' he opened, as he was still climbing to his feet to start his cross-examination.

'As I said, I was on duty with Detective Constable Leyland, dealing with an unrelated matter.'

'What matter?' the lawyer instantly shot back, staring intently at the witness.

'We were surveilling a suspect.'

'Who?'

'Not the defendant.'

'I didn't ask you who it wasn't. I asked you who it was.'

Holden Winchester's obstreperous young lawyer was obviously more than a little bit half-smart, and he was clearly trying to unsettle Detective Senior Constable Dave Hocking, get under his skin. But Dave had given evidence more times than this young bloke had had hot breakfasts, and he didn't ruffle easily. He could play this game all day.

'That's confidential.'

'Why?'

'I told you, it's an unrelated matter.'

'A totally unrelated matter?'

'That's right.'

'Nothing to do with this defendant?'

'Absolutely nothing.'

Moran pulled the lectern closer to him and leaned forward over it, staring at the witness like a cowboy in an old-time movie. Then he screwed his face into a comically incredulous expression.

'Are you serious?'

Dave Hocking felt like climbing out of the witness box, walking over to the bar table, and giving this shithead a good cuff across the ear. But he resisted the temptation, and just offered him a dead bat.

'Yes.'

'You just happened to be outside the defendant's house at the crucial moment?'

'That's right.'

'Pure luck?'

'Yeah. Pure luck.'

'That's a bit fortuitous, isn't it?'

'You could say that.'

They were eyeballing each other with obvious intent. The battle lines now drawn, the lanky lawyer straightened up, curled his lips into a disbelieving pout, and shook his head derisively.

'So this was just a total coincidence, was it?'

'That's right.'

'Are you serious, Detective?'

He was sneering impudently at the witness, taunting him, but Hocking wasn't going to get sucked in.

'Yeah.'

'By some curious quirk of fate, you just happened to be in the exact right place at the exact right time?'

'That's right.'

'You're not serious, are you?'

'Yes I am.'

'You can't be.'

'Well, I am.'

'You can't possibly be, Detective, surely.'

'I am.'

'You can't be.'

It went on, back and forth, entirely unproductively, in the same snide fashion, for several more tedious seconds before His Worship Arthur Oldfield had finally had enough.

'Mr Moran,' he bellowed, so loudly Dave was mildly startled, and the lawyer immediately fell silent, cocking his head at an irreverent angle in the direction of the bench. Oldfield snarled back at him, loudly breathing out his obvious frustration, then turned to the witness. 'I take it, Senior Sergeant Hocking, you contend that if you were to answer Mr Moran's question you would seriously compromise an unrelated and ongoing police investigation, and you therefore seek to claim privilege on the ground of Crown Immunity.'

'Yeah,' he eventually responded, somewhat tentatively at first. 'Yeah, that's right.'

'Granted,' Oldfield barked testily, turning back to the lawyer. 'Move on, Mr Moran.'

Hocking felt a warm sense of smug self-satisfaction at the sight of young Moran getting so unceremoniously slapped down by the crotchety old magistrate. But the pure joy of the moment didn't last. Instead of moving on as he had been directed, Moran straightened up defiantly, and addressed the bench with righteous indignation stirring in his voice.

'Well, with respect,' he protested, not really sounding too respectful at all. 'May I be heard on the point before Your Worship summarily rules against me?'

Arthur Oldfield had been the Chief Magistrate at Southport ever since anyone could remember. He started as a counter-jumper in the old Court of Petty Sessions, and when he was first transferred to the Gold Coast, there was only one beak on the bench at Southport, and that was him. He ruled the roost, and he ruled it with an iron fist. The Southport court was Arthur's court, and in Arthur's court you did as you were told. Play up in Arthur's court and you went straight out on your ear, or to the cells. Sure, some things had changed—Southport was busier these days, there were more lawyers around and Arthur had got more staff, including a deputy magistrate to back him up—but one thing hadn't changed. This was still his court, and in Arthur's court what Arthur said was law.

Of course, this young lawyer was just another ring-in, a Johnny-come-lately, fresh out of law school, and no doubt he didn't know any of that. But Hocking did, so the moment he heard Moran trying to stand the old bloke up, he held his breath, gleefully awaiting the explosion that would surely come.

To his surprise, it didn't. Instead, Oldfield just dropped his head into his hands and let out a long and evidently painful groan. Then he slowly shook his head wearily, and eventually looked up at Moran.

'Mr Moran,' he growled. 'I'll listen to your argument, because I have to.' Hocking was shocked. He had been in Oldfield's court a hundred times, and he'd never seen him sit back and cop anything like this, ever. But the words were no sooner off old Arthur's lips than Moran immediately started shuffling his papers into place, preparing to launch into his argument, as if he had anticipated the response. As he did, Oldfield grumbled on irascibly, but to no effect. 'But I can tell you now, I have no sympathy for your position, and I think you'll be wasting both your time and mine to take the matter any further.'

Of course he was, but that didn't seem to slow Moran down in the slightest. He proceeded to lay out to Oldfield a careful and well-structured submission on the law of Crown Immunity, and its inapplicability to the facts at hand, supported by a long list of decided cases, including High Court and even Privy Council judgements. As Hocking watched and listened to the young man prattling on, wasting his breath preaching to the curmudgeonly King Arthur, who merely moaned and rolled his eyes impatiently, he began to feel a rising sense of precisely what was spooking Frankie Box. This kid wasn't just making this stuff up as he went along. He'd sussed it all carefully in advance. He'd figured something wasn't right about their story, that the cops were somehow covering something up, so he had come prepared with a careful plan, and a well-thought-out argument, with High Court authority to back it up, to ambush Dave about the bogus claim he had just happened to be in the neighbourhood when Holden Winchester OD'ed at the house.

Of course, none of it was of any moment, and it was never going to get him anywhere with a hard nut like Arthur Oldfield. But a smart-arse kid like this had real potential to be very dangerous.

'Yes, thank you.' Oldfield snapped angrily when the lawyer finally sat down. 'I don't need to hear from you, Sergeant. I rule against you, Mr Moran. Now move on.'

So that was how it started, and from there Eddie Moran's cross-examination of Detective Senior Sergeant Hocking resumed, in the same obnoxious and infuriating fashion, from one nit-picking point onto the next, each seemingly more vacuous than the last. He challenged Hocking's identification of Winchester as the person he saw taking the bag into the house because there had been no recourse to a photographic line-up. He asserted the witness's description of the bag as 'an overnight bag' was inconsistent with the nomenclature given by other police to the 'sports bag' in which the drugs were ultimately located, then became nothing short of fixated on whether said bag was black, or blue, or some other different colour altogether. He robustly questioned the Detective Senior Sergeant as to why he entered Winchester's residence without a warrant, or any invitation or authority from the occupier, and by what authority he purported to in turn invite the local police to come into the house, again without permission from the occupier. And then he wrapped it all up with a long and detailed application to the magistrate for an order to exclude all evidence of items located and seized by the police inside the residence, including of course the offending bag—overnight or sports—and the drugs they found therein, on the ground the police had entered and searched the residence without lawful authorisation, and therefore illegally, giving rise to the exercise of a judicial discretion to exclude the evidence on the ground that it had been unlawfully obtained.

Predictably, Arthur Oldfield ultimately dismissed the application. But not without a nervous flutter. Dave could see it worried the old bloke. Moran was quoting binding superior court authority to him, and comparative cases where appeal courts had criticised magistrates' refusals to exclude evidence on similar grounds.

There was a time when Arthur wouldn't have cared. He didn't give a square root what the bigwigs up in George Street had to say. In Southport, Arthur's Law applied. But things were changing. After two solid years of daily headlines in the papers about revelations coming thick and fast out of the Fitzgerald Inquiry, and bleating about systemic incompetence and corruption in high places, everyone was nervous, even Arthur Oldfield.

By the time Frank Vagianni got into the witness box, it was nearly midday, whereupon the same annoying circus sideshow carried on unabated, with Moran taking every pernickety point that he could think of and wringing every ounce of goodness he could get from it, which mostly wasn't much.

Now they had dropped off the admissions, Frank didn't really have too much to say, but Moran kept at him anyway, cajoling and berating him about everything and anything he could. He did the same thing in sequence with Killen, Leyland, and both of the ambos, so by the time the prosecutor closed his case mid-afternoon, everyone in the courtroom was a frazzled ball of stressful exasperation, not least of all His Worship Arthur Oldfield.

And that was when Moran made his big play. Instead of opening the defence case and calling to the stand his client Holden Winchester—who anyone could see was always going to be an absolute disaster in the witness box—he closed his case without calling a single word of evidence from anyone, and submitted to Oldfield that, on the evidence adduced by the prosecution, he couldn't possibly be satisfied beyond a reasonable doubt that Winchester was in possession of the drugs found in the bag.

Once upon a time that one would have splashed off Arthur Oldfield like water off a duck's back. But today, things looked decidedly less certain. Before the detectives in attendance knew it, to their growing horror, the magistrate was sitting up, listening intently, and scratching notes into his notebook.

Moran was arguing the only evidence capable of connecting Winchester to the bag in which the drugs were found was the purported incidental observation by a detective from fifty metres away, at night, in a poorly lit location, of a man carrying a bag, variously referred to as an overnight bag or a sports bag, entering the residence. None of the witnesses could say whether there was another bag fitting that description in the house that night, nor could they say whether any other people, and if so, how many, came and went. The house had a rear entrance, through which anyone could have exited, and it was a known fact that at least one other person—the female who called triple-O—was at the house at the time Holden Winchester overdosed. She at least had left the house without police seeing her, and others may have also. Even if one could infer that Winchester ingested heroin at the house that night—which Moran did not concede—one could never be satisfied beyond reasonable doubt that Winchester, as opposed to some other person, brought the bag, and the heroin in it, to the house that night. The charge as particularised was that Winchester was in possession of the drug found in the bag, but there was simply no evidence whatsoever that either the bag, or any of the drug found in it, was ever under the dominion or control of Holden Waldo Winchester.

It sounded sort of right, even to Dave Hocking, and Arthur Oldfield SM almost looked like he was buying it. Dave didn't like the look of it one bit.

•

When Frank Vagianni saw Dave off in the courthouse carpark after court adjourned that afternoon, the little bloke looked embarrassed and ashamed. They both knew why. From the day they first pulled on the uniform, they'd both been taught good cops stand firm together, shoulder to shoulder, to put the bad guys behind bars. Maybe sometimes some rules had to get bent a little in the process, but a good cop did exactly what was needed. And he never let his mates down. Ever.

Frank's admissions would have got the Winchester case across the line. But now, with nothing else to tie him to that bag, Holden Winchester had well and truly flown the coop, and Dave Hocking had nothing and no one to help him sheet the heroin back to his distributor.

'I'm sorry, mate.'

Frank finally looked him in the eye, and sheepishly offered him his hand.

'Forget it, Frank.' Dave grasped it firmly and shook. 'Winchester'll keep.'

He didn't blame Frankie. Not one bit. Frank Vagianni was a good copper, as loyal and staunch as they came. And he was dead right—no one could afford to take chances these days. That was just the way it was, and whoever's fault it was, it wasn't Frank's.

As he watched Frank and the others climb into their unmarked car and cruise out of the car park, Dave laid one hand onto his side, caressing the mild discomfort that was pulsing gently at the site of his wound. He'd been a copper more than thirty years. He'd been kicked, pushed and punched by drunks and dropkicks maybe a hundred times throughout his working life, hit across the scone on two occasions with a cricket bat and once with a steel rake. He'd been abused, threatened and spat on. One lunatic had even tried to run him over. But in thirty years, Dave had never once been shot before. This was a first.

Things were changing, Dave could see that. And, so far as he could figure it, something was seriously wrong when a half-smart kid fresh out of law school could put the frighteners through a tough, committed cop like Frank Vagianni, and pull the wool over the eyes of a hard old head like Arthur Oldfield. So, Holden Waldo Winchester had walked free, and the chance to lock away a major drug distributor had gone begging. The bad guys had won.

Without even knowing how he got there, Dave found himself sitting in the front seat of his car, his wallet open on his lap, holding a small, dog-eared, colour photograph in both his hands. Absently, gradually, he ran one thumb along the photo's edge, staring at the image of a smiling face. A happy, beautiful young girl with her whole life ahead of her. As the silent seconds passed, sitting alone in the deserted carpark, Dave felt a dull ache gathering in his chest, and a bitter lump tickling painfully at the back of his throat.

He slipped the photograph back into his wallet, pushed it deep into his pocket, and kicked over the ignition.

THREE

The Saturday night disco at the Millen pub wasn't exactly a fancy, top-level turn-out, but on a Saturday night it was the only show in town. Barry Wallace played the records, and did a fair to middling job of it. They had flashing lights and all the bells and whistles, and usually pretty much everyone turned up, once the public bar was closed.

Mason and Jenny Deeds liked going to the disco on a Saturday night, because it was their chance to catch up with a few people their own age. These days, it felt like they were just so busy—between working, and the little one, and all the things that needed done around the place—they never seemed to run into any of their old mates anymore. So, whenever they could, they always made the effort to get down to the disco on a Saturday night. Jenny loved to dance and meet up with her girlfriends on the dance floor, and even Mason—once he'd had himself enough of a skinful to get up on the floor—fancied himself as a bit of a flash, John Travolta type. So, as usual on a Saturday night, the Deeds had an early counter tea with Jenny's parents, then parked the little one with the oldies, on agistment for the night, and went upstairs to kick their heels up at the disco and feel like kids again.

Which is what they did. Especially Mason, as it turned out. When they first got up there it was pretty quiet, so they just sat around, catching up with a few friends over beers. But as the night went on, it got more and more crowded, and at ten o'clock a few of Mason's single mates came up from the public bar. Then, around ten thirty, Ross and Lindy Lewis came in too, with Rowdy McQuillan. Mason and Jenny had seen them earlier in the night, downstairs, having dinner together in the beer garden. Even then, Rowdy looked like he had a thirst on, throwing beers back at a rate of knots. But that wasn't unusual these days. Ever since he'd come back from droving up the Channel Country, Rowdy had been drinking way too much. And by the time he came upstairs with Ross and Lindy, he was obviously as full as a goog.

Naturally, he latched himself straight onto Mason like a long-lost friend. Which they were, of course. Rowdy and Mason had known each other all their lives, grew up in the bush together, riding horses and motorbikes around the scrub, fishing, shooting, playing up, and generally piss-fart-arsing around the place, getting up to no good with their yahoo mates. Jenny liked Rowdy McQuillan a lot, she always had. But he was single, and he drank way too much, and at the Millen pub on a Saturday night, he could be a bad influence on her husband.

It was when Rowdy arrived that Mason switched to drinking rum. That was good at first, because it gave him a little bit of Dutch courage, which meant Jenny was able to get him up and dance with her. But the more rum he drank, the more he fancied himself as a regular little Michael Jackson out there on the dancefloor, and the more he fancied himself, the more rum he drank.

Eventually he was all over the place, dancing with all the single girls, including Jodie Lanham and her slaggy mates, and making a complete dill of himself. Rowdy McQuillan was up there with him of course, bouncing around, all gangly arms and legs, lairising like the big galoot he was, a glass of rum in one hand, and the other waving wildly in the air like he was still out on muster.

The more Jenny watched the two of them up there, playing the fool, bouncing up and down, guffawing like idiots, and bumping into everyone, right, left and centre, the more she began to feel just a little miffed with the cringeworthy antics of her wayward husband. Then, when he started dancing his drunken, down-and-dirty version of *'the bump'* with Jodie Lanham, she had finally had enough, and she quickly set out in a beeline, straight for Mason.

But just before she got there, Jenny suddenly found herself swept up in the arms of the laughing, staggering cowboy, Rowdy, who was now twirling her around him in a swirling circle, howling out a long, soulful wail, like a desert dingo on a moonlit outback night. As she spun around him on the dancefloor, immersed in the kaleidoscope of flashing lights, looking at the lanky, howling cowboy in his silly, drunken stupor, she couldn't help but laugh. And the more she laughed, the more it made her laugh, remembering the old days, playing silly buggers on the dancefloor with Big Rowdy. She loved him, and she loved this town.

By the time Ross Lewis rescued Rowdy from the dancefloor, Mason Deeds and his missus were locked together in a smouldering clinch, shuffling romantically together while everyone around them bounced and bopped to the booming beat of Wham. Meanwhile, Rowdy McQuillan had been reduced to dancing with himself, and was now spinning around erratically in a dizzying circle and starting to tilt dangerously off beam. Rusty caught a hold of him just as he looked set to finally career off uncontrollably into the crowd around him, and he quickly steered the big cowboy back in the direction of their table, where Lindy was gathering up her handbag, saying her good-nights, and swallowing down the last of her drink.

'Lindy and me are calling it a night, mate,' Ross yelled into Rowdy's ear as they walked a crooked line back to the table. 'You want a lift home?'

The big man grunted and nodded simultaneously, without actually uttering a single word, and was soon gathering up his smokes and loose change from the table-top, and stuffing them into his pockets, before he fell in silently behind his friends and followed them submissively down the stairs, and out into the carpark. As usual this time of year, the night air had a cold, refreshing bite to it, and Ross was pleased to see his big mate already walking a straighter line by the time the three of them set out across the gravel carpark, heading for his dual cab pickup.

'G'day Rosco.'

Neville Staffield was sauntering the other way with a bird on either side of him, and Ross knew immediately where he had likely been, and what he no doubt had been up to. Staffield owned the local video store, and ever since his wife walked out on him and took the two kids with her, he'd been living in the attached flat out back of his store, where most weekends he liked to host an intimate little video party with whatever strays he could muster who were silly enough, and/or desperate enough, to want to sit with him through a couple of his latest, new-release movies on video, over cheddar cheese and cheap cask sheila- wine, in the loungeroom of his pokey little flat.

Neville considered himself a veritable patron of the arts and fancied his weekend blockbuster video soirees as the closest thing Millengarra had to a meeting of the 'wine and cheese set'. Ross had always thought of Neville as a complete wanker, but in a town as quiet as Millen it paid to stay on the good side of the local video store owner.

So, Ross and Lindy Lewis exchanged pleasantries with Neville as he introduced the ladies that he had in tow. They were both relatively new in town, but Lindy had previously met the older one at the local hospital. Elaine Barlow was a forty-something-year-old nursing sister, a divorcee who had been living on her own in Millen for the best part of a year, and Ross could instantly see, from the way Neville was fussing over her, he figured he had some sort of a chance of getting in her pants. The other girl was much younger than both of them, and introduced herself as Karen Millard, a primary school teacher, recently transferred up from Brisbane to complete her country service.

As the chit-chat flowed gregariously back and forth between them, Rowdy McQuillan was propped against the pickup truck, nodding silently and staring at the two women as if trying to work out if he knew them. Karen could feel his eyes all over her as she politely batted back Lindy Lewis's cheery banter, and when she was finally introduced to him, she shook his big hand tentatively, and as briefly as she could. He was obviously extremely drunk, and his very presence made her feel timid and uncomfortable.

By the time the girls started running low on idle chatter, Rowdy had begun nodding off like a bobble-head toy, which offered Ross the perfect opportunity to call stumps on the conversation and announce their departure, bundling his big mate into the back seat, and saying their goodbyes. As Lindy drove them out of the carpark, the last they saw of Neville and his lady friends was as they headed out on Colkers Lane in the direction of Karen's house, up on the other side of Castle Street, walking her home. Neville was all over the old sheila, grinning like a Cheshire cat and looking like he figured he was going like a champion.

Meanwhile, Rowdy had suddenly come back to life a bit, and was now slumped forward in his seat with his big, boof head poking in between them, asking dopey questions about Karen—who she was, what she did, how long she'd been in Millengarra. Of course, she'd just finished telling them all that two minutes earlier, and if he'd had his brain in gear he would already know the answer to every question he was asking. But Ross was more than happy to oblige him, and repeat it all back again, in the hope of keeping his friend wide awake for the five or six minutes it would take to drive him home. The last thing he wanted to be doing, at this hour of the night, was lugging a big, sleeping ape like Rowdy McQuillan out of the back seat of his truck.

As it turned out, Rowdy was still awake and still asking silly questions when they eventually pulled up outside Tom Wilson's house, where he was staying. Tom's car was in the driveway, and there was a light on somewhere in the house, so Ross figured he was home, still up and about. He hadn't seen Tom at the pub that night and wondered why he hadn't come along with Rowdy like he usually did. He'd probably spent the night down at the Empire, playing pool.

As Rowdy lumbered his way out of the back seat, he thanked them profusely for the lift home, and then swung the back door shut and leaned untidily in through the front window, saying something soppy to Lindy about what good mates they were, and how much he appreciated everything they did for him, and then insisted on giving her a long hug good night, before they finally got rid of him, and he turned away clumsily and lurched off in a wobbly walk across the road towards the front stairs of the house.

Lindy pulled back onto the bitumen, heading for home. They'd been at the Arms since just after seven, and it had been a long night for both of them.

'Shit,' she said, looking wearily at her wristwatch. 'It's just turned midnight.'

•

By the time Neville Staffield and his friends got back to Karen Millard's place it was close to ten past twelve. Neville reckoned he and Elaine Barlow were getting along together like a house on fire, so when young Karen invited them to come in for a nightcap, Neville jumped at the chance. A few more leg-openers wouldn't do his chances any harm at all, and Karen may as well be paying for the grog. After all, the two women had already downed nearly a full cask of his best wine; it must be just about her shout by now. They'd have a couple of quick ones on Karen, then Neville would walk Elaine home, and by that time, with the few more wines under her belt and a refreshing walk in the brisk night air, he'd be nothing but a living certainty to get the invitation in to stay the night.

Neville was a tad surprised when the young schoolteacher brought out a platter of pâté and crackers, and what looked to Neville like a pretty fancy bottle of red, with a proper cork and everything, along with three actual long-stemmed wine glasses. So naturally he went to some lengths pretending to recognise the label on the bottle, even though he didn't, and talking up the vintage, about which he actually had absolutely no idea. Then he poured, for the ladies first, of course, and then himself, then sniffed in the aroma from his glass and took a mouthful, which he swirled dramatically before swallowing it down with sumptuous appreciation.

'So, ladies, what did you think of *Top Gun*? Fantastic, isn't it?'

Truth be told, the latest Tom Cruise movie, which had featured as the main attraction at Neville's home video party that night, wasn't really Karen's cup of tea. But still, out of courtesy, she said whatever nice things she could think of, all of which Neville gushingly agreed with. Elaine, on the other hand, who by then had already drained most of her first glass, wasn't quite so complementary.

'It's a cheesy kids' show,' she slurred dismissively. 'Whenever the planes are on the ground, all you get is puerile, adolescent crap.'

Naturally, Neville instantly agreed with that as well, while still endeavouring to salvage what little face he could by talking up the counterbalancing redeeming features of the film. Unfortunately, Elaine wasn't having any of it, and between swallows of red wine she launched herself into a robust dissertation on the artistic weaknesses of what she disparagingly referred to as the film's 'paper-thin plot and mindless gibberish passed off as dialogue.'

It all went steadily downhill from there, with Neville trying to retrieve the situation by acknowledging and agreeing with every point she made, but sheepishly offering a possible alternative each time, none of which Elaine was willing to concede. The longer the increasingly one-sided discussion dragged on, and the more red wine Elaine Barlow washed back in the process, the more uncomfortable things started to become, until Karen was eventually searching quite desperately for a way to switch the conversation to another subject as diplomatically as possible.

Suddenly, she gasped audibly, and recoiled in her chair, as if in abject horror. She was gazing wide-eyed, one hand clasped to her mouth, pointing with her other, out through the sliding glass door at something in the front yard of her house.

'Oh shit!' Elaine half-shrieked, as she leapt out of her chair, red wine spraying out across the coffee table and her glass scuttling onto the floor. 'Shit! Fuck, who's that? Who's out there?'

By the time Neville got to his feet and turned to look at whatever the two women were staring at, whimpering with such obvious alarm, his heart was already pumping painfully in his chest and his whole body was on full alert. As he peered out through the glass, into the inky blackness of the outback night, it took a moment for his vision to adjust. Then it gradually came into sight—the tall, rangy figure of a naked man, standing still, ominous, alone in the shadows, a featureless phantom, frozen in the night.

'Who is that? Who the fuck is it?'

'I don't know. I can't see him properly. I don't know who it is.'

'Then get out there and find out. Get rid of him.'

Neville glanced across at Elaine, his face pale and drawn with fear. But she was looking back at him cruelly, insistently, her whole demeanour demanding he take action. Beside her, the young schoolteacher was sobbing like a little child, the fingertips of both her hands pressed frantically against her face.

'We've got to call the police,' he stammered. 'Where's your phone?'

'There's no phone on here,' Karen Millard sobbed pathetically.

Neville had always been a coward, and he felt nauseous now at the prospect of a confrontation with the eerie bogeyman that was lurking out there in the darkness. But when he looked back at Elaine, she was snarling at him, her teeth bared in contempt.

'Get out there and get rid of him.'

There was no option. Neville was the only man in the house; it was up to him to do something. He had no choice. He reached down, took hold of the wine bottle by the neck, and sucked in a deep breath of fortifying oxygen. As he stepped out through the doorway onto the front porch, he called out to the naked statue in a shaky voice.

'Hey. What are you doing there?'

The spectre turned its head to face him, black, hollow eyes fixed on him intently.

'What are you doing? Piss off. Go on, get out of here.'

The man did nothing, said nothing, just stood there motionless, staring passively. Eventually, Neville called again.

'Go on, mate, get out of here. Piss off.'

Neville Staffield had now stepped down off the porch, into the front yard. As the women inside watched him, frozen in anticipation, they could see him inching closer, by tiny increments, towards the tall dark figure, step by step. Each time he called out, the figure stayed completely still, unresponsive, and each time Neville paused expectantly, waiting for a moment, then took another cautious step in the direction of the naked man.

They could hear the video-store man calling out, eventually less stridently and loudly, and then eventually speaking, saying something they couldn't make out, as he drew ever closer to the frozen man. The closer he came, the more Neville seemed to relax, until eventually he was within arms' reach of the mysterious figure, his hand holding the wine bottle now hanging down casually and comfortably by his side. He stood there for what seemed a long time, as Elaine strained her eyes to see what he was doing, standing alongside the tall naked figure in the darkness. It looked like he was talking to him, saying something, but the tall man still stood frozen solid, staring back at him intently, without the slightest movement.

Eventually, Elaine saw Neville reach out, tentatively, as if about to touch a tiger's tail. Suddenly, the statue exploded, wildly flailing his long and muscular arms at Neville, who immediately staggered backwards several frantic steps before he fell down heavily onto his buttocks, dropping the bottle, and half-crawling and half-dragging himself backwards like a panicked rock lizard trying feverishly to claw itself to safety. As he did, the big man followed him, grabbing at him, arms gyrating, snarling and spitting, grunting guttural, incoherent sounds, so loud Elaine could hear them clearly from inside the lounge room. This was a madman unleashed, unhinged and uncontrollable, viciously attacking like a rabid dog.

Suddenly, Neville managed to somehow scramble to his feet, and Elaine immediately dashed for the front door, ready to lock it firmly behind him as soon as he got safely back inside the house. But, to her surprise and dismay, Neville didn't run back to the house. He turned and sprinted off down Castle Street, deep into the darkness, back in the direction of the Millengarra Arms. The two women in the house were now totally alone.

The mystery man in the front yard straightened up to his full height and looked straight towards Elaine standing at the still-open front door of the house. Slowly, vacantly, he began lumbering in her direction. Elaine leapt through the doorway into the house, and slammed the door behind her, fumbling with the latch to lock it. Meanwhile, Karen could now see the fearsome figure closing on the house and had started wailing loudly in her fear and panic. Elaine turned and lunged at her, grabbing both her shoulders and shaking her forcefully.

'Stop it. Stop it.' She was staring straight into the younger woman's tear-filled eyes. 'We've got to get out of here. Now. Is there a back door?'

Karen nodded breathlessly. 'At the side. Into the carport.'

'Where are your car keys?'

'There.'

As Elaine snatched the car keys from the kitchen bench and frantically clutched at her young friend's arm, dragging her physically behind her, she heard a loud slapping sound behind her, which made her half-turn momentarily, to see the wild man from the corner of her eye, his deranged face up against the sliding door, one huge hand clawing at the glass. Her companion's scream was ringing in her ears as she hauled her through the kitchen, into a short hallway, where she saw the side door to the carport. Elaine stopped immediately, pinned her young friend back up against the wall, and jammed her hand over her mouth, muffling all sound. Then she looked straight into her eyes, intently, shaking her head, until Karen stopped making any sound at all. When she was silent, Elaine took her hand away, held her finger to her lips, and shook her head again. As soon as Karen nodded her acknowledgement, Elaine turned and wrenched the side door open.

They were instantly out in the carport, on either side of Karen's car, Elaine feverishly unlocking the driver's door, as quietly as she could, then sliding swiftly onto the front seat and leaning over to unlock the other side. Once in, they pressed the buttons down on all the doors, keeping their eyes pinned to the front corner of the house, hoping, praying, no one would appear.

As she turned the key in the ignition, Elaine held her breath. The starter motor turned over several times, then droned to a stop. Elaine's heart leapt into her mouth, the blood rushing frantically in her ears, as she took hold of the key again and flicked it over. The starter motor turned powerfully, then turned again, and again, and again, before it finally stopped. Now emotion flooded into Elaine's panicked face, and she felt her chin trembling uncontrollably, as an involuntary whimper began seeping anaemically from her passenger's trembling lips. Elaine wrapped her hand around the keys and flicked the switch again.

The engine finally kicked over. She desperately pushed the gearstick into place, but just as she did, a terrifying vision suddenly burst into view from behind the front corner of the house. Elaine Barlow was face-to-face with the long, lanky naked man, sprawled across the right front fender of the car, his big bony hands pawing clumsily on the bonnet. He looked into her eyes with a dazed, vacant expression, and she recognised him immediately. It was the drunken cowboy Neville Staffield had introduced her to, back in the hotel car park.

Elaine put her foot down. As the engine roared and the car careered out of the carport, bouncing erratically across the driveway and out onto the street, she saw the man's big body sliding helplessly off onto the sparse grass of the front yard. She didn't slow down for a second to see what happened to him, she just kept her foot down, speeding back towards town. As they hurtled their way down Castle Street, she quickly clutched at the headlights switch, flicking on the lights, then jammed her hand back onto the steering wheel, gripping it with all her strength, the only way she could control the trembling that was coursing through the whole of her body.

As she drove, she began to make out, up ahead, far away in the yellow light boring deep into the darkness, the figure of another man, all alone, trundling aimlessly in the same direction. The car slid to a dusty stop on the gravel alongside the forlorn, dishevelled figure of Neville Staffield, as Elaine Barlow brutally wrestled down the window and snarled out angrily at her erstwhile escort.

'You fucking arsehole, Neville.'

The video-man looked thoroughly defeated, his fat, flabby chin trembling pathetically.

'That was Rowdy McQuillan.'

'Yeah, I know. We're going to the cops. Get in.'

FOUR

There was only one cop in Millengarra, and Police Constable 1/C Brian Ingles was it. So when the police house bell rang, at precisely 12:21 AM, Brian was the only one around to answer it. Of course he was a bit cranky being woken up at that hour of the morning, but it came with the territory; sadly, he was getting used to it. Saturday was the night when all the shearers, cow cockies, and assorted yahoos came to town from far and wide to blow off a bit of steam, and it was a rare weekend when someone didn't play up like a two-bob watch and end up in the cells behind the station.

But Brian was surprised to hear this time it was big Rowdy McQuillan who had been kicking up a ruckus. From the little bit Brian had seen of him, Rowdy was normally a pretty level-headed young bloke. He liked a drink or two, but he mostly stayed well out of strife.

The two women filing the complaint were pretty shook up, without a doubt, but that was nothing compared to the state of Neville Staffield. The video store owner dissolved into tears the second Brian took his notebook out to take down the particulars of what happened, and from there Neville continued blubbering so badly, and carried on so much, the policeman eventually decided it was best to just leave him with a cup of hot tea and a biscuit at the front desk, while he got what information he needed from the ladies.

As it turned out Karen Millard was just barely holding it all together herself, but Elaine Barlow was a different kettle of fish entirely. She was focused and clearheaded, and she stepped Brian through the story methodically, giving him a blow-by-blow description of the whole event, such emotion as she did occasionally display bottled up and efficiently set aside, so she could get on with the story.

Her complaint, as it came out, didn't exactly sound to Brian like the Crime of the Century; a drunken local getting all his gear off and gallivanting round the town in the wee, small hours of the morning was hardly a unique event in Millengarra on a Saturday night. But as Elaine told the tale, dispassionately and in all the detail she could, Brian Ingles could see that whatever had happened out there in the dark up on Castle Street earlier that night had seriously disturbed the tough, experienced, emergency-ward nursing sister.

'He was gone,' she said eventually, staring blankly, a shaky quaver tickling her voice. 'You could see it in his eyes.' She unclasped her hands and watched a tiny tremble take control of them, then wrapped them tightly back together, and looked him straight in the eyes. 'He was out to kill us all.'

It sounded a little bit dramatic to Brian but, just as a precaution, he took the paddy wagon and did a run down past the Arms Hotel, where Barlow said she had first seen Rowdy earlier in the night. The whole show down at the Arms looked pretty much closed down for the night, and the few stragglers still lingering out front of the pub all looked pretty harmless and subdued. There had been no trouble there, so far as any of them knew or had heard about, and no one had seen Rowdy McQuillan in hours. Brian nodded, suggested they all get off home, and then continued on his way, watching in the rear-view mirror as they climbed into their trucks and utes, cradling their home supplies of beer and spirits.

If that had happened back in Brisbane, he'd have gone back and made them all blow in the bag. But this wasn't Brisbane; it was the bush. Brian had been told the rules. He was a county copper now, and things were done differently out bush.

He cruised on down to the so-called centre of town. It always had a still and eerie feel to it this time of the morning, a single intersection bathed in yellow light flooding from the old town hall, casting long and lonely shadows that made dark places all around. There was something strangely bleak about that intersection once the pubs had shut down for the night and the town had gone off to sleep; it always made Brian feel a tad uneasy. It was an empty, silent place, and he didn't like it.

Sometimes, when he found himself out on that intersection in the early hours on a moonless night like this, he felt like a marooned man, adrift and all alone in a dark and endless ocean. Beyond the buildings, the straight road out of town stretched far ahead, into the inky blackness of the outback night. It felt good to swing the truck around and head back the other way.

Once he got back past the Arms, he took a right turn into King Street, and cruised up past the squat fibro cottages on both sides of the road. There was a dim porch light on here and there, dotted with the usual three-ring circus of moths and other winged insects, but otherwise no life anywhere. The town looked well and truly bunked down for the night.

He slowed, and gradually idled to a stop, winding down the window, looking and listening for anything out of the ordinary. There was just silence and still, sombre night. Up ahead, he could see a dim light flickering on the sign out on the footpath in front of the Starlight Motel. Still no sight or sound of anyone or anything. Brian slipped the engine into gear and moved on. Finally, as he got closer to the intersection, as always, Lance Williams' old bluey, Roger, started up an unconvincing series of half-hearted yelps, before Brian swung the truck left into Haley Road and headed up towards Castle Street. Haley Road was even quieter than King Street—no lights, no noises, nothing.

As soon as he got out onto Castle Street the constable could already see, well up ahead, on the right-hand side of the street, a dull, yellow light glow on the front porch of Tom Wilson's house. There was only a smattering of houses anywhere on the whole length of Castle Street, and the others were all now in complete darkness, so Tom Wilson's porch light was pretty much all Brian Ingles could see anywhere in the street. As he got closer to the house, he made out Tom's station wagon parked in the driveway out front, and what looked like another light on, somewhere inside the house.

When he reached the driveway, Brian Ingles swung the paddy wagon in, pulled up behind Tom Wilson's car, and got out. As his boots crunched on the gravel, in the truck's headlights he could see the car was still loaded with Wilson's work gear—paint tins, rollers, and canvas drop-sheets—as if he'd just got home from a job. Then Brian stepped from the driveway to the front of the house.

The first thing he noticed was the front door, wide open, with just the screen door shut. Then he saw the state of the glass sliding door. It was smashed, with glass spread all over the front porch. Instinctively, Brian lifted his right hand slowly to his waist, and placed it gently on the butt of his service revolver.

'Tom?' he called tentatively. There was no response. 'Tom? Are you there, mate? It's Brian Ingles.'

There was still no sound anywhere. Brian stood still for a moment, looking and listening. Then he moved a little closer, cautiously, peering through the doorway, trying to see into the house. The light on inside was coming from the kitchen, but he couldn't see anyone in there.

'Rowdy? You in there?'

Everything was still and silent, not a sound. He looked back at the front door. When he did, he noticed something out of place. There was a mark on it, a small, dark-brown smear, what looked like an untidy scuff mark, at the centre of the door; and now, on the yellow metal handle, he could see just the suggestion of a faint crimson smudge. He looked down at the porch; there were several tiny, dark-brown spots flecked across the dirty grey cement. Were they paint spots? Or had there been violence here? Was that blood smeared on the door? A dark, uneasy feeling began gathering in his chest. Brian unclipped his holster and drew out his revolver.

'Tom? Rowdy?'

If either of them was in there, neither one was answering. Brian waited, breathing deeply, both hands wrapped around his revolver. Even if that was blood on the door, they'd probably just had some sort of drunken dust-up, and maybe they were both inside, passed out, choked down on the piss. But Brian couldn't quite dislodge the nervous fluttering in his chest. He was all alone out here, his nearest backup hours away. He wasn't taking any silly chances. He breathed in deeply, and breathed out, trying to calm himself, to remember his training, think carefully what he should do next. The first thing was to find out if anyone was in the house, before he ventured inside.

He moved stealthily to the side of the house, descending immediately into deep darkness, penetrated only by thin remnants of light that were managing to reach through from the kitchen, down the hallway, and out through the bedroom windows. He immediately saw the sliding aluminium-framed window of the first bedroom had been smashed in, just like the front sliding door. Brian looked in to where the light creeping from the kitchen down the hallway was half-illuminating a cramped and untidy bedroom, with an unmade bed, and clothes scattered across the floor. There was no one in there.

He moved on, further from the front of the house and deeper into darkness, to a second bedroom window. Like the first, the glass was shattered, from the outside in, and the flyscreen was radically bent out of shape. He peered in, but this bedroom was much darker, further from the kitchen, with only dim reflections of light limping into it.

At first, he could see only vague, unidentifiable shapes, ill-defined forms with no detail whatsoever. But as his eyes gradually adjusted to the interior gloom, he was able to make out a double bed, close to the wall. Like the one in the first bedroom, it was unmade, with its coverings dragged untidily to one side. Just below the pillow closest to the wall, on the light-coloured surface of the sheet, he could see what looked like a dark, maybe shiny, object, a piece of clothing perhaps, or a patch, or something similar.

Then, at the foot of the bed, his eyes were able to distinguish something else, something oddly out of place, a large bag maybe, or a pile of clothes. Or was it something else, something more sinister? Gradually, a clearer outline began forming in the shadows, and Brian suddenly realised what it was.

Someone was lying there, flat on their back, on the floor at the foot of the bed. He could just make out a pair of naked feet, glistening with what looked like some sort of oily moisture. For several seconds he stood totally still at the window, hardly breathing, staring in at the inert, dark object frozen there in the blackness. Then the full realisation suddenly hit him like a hammer.

Brian Ingles darted from the bedroom window, quickly skirting around the rest of the house, checking every window, peering in, alert, listening, satisfying himself as best could that no one was there. When he got back to the front door, he stopped, set himself, and then stepped forward slowly, his gun in both hands at arms-length in front of him. When he got to the screen door, he nudged it open slightly with the gun barrel, jammed in one boot and kicked it open completely, stepping briskly and decisively into the house.

'Police,' he barked, as loudly and forcefully as he could, frantically scanning the lounge-dining area and into the kitchen. 'I am armed, and I will fire on you if necessary. If you are anywhere in this house, come out into the lounge room now, slowly, and with both arms raised above your head where they can be clearly seen.'

Brian's heart was racing as he stared down the narrow hallway towards the dark end of the house. He remained motionless, poised and alert in the lounge room for several long seconds, his gun trained intently on the end of the hallway, waiting, watching and listening. Nothing. Eventually, he began moving forward, slowly and deliberately, step-by-step down the hallway.

As he reached the first doorway, on his left, he kicked the door open, quickly scanning the laundry area. The tiled floor was shimmering with some sort of liquid. Where was it coming from? He moved on quickly, his boots squelching on heavy, wet carpet underfoot as he reached the next doorway, into the first bedroom on his right. Again, he scanned it quickly and efficiently, then moved on to a narrow toilet, on his left, where again a glimmering liquid was pooled on the shiny tiled floor, as it was in the bathroom adjacent, where Brian could hear water trickling from somewhere. He didn't wait to find out where. He moved on to the second bedroom, on his right.

As soon as Brian Ingles looked into the second bedroom, his fears were immediately confirmed. The light sneaking into the room over his shoulder was enough to make out a human body lying deathly still on the floor in the blackness at the end of the bed. He could just make out the outline of a naked arm stretched out on either side, lifeless hands turned palms-up at a curious angle, and further down the long toes of two naked feet, propped up on their heels, protruding into the air. In the darkness, Brian frantically swiped at the wall alongside him with one hand, fumbling for a light switch. When he finally found it, and flicked the light on, he wasn't prepared for what he saw.

Tom Wilson was naked, except for a skimpy pair of black-red-soaked underpants. Every part of his body was bathed in a wet, oily film of shiny red blood that seemed to have exploded all over him, spraying out over the foot of his bed, up onto the walls around him, and over the ceiling. The wall closest to where his head should have been looked like someone had spray-painted it a deep, lumpy crimson colour. Tom's face was all gone.

Later, Brian Ingles would not recall precisely how he got back out to the front of the house. He would simply remember being there, in the darkness, bent over in the front yard, both hands on his knees, dry retching violently, then sucking in deep breaths of air through his mouth and his nostrils, desperately trying to dispel the acrid smell of fresh blood from his airways.

When he eventually regained his composure, he went to the paddy wagon and sat in the front seat for several minutes, breathing deeply, re-gathering, recovering, working out what to do next. This was his first homicide, and he was all on his own; he had to make sure he followed procedure, got things exactly right. He lifted the receiver and radioed through to the CI Branch at Cunnamulla, reporting a suspected murder.

Cunnamulla said they'd get a crew out to him as soon as they could; in the meantime he should secure the premises. Let no one in or out, including himself. When he told them the suspected perpetrator was known and still at large, they just repeated his orders—secure the premises, and wait for the detectives to get there.

It could be a couple of hours. One way or other, it was going to be a very long night. In the meantime, whatever was leaking inside the house would flood the whole place out before the forensics arrived, if he didn't do something about it. Brian flicked on his torch and went hunting around the front yard until he found the water mains tap, then squatted down in the uncut grass and turned off the water supply.

Just as he was giving the tap one last turn, he saw something glistening in the grass a few metres away, at the side of the house. Brian straightened up, flashing the torchlight to where he was looking. There was something there in the beam, something long, straight and narrow, lying on the ground, half hidden in amongst the unkempt tufts of faded grey grass. He kept the light fixed on it as he approached.

The second he got there he immediately realised he was likely looking at the murder weapon. It was a lethal-looking metal bat, grey and silver in colour, but now heavily smeared with what was undoubtedly blood. Even before he leaned down for a closer inspection, Brian could clearly see lumps of blood-soaked hair and tissue attached to it. He studied it intently for several seconds, then straightened up and walked directly back to the truck. He was pretty sure he had left a camera in the glove compartment, and he was hoping he had. If he was right, he would photograph the weapon in situ, then radio through to the CI boys, to see if they wanted him to bag it up straight away, or leave it where it was till they got there.

But when he got close to the cars, Brian Ingles suddenly stopped in his tracks. Up ahead of him, in the dim, reflected glow of the porch light, he saw a tall, naked man, dawdling across the front yard, heading almost aimlessly towards the front door.

'Police. Stop there.' Ingles had his gun trained on the suspect as he barked out directions. 'Now. Right where you are.' Rowdy McQuillan had turned and was facing the Constable, a bewildered look on his face, his hands cupped modestly over his genitals, as Ingles barked again urgently. 'Put your hands above your head. Now.'

'What's going on?' the big man mumbled, as he slowly raised his hands in the air, looking wide-eyed and disorientated. Even in the dull, yellow light, Brian could see an ugly red smear on his cheek, crusty brown lines in the folds of his fingers and long, crimson streaks down both his arms.

'Get down, Rowdy. On the ground. Right now.' As the naked cowboy bent at the waist, into a crouch on his haunches, the policeman strode quickly forward, pulling the cuffs from his belt. 'Right down, all the way, on your front,' he snapped. 'Hands back behind your back.'

McQuillan stretched out on the ground, flat on his stomach, and Brian squatted beside him, jamming one knee heavily into his back, as he holstered his firearm, snatching and yanking at the big man's wrists.

'How's Tom?' Rowdy puffed breathlessly into the dusty grass. 'Is he okay?'

'No mate,' Brian grunted back, as he pulled the two bloodstained hands in together, and clicked on the cuffs. 'I don't think he is.'

•

At just before seven that morning, Brian Ingles stopped in at the big truck-stop out on the road into Millen and ordered a breakfast of fried eggs and sausages. Detective Sergeant Noel Atwood, the Officer in Charge of the Cunnamulla CIB, wanted him back at the station house by no later than 8 AM sharp, so he had about half an hour to grab a quick bite and a cuppa.

Brian had worked through the night, establishing the crime scene, securing it, and then photographing whatever he could of the exterior, and the bat, while Rowdy McQuillan slept it off in the back of the wagon. Then, once the detectives arrived, he ferried the suspect back to the cells, locked him up, and doubled straight back to the Castle Street house to help out as best he could, running errands for the Scenes of Crime guys, and generally trying to make himself useful.

Around dawn, Atwood sent him off to wake up Ross and Lindy Lewis, get whatever detail they could give him, and then report back to the house. By the time he finally left Castle Street, well after sun-up, the police there looked close to all done. They had taken all the swabs they needed, lifted all the prints, photographed everything inside and out, bagged up and tagged all relevant exhibits, and were pretty much ready to roll.

At 8 o'clock, Atwood was fixing to interview Rowdy McQuillan. They'd alco-tested him back at the house, and he went way off the charts, but Atwood reckoned after he had had a few hours' sleep back in the cells, he'd be right and ready to answer their questions come 8 o'clock. Brian Ingles was looking forward to it. There had been so many questions floating around in his head these past few hours, about the horror he saw out there at the Castle Street house, how such a thing could have happened, and why. He could only hope there would soon be some answers.

An hour ago, he had thought he was famished, but now he was just staring vacantly down at his plate, gently nudging the fried eggs around, one way and the other, unable to eat. He couldn't think of food right now. All he could think of was the lifeless, headless sack of bones that was once Tom Wilson, and the fury painted on his bedroom walls around him, laid on thick in blood and bone and gore. What had Tom Wilson done to deserve such rage to be unleashed upon him? Where had it come from? Where had it gone?

Brian looked up at the burbling growl of another massive road train crawling ominously across the tarmac of the truck-stop, slowly easing to a stop. These metal monsters, two and three semi-trailers long, rumbled continuously through the town, day and night, like lumbering giants, their bellies full of moaning livestock press-ganged from the far-flung reaches, heading for the abattoirs and sales yards of the city. As Brian watched the helpless cattle peering out at him pathetically, licking at the metal bars of their enclosure, he felt a hollow feeling forming in his chest, picturing the vague, bewildered gaze he had seen painted on the prisoner's face as he stood there outside Tom Wilson's house, bathed in yellow light and the fresh, warm blood of his best friend. Out there in the cold night air, there was no sign of the frenzy, the unthinkable horror, that was seeping from the walls inside.

Rowdy McQuillan had always seemed a level-headed bloke. Where had it all come from?

When Brian got back to the station house, shortly after seven thirty, he was surprised to see Noel Atwood already sitting at a desk, flanked by several of his colleagues, punching with two fingers on the typewriter, as Rowdy McQuillan sat opposite them, looking tired, dazed and dishevelled. The clothes they had provided him back at the station house—a dark blue, long-sleeved shirt and a pair of white football shorts—were now creased and crumpled after several hours of sleep, and his hair was standing up at awkward angles, giving him an oddly comical, pathetic look.

As the young Constable came into the room, Atwood kept typing but shot him a quick, cursory glance, and nodded in the general direction of a spare chair in the corner. As Brian took a seat, the Sergeant finished typing his next question, rolled the page up off the cartridge slightly so it could be seen, and read it out.

'Ronald, as was explained to you before we commenced this interview, we intend to ask you questions about what happened at Tom Wilson's house earlier this morning. You are not obliged to answer those questions unless you wish to. Do you understand that warning?'

He peered over the top of his glasses at the prisoner. But Rowdy McQuillan was now slumped forward in his chair, staring at the desk in front of him. Eventually, without looking up, he mumbled, almost incoherently.

'Rowdy.'

'What?'

McQuillan looked up at him, sheepishly.

'Everybody calls me Rowdy.'

At first, Atwood said nothing, just stared at him with a tinge of aggravation tugging at the corners of his mouth.

'But your real name's Ronald, isn't it?'

'Yeah, but no one calls me that. Everyone just calls me Rowdy.'

Noel Atwood breathed out impatiently and pushed his spectacles back onto the bridge of his nose.

'Alright.'

He launched into another energetic, double-fingered burst of clattering on the keys, punched out the next stanza, then stopped again, wound up the paper, and read out what he'd typed.

'Question: Do you understand that warning? Answer: Everyone calls me Rowdy. Question: Very well, Rowdy, do you understand that you are not obliged to answer our questions if you do not wish to? Answer: Yes. Question: Given that warning, are you now willing to proceed with this record of interview, and answer my questions?'

He looked up from the page again and stared across his glasses at the suspect. 'So, what's your answer, mate?'

McQuillan silently nodded his assent, whereupon the detective launched into another flurry of frenetic finger-tapping and then, once done, read his work off the page.

'Question: … are you now willing to… answer my questions? Answer: Yes. Question: Very well, Rowdy, we've been told you left the Millengarra Arms Hotel with Ross and Linda Lewis at shortly before midnight last night, and they dropped you home at Castle Street a short time later. Could you please tell me what happened when you got to the house?'

Everyone in the room was staring intently at McQuillan, waiting expectantly for his response. Initially, it didn't come. He just sat there, staring blankly at the vacant space in front of him. But eventually, after several silent seconds passed, he began to shake his head from side to side, before finally mumbling his answer.

'I don't know.'

'What do you mean you don't know?'

'I can't remember.'

The detective breathed in tersely, and briefly cast a sceptical glance in the direction of his colleagues, before he sat back in his chair.

'Why can't you remember, mate?'

'I don't know.' McQuillan shook his head again 'I'd had a bit to drink, I guess.'

Atwood was staring silently back at him, his jaw set in a disgruntled frown. Eventually, he pushed the glasses back onto his nose again, slid forward in his chair, and resumed tapping vigorously on the keys of the typewriter. When he was done, he read out the next instalment.

'Question: Could you please tell me what happened when you got into the house? Answer: I don't know. I'd had a bit to drink. Question: What do you know about the assault on Tom Wilson?'

McQuillan looked dumbfounded, as if he hadn't expected anyone to ask the question.

'Alls I remember is walking into the front yard of Tom's place and seeing Brian Ingles there. He had a gun pointed straight at me.'

He turned momentarily and nodded respectfully to Constable Ingles, who nodded back, then he turned back to face Noel Atwood.

'That was later. What happened earlier on?'

In a disconsolate murmur, McQuillan proceeded to tell his story, such as it was. It came out gradually, with much probing and prompting, in disjointed bits and pieces, but in the typed record Atwood strung it all together, in a narrative anyone could follow.

Rowdy McQuillan remembered being at the hotel earlier in the night, having tea with Ross and Lindy Lewis. They went upstairs later in the evening, and he started drinking with his old mate Mason Deeds, and Mason's missus Jenny, and he remembered being out on the dancefloor for a while, and then after that he got a lift home back to Castle Street with Ross and Lindy. And just before they left, they ran into Neville from the video store, and a couple of sheilas he was with. Lindy was yarning with them for a while, and then they left.

'What happened when you got back to the house?'

Rowdy McQuillan looked stumped for an answer. He sat silent, frowning intently, agonising, as if staring at something somewhere in his mind's eye that he didn't want to see. His mouth was open slightly, his lips moving almost imperceptibly, trying to form words that seemingly just would not come.

'What happened when you got back to the house, Rowdy?' the policeman repeated.

Rowdy looked up at him, wide-eyed and open mouthed, and then just shook his head.

'I don't know,' he almost whispered.

'It has been alleged that a male person with no clothes on attempted to break into a house on Royal Road, adjacent to Tom Wilson's house in Castle Street, shortly prior to your arrest. Can you tell me anything about that incident?'

He dropped his gaze back to the desktop, and slowly shook his head again.

'No.'

'When you were apprehended outside Tom Wilson's house, you were found to have blood on your hands, and on other parts of your body. Can you tell me how that blood got there?'

Rowdy opened both his hands on his lap and stared at them momentarily.

'No, I can't.'

'Tom Wilson's deceased body was located in the house, with extensive damage to the head. Can you tell me anything about that?'

'No.'

'Several windows had been broken in the house. Did you cause that damage?'

'I don't know.'

'What are you mean you don't know?'

'I don't remember.'

'Why don't you remember?'

'I don't know.'

'Do you remember what you were wearing at the Millengarra Hotel earlier in the night?'

Rowdy McQuillan had his head down, staring blankly at the desktop in front of him. He stayed that way for what felt like a long time, as the seconds ticked away on the station clock. Eventually, he looked up and gave a mumbled answer.

'My good Levis, and a white, pearl-buttoned Western shirt.'

'You're currently wearing a plain dark blue shirt and white shorts. Do you recall changing into those clothes?'

He looked down at his clothes, and then over to where Brian was sitting in the corner.

'Brian Ingles gave them to me in the lock-up.'

'Can you tell me what happened to the clothes you were wearing earlier at the hotel?'

He looked back at the detective, staring at him, frowning, as if trying to remember.

'No mate,' he said eventually, shaking his head sadly. 'I don't know where they are.'

'When you were arrested, you had no clothes on. Can you tell me why?'

'I don't know.'

Detective Sergeant Atwood set his jaw, looking exasperated and annoyed, eyeing the prisoner disdainfully. He was getting nowhere with his questioning, and Brian could see he didn't like it one small bit. Eventually, Atwood blew out a long, frustrated breath and slipped his glasses off his face.

'Are you prepared to tell us anything about what happened to Tom Wilson earlier tonight?'

'I can't believe I done it.'

'Done what, Rowdy?'

'Killed him. I can't believe I killed Tom.'

Atwood started typing again, his fingers now charged with more urgency. He sensed a tiny change in McQuillan's voice hinting he may be getting close, may be finally coming within sight of the truth. Without even rolling the cartridge, he read the questions straight off the page.

'Question: Are you prepared to tell us anything about what happened to Tom Wilson earlier tonight? Answer: I can't believe I killed Tom. Question: Are you prepared to tell me in your own words what you mean when you say 'I killed Tom?''

'I can't.'

Noel Atwood was now peering over his glasses, looking Rowdy McQuillan straight in the eye. They were both sitting totally still, face-to-face, staring at each other intently for several long seconds. Then McQuillan eventually lowered his eyes, hanging his head like a penitent sinner. But Atwood kept his gaze trained on him, still saying nothing, waiting to see what this sad, beaten man might say or do next. There was nothing but silence.

'Does that mean you can't because you can't remember,' Atwood eventually said. 'Or because you can't bring yourself to tell us what you did?'

The answer, when it came, was no more than a whisper.

'I don't know.'

Eventually, he looked back up into the eyes of the policeman.

'I can't remember,' he said more firmly. He looked around at the other detectives, then over at Brian. 'I can't remember any of it.'

Detective Sergeant Noel Atwood pursed his lips cynically, staring straight at the suspect. Eventually, he sucked a deep breath in through his nostrils, and blew it out in a long, frustrated sigh. Then he leaned forward over the typewriter and repeated the answer aloud as he typed it onto the page.

'Answer: I don't know.'

FIVE

Ada Morrow's late husband, Bob, paid the grand sum of nine thousand dollars for *Belle Mer*, their cute little fibro cottage on the beachfront at Mermaid Beach. Now, a little over twenty years later, the real estate agents who were pestering Ada to list it for sale all assured her it was worth close to forty times that. Surely it couldn't be true.

It didn't matter much anyway; she'd never sell. Ada loved *Belle Mer*. After Bob's fall, once he'd slowed down a bit and the boys and their wives had mostly taken over the management of Rosalie Station, she and Bob had tried to get off the property and down to the coast as often as possible —— a week every Christmas, and another in August for the RNA Show—and whenever they did, they'd head straight for their beautiful little *Belle Mer*. When it was just them, it was a tranquil sanctuary of old books and lazy sunsets, and when the grandchildren descended upon them in summer it was a joyous, bustling little hub, full of laughter and love. Ada was a country girl, born and bred, she always would be, and Mermaid Beach was as far from Millengarra as any place on earth could possibly be, but *Belle Mer* was definitely her home away from home.

So, every three months or so since Bob passed away, Ada Morrow would make her way down to the South Coast to spend a week, sometimes two, in the beach house. And whenever she did, she would always be sure to catch up with her good friends Judy and Gwendolyn. They were all on their own these days, no longer weighed down by their much-missed menfolk, so they'd take long walks on the beach together, from Mermaid to Miami and back, do all the frock shops in Surfers, and get down to the Tweed as often as possible for a nice counter lunch, and a bit of a flutter on the pokies at Twin Towns.

But today was going to be special. Judy had lined up an appointment for all three girls to each have a session with the exotic Madam Marla Pavlovich. Ada wasn't much of a one for tarot cards, fortune-telling and all the rest of that psychic hocus pocus, but she had to admit that the thought of a private audience with the Coast's most talked-about clairvoyant was more than a little bit exciting. The very thought of it, bubbling around in the back of her brain, was making it hard for her to concentrate on the morning newspaper, as she sat out on the back porch of *Belle Mer*, waiting for Judy and Gwendolyn to arrive.

As usual, she was reading the often-sensationalised stories of all the crazy cases that trooped through the Southport Courthouse on a daily basis, and the silly shenanigans so many people seemed to get up to. Last week the magistrate Mr Oldfield gave a nudity campaigner seven days in jail for flashing her bare bosom at a sergeant of police, and her lawyer—a young solicitor called Eddie Moran, who seemed to always get the juicy cases—claimed in court the sergeant was a regular paying customer at a well-known striptease venue in Surfers Paradise, and therefore should have been downright grateful for the free show, rather than claiming her behaviour was offensive. Ada had a good chuckle about that one. Today there was a story about Mr Moran representing a man who stole a crocodile from one of the theme parks late at night and put it in the swimming pool in the backyard of his best friend's home, just as a joke. Ada couldn't imagine how he'd done it, but thought he probably deserved a medal of some sort for the feat, rather than the three months' jail Mr Oldfield had handed him. Mr Moran was quoted in the newspaper as saying his client would appeal. But then, all Mr Moran's clients seem to appeal when they didn't get the result he said they should. He must have been a very clever lawyer, Ada thought. He was always kicking up a fuss about something or other, and she always loved reading all about his cases, or seeing him on the television.

But lately, with all the terrible things that were happening at home, reading about all these courtroom capers just wasn't quite the same. The stories she once found intriguing, and sometimes amusing, now just left her feeling flat and sadly disheartened.

•

From the street, Madam Marla Pavlovich's house on Isle of Capri, just across the bridge from Surfers Paradise, appeared to be a typical, compact, single garage, three-bedroom brick-and-tile suburban Gold Coast home, with a Poinciana in the front yard, and two brightly-painted gnomes standing sentry in the garden bed on either side of a slightly-chipped, plaster statue of an aboriginal man standing on one foot and leaning on his spear. But at the end of the cracked concrete path that led to her front door, a peculiar, decorative arrangement of small bits of metal, glass and shell hung from the eave, making a strangely unsettling, tinkling sound as it swayed gently in the breeze, suggesting this was no ordinary, average dwelling. On the wooden door behind the tinkle was a rustic circular frame of wood and feathers and, above it, a small painted sign that read, cryptically, 'All the world is queer, except thee and me… And even thou art just a little strange.'

When the door opened, Madam Marla filled the doorway. She was a big lady in a blowsy, flowing caftan, whose full head of long, unruly hair was streaked with strands of grey, and tucked on either side behind her impressively large ears, adorned with even larger brass and blue-bead earrings hanging down to her shoulders. She greeted each of them in turn, in a courteous, but reserved, almost standoffish, fashion, and then led them all to the dining table, where she efficiently disposed of the formalities, taking their cash, and counting it—perhaps a little too carefully, for Ada's sensibilities—before she sat them down and stepped them through the rules of her engagement.

The sessions would be strictly private, one-on-one. Each of them could take written notes of what Madam Marla had to say to her, but no other kind of recording was permitted. While one of them was in session with her, sitting at the dining table, the other two must wait outside on the garden setting at the back of the house. Each session would take roughly twenty minutes.

It was quickly decided by Gwen and Fay that, since this was Ada's first time ever, she should be first. With a flutter of excitement, they quickly wished her well, and scurried off, out to the back patio.

Once they were gone, the maestro moved majestically around the house, flicking off a TV lamp, drawing closed the curtains, and pulling down the blinds. Then she stepped up to the dining table and, with a dramatic flourish of both hands, swept the hair back off her face, before settling herself regally on a chair across from Ada. Placing both hands palm-down on the table, she closed her eyes, and breathed a long and steady breath in through her nostrils.

She held it for several seconds, and then breathed it out again, slowly, calmly, and with complete control.

'Put your hands in mine,' she murmured softly in the semi-darkness, turning both her palms up on the table. Ada reached out across the table and gently laid the fingertips of each hand down on Madam Marla's open palms. They were instantly enveloped in a warm embrace of fleshy fingers as the mystic held her hands tightly in her clasp, and breathed in again, her breath now even deeper, more constant and decisive than before, held it for a moment, and then breathed out steadily, until finally she was still, calm and completely motionless. Her painted eyelids lifted gradually as she opened up her hands, releasing Ada's fingers.

'Give me something of yours,' she said quietly, looking straight into her subject's eyes. 'Anything. Your watch maybe, or something from your bag. Anything that connects with you.'

Ada slipped a bracelet from her wrist and handed it across the table, whereupon Madam Marla wrapped it up in both her hands, closed her eyes, and settled back into a brooding, contemplative trance. As the seconds ticked away, Ada sat in silence opposite her, waiting, feeling slightly self-conscious, wondering what, if anything, she was meant to do, what could possibly come next. From the corner of her eye, she could see a crucifix hanging on the wall behind the big woman's left shoulder. On the hall table below was a brass Buddha and beside that a statuette of Vishnu, along with several sticks of burning incense. It seemed to Ada that Madam Marla had just about all bases covered.

Then the celebrated psychic began talking, as if to herself, rambling erratically in vague and disconnected sentences. As she spoke, Ada silently sat in front of her—watching, listening and wondering—immersed in the shadowy half-light of the dining room, seduced by the sweet smell of incense, and surrounded by strange, exotic gods and idols. And as she sat, and watched, and listened, slowly she began to hear what Madam Marla Pavlovich was really saying to her.

Ever so gradually, Ada Morrow—the country girl from outback Millengarra—began to feel the magic, began to recognise the mystical, mysterious Madam Marla was speaking intimately to her, truthfully, about her, and about her life, all she'd ever been and ever would be. She was reaching deep inside Ada Morrow's soul, remembering, consoling, foretelling, soothing the sadness of her past, and opening a bright window to her future.

•

When Eddie Moran pulled into the bitumen car park outside the old Two Division of the Boggo Road Gaol, he had an uncustomary flutter tickling his innards. Any visit to the imposing, hundred-year-old, red-brick prison on the hillside at Dutton Park, overlooking inner-city Brisbane—its high walls and turrets patrolled by armed wardens—was a bit like running out of petrol on a dark, stormy night outside Frankenstein's Castle. You never knew what you'd encounter when you knocked on the front door.

But today was different to most. Eddie's newest client, Ronald Charles McQuillan, was facing a charge of murder, and that was serious stuff. A conviction for murder meant mandatory imprisonment for life; it didn't get any more serious than that. In his brief but promising career so far, Eddie had done some big cases—including the McCabe kidnapping trial—but he'd never acted for anyone charged with a murder.

As he sat in the car, he sucked in one last drag from his cigarette, and then breathed it out slowly, thinking of what was ahead. Ada Morrow had high expectations, that was for certain.

When she came to his office earlier that week Ada couldn't tell the lawyer too much, other than that her nephew Ronald—who everyone had always called Rowdy, ever since he was just a little kid in short pants— had been charged with murdering his best mate Tom Wilson, who he lived with, out in a little country town called Millengarra, where Ada came from, an hour or so north-west of Cunnamulla, in western Queensland. They'd found Tom's body in the house, beaten to death with a steel baseball bat, with Rowdy's fingerprints all over it. So they charged him with murdering Tom, and he'd been locked up in Boggo Road ever since, waiting for his committal hearing, which was due in the Cunnamulla Magistrates Court in just over a month. But he wasn't guilty, Ada knew that for sure and for certain.

'He told you that, did he?'

Eddie had thought it a pretty fair question; if Rowdy McQuillan was pleading his innocence, hopefully he'd have some explanation about how the deceased wound up dead, with his prints all over the murder weapon. But when he asked it, Ada just looked perplexed.

'Who?'

'Rowdy.'

'Oh no, love. No,' she shot back, now looking even more puzzled. 'I haven't talked to Rowdy about it at all. I told you, he's been locked up in Boggo Road.'

'Well then, how do you know he's not guilty?'

It was a silly question; Eddie should have known that before he asked. The answer, it turned out, was simple. Ada Morrow knew her nephew was not guilty of murder because she had been to see a clairvoyant on the Isle of Capri, Madam Marla Pavlovich, and Madam Marla had told her Rowdy didn't do it.

That was it; that was all she had. Ada knew for sure and for certain her nephew was as innocent as a newborn baby, because Madam Marla Pavlovich had told her so.

Of course. What could possibly be simpler? Case solved, then.

'She said she saw a man running from the house, covered in blood.'

Yeah, right. Any chance that might have been Rowdy McQuillan?

'And that's why I came to see you,' Ada continued, wide-eyed. 'Madam Marla said she also saw a young lawyer.' She leaned forward over his desk and continued in a conspiratorial half-whisper. 'She said he would help us, that he would prove Rowdy didn't do it.' Now Ada paused, as a whimsical smirk settled on her matronly face. Then she continued. 'I knew straight away, Mr Moran. I knew it was you.'

There was a distinct danger of Eddie's early interest in the Rowdy McQuillan case suddenly seriously waning, right then and there, but for the fact Ada Morrow moved on immediately to a much more mundane but meaningful issue—*money*. Ada was comfortably off, she assured the young lawyer, and had already put aside more than enough to ensure her favourite nephew Rowdy got the best legal defence that money could buy. She had retained her family solicitor, Mr Leo Payne of Philips, Wallace & Payne, in Cunnamulla, to take up the case, and Mr Payne had briefed Queensland's top criminal barrister, Mr Dennis O'Dea. But then, not two weeks ago, Mr Payne had announced Mr O'Dea had become unavailable to appear on Rowdy's behalf at the committal hearing, because he was already committed to a major trial due to start in Rockhampton in that same week, so Mr Payne now proposed to brief a junior barrister to stand in for Mr O'Dea at the preliminary hearing. The family was not happy at all, most particularly Aunt Ada, who tightly controlled the purse strings. So, when the marvellous Madam Marla Pavlovich miraculously proclaimed that the brilliant young Eddie Moran would step in and save the day, it all came as an absolute godsend.

Ada had already told Mr Payne, politely and respectfully, he was now sacked, and Eddie was now on the job. She hoped Eddie would forgive her for being so presumptuous, but Mr Payne had assured her he would box up the file, and send it through to Mr Moran, as soon as he received a written authority to do so from Rowdy, which Ada suggested Eddie might have her nephew complete when he visited him at Boggo Road Gaol, which she hoped would be soon. In the meantime, she had brought along with her a copy of some of the police statements, which she would leave with him to help him get started. And, of course, she was happy to write him a cheque, then and there, for whatever fees he thought he would likely incur. It was like music to Eddie's ears.

'Oh, and there was one other thing Madam Marla told me,' Ada suddenly remembered as she was scribbling numbers into her chequebook. 'She said there was a girl involved in it somehow.'

'What girl?'

'I don't know. She didn't say. But I reckon it was probably that Larnie. She was a wild one.'

Ada went on to explain Larnie Mitchell, one of the local girls who had been 'mates with Rowdy for years,' had taken off from the town only a couple of months earlier, and hadn't been seen or heard from since, that Larnie had always been trouble, and there were rumours of her taking drugs. So therefore, by some perverse logic, she must have had something to do with Tom Wilson's murder. And now Madam Marla had all but confirmed it.

As Eddie Moran sat in his car outside the Boggo Road Gaol, he thought about the curious coincidence that one of Rowdy McQuillan's old girlfriends had mysteriously disappeared just a matter of weeks before his best mate was bludgeoned to death. Ada Morrow and Madam Marla might be content to pin Tom Wilson's murder on some poor missing girl, but it seemed to Eddie there was another, entirely different, but equally sinister possibility. From what he had read of the police statements Ada had given him, Rowdy was certainly no stranger to violence.

The police had got a statement from a twenty-one-year-old farm labourer, Wayne Grantham, who had rented a room at the Castle Street house for several months. Grantham described Rowdy McQuillan as having an 'explosive' temper, which was much in evidence throughout his time at the house. According to Wayne Grantham's statement, if McQuillan ever thought either of his housemates had touched any of his possessions, he would fly into 'an uncontrollable rage,' and on one particular occasion, having convinced himself someone had taken some of his beer from the communal fridge, and seeing Tom Wilson asleep and obviously inebriated on a beanbag in the lounge room, he had attacked him, punching and kicking Wilson into unconsciousness, in what Grantham described as 'a brutal and despicable attack on a defenceless man.' The young labourer finally left the residence just weeks before Tom Wilson's death, because he could no longer stomach Rowdy McQuillan's violent attacks on his good mate Tom.

The statement drew a damning picture of a flawed and dangerous bully, a big, powerful man with a very short fuse, given to excessive drinking and terrifying bursts of spontaneous violence. It was a picture that fitted the police case theory perfectly. McQuillan's blood-alcohol level on the night of Tom Wilson's murder had come in at .235%, a dangerously high reading. The prosecution would allege that he became highly intoxicated, and at times violent, during the course of his long bout of drinking at the Millengarra Hotel that night, before he was finally dropped off at the Castle Street house by the Lewises just prior to midnight. When he got there, Tom Wilson was already home, and also in an advanced state of intoxication, and when Rowdy McQuillan staggered in, full of booze and bad manners, the pair quarrelled about something, causing the cantankerous cowboy to fly into a wild, uncontrollable rage, whereupon he savagely attacked the smaller man, ultimately beating him to a pulp—almost literally—and leaving him dead on the floor. Covered in his housemate's blood, he then stripped off his clothes, attempting to wash the incriminating blood off them, before staggering out into the night, to continue his alcohol-fuelled rampage at the home of Karen Millard. When police entered the residence, they found Rowdy's blood-stained clothes, still soaking wet, on the floor of his bedroom.

It was an overwhelming Crown case. Without doubt, Rowdy McQuillan had killed his friend and housemate Tom Wilson; the only question was why. Eddie stubbed the last remnants of his cigarette out in the ashtray, wound up the window, and climbed out of the car, his mind flicking over the disturbing images the police crime scene photographs had captured. So far, he had only seen black-and-white photocopies of the real thing, but they showed him enough to conjure up the true horror of what had happened that night. Even in black-and-white, the shimmering, sticky ooze of blood and tissue that was splattered all over Tom's bedroom, dribbling down the walls in ugly patterns and pooling against the skirting boards, bespoke an attack of almost unthinkable ferocity. What could possibly have unleashed such brutality?

There was no doubt Rowdy's blood alcohol level was seriously high, to the extent he would have had real difficulty forming any positive intention to kill. And the crime scene suggested a blind, irrational rage. But voluntary intoxication was no defence in itself, and even if a jury accepted he was too drunk to form an intention to kill, that just reduced murder to manslaughter, which still carried life imprisonment as a maximum; for a cold-blooded, drunken manslaughter like this one, Rowdy McQuillan would draw some very long time.

But Madam Marla had proclaimed his lawyer was going to save him, so now it was all up to Eddie. *What else was left? Insanity?* Unsoundness of mind was a full defence to any criminal charge, but not if it was caused by voluntary intoxication. If Rowdy McQuillan just drank himself silly, which he almost certainly did on the night, to the point where he was so drunk he was completely out of his mind, that didn't count as insanity. It was just plain voluntary intoxication, and that didn't count. Voluntary intoxication, even to the extent of complete delusion and unsoundness of mind, was no defence to anything. It just brought him back to the same result—manslaughter—which in this case meant at least ten years behind bars, and probably a whole lot more.

But Ada Morrow had let slip to Eddie that the legendary criminal law barrister Mr Dennis O'Dea had recommended Rowdy be examined and assessed by the renowned, Melbourne-based psychiatrist Dr Waylon Penfold, and that strongly suggested to Eddie that O'Dea was at least keeping an open mind about the possibility of raising an insanity defence. Just how all that might work out for Rowdy McQuillan, Eddie wasn't quite certain at first. Ada had assured him her nephew had never been treated for any sort of mental health issues, and she seemed downright insulted that the barrister had even suggested a consultation with the famed Dr Penfold. But when Eddie looked into it further, he found something very interesting. Dennis O'Dea had worked on several cases before with the eminent psychoanalyst, including the successful defence of a man called Philip Malone.

Malone, a hard-working father of three young boys, had been charged with the murder, and near-decapitation, of a man called Roskin, whom he suspected of sexually assaulting his eight-year-old son. After drinking heavily at home one night after work, Malone had gone to Roskin's residence and stabbed him twenty-three times with a fishing knife. In conducting his defence, Dennis O'Dea argued an insanity case, claiming his client, who worked by day in a chemical factory dealing with volatile liquids, had suffered a temporary psychotic episode after inadvertently inhaling noxious chemicals at work, causing him to lose touch with reality and experience psychotic delusions not amenable to rational discernment. In support of that novel defence, Mr O'Dea called the highly acclaimed, Canadian-trained Dr Penfold to give expert medical opinion evidence to prove the phenomenon of inadvertent intoxication by inhalation of toxic substances.

Eddie figured he might just know where Dennis O'Dea was going with this, and it gave him a glimmer of hope about the Rowdy McQuillan case. Tom Wilson was a house painter by occupation, and for the couple of months prior to his death, his regular offsider was none other than his housemate Rowdy McQuillan. House painters regularly worked with paint thinners, and some of those substances could no doubt be highly toxic. It was all a long shot for sure, but if Eddie was ever going to live up to the high expectations of Aunt Ada Morrow and Madam Marla Pavlovich, it was something he needed to at least keep firmly in the back of his mind.

Eddie pulled a twenty-cent piece from his pocket and used it to rap several times on the high steel gate of the old Two Division, layered thick with successive generations of shiny green paint. An eyehole swung open, a warder peered out, and the eyehole swung shut again. Then, as always, a key clanged and clattered in the heavy steel lock, a green metal door within the green metal door creaked open, and a khaki-clad warder ushered him into the gaol.

As Eddie dutifully followed the familiar routine, making his way across the quadrangle to the interview rooms, the images of Tom Wilson's bedroom turned over in his mind's eye, and the strange feeling kept fluttering inside him. What kind of man was he about to meet? Where was this journey going to lead?

Eddie's first impression of Rowdy McQuillan was not a good one. The tall, rangy man arrived at the door of the interview room dressed in the usual light-brown-coloured prison garb—a T-shirt, short matching shorts, and a pair of worn rubber thongs—but his face was twisted into a cynical half-snarl, his upper lip curled disapprovingly at the very sight of the suited-up lawyer.

'How're y'goin?' he drawled from outside the doorway, looking in without entering. 'What can I do for you?'

He looked like he already disliked his new lawyer. If he did, too bad, the feeling was mutual. Eddie didn't get up, but he certainly wasn't going to let some oversized hayseed stand over him.

'I'm a lawyer,' he said, opening his work folder. 'Your Aunty Ada asked me to come out and see you.' He pulled out a cigarette, lit up, and then lobbed the packet onto the narrow desk in front of him. 'Help yourself.'

If the tundra ice pack between them was to be thawed, a packet of tailor-made cigarettes was as good a way as any to do it. Every inmate was entitled to his ration of prison tobacco, but that only came in the form of a can of White Ox; it didn't extend to anything fancy, and certainly nothing tailor-made, cork-tipped or filtered. Eddie knew from experience the offer of a tailor-made smoke was too good to pass up in prison. If Rowdy McQuillan was a smoker, he'd bite.

He was, and he did, and it didn't take long. The packet had no sooner hit the desktop than McQuillan stepped forward and slipped out a cigarette, then pulled up a chair opposite the lawyer, and leaned over the desk as Eddie clicked on his lighter.

'What happened to Old Man Payne?' the prisoner puffed out with a smoky breath.

'She sacked him.' Eddie was looking him straight in the eye, keen to gauge his reaction. When there was none, he slipped out a business card and flicked it flat onto the desk between them. 'He's out, I'm in.'

The prisoner picked up the card and mumbled the name.

'Moran.'

'Eddie.'

The big man looked up at him, nodded, then repeated.

'Eddie.' He nodded again, pensively, still holding the lawyer's gaze. 'I'm not fuckin' crazy.'

'What?'

'I'm not fuckin' crazy. That idiot Payne reckoned I was. Made me talk to a fuckin' psychiatrist.'

It was a bad way to start. So far as Eddie could see, Rowdy McQuillan was an angry man, and he didn't like anyone, particularly some pesky lawyer, suggesting he might have a few roos loose in his top paddock. Eddie was strictly a city boy; he'd never been west of the Parramatta Local Court. But he figured it was a pretty safe guess that out there where Rowdy hailed from—home, home on the range, where the deer and the antelopes played—it didn't go down well for a straight-shootin,' rootin'-tootin' cowboy to own up to being absolutely, stark-raving bonkers. But the way Eddie saw it, his cranky client didn't have a whole lot of options available to him right now, and to be ruling out anything that might save him spending the rest of his days behind bars, would be just plain dumb.

It was time to gently explain the simple facts of life to Mr McQuillan, without upsetting his obviously ever-so-tender sensibilities. Eddie sat forward, cupped his hands comfortably on the desktop in front of him, and eased into a quiet, confidential dissertation.

Firstly, no one was suggesting Rowdy was crazy. Not at all. They were just covering the bases. This was an extremely serious charge—as serious as it gets—and his lawyer's job was to do everything he possibly could to investigate any and all available defences. One such defence was self-defence, for example, or defence of another. They'd be looking at that, very closely, at the committal hearing, cross-examining all of the witnesses to see if there was any evidence that might support such a defence. But there were others as well, and any competent lawyer was duty-bound to consider them. That's all Leo Payne and Dennis O'Dea were doing. They were looking to explore all possibilities, keep all the balls in the air. The fact they asked him to talk to a psychiatrist didn't mean they were saying he was crazy. They were just covering the bases. Who knew? The psych might just come up with something of use, and at the end of the day the stakes were way too high to be turning his nose up at any lifeline that might fall into his lap. Under section twenty-seven of the Queensland Criminal Code, insanity was a complete defence to any criminal charge, so obviously it would be foolish not to keep it in mind.

'I'm not fuckin' pleading insanity.'

McQuillan was now glaring at his lawyer, wild-eyed, snarling angrily like he was about to leap over the desk and claim his next victim. Eddie sat back in his chair to create a more comfortable distance between them, then leaned back as nonchalantly as he could manage in the circumstances, at the same time flashing a quick glance in the direction of the only available exit. For the briefest moment he was considering his options, but then reminded himself of the big fat fee Aunty Ada had left sitting in his trust account, just crying out to be spent.

'Okay,' he shrugged eventually. 'I get it. You're not pleading insanity.' He clicked on his pen and sat forward over the desk, waiting expectantly, like a secretary poised for dictation. 'So what are you pleading, pal?'

'I'm pleading not guilty.'

'On what basis?'

'I didn't fuckin' do it.'

The lawyer smiled wryly to himself, staring silently at the blank page in front of him. Eventually he nodded slowly and looked back up at his client.

'Okay,' he said pensively. 'So tell me what happened.'

He was looking his client straight in the eye, awaiting the answer. But the big man just faltered and eventually averted his eyes, looking down at the desktop in front of him, shaking his head.

'I don't know,' he muttered, almost incoherently. 'I can't remember.' He raised both hands to his head and poked his big fingers deep into his long, tousled hair, slowly and silently scratching his scalp for several long seconds. When he finally stopped, he looked back up at Eddie Moran. 'That's why I've got you,' he said resolutely. 'To find out.'

The wry smile returned to the lawyer's lips. This guy didn't need Eddie Moran, he needed Madam Marla Pavlovich.

SIX

'Quiet please, fellas. Come on now, let's have a bit of shush, thanks.'

Retired Police Inspector Lenny Arthurson was standing in the corner by the drinks table, clinking a couple of empty beer glasses together, doing as well as his frail, crackly voice could manage over the general boisterous din of the drinkers, all cramped together in the small, smoky function room. But from what Dave Hocking could see, there must've been well over sixty coppers in there, and they'd all been drinking free beer for the past couple of hours, so they were well on their way. Poor old Lenny didn't stand a chance. He'd been out of the job for so long half of the young blokes didn't even know who he was.

'Quiet,' Mick Balderston's thunderous voice suddenly boomed out over the babel. 'Shut up, the bloody lot of youse.'

It didn't matter how young or stupid they were, they all knew Mick Balderston. He was still one of the most experienced and respected detectives around; eight years in Homicide, six in Armed Robbery, and nearly as long in the Drug Squad. When Big Mick said 'Shut up,' you did as directed.

So, as the unruly rumble quickly died down, Detective Sergeant Warren Teale good-naturedly resumed his speech from the front of the room.

'Anyway, just to finish off,' he said at the top of his voice, swaying slightly from side to side without spilling a solitary drop of his beer, 'And speaking seriously, if I may, for a moment, Dave.' He looked to his right, where Dave Hocking was standing, beer in hand, alongside him, suddenly feeling slightly less comfortable, sensing the jocular sledging was about to give way to more serious stuff. 'I want to congratulate you, mate, on the Bravery Commendation that was awarded to you today.'

The collected crowd broke into spontaneous applause as Dave lifted his glass to acknowledge them, then knocked back a celebratory swallow. As it washed its way down, it cooled the sad, empty feeling that had sat in his stomach all day. He felt tired and distracted, the muscles behind both ears aching with the strain of sustaining a humourless smile, as he looked around the sea of familiar faces in front of him, bobbing with laughter and raucous hilarity.

It was official. He was a hero. The Trindall shooting had happened well over a year ago. But now, after all the internal enquiries had taken their course, and the Coroner's file had been closed, the Commissioner's office had finally declared Dave Hocking a dinky-di, first-class, certified champion. He was happy with that, he supposed. But somehow, it didn't feel like it ought to. It just felt like he hadn't had a decent night's sleep in too long, and the only real comfort he'd felt in months was the occasional pain in his side where the bullet went through him. It reminded him he was alive.

'I think we'd all agree that there is no better copper on the force than Old Mate here.' Warren Teale's croaky voice was suddenly wavering with emotion, and Dave looked over to see moisture glistening in his old friend's eyes. Clearly, he'd had a few beers too many. 'And I can certainly say, on a personal note, having worked with the bloke for every bit of thirty years, including a few very sticky moments here and there...' With that, the whole room erupted into a renewed bout of raucous jocularity and catcalls that lingered too long. But it had been a long, tough couple of years for the Force, and every copper who had ever walked the beat had had to cop some sort of crap from someone in recent times, so Mick Balderston let it go on till they'd all got it out of their system, before he eventually again bellowed the command to be silent. When the crowd settled down, Teale turned back to Dave, looking even more teary, and added, quietly, 'And a few very sad moments for you too, of course, Dave, along the way there.'

Dave Hocking looked back at his old friend, feeling numb. Warren Teale, and so many others as well, had started with Dave in one place, together, young men full of dreams, hopes and bravado, and they had since lived a life. Sometimes, briefly, it felt like they were all still there, poised in the starting blocks, raring to go, but so much had happened. Everything had changed.

'Anyway,' Teale continued, swallowing hard and blinking his emotion away, 'Having known him that long, I can honestly say...' He paused again, looking around the room at the faces staring solemnly back at him, his face now stretched into a bitter, resentful scowl. 'Regardless of all the bloody bullshit that's being spouted at the moment by some people…' He looked back at Dave with his jaw set defiantly, then continued. 'When the bad guys put on a stink, there's not a man in the job you'd rather have standing beside you, shoulder to shoulder, than that man right there—my good mate Dave Hocking.'

The spontaneous applause that followed was a distant echo in Dave Hocking's ears an hour later, as he drove through the black, sleeping back-streets towards his modest family home in the quiet, southern Brisbane suburb of Camp Hill. The white, overhead streetlights created a strange, dreamlike state he now cruised through, alone and adrift, silently into the night. Familiar faces were there as he drove, suspended in the light, floating like hazy, ill-defined spectres, the fresh-faced rookies and all the old hands, the mates who had come and gone year after year, good men and bad, the ones he once looked up to, the ones he still did, the ones who had failed and betrayed him. And now and then, through it all, the crazed, scary, murderous face of Mark Trindall, the man who had made him a certified hero.

Poor old Warren had drunk way too much. It wasn't the first time, and Dave understood why. Warren Teale was a decent bloke, but he wore his heart on his sleeve. In this job, you just couldn't do that. If you did, it eventually got the better of you, and it had got the better of Warren a long time ago. By the time they turned off the beer at the end of the night, Warren Teale was a gibbering mess. He had the wobbly boot on well and truly, and was still running off at the mouth, carrying on about what a good bloke Dave was, when the hall had all but cleared, and Laurie Morris and Paul Ballard were doing their best to steer him out through the side door, out to the car park.

'I love you, mate. I fuckin' love you,' Warren had called back over his shoulder to Dave, as Ballard held the door open for him with one hand, yanking him out with the other. 'I fuckin' love that man,' he added, to Marsden, on his way out. 'You know that? I fuckin' love him.'

'You too, Woz,' Dave called after him, as they shuffled him out through the door. 'You too, mate.'

'You're not driving tonight, are you?'

Dave turned to see the smiling face of his old pal Roger Page at his shoulder, a half-empty glass in his hand. As always, the Inspector-in-Charge of the Woolloongabba CIB looked sober, composed and controlled. That was Rodge. He and Dave had been friends for the best part of thirty years, pretty much ever since Dave first kicked off in the job, but through all those years he could only ever once remember Roger Page looking anything but cool, calm and collected.

He knew what his old mate was asking, and why. There was a time when a Queensland copper couldn't get done for drink-driving unless he walked into Police Headquarters with his hands in the air and surrendered. But not now. Not since the Fitzgerald Inquiry. You had to be careful these days. And, in particular, Dave Hocking had to be careful. For months now he'd been under investigation by the newly formed Special Prosecutor's Office, the mob who had taken over the job from Fitzgerald of making life hell for any poor copper ever suspected of so much as whistling in the pictures. The Inquiry's investigators had got it into their tiny little brains that Dave had snipped four grand out of the dresser drawer of some little druggie, and they'd been stomping all over his peace of mind ever since.

It all started more than a year ago, when Dave executed a warrant on a fleapit in Kangaroo Point, along with Laurie Morris and Paul Ballard and a couple of young uniformed blokes. They had good information the bloke that lived there—a grubby little rat by the name of Peter Penisi, with a list of priors as long as his arm—had a hydroponic grow-room all set up in his second bedroom and had been peddling pot all around the town. Unfortunately, somebody must have tipped him off in advance because, by the time the cops knocked on his door, the joint was as clean as a whistle. They still pinched Penisi for a bag of smoke and an old outstanding warrant, but that was the last Dave heard of it.

Then, months later, with everyone bagging the coppers day in and day out in the Fitzgerald Inquiry, Penisi belatedly came up with the story the detectives who pinched him that day had swooped on four grand in folders he had stashed in his bottom drawer, saving up to buy himself a new car.

Once upon a time, he would have been laughed out the door. But when he took his complaint to the Inquiry, they got all excited and started sniffing around, asking questions, so Dave and the detectives all made statements denying there was any cash on site, and of course Penisi couldn't prove otherwise, because any dough he'd ever laid his hands on was dodgy anyway. So it all died down again, for a while. Then, a few months back, when the Inquiry finally wound down, they handed Penisi's complaint over to the Special Prosecutor, who proceeded to whip himself into a lather about it, all over again.

By then, after two years and more of Fitzgerald turning them over, every copper in town was diving for cover, lining up in the streets to dog on each other. So, when the Special Prosecutor investigators fronted the young uniformed constables who had helped execute the Penisi warrant, one of them suddenly remembered seeing a detective with a bundle of cash in his hand that day and, when he did, the other uniformed bloke came down with a bad case of the screaming Hail Marys himself, pouring his heart out, and telling the investigators he saw Laurie Morris thumbing his way through a big wad of cash. He even thought he remembered seeing Laurie stuff some of it into his pocket.

It was embarrassing. Coppers selling down coppers. Dave couldn't believe it. He remembered when Rodge first called him into his office and broke the bad news to him. His face was as white as a sheet. He went through it slowly, explaining that the Special Prosecutor blokes had been in to see him, showed him signed statements from both of the uniformed constables. It was all there, not just Penisi's say-so, but signed statements from two police officers confirming the story, chapter and verse, enough to put Laurie Morris out of the job, and behind bars. Coppers giving evidence against coppers.

'It's a new ballgame these days, mate,' Rodge said to him, ashen faced. 'You know that.'

Dave nodded silently to himself, feeling sick in the stomach at the thought of it. As he did, Roger Page watched him silently for several long seconds. Then he spoke again, quietly, almost confidentially.

'Is there anything you want to tell me, Dave?'

Dave Hocking looked up at him, at first uncomprehending. He was looking his old friend straight in the eye, searching his face for what he was trying to say. When he eventually realised, his lip curled into an angry snarl.

'You working for the Special Prosecutor now, are you, Rodge?'

Roger Page's feeble chin began trembling, as if he'd been mortally offended.

'That's a shit of a thing to say to me, Dave,' he eventually protested, his voice quavering with emotion. 'After all we've been through together.'

It was true, they'd been through plenty together. That's what made it all the more painful. Dave gritted his teeth, seething, and pushed his chair back from the desk.

'You know something, Rodge?' he growled angrily. 'I remember when I first came into this job. I was just a hairy-arsed kid from the sticks, brand-new in uniform, didn't know shit from breakfast.' He put one hand on either armrest and leaned forward accusingly. 'Every time we went out on a bust you and all your mates in plain clothes would say to us uniforms "You blokes just wait outside while we go in first and secure the premises, then when it's safe we'll give youse the nod to come in." Remember that Rodge?' His teeth were bared like a rabid dog. 'Mate, I thought youse were all fucking heroes,' he hissed disdainfully. 'It wasn't until I got into plainclothes myself that I realised the first blokes through the door get their hands on all the goodies.'

The Inspector stared back blankly, as if he didn't know whether to be insulted or ashamed. Eventually, his eyes seemed to glisten with emotion. It was the first and last time Dave had ever seen Roger Page look anything but calm and collected.

'What do you want from me, Dave?' he said breathlessly. 'All I'm trying to do is help you, mate.

He looked so pathetic, Dave almost felt sorry for him. But not quite.

'How many times you reckon a copper's snipped a bit of loose cash from a grub like Penisi, and whacked it in his cunning-kick, Rodge?'

The Police Inspector sucked a deep breath in through his nostrils, setting his chin resolutely, and eventually restoring his cold, customary composure.

'Like I said, it's a whole new game, Dave. A whole new fucking game.'

He was right, and Dave knew it. That's just how it was. No point in whinging or wishing it wasn't.

After that, they hardly spoke again for several weeks, partly just because it had been a tough conversation that had opened up doors nobody wanted to go through, and partly because Dave Hocking genuinely regretted having upset his old mate, ashamed he'd attacked him the way he did. He shouldn't have. It was true, Roger Page was just trying to help him, doing what he could to offer his friend an easy way out. But now the genie was out of the bottle, it was hard to put it back in. They both knew, without doubt, in the brave new post-Fitzgerald world, Dave Hocking was a liability for his old mate, an embarrassment Inspector Roger Page didn't need in his life.

Rodge had come up with the plan to send Dave out of town for a while, and they both lied to each other that they thought a trip out of town for a while would be the best thing for Dave. Cunnamulla police needed a hand with a murder case they were preparing for committal proceedings in the Magistrates Court out there. The crime was committed out woop woop in Millengarra, where the only cop in the one-man station was a young junior Constable who'd never even prosecuted so much as a parking ticket before. Somebody needed to steer the young bloke around the park, help him get statements from all relevant witnesses and put a proper brief together for

Police Prosecutions in Cunnamulla. But it needed someone with a few rings around his arse, and it would probably take at least a couple of weeks to get the job done. Cunnamulla couldn't really spare any experienced detectives that long, so they were hoping Brisbane might be able to send someone out there to help out.

It was perfect for Dave right now, Roger assured him. It would give him a chance to get out of Brisbane, keep the investigators out of his hair, maybe even help clear his head a little bit. It would just take the heat off him, all around. In the meantime, Rodge had already talked to Police Media Liaison, and they were going to try to get something in the Sunday paper about Dave's bravery award—a nice little story about the whole Trindall shooting, a photo of the kids, maybe a quote from the Commissioner's speech—just to put a little bit of pressure back on the Special Prosecutor.

Roger Page was doing his best to help his old friend out. So, as the function room cleared, and Rodge asked his old mate Dave if he was planning on driving that night, Dave knew exactly what he was asking, and why. The last thing either of them needed right now, when the Inspector had gone to such trouble to arrange for the Sunday papers to write up one of his top detectives as a gilt-edged, certified hero, was for Dave Hocking to blow it all completely by getting himself pinched for drink-driving. Dave got it. He knew exactly what Roger was asking, and why.

'Mate, I've only had three drinks all night.'

It was true. Dave was a rum drinker, but police union funds didn't stretch to spirits for an impromptu piss-up like this, so it was a beer-only function. A couple of beers was more than enough for Dave at the best of times, and this definitely wasn't the best of times. He'd been feeling on edge all day. Apart from everything else going on, he hated being the centre of attention, and all the speeches and backslapping just weren't his go. Dave was glad it was just about over.

'When do you go to Millengarra?'

'I'll probably head out at sparrows' fart tomorrow morning.'

'Fair enough.'

Roger Page nodded pensively, looking him straight in the eye, his lips stretched into a gentle, affectionate grin.

'Congratulations on the award, mate,' he said eventually. 'You deserve it.' He offered his hand, which Dave Hocking accepted, and shook. 'You're as good a copper as I ever worked with.'

'Thanks mate.'

So there it was. Dave was as good a cop as Inspector Roger Page had ever worked with. What an honour. He could see his old friend's smiling, benevolent face, even now, feel the warmth of his palm in his hand, as he drove all alone through the night, down suburban backstreets bathed in a hazy white light. There was another face there too, a memory he quickly and purposefully pushed well out of his mind, as he swung his car into the driveway and pulled up in front of the tilt-a-door.

When Dave pushed in through the front door, into the house, Denise looked up from the television with a soft, welcoming smile.

'How did it go?'

'Yeah, all right.'

'Did you wear your medal?'

She was a cheeky bitch, always had been. He loved that about her.

'Yeah, right,' he scoffed, as he slumped into the other armchair, feeling his whole body relax, for the first time in hours.

'I left some dinner for you in the oven.'

Dave grunted. He didn't feel hungry, but it was comforting to hear she had put something out for him.

'What are you watching?'

'Oh, I don't know.' She said it without even taking her eyes off the screen. 'Some silly thing.'

Dave sat in the softly lit room, alongside his once-glamorous wife, the woman he had lived with for most of the past thirty years, staring blankly at their tiny television set. What was she watching? He slowly allowed himself to become mesmerised by the colour and movement in front of him, the dull sound of meaningless dialogue droning on as he felt himself melting, seeping further and further into the seat, almost right through it. His mind was clear now, quiet and vacant, for the first time all day. It felt good. But then, even as he tried to relax deeper and deeper into the armchair, he felt a familiar tingling begin in his feet and his fingers, and he suddenly started to sense himself becoming unsettled again. He always looked forward to arriving home to this little house they had owned together for so many years. But now he was there, like so often in recent times, he began to feel a sad, empty feeling gathering, deep down within him. He looked up at the wall clock above the TV. It had just turned seven o'clock. The prospect of another long, sleep-disturbed night lay ahead.

'I might try and get a start tonight, I think.'

'Oh, not tonight, darl.' Denise turned to him, her face lined with concern. 'It's late.'

He couldn't look at her.

'It's only seven,' he shot back, pulling himself out of the chair. 'I should make Dalby by ten, easy. I'll stay there overnight.' He didn't look back until he got to the entrance to the hallway, where he stopped and turned, and faced her for the first time. They were staring benignly at each other now, eye-to-eye, silent, across the little lounge room, as Dave gradually stretched his lips into a flat, humourless smirk. 'It'll break the trip up a bit.'

Denise knew how he was feeling, what he was going through, what he needed. She couldn't help him. He needed to go; she understood that. She nodded sadly, and went back to watching the television.

•

By the time Dave saw the first faded billboard advertising motel accommodation in Dalby, he was still a good half-hour east of the town. He'd been driving for over two hours, staring at the long, narrow tunnel his headlights were boring into the blackness ahead, the incessant, broken white line-marks leaping, on and on, into the light-shaft ahead of him, as if counting down every kilometre of his journey into the outback. With just one brief stop at a servo at the top of the range, to fill up the tank and grab a quick bite to eat, then one more at the pub on the western side of Toowoomba, to stock up on bottles of rum, he was making good time.

In a way, it was almost less painful now, all on his own, wallowing in his own thoughts, thinking things through. At least now he could feel like he was doing something worthwhile, heading out for a job, doing what he always did best, being a cop. He had read the crime reports on the McQuillan murder case, and he was already thinking through what the job would require. It sounded like a pretty standard incident for this part of the world; another crazy, drunken dust-up gone completely out of control. Bluff and bluster turn into a push and a shove, turns to homicide. Piss-fuelled insanity. All too familiar out here in the bush. But there were no eyewitnesses to this one, and no confession, and that meant they would have to do plenty of work to make the case watertight.

He noticed the detective in charge of the investigation was Bruce Atwood. He wouldn't be much help. Atwood was sent out to Cunnamulla for a very good reason; he was useless as tits on a bull. It was going to be just Dave out there, working it up with some young, local constable who didn't know one end of a court brief from the other, so Dave was already thinking it through, working out systematically what ground they would need to cover off in the brief.

It was good to be working, to have something to plan, to help him forget, to push to the back of his brain a whole lot of stuff he didn't need in his head. It was good to be all on his own. No one out here wanted to shake his hand, slap his back, or congratulate him. And, best of all, there was no one out here to feel sorry for him. There was just Detective Senior Sergeant Dave Hocking, all on his own, out on the job.

The former Gold Coast detective, Frank Vagianni, had looked like a broken man when he showed up at the function earlier that night. He'd been suspended from the Force for months, ever since the Special Prosecutor's Office had announced its investigation of official corruption allegations over the Waterworld robbery proceeds. Dave had to hand it to Frank, it was ballsy of him to show up when so many blokes in the job had dropped off him lately, talking about him behind his back and generally treating him like Lazarus the Leper.

It was funny how short some people's memories could be. But Dave remembered. He knew why Frank had turned up, and he appreciated the gesture. He was a loyal little bloke and, whatever he might have done wrong, or not, he'd always been a good cop, and a good friend to Dave.

Frank Vagianni hadn't stayed long that night, but at least he turned up when a lot of other blokes in his situation wouldn't, and he'd made a point of corralling Dave, shaking his hand, and congratulating him on the award. Admittedly, when he did turn up, he looked like a shadow of his former self, and Dave couldn't help reflecting on how quickly a bloke who'd been kicked to the kerb like Frank became Yesterday's Man. He'd lost a heap of weight, and seemed to have aged years, even in the few short months since Dave had last seen him. It wasn't surprising; he was off the Force, and firmly out in the cold. But he still had that broad, Italian-boy grin, and the cheeky glint in his eye that suggested he wasn't quite out for the count just yet.

As Dave Hocking pushed on into the night on the flat, dark Warrego Highway between Bonneville and Dalby, he thought a lot about that curious look in the little bloke's eye. Seeing Frank there that night had initially released a whole bunch of butterflies in Dave's stomach, reminding him of his own Special Prosecutor problems. But, strangely enough, looking back now, he realised he'd found those few minutes alone with Frank quietly comforting.

'How's that Special Prosecutor thing going?'

Frank looked completely unfazed by the question.

'Mate, they've got nothing,' he pronounced with consummate confidence. 'I'll be back in the job in no time.'

Dave smiled and nodded his head warmly, appreciative of Frank's deliberate lack of candour. They both knew it wasn't as simple as that. Frank had a whole world of heartache ahead of him. The stakes for any cop charged with a serious criminal offence like corruption were sky-high. If he was convicted, for starters his career would be over forever, and even once he got out of the slammer, he'd be scratching around for a living for the rest of his life. If he got out of the slammer. For a cop, any cop, and particularly one like Frank, who had played the game hard all the way, any time spent inside was hard time, and there'd be plenty of lunatics lining up to take a shot at him if he ended up behind bars. It had to be a daunting prospect for anyone, even a tough little Italian boy like Frank.

'Are you lawyered up yet?'

'Yeah.' Frank's fat little face lit up comically as he glanced theatrically over each shoulder, then continued in a hoarse, confidential whisper. 'I got that Moran.'

'What?' He was talking about Eddie Moran, the young upstart they'd both had so much trouble with down in the Southport Magistrates Court. 'Are you serious? The bloke's a complete arsehole.'

'Yeah, I know,' Frank said, wide-eyed and grinning like a Cheshire cat. 'It's good, isn't it?' His obvious delight was so deeply absurd and deluded Dave couldn't help breaking into a spontaneous smile at the sight of him, and soon found himself chuckling illogically in unison with Frank. But the senseless glee soon petered out, leaving Frank silent and still, looking quietly resigned.

'Fuck 'em,' he said, shrugging his shoulders nonchalantly. 'If I'm going down, I'm going down swinging.'

Perhaps it wasn't as silly as it sounded. The Force had turned its back on Frank; even the Police Union had abandoned him. The tide had turned on them all with Fitzgerald. Nowadays, any cop accused of anything was automatically considered guilty, on the nose just as much with the Force as with the journos and the general public. They were out on their own. The old rules were out the window. So why not go with a wildcard like Moran, a loose cannon on the deck, the one lawyer every Queensland cop hated more than any other, someone who would kick up as much dust as possible, and upset everyone they conceivably could in the process? When the odds were stacked completely against you, as Frank said, you may as well go down swinging.

Dave pushed the thought from his consciousness, trying hard to focus on the job ahead, the job he'd been sent out to do. It would be pretty straightforward. Everyone knew everyone, and everyone's business, in a small country town. The first thing Dave and the young local constable needed to do was get around to all the locals, speak to anyone who knew these two blokes—McQuillan and the deceased—anyone who could talk about their relationship, how they got on, whether there'd been any previous violence, any ongoing malice between them. Two dopey young drunks living together out back of woop woop would likely have plenty of form. If either of them was in any way punchy, which most young country blokes were, there would have been plenty of drama already between them. Anything anyone could tell them about that sort of stuff would be gold.

As his brain absently drifted around the thought of two violent young men, Mark Trindall suddenly leapt into Dave Hocking's consciousness, screaming blood-curdling threats and baring his teeth like a crazed, mangey dog. He squinted painfully as his heartbeat began to race, and thumped the wound in his side, forcibly pushing the image out of his brain, intently trying to return to the idea of other, alternative avenues of inquiry they should be following on McQuillan and the deceased. But instead, unexpected, uninvited, the Trindall children materialised there in his thoughts, sad and pathetic.

Then, as he tried to think them away, out of nowhere, his own daughter came to him, young, beautiful, full of life and unbounded promise.

Dave opened his eyes wide and fixed his vision intently on the distant glow of oncoming headlights up ahead of him, faraway over the western horizon. He glared at it, concentrating hard, focused on it as he sped, determined, towards it. At first it was just a benevolent beacon lighting the way, but then gradually, increasingly, it grew in intensity with each passing second, escalating steadily from a warm, far-off glimmer into an ultimately ominous threat of harsh, blinding light. Now, as Dave watched it coming, he flicked his lights down onto low beam, and waited.

When the glow continued advancing, undiminished, he angrily flicked his beam switch again, up-and-down, up-and-down, several times. The approaching lights remained constant, surging unrelenting towards him for several more seconds. Then, just as they were about to break over the horizon, the driver adjusted them down, a split second before they finally burst into view.

Dave grunted his indignation, squinting again into the now-visible oncoming headlights, momentarily considering the prospect of pulling the driver over and conducting a vehicle inspection just to teach the ignorant prick some manners. But the urge quickly passed, as the oncoming car came and went, eventually zipping past him in the opposite direction. He had a long way to go, and a long night ahead. He glanced disdainfully into the rear vision mirror, watching the car speed away, into the distance.

Dave looked back at the road ahead for a second, and then back at the mirror. As he did, he saw the other car's brake lights come on. He watched as the vehicle swung into a tight, hurried U-turn, and then fell in behind him, several hundred metres back. Soon he could see it was steadily gaining on him.

Dave was mildly intrigued, almost interested, until he saw a blue light briefly flash into his rear-view mirror, and heard the quick wail of a police siren, flicked on and back off immediately. He scoffed impatiently, shaking his head, as the vehicle fast approaching behind him flashed its lights onto high beam and back down several times.

He didn't have time for this shit, but it wouldn't take long. He pulled over onto the verge of the highway and watched as the headlights pulled in behind him and quickly came to a stop.

As the young uniformed officer climbed out of the car and sauntered towards him, a notebook in one hand and flashlight in the other, Dave wound down his window, then leaned across and flicked open the glove box. His hand pushed past his service revolver, delving deeper and rummaging around for his ID, as he heard the crunch of police-issue boots on the gravel edge of the roadway, walking up to the window.

'How're you goin'?'

The young officer had his pen out and looked like he was already starting to write out a ticket. Dave had bad news for him.

'Good,' he said, as he flipped his wallet open on his lap, ready for the big reveal.

'Do you know you were doing over a hundred and forty in a hundred zone back there?'

Dave held up his wallet, allowing it to fall open in his hand, displaying his police badge and ID.

'Mate, I'm a copper,' he said, matter-of-factly. He was surprised when the officer took the wallet from his hand anyway, and carefully inspected it. 'I'm with the CI Branch, out of Brisbane. I'm on my way out to Millengarra on a murder investigation.'

'Fair enough,' the young man eventually said. He jotted down several more notes before closing the wallet and handing it back. 'Tell you what, I'll put it through as fifteen Ks over, then; okay?' He was now back to writing again. 'Just make sure you knock it back a notch, alright?'

'What?'

'I'll write it down to exceeding the limit by fifteen clicks.'

'What do you mean, exceeding by fifteen?'

'Mate, you would have been doing easy twice that.'

Dave Hocking screwed his face into an incredulous, uncompromising grimace.

'You're kidding, aren't you?' he snapped back. 'You're going to write me a ticket?'

The young man stopped writing and looked up at him with an expression of mild indignation.

'You were doing nearly one and a half times the speed limit.'

'Mate, are you fuckin' deaf or something?' the detective erupted. 'Didn't you just hear me? I'm in the fuckin' job, mate, I'm a copper.'

The uniformed officer looked back at him, silently, for several long seconds, before he eventually spoke up again.

'Were you in pursuit of an offender?'

Dave curled his lip into a threatening scowl.

'Fuck off,' he growled angrily.

The young man went back to writing his ticket, studiously ignoring the senior detective's continued complaints.

'How long have you been in the job, sport?' The question was left unanswered. 'Probably about two fuckin' minutes, have you?' Still no answer. 'Yeah, that'd be right. I've been in the job thirty fuckin' years. And you're telling me you're going to book another copper for speeding?'

The young man tore off the ticket and handed it to him efficiently, not waiting for any response. As he turned on his heels and strode back to his car, Dave pushed his head through the window and angrily yelled after him.

'It's pricks like you that've ruined the fuckin' force.'

By the time the police car had pulled into a U-turn, back onto the eastern-bound lane, Dave was out of his car, calling after him.

'No wonder we're all getting round lookin' over our fuckin' shoulders, you arsehole.'

The car swept away, into the night, leaving Dave Hocking standing alone on the roadside, in darkness, feeling betrayed, broken, and breathless with anger. He leaned forward in the doorway, onto the roof of the car, trying to settle his breath and calm himself down. Eventually, he turned, pushed the door further open, and slumped back into the seat.

'You'll fuckin' keep,' he said aloud to himself, then added, almost as an after-thought, 'You shithead.'

Dave looked down at the crumpled speeding infringement still clasped in his hand. It was for fifteen clicks over. He shook his head. Coppers booking coppers for speeding. How the hell had it come to this? As he looked back up at the road ahead, stretching out to the dim, distant lights of Dalby, he knew he wasn't going to sleep tonight. Certainly not in some fleapit in Dalby.

He reached behind him and lifted the brown paper bag off the floor at the back of the passenger seat. Then he slipped one rum bottle out and screwed off the top. It would be a long night. Cunnamulla was a good six hours drive away. If his demons didn't keep him awake, the sugar in the rum surely would.

SEVEN

Mark Trindall had a painful lump in his throat as he pushed through the narrow wire gate and strode purposefully up the cracked-cement pathway to the front door. This had been his home, the one place where for a brief time he had once felt happy and totally secure in his life. This was where his family was, where he ought to be.

'What do you want, Mark?'

Blair Ainscoe was a big, raw-boned man, and his bulky frame filled the doorway completely as he leaned one tattooed arm on the frame and glared menacingly down at the smaller man. But Mark Trindall wasn't feeling cowed or intimidated. All he was feeling was the same stinging pain that had gnawed at his innards for days. He had been up all night thinking about this very moment; he wasn't going anywhere.

'I want to talk to Cheryl.'

The starch in the little man's voice immediately irritated Ainscoe, and he bared his teeth angrily, scowling with utter disdain.

'Well she doesn't want to talk to you,' he growled. 'She's already told you that. Now fuck off.'

The demand was emphatic and final, but Mark Trindall didn't move an inch.

'I want to talk to Cheryl.'

That was enough for Ainscoe, and he leapt into action. But, as he pushed the door fully open and launched himself forward, furious, out onto the landing, Cheryl Snape suddenly appeared alongside him from nowhere, pulling him back as hard as she could.

'Leave him Blair, leave him. He's just a fucking dickhead.'

She quickly stepped around her new partner, and got up in the face of her ex.

'Fuck off, Mark,' she screamed angrily at him. 'I told you I don't want you coming around here no more.'

Trindall's eyes were now filled with tears, his chin trembling feebly.

'But I want to see the kids, babe,' he said softly, into her face. 'I just want to talk to them, give them a hug.' For the briefest moment, standing there, face to face, she almost felt sorry for him; he looked so helpless, so lost and alone. Mark Trindall loved his children—she knew that—and in his own way he really had tried to be a good father. But then, as she stood there, staring into his tear-filled eyes, her resolve wavering, her ex-partner plaintively added 'I want us to all be together again.'

It couldn't happen; he should know that. It just couldn't be that way. It was over; there was no going back. He had to get that into his head.

'No, Mark,' she snapped angrily. 'You fucking heard me. I don't want you here. Piss off.'

It was so brutal he felt like she'd physically struck him. He reached out and snatched at her forearm, pleading with her.

'Please, babe. I love you. Please.'

The next thing Mark Trindall knew he was on the ground, his head spinning, and his left ear ringing painfully. Blair Ainscoe had hold of his shirt collar and was slapping him, hard and repeatedly, open-handed, over the head. He felt himself being dragged onto his feet and frogmarched up to the rickety front gate, before it was wrenched open, and he was given an almighty shove onto the roadway.

'Get the fuck out of here, you pathetic little piece of shit,' Ainscoe bellowed at him, and then, as a parting gesture, he delivered a heavy kick to the smaller man's buttocks, sending him sprawling headlong across the bitumen towards his parked car.

'And don't fucking come back.'

As Mark Trindall settled into the driver's seat of his car, he watched his former lover and her new boyfriend step back into his one-time family home, and slam the door shut firmly behind them. The sight of that little door closing, shutting him off from all he held dear, sent a piercing pain deep into his chest. He couldn't feel the lump on the side of his head, his bruised buttocks, or the gravel rash on his palms, all he could feel was the ache at the back of his throat and that piercing pain in his chest.

He sat motionless, numb, staring blankly towards the house. Several doors up, the short, balding, middle-aged man he hardly knew had resumed mowing his front lawn, but was still cautiously casting occasional glimpses over his shoulder. Old Wally next door had pulled his front curtains closed, but Mark knew the old man was still there, no doubt watching and savouring the humiliation that had been handed out, just like the rest of the neighbours undoubtedly were too. He was an outcast now, gone, out of their lives, all of them. Somewhere behind that closed door were his children, and their new life, with their mother's new lover. They were probably all inside together now, laughing at how thoroughly he had disgraced himself. His children would grow up learning about how their father was nothing but a pathetic little piece of shit, who had been pushed and kicked and shoved right out of their lives.

Without thinking a thing, Trindall was out of his seat, walking towards the rear of his car, opening the boot, rummaging around until he laid his hands on a familiar object, cold but nonetheless comforting. He pulled the rifle out of the boot and slipped a .22 cartridge into the breach.

●

Dave Hocking was in the main CIB office area, doing paperwork, when the call came through from the Radio Room that there had been a shooting at a house in the nearby suburb of Buranda, and there was currently a siege in progress. All the information the police had at that stage was that the shooter's name was Mark Trindall, an out of work boilermaker recently separated from his de facto wife and two kids, who were all believed to be still in the house. It was still unclear just who had been shot, and why.

By the time Dave arrived at the scene, there was a veritable fleet of marked and unmarked police cars in attendance, and the uniformed boys had already closed down the street and cordoned off the whole area. What looked like a big man was lying half on the landing and half in the front garden bed, face down in a pool of blood, and the obvious suspect was standing not far away from him, framed in the front doorway, with his left hand holding a rifle and the other arm wrapped tightly around the neck of a diminutive female who was clearly in all kinds of bother. The suspect was shaking the woman around and screaming something Dave couldn't quite make out it first.

As soon as he found Paul Ballard, crouched down behind a police car at the kerb on the opposite side of the street, he slipped in safely alongside him.

'What's his problem?'

'Lover's tiff,' Ballard answered, nodding towards the prone figure sprawled over the landing. 'Looks like that's the new boyfriend.'

'Do we know his condition?'

Ballard shook his head.

'It doesn't look good. He hasn't moved an inch that I've seen.'

At that moment, the suspect screamed out again, and this time Dave heard him, loud and clear.

'Get the fuck away from here, all of youse. I'll fuckin' shoot her if youse come any closer. And the kids.'

Trindall's hostage had tears streaming down both of her cheeks, and she groaned loudly in obvious terror at the mention of her children.

'Mark, please don't do it,' she blubbered hysterically. 'Please, baby, please.'

With that, the suspect jammed the gun barrel under her chin, screaming at her.

'Shut up! Fuckin' shut up!'

He had his finger planted firmly on the trigger, the gun barrel dug deep into her throat, as he moved back and forth erratically in the doorway, now bellowing out at the police cordon surrounding the house.

'Get away, all of youse. Get away or I'll fuckin' kill her, you understand me? I'll fuckin' kill her.'

This was a man on the edge, a crazed lunatic with his finger wrapped around the trigger of a loaded gun. It was an accident waiting to happen, at the very least. They had to do something, and soon. When Trindall yanked the woman out of the doorway, back into the house, out of sight, Dave turned back to Ballard.

'Has anyone got onto SERT?'

The Special Emergency Response Team would at least have some sharp-shooters, and hopefully negotiators, specially trained for this kind of hostage-type situation.

'They're trying to get a TRG team here asap.'

The words were no sooner out of Paul Ballard's mouth than a gunshot rang out inside the house, accompanied by the bloodcurdling sound of a woman's shrill scream.

'Fuck!' Dave Hocking's heartbeat was now racing. There were two little kids still in the house. 'We might not have time to wait.'

He shoved his service revolver into the waistband at the back of his trousers, stood up with his hands in the air, and began walking briskly across the road towards the house. As he pushed in through the front gate, and slowed his gait on the pathway, he called out cautiously.

'Mark? Mark, it's Dave here, mate. Mark? Are you there, mate?'

As he neared the front landing, he stopped, looking down at the body of Blair Ainscoe, lying face down in his own blood on the doorstep. Paul Ballard was right, the boyfriend was dead, for sure and for certain.

'Mark? You there, mate? I just want to have a yarn with you. Alright?'

Mark Trindall suddenly appeared at the open window alongside the front door, only feet away from him, brandishing a gun pointed straight at Dave Hocking.

'I told you to fuck off,' he yelled frantically through the window. 'Get back or I'll fuckin' shoot you. I'll fucking shoot all of them.'

They were now looking each other straight in the eye, and the detective could see the fear and panic in Mark Trindall's face. He didn't look like a man who wanted to die in a police shootout.

'Hang on, mate,' Hocking said, as calmly as he could. 'You're going to have to settle down a bit, okay?' As Trindall stared back at him, wide-eyed and panting, looking stunned and confused, the detective continued talking to him, as quietly and matter-of-factly as possible. 'I just want to have a bit of a yack with you, that's all. Okay?'

But Trindall erupted again.

'I'll fucking kill 'em,' he screamed.

'Yeah, okay, mate, okay. Just, settle down. Okay?' Dave had his hands held up high, up over his head, palms forward, trying hard to keep his composure. 'I'll just come to the door. Okay, Mark? That way we can properly hear each other. Okay?'

'Fuck off!' Trindall shrieked, suddenly wrenching himself away from the window and disappearing from sight.

Dave's heart leapt into his mouth. Trindall was on the move, and that meant the kids were in danger. He had to do something to stop him, right now. He pulled the revolver from his waistband and sprinted towards the landing, charging in through the doorway, swivelling to his left as he did, his gun trained at the sound of crazy footfalls scuttling frantically somewhere inside the house. But the second he cleared the entrance hallway and burst into sight, facing into the lounge, a deafening bang exploded from a white flash that knocked him off balance into the wall behind him, as he simultaneously peeled off a shot of his own. He hit the wall with a thud and dropped down onto his rump, the impact knocking the air right out of his lungs leaving him slumped on the floor, disorientated, gasping for breath and unable to move.

His right hand, still holding his gun, was lying limp in his lap. Just above it, on his left side, there was a ragged patch of dark crimson soaking into the front of his shirt. When he saw it, the adrenaline suddenly kicked back in, clearing his brain. He looked up frantically, scanning the loungeroom, waving his revolver indiscriminately across the wall in front of him.

Then he saw him. Trindall was there on the floor, lying on his side in the empty loungeroom, whimpering, curled up and clutching his blood-soaked stomach.

He was looking directly at Dave, his face crumpled into a sad and pathetic expression, eyes filled with glistening tears, as he puffed out short, staccato-like breaths. The rifle was lying on the floor alongside him, just inches out of his reach. The detective trained the revolver on him and tried to speak as firmly but calmly as possible.

'Don't move, Mark,' he said, holding him in his sights. 'Just stay there. We'll get someone to you in a minute.'

Dave looked to his left, out through the doorway, to where he could see several heavily armed police now on their feet and in the clear, tentatively approaching the house. When he looked back, he saw Trindall inching forward, reaching out for his rifle.

'Leave it,' he barked at him urgently. 'Leave it Mark. Don't fucking touch it.'

The wounded man stopped and looked up at him, staring straight into his eyes, his expression now totally hollow and devoid of emotion. Dave was transfixed by his gaze, somehow deeply intense, but completely empty. As they stared straight at each other, eye to eye, Dave could see nothing. The fear and panic were now gone; there was no pain, and no anger. Just a weird, vacant look, of surrender perhaps, or resignation. He felt like he was almost looking right through him.

Now, more than twelve months and six hundred kilometres away from that humble home in suburban Brisbane, plunged deep in the dead of the night, the tyres of his car monotonously droning on a narrow strip of bitumen that tunnelled incessantly into the blackness ahead, visions of that vacant look in the eyes of Mark Trindall were rattling around in the back of Dave Hocking's brain. He was haunted by them.

How did that poor bastard get there, lying on the floor of what was once his own home, with murderous blood on his hands and his kids in the corner, cowering in terror? What was behind those cold, hollow eyes in that instant? What was going through his brain?

Dave Hocking lifted the bottle to his lips and guzzled down several swallows. He reckoned he was no more than twenty-five K's east of Bollon now, which meant he'd easily make Cunnamulla by sun-up. He was making good time.

The straight rum felt good as it burned a path to his stomach, refocusing his eyes on the shaft of light that was leading him into the night. On the edges of the burrowing beam, big red kangaroos occasionally appeared in the flat, dusty scrub bordering the roadway, bounding alongside the long, straight road in packs of four or five, before eventually disappearing back into the night.

He knew from experience he had to keep his eyes out for these big, crazy bastards. They could get up to speeds of around seventy Ks, leaping six feet up in the air and twenty-five feet at a time, and they had the dangerous habit of every now and then deciding it was a good idea to cross over the road in front of a moving car. They were big, lean, barrel-chested bludgers, some of them well over six foot tall and more than ninety kilograms in weight, so Dave knew all too well, with no bull bar on the front of his car, a collision with one of them could prove pretty disastrous. He took another swig of rum, shook his head clear and stretched his eyes open, as wide as he could.

The tunnel of light boring endlessly into the night was almost mesmerising. Any line marking had long ago disappeared from the bitumen strip, and the red dust edges were encroaching increasingly as each successive kilometre swept past under the front of his car.

Dave reached out to the dial on his radio, realising he had been listening to nothing but static for the past half an hour. As he turned the dial one way, then the other, the crackling wavered, momentarily giving way to something that sounded like music, then conversation, then static again. He spun the volume dial, winding it up as far as he could, straining to hear what sounded like somebody talking, far away, deep behind a hissing, abrasive wall of white noise.

It was futile. He stabbed at the off button, then reached again for the rum bottle. Bollon couldn't be far away now. Another couple of hours and he'd be within sight of Cunnamulla. He settled back, watching the straight, slender strip ahead, illuminated in the headlights. As he drove, on and on in the same, long, straight line, the darkness began to close in all around him, weaving a spell, turning the tunnel of light into a dull, slender shaft that seduced him, and eventually hypnotised him.

Bang!

The collision hit like an explosion inside his head, jolting his eyes open and wrenching him instantly awake. Everything was moving, in every direction, weird, indiscernible images careering in giddy tangents before his eyes, as his brain struggled to comprehend. He was desperately gripping the steering wheel with both hands, squinting against the sting of shattered glass spraying into his face, as the car fiercely lurched, rattling and bouncing all around him, out of control, careering off the highway into the dark, dusty landscape. For a momentary millisecond there was a strange, silent feeling of total suspension, and then a horrible, metallic crunch as the car slammed to a sudden stop, catapulting him forward into the dashboard.

•

When he came to, Dave Hocking could feel the warm stream of blood flowing down onto his face. Slowly, warily, he sat back in his seat and reached up, tentatively touching his forehead. It was no more than a split in his scalp, just above the hairline. Like any scalp cut, it was bleeding like a leaky tap, but it was nothing serious. He pulled a handkerchief from his pocket, wiped the blood from his face, and then held it down on the wound. Everything else felt okay. He moved his head carefully from side to side, then rotated his shoulders and slowly lifted his elbows, moving his arms up and down. No pain anywhere, no problem.

He looked out ahead, through what had once been the windscreen, to where a tight pool of light from the headlights was now splashed over a still, empty vista of grey, stunted scrub reaching out into black night beyond. The jagged edges of the smashed windscreen were spattered with tiny flecks of what looked like blood, and the dashboard was covered with fragments of shattered glass. He looked down at his lap. His clothes were dotted with glistening specks of glass particles; with his one free hand he swiped at them indignantly, dusting them away from him.

As the glass fragments tinkled onto the floor and the seat alongside him, Dave suddenly thought he heard something else, outside, not far away. He wound down the window and peered out into the blackness, waiting and listening. Then he heard it again, a scraping, grappling noise, then a groping and scuttling, like something out there was now on the move, running clumsily away from the scene.

Dave flicked off the seatbelt, leaned over and pulled his gun out of the glovebox. The car door resisted, then made a loud, banging noise as he shouldered it open and climbed out, onto the uneven earth. Now he could see whatever it was, something large and stooped over, swaying and staggering in the darkness, maybe fifty metres away from the car, and heading deeper into the distance. He checked the cylinder of his handgun to ensure it was loaded, clicked off the safety, and then set off after it at a brisk walk.

Whatever it was, it was in a bad way, lurching awkwardly off course now and then and occasionally falling down onto the ground, lying still for an instant, then scuttling to its feet and taking off again. Dave broke into a jog, keen to put a swift end to its misery. But it was hard going, trudging through the rough, craggy terrain. He was soon puffing heavily, but he could still hear the creature up ahead of him, now panting a soft grunting noise, and still wavering erratically.

Eventually, it fell one last time, and lay wheezing pathetically in the long stringy grass, scratching hopelessly at the dry ground, trying to get to its feet. Dave slowed to a walk, and gradually approached to within around ten metres of it. As his eyes finally focused on it, in the pitch dark of that moonless night, a profound sense of horror descended upon him.

He could almost smell its fear and panic, hear the pain in the wheeze of its dying breath. He stopped and stood still, now only metres away, raising his gun at arms-length and training it down on the dark, writhing form on the ground ahead of him. He hesitated for a moment, horrified, then pulled the trigger. The deafening crack of the gunshot startled him, and then gradually evaporated into the open expanse of the outback.

There was no more wheezing or whimpering, no scratching. Now there was just peace and silence. To be sure, he squeezed the trigger one more time.

The moment Dave Hocking slumped back into the driver's seat of his car, he reached for the rum bottle and gulped down several deep swallows. As it drained down into his gullet, he sat stunned and motionless, staring out through the shattered windscreen at the flat, desolate patch of plain ahead, bathed in the yellow glow of his headlights. Eventually, he lifted one hand and punched off the light switch, plunging him into a thick, impenetrable darkness.

The horror had subsided now as a sadness enveloped him, seeping into his throat and his chest, stinging his eyes until he eventually closed them. He felt utterly alone, adrift in a sea of dark and regret.

As his chest rose and fell with the slow, rhythmic tide his breath, he allowed himself to think of his daughter, imagining her as a child again, playing blissfully in the backyard. But soon, other ugly, bitter memories began to intrude, and he pushed them away, opening his eyes momentarily to take another long swig from the bottle. When he closed them again, he felt the rum dull his consciousness, tapping into an overwhelming sense of fatigue that slowly, and increasingly, numbed his brain and his body, until he eventually drifted into a deep and dreamless sleep.

•

Several hours later, as a soft orange dawn cracked over the distant horizon, Dave Hocking opened up one eye. He had a thumping headache, and a stiff, aching cramp in the side of his neck. He had slept sitting up, and the blood that had seeped from the gash in his scalp was now crusted and caked onto the side of his face. The car was a good twenty metres away from the bitumen, marooned in amongst the stunted, straggly tufts of grey grass that grew around it, and stretched out on all sides into the distance, as far as the eye could see. He reached down to the ignition, took a firm grasp of the key, and kicked the engine over.

It was well after eight in the morning by the time Dave's crumpled car finally rolled into the main street of Cunnamulla, its driver squinting into a strong headwind that was now blowing hard in through the hole where the windscreen once had been.

It was years since Dave had been out to Cunnamulla, but from what he saw so far it looked like nothing much had changed. With a population of close to 2000, the rural centre of the vast, 47,000-square-kilometre Paroo Shire was as close to the Big Smoke as any town got in these far-flung parts; but it was still just a sprawling little tree-lined hick town, and at this time of the morning you could fire a shotgun down the main drag without serious risk of hitting anyone.

He cruised down past the Shire Council Chambers and headed in a bee line for the New Jumbuck Motor Inn. When he got there, he saw immediately the New Jumbuck didn't look a minute newer than it did ten years ago, but it was good enough for what he needed right now—a hot shower, breakfast, and hopefully a couple of hours decent sleep. He swung into the driveway, killed the engine, and wrestled his way out of the car.

As he stepped into the shade of the awning out front, Dave could already see the owner inside the front office, perched on a high stool at the front desk, hunched over his morning newspaper, and gently blowing the steam off a hot cup of tea.

'G'day,' Dave said as he pushed in through the front door.

'How're y'goin'?' the proprietor drawled back at him.

'Yeah, not bad.'

'Hit a roo, did ya?'

Dave turned and looked out at the car. The blood-spattered bumper was pushed badly out of shape, the bonnet buckled and bent, and the windscreen now non-existent. It didn't look too good.

'Yeah,' he nodded absently. 'Something like that.'

'Pricks of things, they are.' The proprietor nodded philosophically, silently assessing the state of the vehicle for several seconds, then turned his attention to the motel register, running his finger down one column. 'How long're you in town for?'

'Just the night. I head to Millengarra in the morning.'

He arched his eyebrows and nodded again, as if the answer had some sort of significance, then went back to the register. Dave knew what he was thinking. Millengarra was only about a hundred and twenty clicks down the road from Cunnamulla. It was mostly a dirt road, of course, but in these parts a hundred and twenty K drive anywhere wasn't much more than a leisurely outing. *Why would you need an overnight break before pushing on to Millen?* But Dave wanted a few hours R 'n' R in Cunnamulla; he had an old mate he was keen to catch up with.

'Anywhere I can get the car cleaned up?'

The proprietor looked up at him again.

'Yeah,' he said slowly, with yet another pensive nod. 'There's a hose and brush just down the side there, at the end of the driveway. Anything more than that you'd be best to try Rooney's Garage over in Wicks Street.'

'Wicks Street.'

'Yeah.' He sat silent for a moment, staring into space, and then added 'But you'd have to wait a few days if you're after a new windscreen, I'd say.'

Dave didn't have a few days to sit around taking in the sights of beautiful, down-town Cunnamulla, even if there were any. By the time he'd scrubbed the car down, unpacked his gear, had a shower, made a couple of calls and changed his clobber, then convinced the maître d' to whip him up a toasted ham and cheese sandwich in the kitchen, it was time to get going down to the local Police Station.

He needn't have bothered combing his hair before he left. By the time he'd done the quick eight hundred metres drive down to the station, without a windscreen, he looked like he'd just sky-dived from fifteen thousand feet.

The overall impression that short drive created wasn't lost on Senior Sergeant Bruce McKinley, sitting at his desk in the day room of the Cunnamulla Police Station, overlooking the main street, as this new stranger in town wrestled with the front door of his car, parked at the kerb out front of the station, then forced it open with his shoulder and climbed out with a bang, his hair and clothes dusty and windswept. Bruce couldn't help but chuckle to himself as he got up from the desk and strolled out onto the front veranda, just as an old familiar face pushed his way in through the gate and trudged down the path towards the front door.

'Holy shit,' the Senior Sergeant laughed. 'Who's this bloody desperado? Someone throw a muzzle on it, for Christ's sake, before it bloody bites some poor bastard.'

Hocking reached the end of the path, stopped, and looked up at Bruce McKinley with a broad, affectionate smile.

'G'day Brucey.'

He held his hand out, and his old friend grasped it firmly.

'G'day matey.' He looked so happy, he almost had tears in his eyes. 'Good to see you, champ.'

It was good to see him too. Dave had almost forgotten just how good. He and Bruce McKinley had been best mates ever since they started out, back in the old days in the Valley station. Dave was just a hairy-arsed kid fresh out of the Academy back then, and Bruce wasn't all that far ahead of him. They walked the beat together from day one, and from that day on they had each other's back. Brucey taught young Dave everything there was to know about the job, including all the lurks and perks. They must have pinched a thousand pros, pissheads, pimps and pickpockets in their time in uniform together. By the time they made detective they were already best of mates, and after that they'd worked together in plain clothes, side-by-side, for nearly fifteen years. They'd shared a lifetime in the Force, tough times, close calls, weddings, kids' christenings, the whole nine yards, both good and bad. As far as Dave Hocking was concerned, there was no better copper in the job than Bruce McKinley, and no better friend.

'So you're a desk jockey these days?' Dave couldn't help but take a cheap shot at his old mate as they settled down with their coffees on either side of the Senior Sergeant's desk. 'Your own office and everything.'

Bruce was back in uniform, only with more pips on his epaulets these days, heading up Police Prosecutions at the Cunnamulla Station. The way his girth looked to have grown since they had last seen each other, Dave figured he was pretty comfortable in the role.

'Yeah mate,' Bruce said with a contented smile, his face almost flushed with a tiny touch of embarrassment. 'Too old and fat for the mean streets of Cunnamulla.'

They both smiled wistfully and sipped at their coffees. Dave knew it wasn't true. Bruce McKinley was a tough little bastard who could mix it with the best of them. It wasn't the crooks that worried Brucey.

'No,' Bruce said eventually, staring down into his coffee cup. 'The way things are going these days, this might just about see me out I reckon. All I want to do is just hang in long enough to get my super.'

Dave understood. It had been a tough couple of years to be a copper in Queensland, and it didn't look like getting any easier. The old days were gone, and things had changed forever. To do the sort of things that needed to get done out there on the streets, sometimes you had to cut corners. And cutting corners these days was a very risky business. Bruce McKinley was only a couple of years short of retirement age. The last thing he needed now was for the old times to jump back up and bite him on the arse.

They were both more comfortable when Bruce McKinley changed the subject.

'So you're going to help put this McQuillan brief together, are you?'

'Yeah.' It was a murder case and, thankfully, murder cases didn't come up every day, particularly in a place like Cunnamulla. As the local head of Police Prosecutions, Bruce would have the job of presenting the police case to the magistrate at the preliminary hearing.

'You might have a bit of work to do. I see that idiot Atwood was the arrester.'

Brucey didn't like Noel Atwood. Not too many coppers of their vintage did. Atwood was a big, dumb, lazy boofhead, and those were pretty much his better qualities, as far as Dave Hocking was concerned. All through his lacklustre career Atwood had done his best to side-step all the tough stuff, the hard jobs and the sticky moments, quick to blame everyone around him when anything went wrong, but the first to step up to the stage when it came time to take a bow. Atwood was out for himself, not to be trusted, and no one who really knew him was a bit surprised when he bobbed up, late in the Inquiry, volunteering evidence about suspect behaviour by the former Police Commissioner. The press wrote him up as 'the last honest cop in Queensland,' but anyone who'd worked with him knew better. Noel Atwood was nothing but a shallow opportunist who knew how to sniff the winds of change. And it had worked for him. His stint in the Inquiry eventually saved him from languishing permanently out there in Cunnamulla—where he had been banished for being such a dope—and got him transferred back to Police Headquarters in Brisbane, as a personal assistant to the new Commissioner. But no doubt, as usual, Atwood would have left all the hard work in the McQuillan case to others.

'What do you make of it?'

Dave was comforted to think his old friend might know something of the case, because there was something about it that was troubling him. McKinley simply shrugged his shoulders idly and pursed his lips.

'Just another drunken blue between two boofhead country boys, I'd say.'

'Maybe.' Dave had read and seen enough to have his doubts. There was more to the McQuillan case than just some mindless, alcohol-fuelled brawl between two housemates. McQuillan's seemingly benign, innocuous behaviour at the pub, and on his way back home to Castle Street, followed by the terrifying fury depicted in the photographs of what he had unleashed inside the house, his bizarre behaviour afterwards at Millard's house, and the obvious confusion and despair he showed in his police interview, had unearthed a host of dark, disturbing questions in Dave Hocking's mind. 'But if the witnesses are right about their times, Bruce, he had less than twenty minutes in that house. Twenty minutes mate. That's fuck all, considering what he did in there. What the fuck happened? What was it set him off?'

'Mate, who knows?' Bruce McKinley looked bemused. 'Probably just some stupid bloody argument, I suppose. These young blokes out here have more fights than feeds.'

'But did you see the crime scene photos?' The sudden urgency in Dave Hocking's voice unsettled his old friend. There was something troubling him deeply, Bruce could see that in his face, and hear it in his voice, but he wondered if it went way beyond the McQuillan murder case. They hadn't seen each other face to face in months, and they'd had precious little time to talk of late. But Bruce knew all too well how much his old friend had been through in these past few years. He didn't like the distressed sound of his voice. 'Did you see the unmade bed, the big pool of blood on it? What does that tell you? The deceased was stripped down to his undies, Bruce, in his own bedroom, lights out, after midnight, like he'd already hit the sack.'

Bruce could see what he was getting at. He just wasn't quite sure why.

'You think McQuillan attacked him in his sleep?'

'Yeah, I do.' Dave was now leaning forward on the desk, looking plaintively into his old friend's eyes. 'Why would someone do that, Bruce? Why would anyone calmly say good night to one mate, and then walk inside and just viciously attack another mate in his sleep, for no reason? Why would he do that? It's like something snapped, I reckon. Like something's just gone off in his head.'

Bruce calmly took a sip of coffee from his cup and allowed a gentle smile to seep onto his face.

'Mate,' he said quietly. 'I think you might be overthinking things a bit, don't you?'

Dave Hocking blinked, then averted his eyes and slid back in his chair. It had been a long night, maybe he had let things get to him a little.

'I don't know,' he mumbled self-consciously. 'Maybe.'

Bruce nodded patiently and took another sip of coffee.

'All we have to do is prove he did it, Dave. We don't have to work out why.'

He was right. Of course he was right. Who cared why he did it? *He did it. That's all that matters.* Dave suddenly felt strangely alone again. He looked back up at the Senior Sergeant sitting across the desk from him and nodded awkwardly.

'Yeah, mate. You're right.'

McKinley was staring straight back into his eyes, the soft smile still curling the corners of his mouth.

'You okay?'

The detective's eyebrows knitted into an incredulous frown.

'Yeah. Of course.'

Bruce could see he wasn't. Not really. But he'd work it out eventually. His old mate had been through more than most blokes could bear, but Dave Hocking was as tough as they came. He'd get on top of it, sooner or later. These things took time.

'Good,' the Senior Sergeant announced, as cheerily as he could possibly manage, sitting up straight and slapping one hand flat down on the desk. 'Because you and me've got a power of piss to knock back tonight.'

Senior Sergeant Bruce McKinley was working an eight to four shift, and he wasn't exactly run off his feet with work, so by the time he'd clocked off for the afternoon, stopped in at the butcher to pick up some steaks, and then at the bottle-o to replenish his home supplies, it was still only just after half past four by the time he pulled into the New Jumbuck Inn to pick up Dave Hocking.

Dave had done his best to grab a couple of hours shut eye in the meantime, but he hadn't had too much success. Even with all the shades drawn, the stark outback sunlight had streamed into the room, along with the ghosts and the phantoms that haunted him.

He eventually gave up, stripped down to his jocks, and pumped out as many push-ups as he could possibly manage, leaving him lying, sweaty and breathless, flat-out on the carpeted floor. Then he slipped on some joggers and went for a run in the sweltering heat of the afternoon sun, to the edge of the town and beyond. When he finally found himself out there, puffing and panting, looking out at that same, grey, featureless vista of low-lying scrub stretching forever out to the far-flung horizon, he turned around and ran back as fast as he could. By the time Bruce McKinley arrived, Dave had showered and changed, and was sitting at the table and chairs outside the door to his room.

Bruce and his wife Judy lived in a police house on the edge of the other side of town, but the trip down the tree-lined streets of Cunnamulla, through the town and out to the other side to Bruce's home, took no more than about five minutes. It was a compact little Queensland farmhouse, set up on high stumps, with a narrow set of central stairs reaching up to the broad front veranda, and as they pulled up out front, Dave could already see Judy at the top of the stairs, shading her eyes from the sun with one hand as she waved with the other.

As Dave and Bruce climbed out and got to their feet, the driver called out to his wife over the top of his car.

'Look what the cat dragged in, mother.'

Judy McKinley waited and watched with a warm, tender smile lighting her face, as Dave Hocking led the way up the front stairs.

'Dave.'

When he got to her, he stopped and smiled fondly.

'G'day Jude.'

They wrapped their arms tightly around one other. It felt good. Soft and warm. Comforting. She clung to him, holding him firmly, for almost too long.

When she finally stepped back and held him at arms' length, looking into his face, her eyes were glistening with tears.

'How are you darling?'

Dave loved Judy—he always had—but he wasn't ready for a soppy outpouring of female emotion. He smiled, nodded, and shot back a firm reply.

'Good.'

'Really?'

'Yeah,' he scoffed impatiently. 'Of course.'

With that she launched herself at him again, wrapping her arms around him, and holding him close. Again, it felt good. But this time it didn't last long.

'Righto,' Senior Sergeant McKinley barked from the staircase below. 'Move along, you two, before I book youse both for loitering.'

•

The rest of the afternoon, and into the evening, was spent catching up, reminiscing, firing up the barby, and talking old times. They had lived a life together, the three of them and Dave's wife Denise, through good times and bad, work and play, parties, promotions and postings, watching all the kids grow up, celebrating the milestones and copping the curve balls that came.

They had a lifetime to talk about, and all night to do it, so they did. And, as expected, Brucey had too much to drink, did a lot more talking than tending the barby, and managed to murder the steaks, as always. Then, after dinner, he cracked open a bottle of scotch and insisted on launching into yet another in-depth post-mortem on the whole Fitzgerald Inquiry debacle, the long list of precisely who had dudded whom, and how the whole show was generally going down the dunny in a hurry.

By ten thirty, Bruce was slumped in his favourite armchair, his head sprawled back over the backrest, mouth open as if he was trying to catch flies, a soft snore droning in and out along with his breath. Watching him there in the loungeroom, as Judy tinkered in the kitchen with coffee cups, Dave couldn't help thinking about the wild old days, when Brucey McKinley would work twenty-four hours straight on a pinch, drink through all night with the boys, and then back up next morning for court. They'd all gotten old. Pinching crooks was strictly a young man's game.

As he and Judy sat together over coffees, speaking in whispers opposite the snoring senior sergeant of police, Judy finally broached the question she'd obviously been sitting on all night. What about their daughter? What had they heard? *Nothing. Absolutely fucking nothing.* What more could he say? There was nothing to see, and nothing to tell. They just had to wait, and hope, and keep on going.

It was late. There was nothing more to be said. It was time to go home.

When Judy McKinley pulled up in the driveway of the New Jumbuck Motor Inn, she pushed the car into park and laid one hand gently on Dave's. He knew what she was feeling, what she wanted to say, and he loved her for that. But it was all pointless; nothing anyone could say would change a thing. He turned to face her, a sad, wistful smile on his lips, and said nothing. They just sat opposite one another, silent and still, staring blankly for the longest moment, before Judy finally spoke.

'How's Denise?'

It was a tough question. He searched for an answer briefly, but it didn't come.

'I don't know.'

As she looked into his eyes, a tiny tremble began to tug gently at her chin.

'We love you guys, Dave,' she eventually said. 'You know that, don't you?'

He nodded silently, then leaned over the console and kissed her lightly on the cheek.

'Thanks, love.'

'You take care of yourself. Okay?'

'Sure.'

She held firm to his hand.

'Promise?'

Dave Hocking sat silent for a moment, then nodded reassuringly.

'Promise.'

EIGHT

The more Eddie Moran thumbed his way through the police scenes-of-crime photographs from the McQuillan case, the more questions came into his head. According to Lindy Lewis, straight after she and her husband Ross dropped Rowdy off at his home that night, in apparent good spirits, she looked at her watch. And her watch said midnight. She was sure of that, no question about it. Ross Lewis distinctly remembered her telling him too; twelve o'clock was a late night for the both of them. And there was no question Neville Staffield, Elaine Barlow and Karen Millard all arrived at the police station at precisely 12:21 AM. In the meantime, Rowdy had had time enough time to run amok at the young school-teacher's house, terrorising Staffield and his two lady friends, and they'd had time enough to make their way down to the station to lay their complaint.

On any view of the version they all gave the police, McQuillan couldn't have been at Karen Millard's house for less than a full five minutes, and surely it would have taken the occupants at least a couple of minutes to get to the station, get out of their car, and ring on the bell. That left Rowdy not much more than about ten minutes to do what he did at the Castle Street house—go from one to a hundred and ten, from a dazed, happy drunk to a crazed, homicidal maniac, completely out of control, to the point where he literally smashed his housemate's skull into a pulp.

This was madness. Terrifying, sudden, unforeseen madness. Something snapped inside Rowdy McQuillan's brain that night. But what, and why? And would he admit it, even if Eddie could find out the answers? The big cowboy seemed so much more frightened of being labelled a madman than he was of being convicted a murderer. It would be one or the other, Eddie knew that, and the way things were going, he had a terrible feeling he also knew which one it would be.

For once it was almost a relief when the reception line on his office phone buzzed abrasively, jolting him out of his thoughts. He picked up and grunted into the phone.

'Yeah, what?'

'Your creepy Phil Spector mate's on line one.'

Eddie's new secretary, Kirsten Foster, had all the delicate telephone etiquette of a runaway rugby prop forward. He figured she must have learned all her silky receptionist skills dealing with bone-brain truckies at the tyre company she'd worked at for the past few years down in Parramatta, and she still hadn't quite got the message her pithy patter wasn't necessarily the ideal image for a salubrious Gold Coast solicitor's office like Eddie Moran's.

But that was okay, he'd make allowances. He always had. They'd known each other ever since they were kids, growing up together in Sydney, back when he and her big brother Terry used to train together down at Kelsey's gym in the city. She was always hanging around, giving cheek to her brothers and their half-smart mates, particularly Eddie Moran. He liked her bad attitude right from the jump. If she couldn't cop someone, she didn't hold back. And she couldn't cop Eddie's slimy band manager, Barry Poe, one little bit.

'I told you before, Slick, Spector's a producer, not a manager.'

As a kid he'd christened her 'Slick,' just to give her the shits, and it had pretty much stuck. Slick was smart as they came, and she could sus out a fraud like Barry Poe as quick as look at him. Barry had the gig to manage Eddie and his ballsy, New Wave punk rock band, The Drools, and he had been promising them they were on the verge of great things, about to crack the big time any minute, ever since he first started topping up his dole cheques with a twenty per cent manager's commission.

'Yeah, well they're both just as creepy.'

Eddie smiled to himself. Slick knew a creep when she saw one. She learned the tough way, through the School of Hard Knocks. Unfortunately, for all her smarts, Slick hadn't exactly always made every post a winner. When she turned fifteen, she quit school just like all her mates, did the mandatory typing course, then took off on her own out to Parramatta, where she jagged a job with a tyre company, typing bills and trash-talking truckies. Then, at the tender age of nineteen, she fell for a good-looking, sweet-talking, no-good skunk called Trevor Ellowe, a first-class, certified creep of the first order. Trevor was nothing but a lowlife junkie conman. But he stole her heart, and then most of her money, and by the time she woke up to him, Trevor had pretty much chewed up the best part of ten years of her life. The only favour he ever did for her was to get himself killed in a car crash down in the Cross one night, whacked out on smack.

So now she'd come up to Queensland, the merry widow with a pocket full of cash from her big insurance pay-day, ready to start a brand-new life. And she wasn't about to make any more dumb choices. Slick's creep-metre was well-tuned and working overtime, and she certainly had the Drools' manager Barry Poe well and truly sussed.

'Okay. Put him through.'

As usual Barry wasted no time in getting straight into his sales pitch.

'Mate,' he began ebulliently, 'I've got yez an East Coast tour all lined up. Can you believe it? All locked and loaded, brother. Thirteen gigs over three weeks, ten venues in all, pubs and clubs, including two nights in Melbourne CBD.'

'How much?' Eddie interrupted.

The other end of the line went deathly silent for a moment.

'Argh, come on Eddie.' Barry Poe could switch from winner to whiner without missing a beat. 'Don't be like that, mate.'

'How much?'

There was another brief moment of silence before he finally came out with it.

'Average around sixty a night.'

It was precisely what Eddie had expected, and he spontaneously breathed out a painful sigh. The Drools' manager skimmed his twenty per cent lick straight off the top, before expenses.

'Last time it cost us more than that in travel and accommodation.'

'Don't worry about that, mate.' Barry was now firmly back up on the front foot. 'I've got it all sorted. No worries. Youse can take Lester's van. Plus, three of the pubs are going to throw in a free room for the night.'

'One room?'

'Yeah, two singles and a couch.'

'So, who's on the floor?'

'Don't know. You'll have to work it out between yez. But they'll all have carpet on the floor, for sure.'

'Great.' The music was everything. Any one of them would gladly play the gigs for free. But there was a whole lot more to it than that. 'So that's three nights. What about the other eighteen?'

'Sleep in the van, mate. We'll get yez a foam mattress for the back.'

'All four of us?'

'Jesus Eddie, come on, man.' Barry Poe had flicked back into whiner mode. 'It's only three bloody weeks. What's your problem?'

Eddie groaned again. He knew precisely what he had to do, even though he didn't want to do it. He was coming to the end of things, and he just had to pull the plaster off. It had worked okay when he first got out of university and threw the shingle out, scratching around for rats and mice, doing drink driving pleas and the occasional one or two-day trial. In those days he could disappear, take whatever time he wanted to play music, get away every now and then, down south to Sydney, Melbourne or wherever, lay down some tracks or do some gigs. The money didn't matter. He was doing what he loved, and the boys in the band were content to fool themselves that some day they would all crack it big-time.

But now things had changed a bit. These days Eddie had an office of his own, with rent to meet, and bills to pay. He even had a fulltime secretary to feed. And in recent years he had started pulling in some pretty serious legal work. Right now, not only did he have Aunty Ada's cash burning a hole in his trust account, demanding to be to spent on somehow saving her big, crazy, boofhead nephew from a murder charge, but for the first time ever he had jagged a job to represent a cop on some pretty serious corruption charges.

The prosecution of the Gold Coast detective Frank Vagianni was a big deal, a super-high-profile job, and the Queensland Police Union was picking up the tab for all his fees. This was Eddie's chance to go to the next level. It was no time to go AWOL, notwithstanding Barry Poe's very tempting offer of three weeks' fully paid, first-class accommodation in the back of Trevor's van.

'Sorry bud. I'm out.'

'What do you mean, you're out?'

'I'm out. I can't do it.'

'What?' Barry sounded like he was on the verge of tears. 'Come on, man, what are you talking about? It's an east-coast tour. The guys need you. You can't just leave them in the lurch. Not now. The Drools are on the verge of big things, man.'

'They'll just have to get another lead guitarist.'

'Are you kidding, man? Eddie, you're the best there is.'

It was true. Eddie knew it, but it was still kind of satisfying to hear Barry Poe acknowledge it out loud. He also knew Barry and the boys had already had some quiet words with Phil Pascoe, the leader guitarist with the Hearts and Howlers, just in case. Phil wasn't half the picker Eddie was, but he was a casual, easy-going guy and, truth be known, it was never going to work long-term with Eddie. They all knew that, even their lanky lead guitarist. Eddie didn't play so well with other children. Deep down, he was strictly a soloist.

By the time he finally got Barry off the phone, Slick was sitting in a client chair across the desk from him, impatiently drumming her long, painted fingernails on the desktop. As usual, she had pushed her way into his private office uninvited, settled into his comfy client chair without the slightest *by-your-leave*, and eavesdropped on his conversation unabashed. What else would he expect? He set down the telephone and sat back, staring silently at her for several seconds, before he finally spoke up.

'What?'

She stopped drumming her fingers.

'You okay?'

'Yeah,' he shot back, a pained expression on his face. 'Of course I am.'

She screwed her ruby lips into a whimsical, exaggerated pout.

'Even little-boy-lost rock 'n' roll stars have to grow up sometime, right?'

Eddie propped one bony hand on the armrest of his chair and cocked his head at a disdainful angle.

'Did you have something you need to talk to me about?'

'Yeah,' she snarled back at him, with daggers in her eyes. 'As a matter of fact, I do.' She lobbed a pile of papers up onto the desk in front of him, where they landed with an audible slap. 'Temporary insanity resulting from involuntary intoxication. I looked it up, like you told me.'

It was true, he had invited her to check it out when she questioned his unformulated ramblings around a possible defence in Rowdy's case, but he didn't for a moment think she'd actually get around to doing it.

'And?'

'Nothing in Australia I could find. But it turns out there's a bunch of hot-shot judges in America that are absolutely crazy for it.' She pointed one deep crimson, varnished fingernail in the direction of the wad of paper on the desk in front of him. Without moving a muscle, Eddie peered down at the bundle. He could see the top page was a decision of the Florida Supreme Court. 'You should take a look,' Slick added. 'They make real interesting reading.'

Eddie reached down, carefully picked up the papers, and started leafing through them, skimming their contents. They were mostly US appellate court decisions, and some journal articles, dealing with pleas of temporary insanity induced by involuntary intoxication. He quickly picked up multiple references to ingestion of medication like Prozac, Halcion and other selective serotonin reuptake inhibitors, where the psychological reaction had been proven to be unanticipated and ruled pathological in nature. This could be very useful stuff in the McQuillan case. So far as Eddie could remember, American cases were not binding on Australian courts, but if there was no binding authority on point, they could be relied on to persuade a Queensland judge which way to jump.

'Where'd you get this stuff?'

'From the library, like you said.'

He had to give it to her, she was one smart cookie. Right after she started working for him, Slick had asked him how he managed to keep all that law he kept spruiking in his head, and he told her that he didn't, that mostly he just looked it up as he went along, case by case. So then of course she insisted on knowing how all that worked, and she pestered him until he schooled her up on a few rudimentary principles of case-based legal research. Now, a couple of weeks later, here she was, quoting US case law to him on a potentially obscure application of the law relating to intoxication and insanity.

The more he read, the more he liked it. According to this material, US courts had consistently accepted that the effects of intoxication were indistinguishable from other disabling causes of cognitive dysfunction, and had repeatedly ruled inadvertent consumption of or exposure to toxic chemicals could be a valid basis for a temporary insanity defence.

In one of the cases in Slick's bundle, a guy charged with murdering his neighbour in the front yard of his house had successfully argued an acetylcholinesterase inhibitor in the lawn-care product he was using at the time had poisoned his nervous system, affecting his ability to control his temper. That was starting to potentially sound a whole lot like the killing of Tom Wilson. If Eddie could scrape up some sort of expert evidence to link the chemicals contained in any of Tom Wilson's house-painting products to a potential adverse psychological reaction in someone who inhaled them, these US cases might just be enough to convince a judge to allow a defence of insanity resulting from involuntary intoxication to go to the jury.

The penny having firmly dropped, Eddie looked up from the photocopied caselaw to see Slick sitting back comfortably, staring at him with a self-assured smirk plastered all over her face.

'You're welcome,' she said smugly.

Eddie nodded silently at her, still calculating his next move.

'I think I'd better get up to the gaol and see our client.'

•

The bitumen ran out a couple of kilometres north of Millengarra. From that point on, Castle Street was just a graded, gravel strip—known locally as Station Road—stretching straight across the dusty scrub all the way up to the edge of Castle Station, around 100 kilometres away, way up in the Channel Country. When he did his daily drive-around, Constable Brian Ingles rarely ventured past the end of the bitumen. The roads were rough enough out here, even in town, without swallowing dust for no good reason. But as he came past Junction Road that morning, he could already see the patchwork, battered panels of Alby Thompson's beat-up Holden station wagon, parked on the muddy banks of the town bore, up ahead in the distance. So Brian thought he might keep on going, just to check what Alby might be up to.

As he got closer, he could see Alby had found himself a nice, shady spot under the old Mulga tree that hung forward like a bent-over, arthritic old man, casting its shadow across the slender patch of water people liked to call Millengarra Creek. He had a mate there with him too, and it looked like they were handing around a flagon. Two blackfellas camped on public property, with nothing more to do than drink the afternoon away. That looked to Brian Ingles like trouble just waiting to kick in. He figured he might move those boys along.

They must have been half-shot already, because they didn't seem to spot the marked police four-wheel-drive vehicle until it turned in off the road, but when they did they kept their eyes glued to it as Brian steered his way along the bumpy track from Castle Street up to the bore pipe. He could soon see who Alby's mate was—Darby Sands, a sixteen-year-old local boy who had been in more strife than Flash Gordon. He'd just done six months in the Westbrook Youth Detention Centre for unlawful use, and Brian was pretty sure his sitting around consorting with the likes of Alby Thompson, drinking cheap plonk on the banks of Millengarra Creek, would breach just about every possible one of his parole conditions.

'G'day Alby,' Brian nodded, as he stepped out of his truck.

'G'day, Mr Ingles,' Alby croaked, squinting past a craggy hand shading his eyes from the harsh sunlight.

'G'day Darby.'

Darby Sands had his head hung down, eyes averted, like a guilty man.

'G'day boss,' he mumbled, almost incoherently.

'What're you up to, fellas?'

'I'm having a drink, Mr Ingles.' Alby flashed a broad smile, obviously trying to sound chatty. 'Just to cool meself down a bit like, ay.' Then he added, as an afterthought, 'Darby just sittin' with me, keepin' me company like, is all.'

Sands just kept his head down, looking at the ground in front of him.

'You're not drinking are you, Darby?'

'No boss. Not me.'

''Cause that'd be a breach of your parole.'

The young man just shook his head silently.

Brian had been out to Westbrook, once. But even before that, he well knew its reputation. The state-run penal facility for boys, located outside Toowoomba, up on the Darling Downs, was a notoriously tough place, where poor, abandoned kids and wards of the state found themselves locked up, shackled, and—if the rumours were right—put through the wringer, physically and in every other way possible. The infamous prison farm first opened its barbed-wire gates at the turn of the century, when wayward kids were seen and not heard.

At first it was named the Westbrook Reformatory School for Boys and then, after World War One, it was renamed the Farm Home for Boys, in the hope of deflecting dark rumours already filtering out. By the sixties it acquired the efficient, respectable tag of the Westbrook Training Centre— although training in what was the unanswered question—and finally, in '87, it became the Westbrook Youth Detention Centre.

The truth was, for all its progressive name changes, Westbrook had never changed; it was what it was. The one time Brian went there, to drop off a couple of fresh-faced offenders set to start their sentences, he saw dozens of those poor little bastards lined up, working in the fields, cold and hungry, some of them still bruised and battered from the daily floggings dished out by the warders and the bigger, older boys, and all of them looking lost, worthless and totally unwanted. It was no place for kids to be.

'All right.' Ingles ambled over to where Darby Sands was sitting and stood over him. He had no interest in sending Darby or anyone else back to

Westbrook. 'Well, I'll tell you what, just so you don't get tempted on a hot day like today, I might drop you home. What do you reckon?'

As Darby climbed submissively onto his feet, the policeman nodded his head in the direction of the police four-wheel-drive.

'Jump in the back, mate.'

As he drove back south towards town, Brian was watching the dark-skinned boy in his rear-vision mirror, just to make sure he didn't suddenly get any silly ideas. It was unlikely. Darby was small and thin for his age, and painfully shy, it seemed, like a lot of the other indigenous kids. But there was no real harm in him, so far as Brian could see.

His parents were long gone, goodness knew where, but he lived with his nan and a couple of cousins on the southern outskirts of town, and he had always seemed to Brian to be a pleasant, happy-go-lucky kid. Until he went into Westbrook, that was. When Brian first pinched him around twelve months ago, for unlawful use of a motor vehicle and dangerous driving, he was surprised to learn the boy had a string of Children's Court priors—everything from truanting to a couple of low-level B and E's—and he was even more surprised when the Magistrate in Cunnamulla decided to bin him for six months in Westbrook for the unlawful use.

Darby was obviously pretty shaken up by the whole affair and, when he eventually came out of Westbrook, he was a totally different kid. Whenever Brian saw him these days, he always seemed to be moping around, looking surly and at a loose end, often with glazed-over eyes, as if he might be on the grog, or maybe even something worse. Brian hoped not. That was a one-way road to nowhere, especially for an indigenous boy with a bit of form like Darby, and especially out here. It made Brian Ingles wonder what Children's Services were doing, sitting back in their air-conditioned offices in Cunnamulla. But then, the Big Smoke of Cunnamulla was a long way from Darby's hometown.

'You're staying away from the grog I hope, are you, Darby?'

'Yeah boss.'

Brian hated the way the kid called him 'boss.' He didn't used to, not before he went away to Westbrook.

''Cause you look a bit bleary-eyed to me, mate.'

The boy screwed his mouth into an exaggerated frown and shook his head emphatically.

'Ain't been sleepin', boss. That's all.'

'Yeah? Why's that?'

Darby Sands was now gazing blankly out of the window, across the flat, featureless landscape that stretched out to the far horizon.

'Dreaming, boss,' he mumbled.

'Yeah?' Brian had heard all the New Age waffle from white blackfellas spruiking notions of Alcheringa and the Dreamtime. 'What kind of dreams is that?'

'Bad ones.'

He said it softly, and sadly, as if to himself, still staring intently out through the back window. As Brian watched the handsome young boy's reflection shaking erratically in the rear-view mirror, he realised he wasn't speaking of strange gods or Everywhen; these were real-life demons that were haunting him, disrupting his sleep and tormenting his dreams. Brian was reminded of the look in the eyes of those boys lined up in the fields, crammed together, shoulder to shoulder, packed in tight, but every one of them still on his own, isolated and abandoned. It was the same look he now saw in the vacant eyes of Darby Sands, the boy who now called him boss, and he felt guilty about it. After all, it was he who had personally delivered Darby into the hands of those demons.

There was an abrasive thump as the front wheels of the police truck hit the bitumen and the gravelly rattle of the dirt strip turned into a tidy whirring of rubber tyres on the road. As it did, Brian Ingles could already see, up ahead, the intersection of Junction Road, where a dark blue, four-door sedan was straddling the roadway, negotiating a tight U-turn, about to head back in the opposite direction, south on Castle Street.

Even at this distance, it occurred to Brian there was something odd about this car. It seemed to have extensive front-end damage, and the bonnet appeared slightly buckled in the middle, as if it had been recently in a collision. Brian dropped his speed back as he came towards the town, steadily gaining on the vehicle up ahead, which was now straightening up and gaining speed, heading in a southerly direction.

It was a late model Ford, with a single male occupant visible in the driver compartment, but neither the vehicle nor its occupant looked in any way familiar to the constable. Both of the back mudguards were visibly caked in dust and grime, as though the car had come some distance recently, and the driver was now peering all round him, looking like he might be lost. In the process of so doing, he had one arm perched up on the window frame, his elbow protruding illegally from the vehicle, and from the way his hair was blowing all about, even from behind it looked to Brian like his windscreen might be out. As the only copper in a one-cop town, it was Brian Ingles' business to know who the stranger was. He flicked his siren briefly on and off.

When Detective Senior Sergeant Dave Hocking heard the momentary howl behind him, he looked into his rear-view mirror and breathed out a deep sigh of frustration, before eventually he pulled his vehicle off onto to the gravel verge of Castle Street and stopped. With the engine softly idling, he watched in the rear-view mirror as the uniformed constable stepped out of his vehicle, closed the door, and efficiently pulled his police hat on.

All Brian Ingles could make out of the untidy stranger in the car in front of him was his right elbow poking out, with one dusty, unbuttoned shirtsleeve hanging loosely from it. He was sitting motionless in the idling car, but Brian could see the wild-haired driver's eyes glued to his rear-view mirror, watching him intently. Something about this man spelled trouble, and Brian reached down to his hip and placed one hand on the butt of his police service pistol as he cautiously approached. Once he got within a couple of metres of the driver's window, he called out firmly.

'Step out of the vehicle, please, driver.'

When Dave Hocking saw the young Constable behind him, now stationary, poised and primed for action, one hand on his gun like Dirty Harry, he groaned and rolled his eyes.

'Fuck off,' he said quietly to himself, into the rear-view mirror.

'Step out of the vehicle, sir,' the constable called again. 'Do it now, please.'

Hocking growled, then groaned again, then reached his left hand forward for the handle, and pushed his right shoulder up against the door. As usual, it opened with a sudden bang, startling the young officer behind, who immediately stepped back, clumsily snatching to retrieve his pistol from its holster. But before he had the chance to draw it, Dave Hocking had already heaved himself up onto one foot as he attempted to climb out of the car. In doing so, he lost his footing on the gravel on the roadside, his foot sliding awkwardly underneath him on the stones and loose soil of the verge, sending him teetering off-balance as his leg buckled badly and launched him sideways, causing him to roll painfully over onto his right ankle.

'Argh,' Dave cried out in agony as he grasped desperately at his ankle, hopping and bouncing around erratically on his only able foot. 'Argh, fuck! Shit! Fuck!'

As the big man stumbled and staggered, lurching in a crooked line towards the constable, Brian Ingles finally freed his pistol from the holster and held it in two hands, pointing it directly at the stranger as he took a half-step back, steadied himself, and barked out a loud and clear directive.

'Stop! Stop there! Stop, right now!'

Dave Hocking stopped, instantly released his ankle, and allowed his foot to drop back down, balancing on it tentatively and gingerly, as he stood aghast, staring at the barrel of the pistol now pointed straight in his direction.

'What?' he said incredulously to the constable. They were both now looking at each other in abject bewilderment. 'What the fuck do you think you're doing?'

'Turn around now! Get both your hands up on the car, where I can see them. Straight away.'

'What?'

'Do it! Turn around! Right now!'

'Oh, for fuck's sake.'

Dave Hocking turned around and slumped himself forward, his hands palm down on the roof of his car, waiting silently until the constable eventually stepped forward. With one hand Ingles reached out and efficiently patted down his shirt and trousers, then slipped the wallet out of his back pocket. Dave waited long enough for him to flip it open and see his police identification. When he figured the penny must finally have dropped, he slowly turned around and faced the constable. Brian Ingles looked duly embarrassed.

'I was expecting you yesterday, Senior Sergeant.'

He had never met the renowned Detective Senior Sergeant David Hocking, but he had heard a lot about him. The bloke was a living legend in the Force. He had been a plainclothes detective for as long as anyone could remember, had done a bunch of years in the old Armed Hold-up Squad, plenty more with the Drug Squad and the CIB, and reputedly had more homicide convictions than any other copper in the job. To top it off, just recently he'd lined up for a Commissioner's bravery commendation, after he got shot through the stomach at a siege and saved a woman and her kids by taking out the bad guy. It was true, there had been a few stray rumours about the Special Prosecutor's Office sniffing around him for something or other, but since Fitzgerald, what copper wasn't having some sort of bullshit said about him? Dave Hocking was a legend, and when Brian heard he would be working with the veteran detective to prepare the McQuillan murder case, he couldn't have been more excited. This wasn't quite the way he'd hoped to kick off their relationship.

'So, is this your standard procedure for conducting routine vehicle checks, is it, constable?'

Brian sheepishly handed back the wallet and watched as Hocking pushed it deep into his pocket, then slumped back onto his buttocks on the front seat of his car.

'You were unidentified and behaving erratically. You might've been armed. The Queensland Police Code of Conduct specifically states…'

He didn't even get the words out.

'Fuck the Code of Conduct.' Hocking was clearly in pain and feeling cranky about it. 'If you can't pull up a grub without having to draw your firearm, you shouldn't be in the job.'

It didn't exactly sound like regulation QPS procedure, but Brian thought it best not to argue with the senior sergeant, under the circumstances.

'Have a disagreement with a roo, did you?' he said, trying to make light, nodding at the dented front bumper. But Hocking was vigorously rubbing his ankle and grunted his answer without even lifting his head.

'Yeah.'

'Looks like the roo won.'

The smirk quickly faded away from the constable's lips as the senior detective turned on him, a look of palpable disdain splashed over his face. But then he looked past him, distracted, over his shoulder, back at the four-wheel drive.

'Who's the kid?'

'Young bloke, just fresh out of Westbrook.'

The detective still had his eyes trained on Sands as he nodded pensively, at first without saying a word.

'Shithole joint,' he eventually observed, vacantly, as if to himself. 'What'd he do?'

'Pinched a car and rolled it, out there on the Station Road.'

'Pissed?'

'I'd say so. We didn't find it till a week or so later. But there's not a kink in that road between here and the Gulf. You'd have a hard time rolling it sober.'

Hocking nodded again, then breathed out a deep, painful sigh, squinting upwards and outwards, into the glare.

'Alright constable,' he eventually snarled, rubbing his ankle again. 'So solve the mystery for me. Where the bloody hell are they hiding the Starlight Motel in this dump?'

Brian nodded in the general direction.

'Second on your right up ahead, then first left into King Street.'

Hocking grunted a begrudging acknowledgement, then pulled his foot up and into the car and swung the door closed behind him.

'Righto, he said, kicking over the engine. 'Give me an hour to check in and get myself settled. Then let's you and me get to work on this murder brief.'

NINE

Dave Hocking had his mouth firmly shut, his eyes squinting and his head tilted forward, doing his best to avoid breathing in any more dust, gravel and flying insects as the hot, dry air rushed in and buffeted him, all the way up to the Starlight Motel. It was only a few hundred metres from where he had left the local police constable, but by the time he drove the short distance along Castle Street, turned right into George, then left into King, and eventually rolled into the motel driveway, his ankle was already aching from holding down the gas pedal, and the thirst that had plagued him half the way from Cunnamulla had returned with a real vengeance.

He had risen early that morning from a fitful sleep, plagued with the usual bad dreams and sad memories, and had aimlessly walked the deserted streets of Cunnamulla until the first milk bar opened, dragging him inside with a promising whiff of fried eggs, chips, and bacon sizzling on the plate. He had washed it all down with a pot of hot tea, then did his best to idly distract himself with a leisurely trawl through the local newspaper, trying to kill time before he set out on the road to Millengarra.

Dave had figured the drive up there shouldn't take him too much more than around an hour and a half, which would put him in good time to book into his motel, then go find the local copper. But he hadn't counted on the tough state of the narrow, rutted, unsealed road he had to take to get there, or the challenge of avoiding the occasional lumbering, rattling road trains clawing their way south, all the way down from Castle Station and beyond, each one surrounded by a billowing cloud of dried cow-shit, sticks and bouncing stones that filled his car, as they passed by, with a thick and gritty fog of blinding, choking dust. The trip had taken him twice his estimated time, and when he finally got to Millengarra, the parched aftertaste of salted chips and bacon was stuck painfully at the back of his throat.

As he stepped gingerly from his car, Dave felt the bite of the harsh midday sun on his forehead. He leaned on the open door and looked around the tiny, well-manicured patch of almost-green grass outside the motel manager's front office, and the tidy grounds adjoining, complete with a shallow, light-blue-painted, cement pool of water, a mock oasis surrounded by fading, miniature, plastic palm trees. The sight of water made him swallow uncomfortably with thirst, so he quickly pushed the car door shut, and hobbled the short distance to the front office. By the time he got there, he was already puffing uncomfortably and his dusty, sweaty shirt was sticking to the small of his back.

The glass door pushed open with a shrill, efficient ring and, as it swung back closed behind him, Dave found himself instantly immersed in a soothing pool of cool, refreshing air. On the opposite wall, a compact air-conditioner was softly whispering a quiet, beguiling tone of total calm and comfort. He stepped forward and stood underneath it, pulling his shirt out from his body and flapping at the cool air as he looked around the little office. On the wall behind the front desk was a portrait photograph of Princess Diana and her two young boys, alongside a souvenir ceramic wall-plate from the Scottish Highlands and, beside that, a painted wooden keyboard, which evidently had all eighteen motel room keys hanging neatly in place.

Dave tapped once on the chirpy little desk call bell, and waited, expecting someone to appear. But no one did. On the desktop, behind the front counter, he could see, within easy arms' reach, a frosted carafe of what looked invitingly like cool, thirst-quenching water, but there were no glasses or cups anywhere in sight. He swallowed hard against his sticky, dust-encrusted throat, and tapped the bell once again. Still no response. Through the open back door of the office he could see what appeared to be a modest home dining area, and beyond that, through the sliding glass door at the back of the building, a compact little garden bed abutting the side fence. But there was still no sign of life. He tapped the bell again. Nothing. Then he looked back at the cold carafe of water. He tried to swallow, but his raspy throat was clogged and raw with thirst.

With one eye on the back door to the office, Dave reached down and took hold of the carafe behind the desk. It felt tantalisingly frigid to his touch. Before he knew it, he had it to his mouth, his head tipped back desperately, pouring the cold, invigorating water over his lips and tongue and down into his desiccated throat, gulping and guzzling as it spilled across the corners of his mouth and dribbled down the sides of his neck, renewing and rejuvenating him.

'Excuse me.' The voice was sharp and indignant. 'Can I help you?'

With a startled splutter, Hocking straightened up to see a straight-backed little woman in the doorway to the back room, clutching a bunch of freshly picked wildflowers to her breast.

'Oh yeah,' he grunted, swiping at his chin as he sheepishly replaced the carafe back up onto the desktop counter. 'Yeah, my name's Hocking. Dave Hocking.' He pulled a handkerchief from his pocket and mopped the moisture from his neck. 'I'm a policeman.'

'Really?' the little woman shot back, her voice laced with a mixture of incredulity and disdain, as she stepped forward to the desk, picked up the carafe—which Dave could now see was actually a vase—and carefully squeezed her bunch of wildflowers into it.

'Yeah,' he said, watching as she arranged the flowers just exactly as she wanted them. He pulled out his Police ID and laid it on the counter. 'Brisbane Headquarters should have rung through, did they? Made a booking for me?'

She looked up from the flowers, inspected the ID, then coldly shook her head.

'News to me, I'm afraid. No one's called.'

'Shit,' Hocking grumbled miserably, half under his breath. 'That'd be right.'

It wasn't the first time Headquarters had stuffed up his accommodation on one of these away jobs, and it probably wouldn't be the last. But the one thing he didn't need right now, after three hours on the road, swallowing flies and coughing up dust, was to find himself stuck out here, out back of Bourke, with a crook ankle and a busted windscreen, and nowhere to even lay his head down. What else could go wrong?

'You look like you walked all the way from Brisbane,' the manager said dryly.

Dave looked down at his dusty trousers and grimy, sweat-stained shirt, feeling suddenly self-conscious.

'I done a windscreen.'

The terseness of her expression melted slightly, replaced by the beginnings of a tiny smirk settling at the edges of her mouth. She looked him up and down, wryly.

'Hence the rugged, windswept look, I suppose. Most becoming.'

The joke was on him.

'Yeah.'

Or was it? He looked at the tidy motel keyboard on the wall, the eighteen shiny keys all hanging there expectantly, as if waiting for someone to use them.

'Anyway,' he said, recovering his composure, and poking one finger in the general direction of the keyboard. 'You don't look like you're exactly run off your feet around here. You reckon you can squeeze me in, or what?'

It was a cheap shot, and he could see she didn't like it; but he did. The smirk instantly faded away from her face, and a corresponding one settled on his, as the manager opened up the booking register on the desktop and ran her finger down the page.

'Maybe,' she said curtly. 'How long were you hoping to stay?'

'A couple of weeks maybe. Just up on a job.'

She looked at him over her glasses.

'That Rowdy McQuillan business?'

'Yeah. You know him, do you?'

She said nothing in response at first, just stared silently at him for a moment, with what seemed like a tinge of sadness in her eyes, then looked back down at the register.

'Not really.'

He picked up the faintest waft of her perfume as he leaned onto the desk, watching her move one carefully sculpted fingernail slowly down the page. She was a handsome woman, trim and fit-looking, but she was no spring chicken. She had to be somewhere in her fifties, probably not much younger than Dave himself. But her attire was neat and particular, almost elegant, not like any country hick he'd ever laid his eyes on. She looked out of place in this backwater dump, and the copper in him was already wondering what her back-story was. She had a trace of some sort of accent, British or maybe even Kiwi. The gold wedding band on her left hand looked like it had been there forever, but something about her manner and style made him think she was all on her own, a widow perhaps, or maybe the ever-loving spouse of some dud who had long since gone missing in action.

'Any preference?'

When she looked up from the register their faces were almost too close, and she automatically shuffled a self-conscious micro-step backwards. Hocking stayed where he was.

'How about something with a view of the ocean?'

She stretched her lips into a humourless smile, then turned her back to him, selecting a key from the board. Dave couldn't help but notice she was in pretty good shape. But as she turned back to face him, he was looking her straight in the eye.

'Room Fourteen's probably got the best air-conditioner,' she said politely, proffering a small, brass-coloured key.

'Room Fourteen it is then.'

With key in hand, Dave stepped to the office front door, then propped and turned back to face her.

'Sorry, what was your name?'

She looked surprised to be asked.

'Carol,' she said, tentatively. 'Carol Graham.'

He thought about that for a moment, then nodded a courteous smile.

'Thanks Carol.' As he pulled the door open it gave out the same perky ring. 'You can call me Dave.'

'Oh,' she replied, as the policeman disappeared out through the door. 'Right.'

•

When Dave Hocking got out of the shower, he felt like a brand-new man. The first thing he did was climb back up onto the bed and give the air conditioner another hearty thump, still hoping he might be able to somehow quieten it down. But the noisy whirring and rattling persisted unabated, and he cursed it under his breath, snarling and gritting his teeth. If Room Fourteen had the best air-conditioner in the joint, he wouldn't want to see the worst. He couldn't help wondering if this was just another of the manager's half-smart jokes. Admittedly, he had cranked the air up to absolute maximum, and by the sound of the rattle it was having trouble maintaining the pace, but it would just have to stay that way until the temperature dropped down to something halfway fit for human habitation.

Dave climbed back down off the bed and limped across to the fridge, where he pulled out the icetray, and cracked a bundle of cubes into an open tea-towel. He rolled the towel up, wrapped it tightly around his ankle, and tied it into a knot. With his icepack firmly attached, he slumped into the only armchair, propped his foot up onto the bed, and opened the McQuillan murder file.

He had a fair idea where he wanted to start. Most of the police statements and forensic stuff was already there, although some of it needed some cleaning up. Noel Atwood wasn't exactly a genius, so with him leading the investigation, predictably there were a few glaring holes in the brief that needed to be urgently plugged before the committal, but that would be straightforward enough. Dave had already written out a list of the points he wanted young Ingles to cover off with a few of the police witnesses, and get their statements tightened up and re-sworn. It was all pretty routine stuff.

The more pressing issue they needed to address was the evidence of the civilian witnesses. Atwood had taken statements from a couple of young blokes about the defendant's bad temper and his penchant for violence. Gary Winthrop, one of the yahoos who were drinking with McQuillan at the pub on the night of the murder, had described how Rowdy had punched him, repeatedly and without provocation, earlier that night; and a former housemate of the defendant, Wayne Grantham, had given Atwood a statement claiming that, weeks earlier, McQuillan had assaulted the now-deceased, Tom Wilson, pretty viciously and completely out of the blue.

That was useful enough stuff, but it still didn't entirely explain McQuillan's apparently sudden, explosive attack on the deceased at the Castle Street house. Dave was more interested in what Ross and Lindy Lewis had to say. They had been with the defendant most of the night in question, and from what Dave could make of the police notebook accounts they gave to the detectives that night, and to Brian Ingles, McQuillan was in a pretty placid state, and pretty drunk to boot, when he was dropped off at the house. Even more interesting was the fact they seemed to be certain he didn't get there until just before midnight, which didn't leave him much time at all to have gone from one to a hundred.

Maybe the answer was somewhere in what Wayne Grantham had to say. Maybe McQuillan just had a screw loose, some sort of psychiatric condition that set him off, without notice. But then, that raised a potential insanity defence. The other possibility was Ross and Lindy Lewis had simply got their times wrong. After all, they were drinking for hours that night; they could have lost track of things. Maybe they actually dropped the defendant home earlier than they thought, so maybe he and Wilson had a lot more time together to work up an argument with each other, and then get down to the rough stuff. As things stood at present, with the Lewises' account of having dropped him off right on midnight, and the police station records showing the first complaint came in at 12:21 AM, McQuillan couldn't have been there for more than around ten minutes. That left a bunch of unanswered questions floating around. But if the Lewis's time was wrong, if they actually dropped him home much earlier, those questions would disappear. Somebody needed to talk to Ross and Lindy Lewis immediately, go through their whole story with them with a fine-toothed comb, get a proper statement out of both of them, and pin them down to precisely what they could and couldn't say about McQuillan's ETA at Castle Street.

The moment Dave saw the police truck pull into the driveway, he emptied his make-shift icepack into the sink, pulled on a sock and shoe, shuffled together his murder case file, and hobbled out to the car. As he wrenched the door open and pulled himself onto the passenger seat, he was instantly assailed by the wail of some song by Madonna blaring out from the radio. Settling into the seat, Dave looked over at Ingles with a painful wince on his face. But the constable seemed totally oblivious, and was sitting bolt upright, both hands on the wheel, a picture of efficient attentiveness, staring straight back at the senior detective with a look of anticipation.

'What?'

'Seatbelt, Senior Sergeant.'

Dave could see this was going to be painful. Ingles was obviously one of these hot-shot young blokes who knew all the rules and procedures but couldn't tell his arse from his ankle. He was no doubt one of the New Wave, post-Fitzgerald recruits, who'd learned all there was to know about being a cop from doing some course at the university. *Good luck with that, sonny.*

Hocking scowled at the young man as he pulled down the seatbelt and fastened it, firm at his hip. At the sound of the click, Brian Ingles turned the key and kicked over the engine. At the sound of the engine, Dave Hocking reached across, still scowling, and turned off the radio.

Ross Lewis worked as a roller operator with the Paroo Shire Council, working remotely, living out of camp accommodation on a ten-day roster, with four-day weekends at home. The good news was he was on days off at the moment, and Ingles had arranged for them both to meet Ross and his wife at their place out on the Cunnamulla Road.

The house was a typical, country-town shack, propped up on stumps, with a tin roof and weather-board cladding, a half-rusted truck out the back and two scrawny dogs barking out front. When they drove in through the front gate and up to the house, Dave couldn't help thinking, from the look of the joint, the Lewises were going to be a couple of hillbilly hippies whose time estimates would be about as reliable as a cheesecloth condom.

But as it turned out, Dave was wrong. Lindy Lewis immediately impressed as a sensible, straight-up-and-down, no-nonsense country girl, and she had the inside of the place as neat as a pin. Her husband was a bit of a hayseed, a long, lanky, slow-talking bumpkin, but between them they both told a pretty clear tale of what happened on the night of the murder, consistent in every respect with all of the police notes taken of the versions they gave at the time.

They had picked Rowdy up from Tom Wilson's just after seven and went straight to the Millengarra Arms Hotel. According to Rowdy, Tom had already headed off to the Empire, where Ross knew he often played pool with his mates for hours on end, but Rowdy was keen to go to the Arms that night for the disco, and so was Lindy. All the young people from around the district normally got to the pub for the Saturday night disco, and Lindy liked catching up with her mates. So they had arranged to pick Rowdy up, have a few drinks and some dinner downstairs at the Arms, and then head up to the disco once it got going.

Lindy drove. She wasn't planning to have too much to drink that night, because she had to be up early the following morning. It was the third Sunday of the month, when old Father Cooke made the trip up from Cunnamulla to celebrate mass for the faithful, and Lindy's Aunt Peg was one of them. So Lindy had to be up bright and early next morning to drive her aunty to church. That's why she didn't plan to drink much that night, and that's why she drove.

They got to the hotel around a quarter past seven, had a couple of drinks in the front bar, then got a table out in the beer garden for dinner. Rowdy was in good spirits. They didn't notice anything out of the ordinary about him. He and Ross were drinking shout-for-shout at first, but then Rowdy got onto the rums and went his own way.

As things turned out, they didn't end up ordering their meals until well after eight, which was a pretty late dinner for all of them. Ross and Lindy ordered a bottle of wine to have with their tea, and Ross drank most of it. But Rowdy stayed with the rums and was putting them away at a fair old rate.

By the time they headed upstairs to the disco, it was getting on close to ten thirty, and Ross had to admit he was feeling pretty full by then, so he hated to think how Rowdy was travelling. But he looked all right, and he was behaving himself okay. Rowdy always could hold his grog, and he was generally a pretty happy drunk. He looked to Ross and Lindy that night like he was just having a fat time, as usual.

As Dave Hocking questioned them closely, and Brian Ingles operated the cassette tape recorder, the Lewises recounted their story of how they had marched Rowdy out of the pub, close to closing time, then stopped in the car park chatting briefly with Neville Staffield and his two lady friends, then dropped Rowdy back at the Castle Street house. When he got out of the car to leave, Lindy remembered, he got all emotional and gave her a hug and a kiss.

'Was he upset about something, do you think?'

'Nah.' Lindy Lewis smiled wistfully, with a shake of her head. 'That's just Rowdy. He's a big softy, always has been.'

A big softy. An ugly image of Tom Wilson's mutilated body popped uninvited into the back of Dave's brain. He quickly pushed it away.

'So then what?'

'That's when I looked at my watch.'

'Why?'

'It was late. I had to be up in the morning.'

'What watch were you wearing?'

Lindy held out her left wrist, showing a digital Casio. Dave checked it against his own; the time was spot on.

'What time did it say?'

'It had just clicked over onto midnight, just as we were leaving Rowdy's.'

'You sure?'

'Absolutely certain. I think I said as much to Ross at the time.'

She did, and Ross Lewis remembered her saying it. Even allowing for the four thousand odd beers Ross had drunk that night, and discounting his recollection entirely, Lindy Lewis's evidence on the timing of Rowdy McQuillan's arrival at the Castle Street house was about as rock-solid as a time estimation could be. That meant McQuillan had only around ten minutes to wreak the absolute havoc he had in that house.

'Let's go back to the hotel. Up there at the disco, did he do anything, say anything, that suggested he might be upset or angry about anything?'

'Not really.' Lindy Lewis was pensively shaking her head. 'But we weren't with him the whole time up there, ay. He was mostly drinking with Mason.'

'Who's Mason?'

'Mason Deeds.'

Nowhere in any of the police statements, notebook entries or investigation logs, was there any mention whatsoever of the name Mason Deeds, but according to Lindy Lewis and her husband, Rowdy McQuillan had spent a good hour or more drinking with Deeds and his wife just before he left the hotel that night. That made Mr Deeds someone they needed to talk to.

As they drove back out through the front gate, loudly farewelled by the two barking dogs, Dave Hocking was rattling off instructions to Ingles to get a full witness statement typed up for each of the Lewises and get him a draft by the morning. Ingles nodded efficiently and then, as they got to the gate, pulled the car up in the driveway, turned off the engine, undid his seatbelt, pulled his notebook from his back pocket, then his pen from another, and scribbled down a careful note of the instruction.

The detective rolled his eyes and shifted impatiently in his seat, waiting while the constable finished his note, unclicked his pen, pushed notebook and pen back into his pocket, clicked on his seatbelt, then re-started the car.

'Are you going to stop every time I tell you to do something?'

Brian Ingles looked shocked, and a little bit hurt.

'Just thought I'd make a contemporaneous note in my official police notebook, Senior.'

'Listen, champ,' the detective spat back, baring his teeth like a rabid dog. 'At my age there's only so many years left. If you can't drive a car and think at the same bloody time, we'll both be long dead and gone before we get this job done. You understand me?'

'Yes Senior,' the constable shot back, nodding urgently. 'I'll have draft statements for you by morning.'

'Good,' Hocking huffed, settling back in his seat as Ingles steered the police vehicle onto the roadway. 'Now what about this bloke Mason Deeds?'

'He works at the roadhouse. I saw him out there this morning.'

Mason Deeds worked as a short order cook at the BP truck stop a couple of kilometres south of the town, out on the Cunnamulla Road. Ingles didn't know him well, but he'd spoken to him often enough, in the servo, just to order a burger and a carton of chips now and then. He was a quiet young bloke, never in any sort of trouble so far as Brian was aware. He grew up in the Millengarra area apparently, and was married to a local girl, Jenny, whose parents ran the post office. He was probably around the same age as McQuillan, although Brian didn't know they were mates.

When the constable enquired whether he should ring and get Deeds into the station, Dave Hocking just shook his head. They'd be passing straight by the roadhouse on their way back into town; it was coming up for four in the afternoon, so the rush-hour was long gone by now, and the roadhouse diner was as good a place as any to ask a few questions. Besides, Dave Hocking hadn't had a bite since breakfast, and right now he could murder a carton of chips and a coffee.

For a quiet young bloke who'd never been in any sort of trouble, Deeds looked curiously nervous to Dave as he arrived at the front counter, wiping both hands on his grubby white apron. As Brian Ingles made the introductions, the burger-flipper bounced back and forth from one foot onto the other, looking as jittery as a long-tailed cat in a room full of rocking chairs.

'Yeah,' Ingles eventually summarised. 'So the sergeant was just hoping to ask you a couple of questions about what happened that night.'

'Nothing,' Deeds shot back instantly, looking slightly rattled. 'Nothing happened.'

Dave Hocking smiled wryly and looked him in the eye, silently, before he eventually spoke up.

'I'm just interested in what you two might've talked about, that's all.'

'Nothing,' Deeds shrugged, looking over at Ingles, and then back at Dave again. 'We didn't really talk about nothing. We just had a drink together, that's all.'

'You must've talked about something.'

'Not really. We were just drinking, is all.'

Dave was intrigued by Mason Deeds evident reticence. In these parts, any stranger in town was likely to be treated with caution, and a strange cop asking questions was roughly akin to a Martian who'd just landed from outer space, but Deeds' reaction was something else again. This wasn't just wariness; he looked to Dave like a man who had something to hide.

'Did you hear anything, see anything happen, might've made him upset in any way?'

Mason Deeds pushed his lips into an exaggerated pout and shook his head pensively, as if trying to recollect. For a second or two he was looking the detective straight in the eye, but then he blinked self-consciously, and dropped his eyeline down to the floor.

'What about your wife?'

The young man's head bobbed back up urgently.

'What do you mean?'

At first, Dave Hocking said nothing, just stared back blankly at him. Then a humourless smile seeped onto his lips.

'I mean "what about your wife?" Did your wife talk to him at all?'

'No.'

'What, not at all?'

'No.' He was glancing, wide-eyed, from one policeman back to the other, a curious tremor now straining his voice. 'She wasn't talking to him. They didn't get on.'

'That's funny,' Hocking quietly replied, staring him straight in the eye. 'We'd heard you were all good mates.'

Deeds' mouth dropped open, and for a moment he just stared back silently at the detective, as if searching for something to say. When he eventually found his voice, the words leapt out on top of each other, as if competing to be first out of his mouth.

'We used to be, but not anymore.' Mason Deeds was shaking his head insistently. 'Jen doesn't like him no more. She reckons he drinks way too much nowadays. Ever since Larnie took off.'

'Larnie? Who's Larnie?'

'Larnie.' Deeds stood gap-mouthed and wide-eyed again for a second or so, then turned to Constable Ingles for back-up. 'You know, Larnie Mitchell.'

'Just one of the local girls,' Ingles informed the Senior Sergeant. 'She used to be mates with McQuillan. Took off about four weeks before all this happened.'

'Took off where?'

'Well, we're not actually sure just yet. She's currently still listed as missing.'

By the time Dave Hocking had limped back out to the car, spilling half his coffee in the process, and climbed back into the passenger seat, alongside Brian Ingles, he was crankier than he had been all day, and that was saying something. According to Mason Deeds, Ronald McQuillan and Larnie Mitchell had been good mates for years. There were even rumours around they were rooting each other. Then McQuillan suddenly goes bush—no one knows why—and then he lobs back into town just as suddenly, and within a few weeks Larnie Mitchell mysteriously goes missing. And no one's seen hide nor hair of her since. A month later, McQuillan beats his housemate to death. Yet no one makes any connection.

As Ingles pulled out of the truck stop and onto the road back to town, Dave was already firing angry instructions at him. He wanted the full missing persons file on Larnie Mitchell—that afternoon—including any statements he'd taken from her parents and all of her mates, and he wanted an update check done on the crime indexes and Social Security records, and renewed inquiries made with all of the trucking companies and bus services running between Millengarra and Brisbane. If Larnie was out there, he wanted to know where, and if she wasn't, he wanted to know why.

Meanwhile, he wanted the constable to get Mason Deeds into the station as soon as he knocked off work, and get a full statement from him about everything he knew—what he'd seen, what he'd heard, and what people were saying around town, not just about McQuillan and the night of the murder, but about Larnie Mitchell, what was going on with her and Rowdy, and anything else at all—news, gossip or scandal—about where she might've ended up. A healthy young woman doesn't just disappear into the ether without leaving a trace.

So far, at least, they'd learned one thing from Mason Deeds: before she disappeared, Larnie Mitchell was doing a bit of casual bar work at the Empire Hotel, where Tom Wilson was drinking on the night of his murder. It sounded to Dave like a good place to start.

•

Bob Proctor, the publican down at the Empire, was a man in his mid-to-late-forties. A big, heavy redhead whose ruddy face and impressive potbelly suggested he didn't mind sampling his own wares from time to time. When Constable Ingles introduced them across the public bar, Bob took Dave's hand in a vice-like grip that almost brought tears to his eyes. Then the welcoming smile faded away from his chubby face as he resumed wiping down the bar.

'You're here about Tommy Wilson I suppose. Bugger of a thing. He was in here that night. But I wasn't around, unfortunately.'

Dave already knew that. Bob Proctor and his wife spent the weekend of Wilson's murder down in Cunnamulla for his brother-in-law's wedding. Noel Atwood's boys had covered all that and had taken statements from all of the staff who were on duty at the Empire that night, although none of them had had too much to say. That wasn't what Dave was there for.

'We were actually hoping to talk to you about Larnie Mitchell.'

'Larnie?' Proctor looked puzzled. 'She turn up, did she?'

'No, just following up on her, that's all.'

Dave figured it would take about two minutes in a town this size for rumours to start circulating about a possible connection between Larnie Mitchell and the McQuillan case. That was alright. It was surprising how much you could sometimes learn once you got the small-town gossip going. But for his part, Proctor looked largely uninterested. He shrugged it all off as if he wasn't too fussed either way but was happy to pull out her employee file for them, complete with pay sheets and rosters, which he set down on one of the tables out in the beer garden, for the detective to inspect for himself.

'She was actually rostered to work on the Saturday,' he said, sifting through the papers until he found the relevant sheet. 'But, you know, if I had two bob for every time one of these young sheilas has let me down, I'd be a millionaire today, I can tell you.'

As he slid the open file over the table in front of Dave Hocking, the detective plucked out a single-page letter with a small colour headshot paper-clipped to the front of it. He slipped the image from the page and held it up close. There she was—Larnie Mitchell—young, attractive and alive, in every way, smiling out from the photograph, not a fear or care in the world.

As he stared at her picture, her smiling green eyes staring straight back at him, he felt a sad, painful ache in his chest. Larnie Mitchell looked like every young girl of her age should look—safe, happy and confident. So where the hell was she?

'Can I get youse a beer while you're at it? On the house.'

Dave looked up from where he was sitting, hunched over the photograph, but before he could answer Bob Proctor's question, he was distracted by the sight of a long-haired, tattooed, moustachioed man in his fifties, wheeling kegs of beer up a ramp, in through the back door to the public bar.

'Jimmy Rawlings,' he bellowed at the top of his voice.

The moustachioed man stopped in his tracks, and turned quickly to face the detective, frozen like a deer in the headlights. The instant recognition was obvious. Hocking straightened up, with a disdainful sneer stretching his face, as the newcomer nodded respectfully, then wandered slowly towards the policeman. Bob Proctor intervened tentatively.

'You know my bar manager Jim Rawlings then, do you, Dave?'

'I should do. I've pinched him enough times.'

James Edgar Rawlings was an ex-professional pug who trained for years under Lester Mathers down at the Stanley Street Gym. He'd come up tough as a Ward of the State, spent some time in Westbrook as a kid, and then moved up with the big boys to Boggo Road Gaol. He was in and out of anything going for years, until Lester Mathers got hold of him. The old bloke kept Jimmy on the straight and narrow for a while, first as a fighter and then as a ring man, but when old Lester eventually hung up the spurs, Jimmy Rawlings went back to the old ways.

'That's a long time ago now, Mr Hocking.'

Dave Hocking was staring him down, the same look of disdain in his eyes.

'Yeah, well, as you know, Jimmy,' he said slowly, 'I've got a long memory.'

James Rawlings looked abashed and pathetically powerless, but he kept his head up, his chin jutting out, refusing to look away. As the silent seconds ticked over, Bob Proctor shifted uncomfortably in his seat.

'So, what about that beer, Dave?'

The look in Dave Hocking's eyes slowly softened. Eventually, he turned to the publican and nodded.

'Yeah, what a good idea.' Then he turned back to Rawlings. 'Your shout, Jimmy.'

Proctor gave the manager a perfunctory nod, now back to being a bundle of business.

'What about you, Brian?'

Brian Ingles glanced across the table towards the senior sergeant, who ignored him completely, then shook his head in reply.

'No thanks,' he mumbled. 'I'm on duty.'

•

Carol Graham opened her eyes in the darkness. She had been awake for a long time now, desperately tired and willing herself back to sleep, but it just didn't work. The longer she lay there, the clearer it was. She was awake. There was no point pretending otherwise.

As her vision adjusted, Carol looked out into the shadowy corners of the familiar, comfortable bedroom she had slept in alone for the past six years. She felt safe and assured, had always felt so, in those soothing surroundings, adorned by the curtains Peter and she had picked out together, the pieces of furniture they'd planned for and searched out—the bed, the side tables, the dresser, all carefully chosen and cherished. The pillows, the bedcovers and cushions, even the door handles; everything, right down to the paint on the walls. It was theirs, they had selected and assembled it, piece by piece, made it their own. And now it was hers, all alone. Through the darkness she stared at the smiling picture of Peter and her, together in happier days, before his illness, before all the pain and the sadness, before everything changed.

She threw the sheet back off her and puffed audibly into the empty room, emphasising the point to herself. It was a stinking hot, breathless night, and she was melting away to a sweat stain. She could feel the hair pasted to the back of her neck, and the pillow below it, damp and sticky. Since the onset of menopause these hot flushes had become increasingly frequent and far more intense, disturbing her sleep and so often leaving her anxious and irritable. She hated them. They were a cruel reminder of all she had lost, and would lose, of her life changing, deserting her, day by day, leaving her more and more on her own. She lifted her knees, spread her arms out and legs apart, and lay there, flat on her back, as if rehearsing for something never likely to happen, puffing out short, brutal sighs of frustration.

When she finally settled, she threw her legs off the bed and swung herself up into an upright position, sitting still for a moment, staring down at the floor and sucking in whatever air she could find. Eventually, she snatched at the sides of her nightie and stripped it off over her head, then scrunched it up and used it to mop the moisture from the back of her neck, her face, chest and belly. It felt good, like fighting back, demanding relief, railing against the oppression.

As she stepped into the unlit ensuite and peeled off her pants, Carol felt better already, more relaxed, alone and naked, unseen, in the darkness, the cool, shiny tiles pressed up hard under her feet, surrounded by mirrors and glass. She reached in and spun the tap on, waiting a moment expectantly, and then stepped in under the stream of cold, flowing water. It took her breath away. As it flowed over her head, through her hair, and down onto her neck, back and chest, she felt herself panting short, shallow gulps of air, gasping against the chill until her body eventually adjusted, recovered, and rejoiced in the brisk, re-invigorating freshness. She felt pleasurably renewed and recharged, instantly alive again. As the water flowed over her head and her face, she ran her hands in long strokes, down over her neck and onto her breasts, caressing them, remembering past joys and lost pleasures.

A harsh beam of headlights suddenly and abruptly intruded, spilling into the bathroom through the high window, and splashing abrasively onto the opposite wall. Carol could now hear a car engine idling in the driveway outside, a car door opening and closing, and two men saying something unintelligible back and forth to each other. By the time the taxi eventually reversed out of the driveway back onto the road, she was standing alongside her bed, holding a towel firmly and close to her chest, looking out through the curtains, as her only tenant, Detective Senior Sergeant Hocking, limped untidily across the motel grounds, back to his room. When he got there, he lurched back and forth at the door, rummaging around for his keys before eventually, after a painful performance manoeuvring the key into place, he pushed the door open and stepped into his room, out of sight.

Carol Graham moved quickly in the darkness, pulling open the bottom drawer of her dresser. She pushed both hands urgently in and grabbed the first nightie they touched on, then the first pair of undies, and then she bounced around briefly until she was fully attired. That done, she scurried back to the window, crouched down and peered out through the curtains surreptitiously, trying to see what she could in number fourteen. At first it was completely dark, but then, after a minute or so, the toilet door opened with the sound of a flush, and light spilled out into the room.

The policeman got as far as the bed and then launched himself onto it, fully dressed, his collar unbuttoned and his tie skewed out at an awkward angle, propping himself up against the bedhead with both pillows. She couldn't help noticing he hadn't even bothered to kick off his shoes, and she winced at the thought of what kind of a mess he was making of her freshly laundered bed coverings.

She could see he was holding what looked like a bottle of something in one hand, and something else—something small—in the other. What was it? *A photograph perhaps?* Whatever it was, he seemed to be staring at it intently, studying it, as if in a trance. Eventually, he appeared to abruptly snap out of it, gruffly pushing the item into his breast pocket and wearily dropping his head back against the wall.

He lifted the bottle to his lips, tipped his head back and swallowed down several mouthfuls, then lowered the bottle back down and sat still—absolutely motionless—gazing blankly out into the room. He must be looking at something, but what? The television was off. She watched him, intrigued, wondering what he was doing as he lay there, staring at something, or maybe at nothing at all, straight ahead in the dimly lit room. Eventually, he raised the bottle again and poured more into his mouth.

He looked utterly alone, Carol realised, lying by himself on a bed built for two, in a room by himself, no company, no conversation, not even a television on. Just drinking by himself, alone with his thoughts. Carol felt suddenly cold, and sad, and curiously anxious. Was that her life too, marooned in an empty house far from home, with nothing but memories for company? Was that how she looked?

Then something changed. The policeman took one more hearty swig from his bottle, and then lifted the telephone. He leaned across and dialled in a number. He was ringing someone, reaching out for someone to talk to. He had someone. Who could it be, she wondered? Who would it be for her? Whom would she ring, at this hour of the night? Who would be there to share her thoughts, to listen to her worries and woes, empathise with her, console her?

She closed up the curtains, went back to her bed, and lay down. All alone, Carol pulled the sheet over her, closed her eyes tightly, and prayed she would fall asleep soon.

•

Propped up with his back to the bedhead, in the half-light in number fourteen, the telephone receiver pressed to his ear, Dave Hocking heard the STD beeps announce someone had picked up the phone, but at first no one answered.

'Hello,' he said tentatively.

'Hello?' His wife sounded groggy and uncertain. He had obviously woken her.

'Yeah, Denise, yeah it's me,' he said awkwardly, suddenly conscious how late he was ringing. 'How're you going?'

'Dave?' she said croakily, with a new touch of urgency. 'What time is it?'

The line was scratchy and hard on the ear, the thin, tiny voice fragile and distant, like an astronaut far out in space.

'Oh, yeah, it's...' *What the hell time was it, anyway?* He looked at his watch, but couldn't make it out in the darkness. 'I don't know. It's like, late, I think.'

'Where are you?'

'Millengarra.'

'Are you okay?'

Good question. He wasn't sure. He felt bad he had worried her. He could hear the concern in her voice.

'Yeah, I'm fine,' he said, as reassuringly as he could manage. 'I...' The words stuck in his throat. He had something to say, something he needed to say, but he realised he couldn't say it to her, couldn't ever have said it, even if he knew what it was. 'I was just ringing to say hello, that's all.'

'Is everything okay?'

'Yeah, of course it's okay. I just thought I'd give you a call. That's all.'

'God, what time is it?'

He could hear her groping around for the clock.

'It's pretty late I think.'

'Jesus.' She sounded suddenly panicked again. 'What's wrong?'

'Nothing. I was just ringing to tell you I got here all right, that's all.'

'Well, couldn't you have rung in the morning or something? What time is it?'

'I don't know.'

'Oh God, it's nearly one o'clock, Dave.' She sounded cranky. He shouldn't have rung. 'What are you doing ringing at this hour, for God's sake?'

'I was just…' He really wasn't quite sure. 'I don't know.'

'You been out on the drink or something, have you?'

'Yeah.'

'Oh great.'

She was cranky. She was entitled to be.

'Okay, listen, I'll go, let you get back to sleep.'

'Is everything alright?'

No. Everything wasn't alright. Everything hadn't been alright for a long time. That much was certain. But why? What could he do? What could Denise do? What could anyone do?

'Yeah, of course.'

'You sure?'

'Yeah. I said it was.'

'Okay.'

'Okay. I'll speak to you, then.'

'Okay darl.' Her voice was softer now, tinged with concern. He wished he could see her, and touch her, hold her close. 'Give us a ring in the morning, will you?'

'Yeah okay, love,' he said staunchly.

'Okay darl.' It wasn't much more than a whisper. 'Look after yourself, pet.'

'Yeah, I will.'

Dave Hocking put the telephone down and stared out into the dark room in front of him. A deep sadness seeped into his consciousness now, with the clear realisation even she couldn't save him, nor he her. There was no answer for them. Side by side, they were light years apart. His stomach was churning, demons circling ominously, lingering out there just beyond the light, waiting to come under cover of darkness.

He put the bottle up to his lips and tipped his head back, gulping down several deep swallows, as the rum seared a sweet, fiery track down through his gullet, mercifully dulling his senses and numbing his brain.

TEN

Eddie Moran had come straight from the prison to the Supreme Court. As soon as he was told by the very helpful receptionist at the Melbourne rooms of the eminent psychiatrist Dr Waylon Penfold that the good doctor was currently in Brisbane and scheduled to give expert evidence at a criminal trial in the Brisbane Supreme Court that day, he figured he'd kill two birds with one stone. Firstly he would get out to Boggo Road Gaol and ask Rowdy McQuillan a few pertinent questions needing urgent answers, and then he'd double back into town to the Supreme Court to meet Dr Penfold for lunch, and hopefully extract from him some sort of expert advice on what it all meant.

But, as Eddie sat alone in the court cafeteria, alternately sipping a bad cup of coffee and smoking a Camel cork-tipped, waiting for Penfold to appear with the usual one o'clock lunch-time adjournment rush, he wished he had scheduled his meetings that day in the opposite sequence. If he had seen Dr Penfold first, and got what he needed, he might have gone out to the gaol armed with enough fancy-sounding, scientific doctor-speak jargon to convince his contrary client an insanity defence was his only way out. As it was, Eddie's meeting with Rowdy McQuillan had not gone well.

He had spent the first fifteen minutes, in the cramped confines of the interview room in the old Two Division, carefully stepping his client through the finer points of the concept of involuntary intoxication, and the history of appellate case law, primarily in the United States, suggesting such intoxication could be used as the basis of a plea of not guilty on the grounds of insanity. But, as it turned out, that last word—*insanity*—proved a real sticking point.

'I'm not fuckin' nuts,' the prisoner growled back at him.

'I didn't say you are, buddy. Okay?' Eddie was hunched forward over the desk, looking earnestly into his eyes, doing his consummate best to sell it. 'We're talking temporary insanity here. Okay?'

McQuillan was shaking his head, his eyebrows knitted together in a tight, troubled frown.

'Temporary,' Eddie repeated. 'You just breathed in too many paint fumes at work, that's all. Sent you over the edge. Could happen to anyone.'

There was a moment of silence before McQuillan responded, quietly but firmly.

'I didn't work that day.'

'What?'

'It was Sat'dy. We didn't work Sat'dys.'

'But you'd been in Tom's car, right? Surely, at some stage that day. With all those paint tins.'

'Nuh.' McQuillan shook his head again, even more emphatically. 'I spent all day at home, until Ross and Lindy come to pick me up.'

Eddie was almost out of suggestions.

'Well, maybe it was a hangover from Friday.'

The big man looked down at his hands, laid flat on the desktop. He lifted them up off the wooden surface, placed them palm-to-palm, and rubbed them softly and slowly together, as he looked back up at his lawyer.

'I didn't kill Tom.'

Yeah, right. Eddie had heard it before. There was only one problem about that.

'Then who did, pal?' He was looking the big man straight in the eyes. 'Who did?' McQuillan breathed out a deep sigh and looked back down at his hands. 'And if you didn't do it, how come you ended up with his blood all over you? And your fingerprints all over the murder weapon?'

They both knew McQuillan had no answer to any of that. He just sat with his head lowered, staring silently at his big, calloused hands. When he eventually spoke, his voice was subdued and seemingly resigned.

'I know you're trying to help me.' The next bit seemed to stick in his throat for a second, before he eventually got it out. 'And I appreciate it, ay.' He went silent again for a second, then mumbled disconsolately, 'But I never killed Tom Wilson. I wouldn't do that.'

Great. So now Eddie had his first ever murder case, due to kick off any minute, a fully-funded, private gig, for a client caught at the scene of the crime—literally red-handed—with a definite, rock-solid plea of not guilty, but beyond that not a single instruction, other than *I'm not crazy, and I didn't do it.* Without a crystal ball, how was he supposed to defend a murder charge on that basis? Where the hell was Madam Marla Pavlovich now he really needed her?

As Eddie sat at the narrow desk in the close, humid confines of the interview room, staring at the top of his client's hung-down head, he began thinking about something Aunty Ada had told him, something she said about the one clue her fortune-teller came up with concerning the crime, something about a girl—a 'wild one'—who was somehow involved in Tom Wilson's murder. He flicked through his file until he came to his handwritten notes, where he saw he had written down a name.

'Larnie Mitchell.' As he looked back up from his notes, Rowdy McQuillan was looking him straight in the eye. 'Who's Larnie Mitchell?'

A familiar scowl returned to his client's face.

'She's got nothing to do with it,' he growled ominously. 'Leave Larnie out of it.'

In that moment, as they sat face to face, the big cowboy staring menacingly into his lawyer's eyes, he looked every inch a killer. Without doubt, his instructions were final. That was it. No further discussion.

So now, as he sat alone in the airy, ground floor cafeteria of the Brisbane Supreme Court building, sipping and smoking, waiting to meet with the great Dr Penfold to discuss a prospective defence his client had now expressly and vehemently disavowed, Eddie Moran was all out of answers. The lunch adjournment hour had now finally clicked over on the clock, the rush-hour had begun, and Eddie numbly watched as the straggling procession of faces filed through the front door of the cafeteria—barristers, solicitors, court staff and clients—ambling in, loading up with trays and cutlery, and falling into line to place their orders.

He had never met Dr Waylon Penfold, but he recognised the acclaimed psychiatrist the moment he first ambled through the doorway, looking lost and all alone, all six foot five and fifteen stone of him. He was wearing a brown tweed jacket over a dark blue shirt with leather suspenders and a multi-coloured bowtie, and his wire spectacles, strung around his neck on a silver chain, were perched precariously at the end of his bulbous nose, as he gazed around the room in all directions like he was tracking some unseen, air-born insect. The overall impression was like a cross between Gyro Gearloose and the Cookie Monster; if this guy wasn't a shrink, Eddie had never seen one.

'Dr Penfold?'

'Yup, that's me alright,' the doctor said in a broad American twang, peering through the bottom of his glasses. 'I guess you must be Mr Moran. Am I right?'

They worked their way through all the customary introductory small talk as they lined up with their trays and loaded up on sliced roast beef and vegetables, so by the time they got back to their table, Eddie was ready to launch straight into business. He already figured, the way things were shaping up, Penfold wasn't going to provide the silver bullet he was looking for, so as far as Eddie saw it the less time wasted in the process, the better. He started by laying all the cards down fairly on the table, noting clearly and upfront that Rowdy McQuillan's former lawyers had referred the defendant for examination and assessment by the doctor, which led Eddie to assume, given Dr Penfold's previous work with Rowdy's barrister Dennis O'Dea—in particular as part of the defence case in the Roskin murder trial—that the reason he was being brought into the case probably had something to do with an intended plea by Rowdy of insanity based on involuntary intoxication.

Penfold stopped him in his tracks.

'There's nothing to support it,' he said, stuffing in a mouthful of roast beef and chewing lazily on it like an old bull up in the back paddock.

When he finally gulped it down, and then began meticulously slicing up the next bit on his plate, the doctor proceeded to explain to Eddie matter-of-factly that Mr McQuillan's former lawyers had asked him to explore the possibility of involuntary intoxication resulting from the ingestion of noxious fumes. But when he looked at the contemporaneous hospital records, including toxicology reports, and spoke to the medical staff who examined McQuillan following his arrest, as well as to McQuillan himself, he found no evidence of acute toxicity induced by chemical poisoning of any kind.

'What about his lack of memory? Do you think it's genuine?'

'Oh yes.' Penfold nodded sagely to himself. 'I have no doubt about that. None whatsoever.'

'So what do you put that down to? Alcohol consumption?'

'Maybe.' He crammed in another mouthful and chewed on it for a long time, without uttering another word. Eddie was beginning to struggle with an increasingly irritating impression that the good Dr Gearloose was enjoying being deliberately obtuse, when the fat man finally swallowed, nodded, and then added, 'He certainly had a dangerously high blood-alcohol reading. But in this case, I think there was probably something far more sinister going on.'

'Yeah?' Eddie was starting to get interested. 'Such as what?'

'Well, I think he almost certainly experienced a major psychotic episode.'

Eddie liked the sound of it. With any luck, the doctor was about to serve him up a fully blown insanity defence.

'You think he's crazy?'

'That depends on what you mean by crazy,' Gearloose answered cryptically, before he shovelled in another mouthful, shutting down the conversation while he chomped on his roast beef pensively, and Eddie waited patiently for the next instalment. 'You ever hear of post-traumatic stress disorder?'

Sure he had. PTSD had been a kind of buzz-phrase for the past few years, mostly trotted out as an excuse for strung-out, returned Vietnam War veterans struggling to re-adjust to life on Civvy Street. So far as Eddie understood it, PTSD was just a new, you-beaut term for what the old diggers used to call shellshock, or combat fatigue. But what did any of that have to do with some lonesome cowpoke riding the range way out back of nowhere?

'People exposed to a particularly traumatic event can experience acute or even chronic PTSD, manifested in symptoms of severe psychosis.'

'You think something happened to him, sent him crazy enough to kill Tom Wilson?'

'Maybe,' the doctor said, stroking his fat chin. 'Or maybe the other way around.'

This guy was starting to sound a little bit like The Riddler, and Eddie was already sick of playing Twenty Questions with him.

'I'm sorry, doc,' he said, wincing painfully as he ran his fingers through his tousled hair. 'I don't get it.'

Waylon Penfold pursed his lips, clasped his hands together on his chin, and breathed in a long, deep breath, as if to set himself to loftily pontificate about a matter of great moment.

'Post-grade and anti-grade amnesia,' he began, staring blankly off towards a corner of the ceiling, 'Commonly occurs as a natural defensive mechanism employed by the human body to cope with a potentially devastating emotional reaction to a violent or otherwise traumatic incident or series of events.' He paused for a moment, considering his next sentence, and then continued in the same, carefully measured tone. 'Another common manifestation of such reaction to violent trauma is post-traumatic stress disorder.'

It was an impressive entrée into what appeared to Eddie to be almost intended as a succinct rehearsal of the expert evidence he could give before a court of law. Post-traumatic stress disorder, the doctor methodically explained, was how the body often chose to deal with what otherwise would be the unbearable horror of some trauma it experienced. Examples were often seen in warfare, or in cases of profound personal tragedy. The disorder consisted of symptoms such as re-experiencing, avoidance, hyperarousal, and negative changes in mood and brain function, as well as both acute and long-term psychotic symptoms, such as distressing hallucinations and delusions, and disorganised behaviours including wildly erratic physical actions, grunting or speaking unintelligibly, and doing weird, irrational things. Eddie couldn't help but bring to mind the evidence of Rowdy McQuillan's bizarre and unexplained behaviour at Karen Millard's house on the night Tom Wilson died.

'Are you saying he might have witnessed Wilson's murder, and that's what sent him crazy?'

'I believe that to be a clear and present possibility.' He cupped his pudgy hands together and leaned forward over the table. 'To the extent, in fact, that I decided to further investigate that very possibility.' Now he slipped the wire spectacles slowly and deliberately from his nose, let them fall loose around his neck, and closely looked the lawyer in the eye.

'And that, sir,' he announced, somewhat bombastically, 'led me to a quite extraordinary discovery.'

•

Dave Hocking was starting to feel pretty ordinary. He had not slept well, as usual, and now that the real heat of the day had kicked in, he was beginning to feel washed out, and a little thick-headed. Ingles had surprised him with his efficiency, producing the draft statements Dave had demanded from both of the Lewises first up that morning. He'd done a pretty fair job of it too—not that Dave said so to him—and the Senior Sergeant had pretty much turned them around as they were, with instructions to the constable to get them signed up and Oaths Act-ed as quickly as possible, ready for tender at the committal proceedings.

Meanwhile, Ingles had also got Mason Deeds into the station that morning, and had taken a detailed written statement from him, or at least as detailed as Deeds was willing to give. He retold his earlier story in writing, and dutifully signed on the bottom line, as directed. But it didn't tell them much. According to Deeds, he was half-shot by the time he first ran into Rowdy, up in the disco that night, and from there they proceeded to get on the rums— which Mason rarely drank these days—and were going shout-for-shout for a couple of hours, so it all became a bit of a blur. He couldn't recall much of anything they spoke about, or anything strange or unusual about Rowdy that night.

He was hiding something, Dave Hocking was pretty sure of that. Exactly what was hard to tell, but Mason Deeds was shitting great big bricks for some reason. With a hayseed like him it was probably just something completely mindless, like not wanting to let on he drove home over the limit that night, or not wanting to say how full his old mate Rowdy was when he left the hotel. Maybe the thought of potentially being called to give evidence was just too much for a bumpkin like him to bear. Who knew? Whatever it was, it was something, and Dave figured he'd find out what it was sooner or later.

For now, the only new information Ingles had managed to wring out of the burger boy was about the missing Larnie Mitchell. She and Rowdy had been good mates ever since they were kids, but Deeds confirmed what the Lewises had already told them, that the gossip around town was, not too long before McQuillan took off to go droving, the two of them got a whole lot more chummy than they ever had been. And he went one step further. Though most of the young blokes around town would chew the ear off anyone who'd listen if they got even close to any female, particularly a red-hot sort like Larnie Mitchell, Rowdy McQuillan proved to be the soul of discretion, so his old mate Mason had to prise it out of him. And when he did, the big fella eventually came clean, confirming he and Larnie were head over heels for each other, and had even made plans to take off together, and maybe get married. But then all of a sudden something seemed to go wrong—Mason didn't know what—but Larnie apparently kicked the cowboy straight to the kerb, and after that he just moped around the place inconsolably for weeks, and then he took off, out of the blue, no one knew where. No one saw or heard the slightest word from him for the best part of a couple of years. Then he came back, unexpectedly. And three weeks later, she disappeared.

The updates on the crime indexes and Social Security records drew a blank, and none of the bus services or trucking companies had anything on anyone with Larnie's name or general description. They even checked with the hire car outlets. Nothing. She had no car of her own, and no one had driven her out; at least, if they did, they weren't saying so.

Dave had a bad feeling about where Larnie Mitchell had got to. He had been seeing her photographed face all night, or faces like it, and others, familiar but then not. Strange, changing faces, spectres that floated in and out of his consciousness, disturbing and troubling him, all different but, weirdly, all still somehow Larnie. Where had she got to? She didn't just vanish into thin air. There was an answer to this mystery, and Dave Hocking was sure it had plenty to do with Rowdy McQuillan.

As he stood in the cracked, oil-stained driveway outside Daines' Smash Repairs, the afternoon sun beating down on him, that mystery was swirling around in his brain, hurting his head. With Constable Ingles off at the Lewises', signing them up on their statements, Dave had taken the opportunity to drive his crumpled car the short distance from the police house, down Humeburn Road and right into Connell, to the only mechanical/panel shop in town, to see what he might be able to get done to return it to some kind of drivable condition.

He was already wishing he hadn't. The skinny, grease-covered kid now circling his car at a glacial pace, hunched over like a mangy cat, was doing nothing to relieve his headache, or conjure up the slightest spark of confidence. The only thing about the dirty, ragged young man that gave any suggestion of skill or training was the well-worn state of his filthy, tattered overalls, held together by dried, caked-on spray paint and grime.

'She's pretty cactus, ay,' he eventually drawled, looking soundly defeated before the battle had even begun.

'Yeah, thanks chief. I hadn't noticed. When can you have it fixed?'

'Orrr…' The young man straightened up and leaned back, as if trying to get the car into focus. 'Shit, I don't know, mate. Next Wensdy, maybe?'

The detective's top lip curled into an involuntary scowl. The prospect of relying on Constable Ingles all week for his transport was almost too much to bear.

'Forget it. Just a new windscreen'll do.'

'A new windscreen?' He looked shocked at the very suggestion. 'Shit, that'd push her out to probably Wensdy week I reckon, ay.'

Dave rolled his eyes and breathed out a deep, frustrated sigh.

'Tell you what, champ, just fix the fuckin' radiator hose. Alright?'

'Yeah, man, sure. No worries.'

The young man was now nodding his head with an insipid half-smile, looking almost relieved. He hunched his shoulders and shoved both grubby hands deep into his back pockets, as he watched the policeman scribbling down his name and contact details.

'You're that big top cop up from Brisbane, aren't you? Here for Rowdy's court case.'

Hocking stopped writing momentarily and looked him straight in the eye. 'You know him, do you?'

'Me?' The young man looked horrified. 'Nah. No way.' Hocking was still staring straight at him, his look blank and devoid of emotion. The prospect of any given citizen of Millengarra not knowing any given other was remote, at best. A cynical smirk crept onto the detective's face as he went back to writing.

'I read all about you,' the mechanic continued. 'Heard you was in a siege and that.'

'Yeah, that's right.'

'Shot some bloke or something, didn't you?'

Hocking stopped writing again and looked up at him, his stare now cruel and intimidating.

'What's your name, mate?'

'Kevin.'

'Kevin who?'

'Kevin Daines.' Suddenly he was almost stuttering. 'It's me uncle's shop.'

'Righto, Kevin.' Dave ripped out the note he had written and pushed it in Daines' direction. 'I'll be back tomorrow. Make sure it's done.'

He could feel the sting of the afternoon sun on his forehead as he limped slowly and carefully up Connell Street back to the main intersection. His crook ankle was on the improve, without any doubt, but it still wasn't right, any more than his head was. By the time he got to the Empire Hotel, on the corner, and looked out at the Anzac memorial, and the sadly pretentious Town Hall beyond, the foggy feeling that had been gathering between his ears all morning was settling into a mild, ill-defined ache, the product of no decent sleep and way too much rum.

As he rounded the corner and walked east on Humeburn Road, the town around him seemed vacant and still, the road ahead all but deserted, all the way to the police house and beyond, the only sign of life a single, dust-covered ute in the distance, boring in through the shimmering heat. Across the road, half-hidden in the shadow of the broad doorway to the local snack bar, a wrinkly, brown woman was leaning breathless and sweaty on a rickety, well-worn straw broom. When their eyes met, she nodded courteously, and he did likewise, then she picked herself up and went back to sweeping the floor. Dave squinted up ahead, into the relentless sunlight, then limped on towards the police house.

As the dust-caked utility finally rolled through the empty town towards him, the driver raised one craggy hand in a perfunctory wave from under his broad-brimmed hat, staring distrustfully at the sight of this stranger in town. The sweaty detective nodded and stared back disdainfully, until the driver quickly looked away, and went back to his business. As the vehicle passed by him, Hocking stopped in his tracks and turned purposefully, watching it go, all the way to the intersection and through it. He wanted every nosey yokel in this two-horse town to know he was here, and he had his eyes on every one of them.

Curiously, as the battered utility cruised past the sandstone statue of the Unknown Soldier at the centre of the intersection in the centre of the town, and then disappeared into the dust and the heat of the desert beyond, Dave noticed on its back tray, propped up against the cabin and tied into place, a golf bag filled with what looked like a full set of clubs. There was a time—long ago—when Dave had fancied a good game of golf now and then. But to the best of his recollection, to play golf you needed a golf course, and for a golf course you needed a green, and to have a green you needed some grass. *Where the hell would anyone find a golf course in a shithole like this?*

He was still pondering that question as he limped past what looked like the last shop in town, a small, free-standing wooden building covered in white, flaking paint. Its street presence, such as it was, consisted of a cracked glass front window on either side of twin glass front doors, informatively adorned with a faded, red sign that read, simply, 'OP SHOP.' As Dave passed by the Salvation Army second-hand charity outlet, he glanced incidentally through the front windows at the barely organised clutter inside.

Suddenly, something caught his eye. It stopped him, dead in his tracks.

Dave bent over urgently and pressed his face to the window, squinting in through the glass, trying to make out what looked like something vaguely familiar to him. He was crouched down uncomfortably, peering down into the back of a low, narrow shelf, no more than a foot from the floor, half-hidden below a bulging rack of old dresses and coats overhanging a menagerie of random, unwanted junk, trying to make out precisely the object that had caused his double-take. He knew what it was; he was sure he could make out the heel of a shoe, a tiny, dust-covered slipper, maybe once red-coloured, perhaps even shiny. The faded colour of it stirred a painful, distant memory inside him, one that made his heart suddenly start thumping, quickly and forcefully. Was that what he thought it was?

He straightened up, puffing from the strain of his racing thoughts, his head feeling foggier than ever. Then he stepped abruptly to his right and clutched at the door handle, rattling and trying to twist it, but it remained steadfastly locked. As his eyes focussed on the sign now directly in front of his nose, he read the inscription.

Open Saturday, Wednesday and Friday, 10am – 4pm.

Dave sucked in a draught of thick, dusty air. His head was starting to spin as he allowed his focus to blur on the typewritten words of the home-made sign stuck to the inside of the door, and he steadied himself with his grasp on the handle. He closed his eyes and blew the breath out, breathing deeply now, trying to collect himself. Today was Thursday. The shop was closed. It would open tomorrow at ten.

The sound of a car horn behind him suddenly jolted the detective from his abstraction. Constable Brian Ingles had stopped in the street alongside him in the police four-wheel drive vehicle, engine running. He was obviously on his way back from signing the Lewises up on their statements.

Hocking stepped to the passenger door, pulled it open, climbed in, pulled it shut, turned up the air con, and switched off the radio.

'Okay, let's go.'

•

Dave Hocking had wanted to talk to Larnie Mitchell's parents, find out what they knew about Rowdy McQuillan, whether they were aware he and she were an item at some stage. Had they heard or seen any trouble between them? When did they last see him, and her; what had they heard from either of them, or from anyone else for that matter, since she disappeared? What was their theory about where their daughter had gone? What were their fears and suspicions? He wanted to know what had happened to Larnie Mitchell. Because something in the back of his brain kept telling him, once he had the answer to that question, he'd know why her big cowboy boyfriend had murdered his housemate Tom Wilson.

But by the time the police vehicle pulled into the driveway of the neat, modest home of Lyall and Sue Mitchell, the jittery, distracted feeling in the pit of Dave's stomach had begun to take hold of him, shooting itchy tingles into the palms of his hands and the top of his head. As Lyall Mitchell welcomed them into the house, pleasant and polite, to the point of being almost obsequious, bowing courteously as he shook hands with both of them, Dave felt hemmed in and increasingly unable to concentrate.

When Mrs Mitchell enquired if they would prefer a cold drink or a hot cup of tea, the sad, fearful sound of her voice added to his growing unease, further unsettling him. Like everyone else in the town, the Mitchells clearly knew why Dave Hocking had come all this way. He was here for a murder case, and now they knew why it was he wanted to see them. They had made the connection: if Rowdy McQuillan killed Tom Wilson, had he also murdered their daughter?

Dave realised what he had done, how cruel he had been. As he looked into their eyes, he saw himself hiding there, cringing and terrified, him and his lost, lonely wife Denise. Dave Hocking was the dreaded harbinger of all Sue and Lyall Mitchell had been trying to hide from themselves, fears and nightmares they had desperately hoped to ignore.

'You said your daughter had taken some jewellery?'

'Just an old drop pearl necklace that used to belong to my mum.' Her voice quavered slightly, but she quickly recovered. 'It's not important, though. We just want to know she's okay.'

'Of course.' An item like that could be traceable. He took down the details, then invited Sue Mitchell to draw a sketch of it in his notebook. She did so, meticulously, taking her time, reviewing it, altering it fondly, until she seemed to be sure she'd got it just right. When she was finished, she looked up at him, absently, then suddenly seemed to collect herself.

'Would you like to see her room?'

Dave nodded mutely—he didn't really know why—then left Ingles sitting at the dining room table, studiously taking Lyall back through his statement, and followed Sue Mitchell into the hallway. When she got to the door she opened it carefully, almost cautiously, as if expecting to find someone unexpected inside. Then she turned back, and ushered him in.

Larnie Mitchell's bedroom looked like a shrine, perfectly neat and tidy in every respect, not a thing out of place. On the bed was a floppy rag doll with thick woollen hair tied up in pigtails, propped up against the pillows, on the dresser an assortment of knickknacks and smiling photographs of Larnie and her friends. It felt warm and familiar. Absently, Dave reached down and opened up the small painted box sitting on the dresser. As the lid pivoted back, a tiny ballerina began delicately pirouetting to the soft sound of tinkling music.

'Lyall gave her that.' She was wringing her hands, looking feeble and fragile. 'Larnie was a real Daddy's girl.'

The detective closed the box, and then slid open the top drawer. It was filled with pencils, erasers, cheap costume jewellery, music cassettes, batteries and miniature toys. He reached in with two fingers and fished out a tiny item from amongst the jumble. It was a small, brass mouthpiece for a cannabis bong. No doubt Larnie's parents wouldn't even know what it was for, but any copper would, and Dave could instantly see it had recently been used by someone to smoke weed. *Interesting.* He dropped it back where it had come from, and slid the drawer closed. Then he reached down and opened up the drawer below; again, the same clutter of useless, long-discarded items.

'I was too tough on her really, I suppose.' Sue Mitchell's voice quavered slightly as she finished the sentence, and she paused briefly, sucking in a deep breath to clear the emotion. 'But Lyall's a big softie. Always has been.'

Dave stretched his lips into a flat, empathetic smile as he ran one hand through the drawer. There was something there, at the back, that had taken his attention. He gently clawed it clear at the back of the drawer, as it gradually revealed itself—a small, flat, plastic tag with the word *Hotel* printed on it. As he gently prised it out from under the clutter, he saw it was a keyring of some sort, attached to a bronze-coloured door-key. The full inscription on the tag read *Empire Hotel*. He turned it over. *Room 8.*

'Before she eventually took off,' Sue Mitchell was muttering, 'She came and went for weeks, without even saying hello.' Her voice trailed off feebly, and she stood silent, her head lowered, for several seconds, before eventually continuing. 'Lyall used to leave money out for her.'

She was suddenly a bundle of efficiency and motion as she pushed past Dave and clutched at the back of the dresser. 'He thought I didn't know, but I did. I'd always find it when I was cleaning.'

She pulled the dresser slightly forward, away from the wall, as Dave Hocking surreptitiously slipped the key to Room 8 into his pocket.

'Look at this.' She reached in and retrieved something taped to the back of the unit, then proffered two folded twenty-dollar notes to the Senior Detective. 'Do you believe that? Silly, isn't it?'

Dave took the notes in his hand and straightened them out. Written in black marker ink on the front of one of the notes were the words *Love you. Dad xx.* Dave wondered how her dad would feel if he realised she was probably using the dough he left out for her to buy dope. As he looked back up at Sue Mitchell's face, her eyes were glistening with tears, her chin wrinkled and quavering.

'I'm sorry, it's just...' Her voice trailed off again, as she pushed her fingers into the end of her sleeve, fossicking there for a tissue. 'We never really started to worry until what happened to Tom Wilson.' Her voice was wobbling erratically as she dabbed at her tears with the tissue. 'Not that we think Rowdy would ever do anything like that to Larnie.' Now she looked straight at him, plaintively, her whole face trembling pathetically. 'Surely not.'

As the tears suddenly welled again in her eyes, she grasped at her mouth with both hands, covering it up as if she was trying to stop saying things she didn't want to hear. Standing alone in the room, shaking and blubbering, she looked so diminished, so vulnerable, defeated, Dave found himself moving towards her spontaneously, without even thinking. He wrapped both his arms around her, and she fell instantly into his grasp, sobbing uncontrollably. As her whole body trembled and shook against him, he held tight, enveloping her, holding on desperately, part life-raft and part drowning man.

After what seemed like a long time, she fell still. Eventually, she stepped back politely, efficiently blew her nose into her tissue and wiped dry her tears, then breathed in a deep, settling breath.

'Do you have children?' she said wearily.

He had to think about that for a moment.

'Nuh.'

'You're lucky.'

'Yeah, I guess.'

'Everything's different now. They're all so lost these days.'

Dave Hocking nodded despondently. She was right. They were lost. They were all so lost.

ELEVEN

Eddie Moran wasn't quite sure what to make of what Dr Waylon Penfold told him. It was definitely right out of left field and, let's face it, anything you got from a guy wearing braces and a fruit-salad bowtie had to be definitely open to question. But the good doc had a way of wrapping it all up in big, fancy words that made it sound almost impressive, and if he could even half-way sell it the way he had to Eddie, he might just convince a jury. But, more importantly, if what Dr Waylon Penfold had to say was right, it changed everything.

The first thing Eddie did was pull out the crime scene photographs and have another close look at them. Suddenly, he had a whole new set of questions bubbling around in the back of his brain.

By the time he got to the Queensland Government Health Laboratory in the city it was getting close to four o'clock, and senior forensic scientist Pat Keenan was looking slightly jittery. Eddie figured that was partly because the career public servant didn't want to miss his knock-off time, and the early bus home, but he also knew Pat Keenan didn't entirely trust Eddie Moran. He was right to be nervous. He'd given evidence in plenty of Eddie's cases, and they both knew the lawyer wouldn't hesitate to ambush him, any chance he got.

'In the forensic report you refer to "extensive, partly washed-out bloodstains."'

Eddie was referring to the clothes found in the second bedroom—Rowdy McQuillan's jeans and pearl-buttoned cowboy shirt. It was pretty clear from the crime scene photographs that anyone standing in the room where Tom Wilson was bashed to death would be expected to have ended up covered in blood. The walls looked like they were spray painted with it. But the photographs of Rowdy McQuillan's discarded clothing, found by the police in the next room, showed only pale pink, diluted patches on both sleeves and the front of the shirt, and on both upper legs of the jeans. All the police statements noted the clothing was dripping wet, and the police theory was McQuillan had washed all the blood from his clothing after the murder and before he left the house, stark naked. But having heard what Penfold had to say, Eddie suddenly didn't buy it anymore.

The wet clothes had been bundled into plastic exhibit bags, along with all the other potential exhibits located by police at the crime scene, and sent to Queensland Health for the scientists to look over, and Keenan had documented his observations on them in his forensic report. His reference to 'extensive, partly washed-out bloodstains' played neatly into the police hypothesis, and at first Eddie swallowed it without a second thought. But after his fireside chat with Waylon Penfold, he took another good look at those photographs. When he did, he couldn't help thinking, if someone washed the blood off those clothes, they did a mighty good job of it. If Rowdy McQuillan was in that room when the killing occurred, those clothes should have been—would have been—absolutely dripping with Tom Wilson's gore. And yet, from what Eddie could see, they were pretty close to spick-and-span. Eddie was no laundry lady, but it seemed to him like a whole lot of washing to have done, particularly when McQuillan had not much more than about twenty minutes to get in, get the job done, and get out.

'Yes.'

Keenan's one-word answer had all the cautious circumspection of a man determined not to be ambushed.

'Have you seen the crime scene photographs?'

'No.'

Eddie was surprised. He would have thought the Queensland Government forensic boffins would have wanted to see all the photographs of the scene of the crime. But, then again, maybe not. The scientists' job was just to look at the evidence found, interpret it, and report their findings back to the police. Maybe photographs would just distract them.

The pudgy little man in his regulation, public service grey cardigan and green checked shirt, was sitting forward over the desk, his hands clasped together on the desktop, staring over the top of the half-spectacles strung around his neck, looking the soul of humble integrity. Whatever shortcomings he might have, Keenan was straight up-and-down; if he said he hadn't seen the photos, he hadn't seen them.

'Okay.' Eddie thought carefully before he asked his next question. 'So how extensive were these bloodstains? Was there a lot of blood on the clothing?'

'No.' Keenan answered without hesitation, looking Eddie straight in the eye. He looked like a man with a point he wanted to make. 'The term 'extensive' is not meant to signify the clothes were inundated with blood, or even heavily spattered. It's simply terminology that's generally accepted in the field to signify the presence of multiple patches of blood on the garment.'

So he did have a point to make. But Eddie could also see Keenan still didn't want to be ambushed.

'Okay,' he offered tentatively. 'So what's your point?'

'I saw the body.' Now the scientist had the pained expression of a man resigned to his fate. 'And the clothes. There would have been massive blood loss. Extensive spattering.'

'And?'

Keenan looked down at his hands, which he was wringing gently over the desktop, remaining silent for a moment, before he looked back up at the lawyer.

'I rang Noel Atwood and made my views quite clear to him.' It sounded to Eddie like Keenan was worried the investigating officer might have buried a vital piece of information. He kept his eyes intently trained on him, determined not to let him off the hook. In reply Keenan held his gaze steadfastly, then eventually continued. 'Whoever inflicted those injuries would have been covered in blood and tissue.'

It was exactly where Eddie thought this might be going, and he knew instantly it was potential dynamite for the defence.

'Are you saying these clothes weren't worn by the killer?'

'No.' Keenan blurted out the answer with an urgency that almost startled the lawyer sitting opposite him. 'I'm not saying that.' So what was he saying? Eddie kept his eyes trained on him, awaiting further explanation. 'I'm just saying if they were worn by the killer, they must have been very thoroughly washed after the attack took place.'

Bingo. Unless those clothes were given a thorough washing after the event, Rowdy McQuillan didn't kill Tom Wilson. So far as Eddie figured it, that's exactly what it added up to.

'Washed with some sort of detergent?'

'No. Blood will wash straight out in cold water.' Pat Keenan was adamant about that, but he clearly had something more to say. 'But with that much blood you'd need plenty of it.'

'And you'd need time to do it, too. Right?'

'Yes.'

And plenty of it. And time was one thing Rowdy McQuillan definitely didn't have plenty of that night, even on the Crown case. Things were suddenly starting to look very interesting.

•

Dave's headache had got worse. Boxed into the close and stifling confines of the Mitchells' modest home, he could feel the tingling in his palms and scalp gradually turning into a hot, urgent flush that burned in his face and filled his eyes with an irritating itch. A sudden sense of nausea pushed up from his stomach, turning him away from where Ingles still sat at the kitchen table with the Mitchells, and sent him lumbering purposefully towards the front door of the house, seeking the relief of fresh air and whatever breeze there was.

As he pushed out through the flyscreen door, into the harsh sunlight, his whole consciousness was gripped by a debilitating sense of panic and distress. The tingle had become a thousand needles pressed into his skin, his face a fiery furnace, the nausea tugging at his stomach and pushing up into his throat. When he closed his eyes, he could see Sue Mitchell's torment in the crazy face of Mark Trindall, and in the tortured woman he held tightly in his grasp, as she sobbed and gasped for air, the barrel of a gun pressed against her face. He could see Denise, and Lisa, the smiling photographs of Larnie Mitchell and her schoolyard friends, and the pathetic, whimpering children, huddled together on the loungeroom floor, crying in their terror and their loss, as their father lay dying on the floor beside them. What could he possibly do to assuage their agony? How could he ever save them? Any of them. He couldn't even save himself.

His eyes were open now, but he still couldn't see where he was going. As he bumped against the front gate, Dave Hocking stared down, uncomprehending, wondering how he got there. He felt giddy, lost and unbalanced, his head spinning wildly, filled with weird, erratic images.

'Leave it, Mark. Don't fucking touch it.'

That vacant, empty look in Trindall's eyes was there in front of him, haunting him, consuming him as he stood motionless on the narrow pathway, the cruel sun bearing down relentlessly, baking every bit of him, inside and out. Eventually, he slowly turned, looking back towards the house.

And there he was, Mark Trindall, framed in the doorway, those wild eyes filled with fear and panic, his rifle trained intently, poised to explode at any second.

'I'll fucking kill 'em.'

Through his garbled haze, Dave looked down at the pathway, his eyes following it towards the door, up to where the dead man lay, face down on the doorstep. Face down; but there was no face. There was no head. There was just crushed bone and blood and pulpy tissue laid thick, inches deep, in an ugly, obscene, black-red ooze spread crazily across the landing.

Dave felt his eyelids heavy on his face as a breathless, sickly silence descended over him, his pupils rolling softly backwards into a blanket of blackness, and his consciousness swirling helplessly, out of control. In that moment he could feel himself falling—slowly, it seemed—lifeless and unknowing, into an abyss. He hit the ground hard, but painlessly, before everything quietly faded into nothing.

•

When Dave Hocking gradually opened up his eyes, he was lying comfortably, flat on his back, staring up towards the white light of a long, fluorescent tube attached to the ceiling. He blinked softly, focusing his vision, taking in the strange, benign environment, and gradually collected his thoughts, orienting himself to his surroundings. He knew where he was. He remembered how he got there. Ingles had helped him to the car. He had lapsed in and out of consciousness on the drive back to the hospital, his head pounding painfully, in time with the throbbing ache in his side, and the thick waves of nausea washing over him. He remembered Ingles speaking to the nurse; he remembered that she gave him something, and he remembered lying down, looking up through half-closed eyes into that white light, feeling sick and helpless and fatigued.

When was that, how long ago? Whenever it was, he felt better now, he thought. What time was it? A crisp, white pillowcase was puffed around his ears on both sides of his head, and he was comfortably cocooned beneath a single, heavy blanket, pulled up to his chin. It was quiet in there, and cold. Without moving his head, he strained his eyes towards the gentle whirring to his left, where a clean, white air-conditioning unit was efficiently going about its business. Dave looked back up at the white light overhead and closed his eyes. He definitely felt better.

'You're finally awake, are you?'

The nursing sister reefed the curtain open, touched a gentle hand onto his forehead, and then carefully took hold of his wrist, measuring his pulse.

'How are you feeling now, darling? A little bit better, are you?'

Dave slowly closed his eyes again and nodded wearily. Through the haze he was remembering her kindness and efficiency, the softness of her touch, and her cheery, reassuring voice. She had asked him questions, administered her tests, and insisted that he have a sandwich and a steaming cup of tea, before she laid him down to rest.

'How long was I out?'

'A couple of hours.' She was looking at the watch pinned to her tunic as she counted out his heartbeat. 'That looks to have settled down quite nicely.'

'What happened?'

'You just fainted, love, that's all. A bit dehydrated, I'd say. Too much sun and not enough sleep.'

'So, am I right to go?'

There was a momentary touch of hesitation in the way she looked at him, but then she nodded back efficiently.

'Sure,' she said. 'Just make sure you keep your fluids up. Okay?'

Once Dave Hocking had put his shoes back on, pulled back the curtain and sauntered out to where the sister was now sitting, filling out her paperwork, he could see the Millengarra Hospital was not much more than one big room, cordoned off into a couple of empty treatment areas, a front reception desk and the sister's working station. He wandered over and stood beside her desk, looking at her nametag.

'You're Elaine Barlow, aren't you?'

'And you're the Brisbane detective they sent out for the case.'

She was a witness in the Wilson murder, and he had always planned to talk to her, just like all the others. She was one of the first to see Rowdy McQuillan after the event, along with Neville Stafford and the young teacher, and their evidence was crucial to set the scene. But it was more than that. Elaine Barlow had nursed him back from a scary, unexpected place he never thought he'd ever find himself in. He wondered what she'd learned about him. How much did she know? How much could she tell? He wanted to remind her who he was.

So it felt good to see the instant tinge of trepidation in her eyes when he told her he needed her to answer a few questions for him. It was empowering to watch her fidgeting uncomfortably as he settled in a chair alongside her at the desk and flipped open his official police notebook. It was good to be the one asking the questions, recording her answers, back in charge, controlling the agenda. And as she talked about the harrowing events she went through on the night Tom Wilson died, how frightened she had been, how helpless and confused she felt, he no longer felt like some delirious, sun-stroked patient, some pathetic victim. He was a detective senior sergeant of police, demanding answers, doing his job.

She was an obviously intelligent, no-nonsense woman. She answered his questions in a sensible, straight forward fashion, recounting the events as she recalled them, dispassionately and without embellishment. But he could see she had been rattled by what happened. When she described first seeing the defendant's face in the carport, through the windscreen of Karen Millard's car, as they scrambled to make their escape, her voice wavered erratically and she eventually stopped speaking for a moment, to collect herself.

'How were you feeling at that point?'

'Scared to death.' Her eyes began to glisten, but she blinked her tears away and breathed in deep, refreshing breath. 'All violence is deeply disturbing.' For several silent seconds she gazed blankly at the desktop. Then she blinked again, several times, before she looked back up at him, straight in the eye. 'As you know yourself, only too well I suppose.'

The detective pretended not to know what she was on about. Obviously, he had revealed something to her in his dazed condition, more than he should have. He grimaced involuntarily at the thought of what he might have said, staring blankly back at her, before she eventually elaborated.

'When that man shot at you. You must have been terrified.'

What could he say? She didn't get it. No one did. Getting shot at didn't terrify him. It didn't mean a thing. In a lifetime on the force he had seen every kind of violence anyone could possibly imagine. The aftermath of awful car collisions—screaming, moaning, dying bodies—the slashings and the bashings, burnings, pub brawls, murders, suicides, poisonings and crazy, household bloodbaths. Violence didn't disturb Dave Hocking any more, and it didn't scare him. It made no difference to him. It was just part of the job. Mark Trindall's screams and threats were just posturing, they weren't terrifying. Staring down the barrel of a gun meant nothing, other than the job that had to get done. The explosion of propellant chemicals in a cartridge was no more than loud noise, a bullet spat out of a barrel just the obvious, inevitable consequence of a finger pulled back on a trigger. The Trindall shooting didn't spook him, not when it was aimed at him, not when it came hunting for him, not even when it ripped right through him.

That wasn't what terrified Dave Hocking. The violence just flowed right over him, a legacy of every night and day of the past thirty years, an endless procession of savagery, stupidity, insanity and mindless cruelty. None of that upset him anymore. What terrified Dave Hocking was the hopeless look he wished he hadn't seen in a perpetrator's dying eyes, a look of utter resignation, of helpless surrender to the realisation that his whole life meant nothing, that everything he'd done and everything he'd known was worthless and irrelevant.

'Leave it Mark. Don't fucking touch it.'

When Dave Hocking bellowed his demand, Mark Trindall's hand was only inches from the rifle lying on the floor between them. For a moment the wounded man had stopped moving, and then he slowly raised his face to the detective. But from the moment he looked up at David Hocking, the detective could see plainly how the next few seconds were destined to play out. It was all there, spelt out in those hollow, empty eyes. No panic, no anger and no pain, just a profound, soulless melancholy that coldly dictated what must happen next. As they stared into each other's eyes, Dave felt his finger tighten on the trigger.

Trindall's grab for the gun was deliberate more than sudden. But it was quick, just the same. He had the rifle in both hands before Dave even managed to take aim, and the barrel was almost pointed straight at him before he peeled off his first shot. The way the perpetrator was stretched out, prostrate on the floor and facing him, he presented such a compact target the policeman's bullet almost missed him altogether. But not quite. It struck him on the top of his head, just below his receding hairline. The rifle barrel wavered erratically for a moment and then straightened back towards him, as Hocking re-aligned his aim, targeting the shooter's hands and shoulders. He squeezed the trigger back again. The result was instant, and this time, absolutely final. Dave didn't see precisely where the bullet wound erupted, but it was somewhere on the perpetrator's face, so that his head bounced back in an expanding ball of blood, and then flopped forward immediately, instantly still and completely silent.

At first, with the gunshots still ringing years, all Dave could hear was what sounded like the distant shouts of the policemen, crouched and alert out in the front yard, cautiously striving to assess just who had done the shooting, and at whom. Then, gradually, in the hush of his surroundings, another sound crept into his consciousness, a tiny, feeble sound, no more than a breathless, groaning whimper. He looked around the next room aimlessly until his vision focused on something in the far corner of the lounge room. Two children—a skinny, soft-skinned boy and his pig-tailed little sister—were huddled there together, trembling and in tears, as they looked towards the lifeless, blood-soaked body of their father, lying face down on the floor.

Now, sitting in the cool, sterile surrounds of that little, one-roomed outback hospital, bathed in white, fluorescent light, Dave Hocking could still see that haunted, haunting look that had predicted with such clarity and certainty the awful outcome that would change a family's history, and two children's lives, forever. Why? How had it come to that? What brought a man to that point in his life, to the edge of the abyss? What made him step off into the blank uncertainty awaiting?

He could see from Elaine Barlow's drawn expression she was remembering a similarly crazed look in the eyes of the naked man who terrorised her and her friends at Karen Millard's house.

'What do you think made him snap like that?'

Barlow shook her head, evidently all out of answers.

'I don't know. Drugs maybe.'

Not a chance. Barlow hadn't seen the toxicology report, but Dave had, and he knew there was absolutely no trace of any drugs in the offender's blood when he was tested on the night. Elaine Barlow's guess was clearly wrong, but it was an interesting one, just the same.

'What sort of drugs?'

'Amphetamines maybe. LSD. We had a couple of bad drug reactions come into the clinic around that time.'

'McQuillan?'

'No, not him. But you know what it's like these days. All the kids are dabbling in something.'

Hocking nodded silently. He knew what she was saying, all too well. He flashed on the brass bong-piece he had found in Larnie's dresser drawer. Even in a little fly-spot country dump like this one, way out back of Bourke, in the dead centre of bum-fuck nowhere, drugs were everywhere. It was the first thing he had checked for in the brief. But the toxicology report was crystal clear.

'He'd had a big drink. Maybe he was just mindless on the grog.'

'It was more than that.' She hugged herself as if the air-conditioning was up a notch too high. 'He wanted us all dead,' she said, staring out into the room. 'I could see it in his eyes.'

She was rattled all right. And Dave could see the more she talked about it, the more unsettled she was feeling.

'We weren't the only ones either.' Elaine was still staring at the empty space in front of her, her eyes filling up with tears. 'I heard later he turned up at Jenny Deeds' place too. They were lucky to get out alive.'

'Jenny Deeds?'

'Yeah.'

'When was this?'

'That night. He went to their place as well.'

So that was it. That was what Mason Deeds had been hiding under his hat. His old mate Rowdy didn't just benignly walk out of the disco and disappear into the night. He came back for a visit after hours, and with murderous intent. Dave was careful how he teased the story out of Elaine, anxious not to let her think she was betraying confidences, but it turned out the girlie gossip around town was that after blundering into Karen Millard's house, McQuillan showed up at the Deeds' place in the wee, small hours of the morning, in all his naked, blood-soaked glory, and ran amok all over again.

Obviously, the last thing Mason Deeds wanted was to find himself sitting in the witness box driving nails into his best mate's coffin, so when he learned the next morning what McQuillan had done, and that he'd been arrested and charged with Tom Wilson's murder, he just shut the story down completely, giving his wife Jenny strict instructions not to mention anything about Rowdy coming to their house that morning. The story would be the last they saw of him was when he walked out of the disco, and that's all they knew. Except it wasn't true. And if a pea-brained hayseed like Mason Deeds thought he was going to sidestep the issue by pulling the wool over the eyes of a couple of dopey coppers, he had another thing coming. Hocking would make sure that.

By the time Dave stepped out of the Millengarra Hospital and strode up Connell Street towards the Empire Hotel, he felt recuperated and recharged. He was already plotting his next conversation with the devious little Mr Deeds, and relishing the prospect. But that would have to wait for another day. After all, the good sister said he had to keep his fluids up.

When Dave walked into the Empire, the big, redheaded publican Bob Proctor was slouched across the public bar, in a huddle with a bunch of regulars. Like any good hotelier, he spotted a prospective customer immediately.

'Dave, how are you mate? What are you drinking?'

As Dave put his order in, Proctor casually introduced him around the little group propping up the bar. Darren Martin he already knew; the switched-on young proprietor of Martin's Transport—the only haulage company in town—had assisted their inquiries about Larnie Mitchell, making sure his staff opened up their books and gave whatever information they were asked for. He had impressed Dave at the time as a competent, cooperative young bloke, and as they shook hands at the bar he thanked Martin again for the help he'd given them.

The other two Dave hadn't met. Merv Ahern—a big, raw-boned farm-boy in a broad, flat Bazza McKenzie hat and fancy, moleskin strides—looked like he'd just stepped out of an R.M. Williams boot and clothing catalogue. His family owned Rossleigh, Dave was informed, a big sheep station up Wyandra way. His cow-cockie sidekick Rolly Dawson—for all the world the country hick from central casting—was his trusty manager.

It took them three rounds to get properly acquainted, and it wasn't until Bob Proctor put the fourth shout on the house that Big Merv Ahern finally got around to what was on his mind.

'So,' he drawled, as he set his beer down on the bar and leaned back on both elbows. 'You're up from Brizzie are you, Dave?'

'Yeah.'

'For that murder case, ay?'

'Yeah.'

'And you reckon that missing sheila could have something to do with it, do you?'

It was a curious question. One Dave hadn't been expecting. He glanced across at Darren Martin, who was looking down self-consciously into his glass and shifting his weight from one foot to the other. Dave hadn't picked the trucker for a gossip, but he wasn't fussed one way or the other. He had no beef about the locals chin-wagging to their mates about any titbits they'd picked up about the police investigation. It was hardly confidential most of it, and he knew well enough how quickly gossip spread in any town, particularly ones like this, not much bigger than a ten-cent postage stamp. In fact, he counted on it.

'Just checking all the leads we can, Wal, that's all.'

Rolly Dawson's jaw dropped open.

'But you've already got the bloke, haven't you?'

Dave smiled back cryptically at him.

'Yeah. But she's still missing.'

The cockie stared back at him open-mouthed, looking utterly confused, then looked around the little circle at the other faces, searching for elucidation. None came. Dave Hocking added nothing, just tipped his head back enigmatically, and swallowed down another swig of rum.

'Fuck!' Merv Ahern suddenly erupted. 'You're good,' he guffawed. 'You're fuckin' good, ay.' He was pointing one fat finger in the detective's direction, bouncing his big head up and down. 'You're shit-hot, I can see that, mate. You're a fuckin' gun.'

'Yeah,' the cow cockie chimed in. 'We read all about you in the papers. You was in that siege thing, weren't you?'

Bob Proctor was nodding his head enthusiastically, a big smile spread across his ginger dial.

'Yeah mate, he's a dead set bloody hero, this bloke.'

Dave could suddenly feel the pins and needles stabbing lightly at his scalp again, and a rising itch crawling into both his palms.

'No,' he mumbled, rubbing one hand against his hip. 'Bullshit,' he added, almost in a whisper. 'I'm no hero.'

Ahern guffawed again, louder than ever.

'That's not what I heard. According to the papers, you got shot and everything.'

Dave could feel his heart accelerate, the blood pumping hard into his head, stinging his eyes and flushing his face. He took another swig of rum, then rolled the frosted glass across his forehead.

'It was no big deal.'

Ahern erupted into raucous laughter.

'No big deal?' Bob Proctor was leaning forward over the bar, red-faced, his eyes as big as dinner plates. 'I heard you had to shoot the bloke.'

'You killed him, didn't you?' Rolly Dawson added. 'Is that right? Did you kill him? That's what the papers said.'

Dave Hocking planted his glass down on the bar and abruptly pushed his way out of the circle.

'Just got to take a slash,' he muttered, almost incoherently, as he strode away from them, head down, through the public bar and out into the back hallway that led down to the toilets, and out towards the balcony beyond. As he passed the door to the male toilets his head was already thumping, his eyes burning, driving him straight onwards, down the corridor towards the cool night air outside. By the time he broke out onto the broad floorboards of the old veranda he was sucking in short, staccato gulps, desperately trying to suppress a gagging, retching feeling rising in his throat and stomach. He stopped on the veranda and slumped helplessly onto the long seat propped against the back wall of the hotel, his head hanging down defencelessly, his eyes half-closed, his whole being gripped and overcome by his sudden malady.

As he breathed slowly in and out, and the night air gradually enveloped him, he could feel the needles softening on his skull, the heat draining from his face and ears. He clutched at the dull ache in his side and wondered what was happening. Too much sun. Not enough sleep. That was it. Eventually, he straightened in his seat, slowly and cautiously, and laid his head back against the wooden wall. He felt better now. Exhausted, but better.

His slow, steady breathing was suddenly interrupted by the tock of bootheels on the wooden floorboards overhead. Dave looked up instinctively towards the sound, as a young, blond-haired woman in a short, blousy, low-cut dress and ruby-red cowgirl boots strode across the upstairs veranda and stepped onto the narrow wooden stairway. The night air caught her dress on the way down, pushing it back from her soft white thighs, in a teasing, wafting wave that seemed to almost beckon him. He looked down self-consciously and when he looked back up she was almost upon him, striding for the backdoor of the hotel.

'G'day mate,' she said, with a sexy country swagger, as she sashayed past and disappeared into the hallway.

Who was she? A barmaid? He hadn't seen her in the hotel before. Where had she come from? He traced her path back up the wooden stairs, back to the top storey. Along the length of the first floor, abutting the open upstairs veranda, he could see a row of closed doors, obviously the accommodation wing. Dave stood up, still looking up, and ambled closer to the stairwell for a better view. Now he could see clearly, adjacent to the top of the stairs, the last closed hotel room door in the line. From where he was standing he could just make out the tarnished brass number plate on the front of it—number *8*.

TWELVE

Slick didn't miss her former husband. Too much water had passed under the bridge for that. Too much deception, too many scams, and way too many bitter disappointments. Trevor had been nothing but a cheap and tawdry two-card trick in her life, a beautiful, beguiling apparition she had fallen for, mesmerised by his handsome, smiling face, and broad-chested, suntanned swagger. But from the day Trevor Ellowe first walked into Kirsten Foster's life, when the two of them were still just fresh-faced kids, gazing longingly into each other's eyes across the counter of the tyre company at Parramatta, everything they had was destined to end up in a steaming pile of dog shit. And it did. Trevor broke her heart in every way imaginable, and by the time she finally kicked him down the back stairs of her life, she'd used up every bit of love she'd ever had for him.

So Kirsten didn't miss her late husband Trevor one tiny little bit. But sometimes, especially on nights like this, she couldn't help but think about him. Not the desperate, scheming Trevor, the one whose charming, cheeky grin had long ago become just a shifty and distrustful sneer, but the real Trevor, the original mirage, the young, swashbuckling Trevor, before the drugs, the drinking and the lies. That Trevor sometimes came to her at night, deep in her pleasant dreams. Tall, handsome and upright, flashing that broad and welcoming smile that used to make her heart leap and take her breath away. That Trevor was in her thoughts tonight.

'Hey Slick. What's happening?'

She wasn't surprised when Eddie picked his phone up on the second ring. She knew he'd be awake. Eddie didn't sleep. He was like a vampire, up until all hours of the morning.

'I just broke up with Warren.'

A second's silence passed before he answered.

'Great.' That was pretty much the reaction she expected. Eddie never did like her latest boyfriend, Warren. She knew that from the get-go. She figured it was probably just his white shoes and ebullient real estate sales-pitch patter. 'So, you want to celebrate? I'll crack out the champagne.'

She took a taxi straight from Levsky's Bar and Grill to Eddie's unit on the beachfront, and by the time she got there he was stirring up a storm, re-heating a large wok full of his signature Chinese stir-fry. Behind the apron he was still wearing his crumpled suit-pants and work shirt, sleeves rolled up to the elbows, and his dining table was awash with police statements, photographs and assorted paperwork, so she figured he'd obviously been working through the night and, knowing Eddie, no doubt he'd totally forgotten to eat anything at all until she called.

'Congratulations, kiddo,' Eddie announced, as he handed her a fine, full-bodied red and gently clinked her glass. 'You just ditched another dud.'

She gazed down into the glass, suddenly feeling deeply sorry for herself. A girl would be nothing short of barking nuts to be looking for relationship advice from a screwball misfit like her old friend Eddie but somehow, deep down, she kind of knew he was right. Again. And it really pissed her off. Warren was a loud-mouthed try-hard, and all his fancy cars and flashy lifestyle didn't change the fact he was essentially a boring, middle-aged, recently divorced dickhead, with nothing to really recommend him but a Mercedes Benz sports car and a bountiful bank balance. Still, those were both good things and, for everything he wasn't, Warren was at least some company. But now, because for some reason Kirsten Foster never could quite seem to settle for anything other than the perfect Hollywood romance, Warren was gone.

Her chin began to tremble as moisture gathered in the corners of her eyes.

'I'm all alone again.'

'What are you talking about, doll-face?' Eddie stepped forward and wrapped his lanky arms around her, pulling her in close to him. 'You've always got me.'

'Yeah, great,' she sighed, as she gently rolled her eyes and laid her head against his chest, feeling a familiar comfort. He was right again; she always had Eddie. 'How depressing.'

He was so obviously excited about the feast he had prepared for them, she didn't have the heart to break it to him that by this late hour all the normal people had already eaten hours ago, including her. As Eddie fussed around the kitchen, garnishing and plating up their meals, she recounted, blow-by-blow, the painful, sad account of how she and White-shoe Warren had finally ended the affair, and wrestled with the mess of paper splayed across his table, pushing back enough of it to clear a corner big enough to squeeze a couple of plates in with some chop sticks, a bottle and two glasses.

The stir-fry, as it turned out, was one of Eddie's best, which was saying something, and the red wine they washed it down with got better with every glass. As they talked and laughed and drank, and traded the usual cheap shots and wise-cracks back and forth across the table, Slick gradually forgot about how much she was going to miss Warren's sexy sports car and how sorry she was feeling for herself. By the time Eddie opened up the second bottle she was happy to be just who she was, and where she was, doing what she was doing with just who she was doing it with. She wasn't even thinking about Trevor anymore.

'Shit, I meant to ask,' she suddenly blurted out, as she recognised the mess heaped on the table as the McQuillan murder brief. 'How did you go in Brisbane?'

'Yeah, interesting.' Eddie reached for his cigarettes and flipped the pack open, offering her one. 'Real interesting.'

He clicked on his lighter and lit them both up, then stretched his long legs straight and leaned back on his chair, launching straight into the story. His meeting with their client at the gaol that morning had gone pretty much as disastrously as every other meeting he had had with him to date. The cantankerous, contrary cowboy shot the whole prospect of an involuntary-intoxication-leading-to-temporary-insanity defence straight down in flames. He claimed he didn't work that day, went nowhere near any paint fumes, and didn't even stick his head in Wilson's car. He hadn't had a single, solitary whiff of any toxic fumes of anything from anywhere. '*I'm not crazy and I didn't do it*' was all he had to offer.

Great. All those hours of reading Slick had done of all them high-falutin' Yankee court cases on involuntary intoxication had just gone straight down the dunny without even passing *Go*. She was starting to dislike this cowboy dude, and she'd never even met him.

But then Eddie told her he went from the gaol straight to the Supreme Court, where he had lunch with Dr Waylon Penfold, the Melbourne shrink who sounded, to Slick, like more or less just a fatter, better-dressed version of loopy Doc, from *Back to the Future*. The doctor had ruled out involuntary intoxication too, but he ruled in something else he called PTSD—post-traumatic stress disorder. As Eddie explained the concept to her, as it had been explained to him, it sounded, to Slick, a whole lot like an insanity defence, until he came up with the doctor's final punchline—the PTSD may not have caused the murder, the murder may have caused the PTSD.

So from there Eddie went to see a forensic scientist called Keenan at the Government Health Laboratory in the city, to see if there was anything at the scene that might have pointed to the possibility Wilson might have been already dead when Rowdy got back to the house. And that's when Keenan dropped a total bombshell, one that Eddie figured blew the case wide open—Tom Wilson's murderer would have been covered in blood, a lot more than the police found on Rowdy's clothes.

'So?' Slick didn't get it.

'So, unless he thoroughly washed his clothes out after the murder, Rowdy McQuillan didn't do it.'

'Is that it?'

'Yeah.'

'His clothes were clean?'

'Yeah.'

'So what?' It didn't sound like too much of a bombshell to Slick. 'Is this a guy thing or something? Is it so hard to give your clothes a decent wash?'

'No,' Eddie's chair dropped forward, and he leaned in close to her, his face twisted into a perplexed expression. 'But that would have taken time. He would have had to be there for at least ten minutes.'

'Of course he was.' She splashed another dollop of the red into her glass. 'Wilson was probably out cold that long before the second attack.'

'What second attack?'

'Have you looked at the photographs?'

Slick was no lawyer; she was just a secretary. She didn't get paid to read police briefs or scientific mumbo jumbo. She hadn't read a single word of any of the witness statements, so she had absolutely no clue what any of the prosecution witnesses had said about anything. But how could she resist pawing through those creepy crime scene photographs? They were like still-shots from a horror movie, full of scary, awful stuff you didn't want to look at, but absolutely had to. Horror movies terrified her—always had—which was why they'd always been her favourite.

She reached forward and delved deep in under all the paperwork surrounding them, pulling out the pile of crime scene photographs, bundled together and loosely tied up with pink legal tape. She slipped off the legal tape, shuffled through the bundle and then slapped one down, face-up on the table between the remnants of stir-fry and red wine.

'First attack, right here. See?' It was a close-up photograph of Tom Wilson's unmade bed, and Slick had it skewered to the tabletop with one long, painted fingernail resting on a red-black patch of blood directly alongside a grimy, crumpled pillow. 'A bunch of blood that big means whoever hit him got him good, right there.' It looked to Eddie like a reasonable assumption. *But so what?* 'If he wasn't out cold there and then, he sure must have been real close to it.'

'Maybe, maybe not.'

Slick went back to shuffling the photographs.

'Yeah, maybe not,' she said, still shuffling the pack, before eventually slipping out another photograph and slapping it face-up beside the first. 'But then right here you've got another, bigger one.' It was a wide shot of the whole crime scene, and this time her fingernail was pointing to a broad patch of what looked like blood pooled against the wall beside the bed. 'So I figure, even if he wasn't out cold on the bed, he got up but then fell down again, right here, beside the bed. And that there looks to me like a shitload of blood, right?' *Yeah, she's right, that is a shitload of blood, without any shadow of a doubt.* 'By the look of that blood-stain, I'd say he definitely was out cold by then.'

'Not necessarily.'

'See this?' She was pointing to what appeared to be a long, thin, ruby-coloured line painted on the carpet, curving from the pooled blood back down beside the bed. 'It's an outline, right? Of a body. Someone was lying right there in the blood.'

'Sure,' Eddie nodded. At least that was what it looked like. 'But that doesn't mean he was out cold. He could have just fell and laid there for a couple of seconds, then got up.'

Slick moved her fingernail several inches to the right and left it resting on the headless body of Tom Wilson, lying flat on his back at the foot of the bed, his arms splayed out alongside him.

'The dead guy was clearly on his back when this shit happened. Right?'

'Sure.' There was no doubt about that. All of the wounds were inflicted to the anterior aspect of the body, mostly to the face. As Eddie was still intently studying the depiction of the gruesome scene, she flicked another photo from the batch.

'So how did this get there?'

She was holding up a close-up of the blood-stained tee-shirt Wilson had been wearing on the night of his murder, her finger pointing to a clearly defined pattern of minute squares etched into the left side of the shirt in an oily, crimson paste.

'That's a carpet pattern, right? Made by coagulating blood.' She was right. It was clear and unmistakeable. As the body had lay prone across the blood-soaked carpet, the blood had obviously begun to clot, mirroring the pattern of the carpet in the fabric. 'On the left side of his shirt. Not on his back, where he ended up.' She arched her eyebrows whimsically at him, and he did likewise in reply. 'Which means at some stage he was lying on the carpet on his left side in a pool of blood, long enough to leave that carpet pattern on his shirt.'

Eddie snatched the photograph from her, and held it close up to his face. He gazed at it for several seconds, until he was absolutely sure. She was right. The clotting blood had formed a distinct pattern of the carpet on the left side of the tee-shirt, which had to mean Wilson was lying on the carpet on his left side long enough for the blood on the shirt to start coagulating.

Slick was sitting back now, looking smug and happy with herself.

'It'd take a few minutes for the blood to clot and form a pattern like that.' She was right again.

'How did you know that?'

'Are you kidding? I lived ten years in Parramatta.'

What she didn't know was the prosecution timeline was so tight McQuillan didn't have a single extra second—never mind a few minutes—to spare. The features she was pointing out seemed to make it clear and certain Wilson was hit hard at least once before the killer launched the final, fatal assault. Hard enough to make him fall onto the floor, maybe even pass out, lying on his side for some time, motionless in one position, before he eventually got up and moved, or was dragged, six feet or so to the centre of the foot of the bed, before the killer came again, this time finishing him off, good and proper. All that would have taken time, which on the prosecution case, Rowdy McQuillan simply didn't have.

'So there were two attacks,' Slick added triumphantly. 'The first one here.' She poked her finger at the bloodstain on the bed. 'Then the second one, right here at the foot of the bed, where the real damage was done.'

It was good stuff, and it fed right into the alternative narrative Eddie needed to tell, that between the time Ross and Lindy Lewis dropped Rowdy McQuillan at the Castle Street house around midnight, and when he showed up at Karen Millard's house about fifteen minutes later, there just wasn't enough time for him to have so viciously attacked Tom Wilson—twice, as it now appeared—do to him what was done, and wash his clothes so thoroughly they were virtually spotless by the time the cops showed at the house.

'You're one smart cookie, you know that?'

'A lot smarter than you are evidently, Mr Genius.'

'Who would've thought it?'

'Yeah, right,' she smirked, draining her glass. 'Fuck you too.'

He lifted the bottle, refilled both their glasses, thought about what she'd just told him, and then proceeded to explain to her the stuff she didn't know about the prosecution evidence. The Lewises had put a firm time on precisely when they last laid eyes on Rowdy McQuillan that night, lumbering his way towards the front door of Tom Wilson's house, three sheets to the wind but otherwise apparently sane and docile, at precisely twelve midnight. Brian Ingles made a contemporaneous note on the occurrence log that Neville Staffield, Karen Millard and Elaine Barlow arrived at the police house at spot-on twelve twenty-one AM. That left a window of exactly twenty-one minutes. The version they gave him meant Rowdy McQuillan had to have been at Karen Millard's house for a full five minutes at the absolute minimum, and it would have taken them a couple of minutes at least to get to the police house. It all added up to the fact that McQuillan couldn't have been in the Castle Street house for more than about fifteen minutes tops. That wasn't much time for him to have gone into the house, got into an argument with Wilson, worked himself up into a frenzy, grabbed a baseball bat and attacked Wilson once, and then a second time, beat him to an absolute pulp, and then taken off his clothes and washed them out so thoroughly there was virtually not a single spot of blood left on them.

'So what are you telling me?' Now she was sitting forward on the edge of her chair, wide-eyed and enthralled, like she was watching a cheap murder-mystery on TV. 'You think he maybe didn't do it?'

'Yeah, maybe.'

'But didn't you say his fingerprints were all over the murder thing? And he had the guy's blood all over him. So he must have been there, right?'

Eddie sat back in his chair, sucked hard on his cigarette, and blew out a long, grey stream of smoke.

'Yeah,' he said eventually. 'That's where my day got kind of weird.'

It turned out, Eddie explained, Waylon Penfold wasn't just a one-trick pony. Apart from his well-documented contributions to the study of the causes and effects of involuntary stupefaction, apparently Penfold was also something of a red-hot expert in the field of what psychoanalysts referred to as *repressed memory*. The term, according to the doc, referred to a kind of psychological glitch in people's consciousness, where painful memories were pushed away into the back of the brain and stored in the unconscious mind so that normal, conscious recall couldn't access them. He said it happened all the time with PTSD patients who had been through a particularly traumatic event; they'd lose all memory of what happened to them. Except it wasn't really lost at all, it was just locked away somewhere inside their head, somewhere where they couldn't get at it, as a kind of natural defensive mechanism to protect the mind from the effects of thoughts too horrible to think about.

But the doctor also said these repressed memories could sometimes be recovered, or at least accessed, through hypnosis, at which he just so happened to be also a you-beaut, whiz-bang expert. So, once Penfold worked out his patient apparently had lost his memory of everything that happened—and not because of any kind of involuntary intoxication—he asked him for permission to hypnotise him, in the hope that may assist in recovering some kind of memory of the event.

'And that's where things got really funky.'

'*Funky?*'

'Yeah.' Eddie sucked in another mouthful of his cigarette, swallowed it down with more red wine, and sat silently for several seconds, pensively tapping his cigarette on the corner of the ashtray. 'According to Penfold, McQuillan went straight under—like real deep—so he started asking him to turn him mind back to the night of Wilson's murder. He reckons when he did McQuillan started getting really freaked out, like super-agitated, to the point that Penfold was thinking of bringing him straight out of it.' Eddie paused, almost reluctant to proceed, but the expectant look on his sidekick's face made it pretty clear he didn't have much choice. 'Anyway, he reckons McQuillan then started making weird noises, like grunting, just like a pig he reckons. So he started trying to calm him down, get him to relax, but he was just getting worse, more and more upset. And when Penfold asked what it was eating him, he reckons Rowdy said to him something like *Someone's there*, or *There's someone there*, something like that. Something about somebody being there. And then he says something like *He's going to hurt me*, or *He's trying to hurt me*, just like he was scared or something of whoever it was he was saying was there. And then he starts sort of moaning and grunting again, and then he starts sort of crying and saying, like, *Blood. There's blood everywhere*, something like that. And then he says *He's dead. They killed him.*'

'*They*?'

'That's what Penfold reckons. He says he said *They killed him.*'

For the next couple of seconds Slick just sat there, completely still, her eyes bulging, mouth wide open, the fingertips of one hand pressed against her lips, as she stared straight at her boss.

'Are you shitting me?' she eventually exclaimed, breathlessly. 'Are you fucking shitting me?'

'Crazy, right?'

'Crazy? That's like fucking stark-raving, crawling-up-the-fucking-walls type crazy. Are you serious? What are you going to do?'

He shrugged and sat back in his chair, taking another drag back on his cigarette.

'I don't know.'

'Can you put this shrink guy in the witness box to say what he said?'

'No.' Eddie shook his head disconsolately. 'It's just an out-of-court, self-serving statement. Totally inadmissible.'

'Holy shit.' She was leaning forward, gazing intently at him, her eyes as big as dinner plates. 'So what are you going to do? You've got to get this guy off.'

Eddie looked back at her and nodded silently for several seconds. Then he wearily reached forward to the ashtray and stubbed out his cigarette.

'Then I guess that's what I'm going to try to do.'

●

Dave Hocking was at first stirred gently from his slumber by the sound of something loudly plopping all around him, then suddenly wrenched awake by heavy splashes of cold water on his face and chest. Flailing desperately and gasping like a drowning man, he rolled onto one side and clawed at the ground around him, struggling to get up onto his feet.

'Shit. Hey. What the fuck?'

Carol Graham waved the hose in his direction one more time, sending a new spurt of water at him as he staggered backwards over the uneven garden bed.

'You keep a civil tongue in your head.'

She closed the nozzle off, but firmly stood her ground in the centre of the driveway, holding the dripping hose in both hands, aimed ominously at him, like a sheriff in a B-grade western, bailing up the town bandito. Dave stretched his eyes wide open, then narrowed them again and squinted back at her, trying to regain his senses.

'What's your problem, lady?'

'What's my problem?' She lowered the hose, opened up the nozzle till the stream was flowing forcefully again, and held it pointed at the driveway, poised, locked and loaded, ready to retaliate to his first false move. 'I'll tell you what my damned problem is. My husband built that garden bed.'

Dave looked down to where his feet were buried deep in an untidy clump of flattened flowers and small shrubs, pressed hard against soil. He looked back up, bewildered.

'What?'

'Do you have any idea how hard it is to get petunias to grow like that out here?' The spurt of water was inching ever closer to him. 'And you, you great drunken oaf, along you come and use them for a damned mattress.'

She swished the hose in his general direction as a parting warning shot, which briefly startled him, and then promptly turned away, going back to hosing down her driveway.

'I did?' the dishevelled detective murmured to himself, as he gingerly stepped over the compressed petunias and out of the garden bed.

He did. He remembered now, and unfortunately his grubby, crumpled clothing bore tell-tale witness to the fact. He had slept the night out in her garden bed, one that apparently had been planned, constructed, planted out and cared for by her now absent but obviously still highly-revered ex-husband, whoever and wherever he may be. He felt bad about it. Perhaps it was just a touch of the old Alcoholics' Remorse, but he could tell from the way Carole Graham was aggressively swishing her hose back and forth across the bitumen driveway he had deeply offended her.

'If those flowers die the replacement cost goes on your bill,' she snapped tersely at him as he lumbered back towards his unit.

'Yeah, okay,' he mumbled without looking back, as he pushed in through the open door and swung it closed behind him.

Dave threw himself onto the neatly made-up bed and lay there motionless, staring at the ceiling, feeling like he would soon drift back to sleep, but knowing that he wouldn't. He idly reached into his side pocket, where his police-issue mobile telephone was pressing uncomfortably against his hip, pulled it out, and dropped it carelessly onto the floor. It had been a rough night. He remembered staggering back to the motel, home supplies in hand, his head full of painful memories and questions that he couldn't answer. At some stage he had gone outside, sat on the low block edging of the garden bed, fiddling with the fancy, newfangled mobile phone the QPS had issued him, hoping he might get some sort of clear reception out of it. But it was useless; he couldn't even work out how to turn it on. Eventually he gave up, tipped back the bottle and swallowed down the last of his rum, then lowered himself back down onto the soft foliage behind him. He remembered lying on his back, feeling drunk, looking at a million stars in the black sky overhead, closing his eyes and seeing Larnie Mitchell's pristine room, full of girlie dolls and knick-knacks, and those happy snaps of pretty, smiling schoolgirls.

And Janey. She was there too. When he closed his eyes he saw her there, like she was standing right in front of him.

Dave Hocking rolled off the bed up onto his feet and pulled his shirt off. What time was it anyway? He had to get going, get his mind back on the job, do something, starting with a quick slash, a shave and a cold, refreshing shower. He launched himself into it without further ado, and by the time he'd finished in the bathroom and pulled on a crisp, clean shirt and a pair of strides, he was feeling his old self again. Now it was time to get down to Daines' Smash Repairs and kick some freckle. It was already nearly ten o'clock, so if that scrawny grease-monkey didn't have his radiator hose replaced and his car back on the road by the time he got there, Dave was going to have plenty to say about it.

As it turned out, Kevin Daines surprised him. By the time Dave had made his way down into town and walked up Junction Road to the corner of Connell, he found his car efficiently parked in the driveway of the panel shop, still looking generally bruised and battered, but otherwise ready to roll. The skinny, oil-stained kid was in the workshop, his head hidden underneath the bonnet of a fire-engine red utility with chrome reverse hubcaps all around, and when he heard Dave's footsteps he emerged, wiping his filthy hands with a correspondingly filthy piece of cloth.

'How're y'goin'?'

'I don't know, you tell me.'

'Yeah mate,' Daines laconically assured him. 'She's all good, no worries. Just make sure you keep her topped up, you'll be sweet.'

Dave waited while the young man squeezed the hood down, and gently wiped it clean.

'What year's this thing?'

''73.'

'VJ Valiant.'

'Yeah.' Kevin Daines stretched his lips into a gap-tooth grin as he lovingly looked the vehicle over. 'It's me own car, ay. Just doing her up.'

'Nice.'

As Dave followed the mechanic back towards the office to fix up the bill, he noticed something curious across the road. Over the front door of the all-purpose store on the opposite corner was a bright blue sign with gold coloured writing on it, spelling out in capital letters the word 'Golf.' Below it, to one side, was a small wooden table, covered with a cluttered assortment of potted plants.

Once they had finally finished in the office, and Kevin Daines had handed back his keys, Dave left his car parked in the driveway of the panel shop and walked straight across the road. When he got to the store, he stopped momentarily outside, picked out a pot full of petunias from the display table out front, and then strode on to the counter inside. As he slapped his money down and waited for his change, he stood staring at the sign outside, intrigued.

'What's your golf course like?' he said eventually to the craggy-faced proprietor, now fossicking below the counter for a bag to put the pot plants into.

'She's no St Andrews, that's for sure,' the old man droned back wearily. 'Plenty of good bunker practice but.'

When Dave Hocking got back to his car, he dropped the bag full of petunias onto the front seat beside him and kicked the engine over. As it purred efficiently, he slipped the automatic gearstick into 'drive,' pulled out onto Connell Street, and then left into the main drag, heading for the police house. He was feeling good, under his own steam again, back in charge of his own life.

Then he suddenly spotted something he had all but forgotten. The squat little standalone building with the red sign reading 'OP SHOP' was just there on his left, and its front door was wide open. Dave moved his foot across onto the brake pedal and pulled over to the kerb. He turned the engine off and sat still for a moment, looking back at the little building in his rear-view mirror, thinking what he wanted to do next. Eventually, he pulled the keys from the ignition, pushed the drivers' door open with a bang, and climbed out of the car.

When he stepped in through the front door, Dave could see immediately the cramped Salvation Army second-hand clothing store was even more cluttered than it had appeared from outside. The matronly little woman at the front counter looked excited at the sight of him, and greeted him immediately with what for Dave was fast becoming a customary salutation.

'You're the detective they sent up from Brisbane.'

Like everyone else in town, it seemed, she wanted to talk about the McQuillan case, but like all the others she had no information, just questions he wasn't interested in answering. Dave was in her shop for something else entirely. Yesterday he had seen something in the window, something tucked away at the back of a dust-covered, crowded shelf, all but obscured behind a wall of bric-a-brac and hand-me-downs. It was something potentially important, something he needed to get a closer look at if he could. The vague description he gave of what he was looking for didn't seem to mean much to the pleasant little lady, but when he pointed in its general direction, she energetically began ferreting away until she finally retrieved exactly what he wanted—a diminutive pair of little girls' red patent leather shoes.

'You got little kids at home, have you?' the old lady said sweetly as she handed them to him.

But the detective didn't answer; he was staring intently at the little shoes, turning them over in his hands, inspecting them, intrigued by them, as if searching for some obscure, exotic secret hidden somewhere on their surface.

'Do you remember the girl who brought these in?'

'Girl?' The woman looked confused. 'What girl?'

He looked up from the shoes, at first uncomprehending. He quickly collected his thoughts.

'Where did you get these from?'

'I don't know, love.' She looked contrite, almost apologetic. 'Some of that stuff's been there for years.'

'How many years?'

'I don't know.'

Now the shoes were in his hands, up close where he could touch them, feel them, see them clearly, he couldn't be so certain they were the same. Now they didn't seem quite so familiar. It had been too many years. He wasn't sure.

'I'll take them.'

Dave Hocking drove straight back to the Starlight Motel. As he closed the door to room fourteen behind him, he spun the air con dial up as far as it would go, then slumped down into the armchair, pulling the little shoes out of their plastic bag. Were they the ones? Was it really possible? If they were, what could it all mean? He sat silent and completely still, alone in the room, the shoes lying in his lap, staring at them for a long time, lost in a sea of painful memories and cruel regret, questions and recriminations bouncing back and forth around his brain. Eventually, he stopped; he just couldn't do it anymore.

Dave drew in a cool, refreshing breath, and blew it out again. They weren't the shoes. They were similar, but not the same. He was mistaken. He stood up, walked over to the wardrobe, and stuffed the bag and shoes efficiently into his overnight bag. Then he stepped up close to the air-conditioning unit, and let the cool air blow over him, soothing and settling. They weren't the shoes.

When he stepped into the front office of the motel, the doorbell heralded his arrival, as always, but there was no one behind the counter, as usual. It was probably just as well. The last thing he needed right now was another confrontation with the lady of the house. He waited a few moments, to be sure the coast was clear, and then reached over the front counter, and set down the little pot of blue, purple and pink petunias on the desktop where she would easily find them. They looked good.

As he momentarily admired them, Dave noticed, on the desktop beside the pot of flowers, the motel guest register, its leather-bound cover closed shut. Something suddenly occurred to him. People came and went through these little outback towns all the time. People wandering aimlessly, salespeople, people on holidays, people lost, running away, looking for work. The first place a lot of them would lob when they hit town would be a place like this, right here, the one and only motel in the town.

He reached down, flipped the register open, flicked through the blank pages from back to front until he got to the last entry—Detective David Hocking—and ran his eye up the page from there. Carol Graham wasn't exactly doing a roaring trade, but there were names, plenty of them, some in and out, just overnight, others staying days at a time. When he got to the top, he turned the page and scrolled again, from the bottom upwards. Then he turned the page again, and then again, page after page, until he got to the last entry at the top of the first page of the register. Nothing. That was just over twelve months ago. There had to be earlier registers; he needed to go back further. He peered over the counter-top to where a bundle of papers and books was neatly stacked at one end of the desk, then reached over and began rifling through them.

'Can I help you with something?'

Carol Graham had a habit of sneaking up on people that Dave Hocking was starting to find irritating, and right now he was in no mood to answer her questions. But he had a question of his own, an important one, about something he desperately needed to know. He pulled his wallet out of his back pocket and held up a tattered, colour photograph of a smiling teenaged girl.

'Have you ever seen this girl?'

Carole Graham looked taken aback, almost affronted, as if she was being accused. But when she looked at the photograph, she could see the face was familiar.

'No.'

'You sure?' He was so insistent, almost desperate, she had to feel sorry for him. 'You've never seen her? Anywhere in town.'

'No, never.'

Dave Hocking pushed his wallet back into his pocket, and promptly turned away. The cheery doorbell gave another bubbly little ring as he disappeared out through the door.

THIRTEEN

When Dave finally got to the police house, he was surprised to find a bundle of witness statements neatly stacked up on the spare desk, waiting for the Senior Sergeant to wade through them. Brian Ingles had interviewed everyone he had been told to, as well as one or two Dave hadn't even asked for. And as the Senior Sergeant leafed his way carefully through them, one by one, he soon realised the kid knew how to take a statement from a witness. Not every copper did, that was for sure. Dave had worked with seasoned veterans who didn't know one end of a decent witness statement from the other. But this jumped-up kid, still wet behind the ears, had made a fair-to-middling job of it.

At the bottom of the pile were Sue and Lyall Mitchell's. Dave had told Ingles to get statements from them, even though it looked unlikely they'd have much to offer, and as it turned out he was right; they didn't. They both knew Rowdy and their daughter had been mates for years, growing up together, knocking around the neighbourhood as kids, but nothing more than that. Since Rowdy went away Larnie never mentioned him, even after he came back to town. They'd both seen him once or twice around the town, said hello and that, but as far as Larnie's parents knew, she and her old mate Rowdy had just more or less gone on their separate ways in recent years. There was no trouble that they knew of, no bad blood. They'd just grown apart, as kids sometimes did when they got older.

There was something about reading these two parents' statements that was making Detective Senior Sergeant David Hocking feel increasingly uneasy.

Two loving parents who knew absolutely nothing about their daughter's life, not even whether she was alive or dead. Their witless despair left him feeling sadly hollow and frustrated, more cranky, with every page he turned, convinced there must be something everyone had missed—something going on between the cowboy and his girlfriend that no one had been told.

'What was she spending her money on?' the detective suddenly erupted.

Brian Ingles looked up, startled, from the other desk.

'Who?'

'Larnie Mitchell.' Hocking disdainfully lobbed Lyall's statement flat onto the desktop. 'She was drawing a benefit, plus she was working on the side at the local pub, and her old man was leaving dough out for her. What was she spending it on?'

Ingles looked stumped.

'I don't know.'

'What about boyfriends? She was a good sort. Some young buck around the town must've been getting his end in.'

The constable shrugged absently.

'How would I know?'

'How would you know?' Hocking pushed his chair back and started wandering angrily around the room, waving his arms in the constable's direction. 'Because you're the local fucking copper in this town, that's how you'd know. This is your fucking town.'

Ingles fumbled sheepishly for words.

'People have got a right to privacy though, Senior.'

'Fuck people's privacy.' Dave Hocking could hear himself shouting, but he wasn't quite sure why. He just couldn't help it. He was angry, so angry he just had to shout. At someone, anyone. 'You're a one-man station in a two-horse fucking fly-spot. You should know every boil on every bum in this town. You should know exactly who's up who for the rent, and for how fucking much. Fuck people's privacy.'

He was still angry when he got back into his car and slammed the door behind him. Angry at everything. Angry at this stupid, two-bit town, where everyone knew everything about everybody's business, but no one could tell two parents whether their teenaged daughter was alive or dead. Angry about what he didn't know, and couldn't seem to find out. Angry at that little pissant Mason Deeds thinking he could put one over on the coppers, angry at the CMC, at all the smart-arse lawyers, at Roger Page, at cops who couldn't wait to dog their mates, and at that piece of shit Mark Trindall, who had made the coppers kill him right in front of his own two kids. He was angry that the local gossip group knew all about how a killer terrorised Jenny Deeds in her own home on the night he beat his housemate to a pulp, and yet no one even thought to mention it to the local copper, Brian Ingles. He was especially angry at Ingles, not for anything he did or didn't do, just for the fact he was young, and inexperienced and stupid, like all the others, full of promise, with his whole career to look forward to. One of the new breed who had it all ahead of them, who believed the job was all fair dinkum and they were on the side of right and might, just like Dave once did. And he was angry at himself, for just not being able to believe it anymore, for failing to live up to everything he had once expected of himself, becoming a pale, disappointing shadow, one of yesterday's men. He was angry about the things he'd done and said, and wished he could take back, but knew he couldn't. And most of all he was angry that he couldn't find a lost girl, couldn't find anyone, not even himself.

Dave needed to calm down, stop beating himself up, being angry. He needed to get some time to relax, slow down, grab a bit of R 'n' R. He found himself cruising west on Humeburn Road down towards the Arms Hotel. It was after four o'clock, but still too early to go to the pub, and the thought of sitting in his motel room watching afternoon TV was nothing short of soul-destroying. By now the Brisbane papers should be on the shelves, but only at the newsagency, and the last thing he wanted right now was to run into Lyall or Sue Mitchell.

Dave had another idea; one he knew would help him relax. He hadn't had a hit of golf in years, and the detective in him was still intrigued by that sign that hung over the front door of the all-purpose store. *What the hell would a golf course look like in this part of the world?* There was still a couple of hours' sunlight left and he figured, however dry and dusty the local fairway might be, whacking a few balls would be as good a way as any to blow off some steam.

When he eventually arrived at the so-called course, a couple of kilometres down a dusty track that came off Station Road to the north of the town, he soon saw it was every bit as bad as he had expected. Some enterprising entrepreneur had seen fit to grade and clear enough of the flat, scrubby landscape to accommodate four par-three holes, each one featuring a small circle of patchy, grey grass to tee off, and a corresponding putting 'green,' linked by a fairway sparsely dotted with short, scraggy shrubs. But Dave had it all to himself, and it would be all that he needed.

Before he left the all-purpose store, the old bloke had handed him two keys, one to get into the shed, and the other to open his locker—number three of four—where he would find a buggy and bag, with a wood, a couple of irons and a putter. And finally, he handed him a rolled-up square of artificial turf, fastened with a rubber band.

'You'll need one of these, I reckon.'

He reckoned right. That was clear enough to Dave the moment he stepped up onto the first tee. He looked down at the rough tufts of hardy grass, and then over a broad, barren landscape, where the sandy soil of the fairway stretched an uneven path out to a faraway flag marking the green and first hole. He slipped the rubber band from the mat the old man had given him, and unrolled the little square of artificial turf. It would do the job, almost like it the real thing. It wasn't, of course, but obviously, in this town, if you didn't want to play every ball from the bunker, you had to bring your own grass along with you.

Dave pushed his tee into a tuft, pulled the wood from the bag, and got himself set. It had been a long time, but he told himself it was just like riding a bike. He hunched his shoulders and carefully positioned his grip, adjusting his stance—weight evenly balanced, left arm straight—then swung through for a smooth and effortless practice shot. It felt good. He re-set himself, relaxed, and swung once again. Even better. He was ready, good to go. He moved forward a half-step and carefully addressed the ball, head down, arm straight, eye on the ball. Then he swung through, hard.

The ball made a sweet tocking sound, but then sailed off wildly, at a skewed angle, barely clearing the low shrubs dotted all over the fairway, skipping and bouncing in a zig-zag path before it eventually came to rest on the edge of the fairway. Dave congratulated himself with a gentle nod. It was a start.

As it turned out, he went on much the same as he had started. It wasn't exactly his best day with the clubs, and his wayward shots led him a long and crooked journey around the course. But once he had got to the first hole he was already feeling much better, and he convinced himself the exercise was doing him good. On he went.

By the time Dave reached the tee-off at the fourth hole, the sun was starting to sink into the western horizon, and the light was fading fast. He knew he had a fair walk ahead of him to get back to where he had parked his car—as inconspicuously as possible, in behind the shed and hopefully out of sight of any nosey locals—and he didn't fancy making his way back through the scrubby mulga in darkness, so he decided to skip the last hole and head back to the car.

With the warm western sun at his back, Dave watched his long shadow dancing around erratically on the uneven ground in front of him as he trudged through the orange-tinged country back to his car. When he looked up to where his car was, tucked in behind the shed, he could see up beyond it, far away in the distance, a cloud of dust billowing behind a vehicle moving at speed along a gravel track out on the horizon. As he walked, he watched it sparkling in the early sunset glare, tearing through low-lying shrubs as if racing the dusty cloud, hot on its heels. Eventually, the vehicle slid to a sudden stop, and then remained stationary as the mist gradually settled around it.

As the seconds passed and the cloud eventually cleared, Dave realised he recognised the fire-engine red, VJ Valiant utility he had seen earlier that day at Daines Smash Repairs. Someone was obviously taking it out on the back roads for a thorough test-drive. Then the someone suddenly stepped out of the car.

It was a long lanky streak that looked a whole lot like Kevin Daines. Whoever it was went straight to the open tonneau at the back and lifted something out—a long tool of some kind, maybe a shovel or a crowbar— then rested it across one shoulder and walked away into the scrub. As Dave got to the shed and wrestled the key into the lock, he could still see the faraway stickman trudging off into the distance, the implement protruding awkwardly above his head. After Dave had replaced his buggy and clubs, closed up the locker, and finally emerged out of the shed, he could still see him off in the distance, walking away, now no more than an elongated speck on the hazy horizon. The detective wondered where he was going, all alone, at this hour, out there in the middle of nowhere. *Curious.*

The sunlight was all gone by the time Dave Hocking reached the edge of the town. He hadn't eaten all day, and the exercise had made him hungry, so he decided he'd grab a meal, somewhere out of the way, then hopefully get back to the motel relatively early, watch some TV and hit the sack. He could do with a night off the grog.

When he got to the truck-stop diner he saw Mason Deeds, only briefly, as the short-order cook pushed his way out from the kitchen with a tray-load of steak and chips, spotted Dave on the other side of the counter, nodded sheepishly, picked up next orders from the young girl serving, and quickly retreated back to his hot-plate. Dave nodded back at him coolly. It was Dave's night off; Mason Deeds would keep.

Loaded up with his hamburger-with-the-lot, a carton of chips and a Coke, Dave headed back out to the car. As he ambled across the bitumen tarmac, breathing in the aroma of freshly fried onions and hot, crispy chips, he suddenly picked up a splash of colour in the dim, reflected light of the carpark surrounding his car. *A pair of ruby-red cowgirl boots.*

It was the girl he had seen last night, out on the back veranda of the Empire Hotel. She was still wearing her fancy high-heeled boots, now pulled up over a pair of tight, faded jeans, and was perched on the low wooden railing at the edge of the carpark, alongside his car, her legs tucked in close, both hands clasped modestly over her knees.

As Dave yanked open the car door and unloaded his dinner onto the passenger seat, he noticed the young woman climb to her feet and dawdle towards his car, as if she might have some business with him. He straightened up in the doorway and greeted her with a perfunctory nod.

'G'day.'

She stopped, arms folded across her chest, regarding the damaged front fender.

'Hit a roo, did ya?'

'Yeah.'

'Buggers, aren't they.'

'Yeah.'

She nodded pensively, and then looked back up at him.

'You're the D they sent out for Rowdy's thing.'

'That's right.'

The girl looked like she had something to say, but wasn't sure she was ready to say it.

'Someone said you've been asking round about Larnie.'

As she mentioned the name her chin seemed to waver, ever-so-slightly.

'Did you know her, did you?'

At first, the young woman stood totally still, folding her brow into a deep, troubled frown, as if she was carefully considering his question. Then, after several long seconds, she glanced out around her, into the empty carpark, and back at the diner, as if checking for eavesdroppers.

'Can I talk to you?'

'Sure.' Dave Hocking motioned towards the passenger seat of his car. 'Jump in.'

•

Once Jodie Lanham had introduced herself to Detective Dave Hocking and explained to him she had been best friends with Larnie Mitchell for as long as she could remember, the detective reciprocated, showed her his ID, told her he wanted to find out whatever he could about where her best friend had got to, and why, and offered her up the chip carton. Jodie delved into it without hesitation and came out with several chips, which she promptly stuffed into her mouth and chewed on pensively for what seemed like almost a minute, before she finally had something to say.

'Something's happened to her. I'm sure of it.'

She looked pale and uncertain. Dave could see he would have to take things carefully, one step at a time.

'Why do you say that?'

'She would've rung me,' she blurted out, and then paused, seemingly overcome with a sudden emotion. She was looking down at her hands now, her wrinkled chin trembling pathetically. 'She would've let me know where she got to.'

The reasoning didn't strike Dave as particularly compelling. He'd learned long ago people didn't always do as expected. The one thing you could confidently rely on with people was their capacity to be unreliable.

'Why did she leave Millen?'

Jodie Lanham looked up at him suddenly, almost as if she was surprised to be asked such a question.

'We were always going to go,' she said insistently. 'Her and me. We were going to go down to Brisbane, get out of this dump.'

'So maybe that's where she is then.'

'No.' She was firmly shaking her oval-shaped face from side to side. 'She would have told me. She would have been in touch by now.'

Again, the logic was less than compelling. Dave nodded, took a bite of his burger, chomped away at it slowly, then casually washed it down with a mouthful of Coke. Jodie Lanham had something she wanted to tell him; all she needed was time to get comfortable about spitting it out. He picked up the chip carton again and offered it up to her, but this time she just stared at it blankly, as if counting how many chips were left. When she finally spoke, her voice was charged with a new urgency.

'I heard Tommy Wilson was down at the Empire that night.'

'What night?'

'The night he got…' Her voice failed her momentarily, but she immediately sucked in a breath and continued. 'The night he died. They reckon Tom was mouthing off about Bob Proctor being responsible for what happened to Larnie.'

The conversation seemed to have suddenly taken a radical redirection. For some reason Jodie Lanham was drawing a connection between Larnie and Tom Wilson. What did Larnie's disappearance have to do with the death of Tom Wilson? And what did any of it have to do with Bob Proctor?

Responsible how?

Jodie was looking him straight in the eye, the emotion all gone now, replaced by a steely resolve.

'Larnie was in trouble.' He could see from the look on her face that this was really what she had come to tell him. 'Bob Proctor had given her a room to stay in, down at the Empire.'

'Room eight.'

'Yeah.' She looked shocked. 'How'd you know that?'

Dave Hocking side-stepped the question. For now, it suited him to have Jodie Lanham believe he might be one step ahead of her.

'What's that got to do with her being in trouble?'

'Her and Mozzie had a big heap of speed stashed in there.' Dave figured 'Mozzie' was the same Maurice 'Mozzie' Blane mentioned in Brain Ingles' missing person file as a former associate of the Mitchell girl, but he wasn't about to interrupt Jodie Lanham's narrative to confirm the fact, not while she was being so forthcoming about her best mate dealing in amphetamines. 'I think Bob was getting some of what they sold it for.'

'Sold it to who?'

'Truckies mainly. Out of this joint here.' She waved her thumb in the direction of the truck-stop diner. 'Or down the pub.' She paused briefly, then went on. 'Sometimes we'd go into Cunnamulla, or up to one or two of the stations.'

'We?'

Lanham hung her head briefly, like a repentant sinner, then shrugged and looked back up at him.

'We were just trying to scrape together enough money to get out of here, that's all, maybe get a place together somewhere down in Brisbane.' Tears had begun welling in her eyes. 'We almost had enough too, until someone took off with our stash.'

'Pinched it?'

Jodie nodded silently.

'Mozzie reckoned it was Larnie who done it.' She looked back down at her hands. 'But I know for sure it wasn't.'

'How do you know that?'

'I just know. Larnie wouldn't do something like that. Not to me.' She looked like she was trying to convince herself. 'We was best mates.' She delved into her handbag and pulled out a tiny, black-and-white photograph, obviously taken in an arcade photo booth somewhere. It showed two giggling girls, pressed together, cheek-to-cheek, pulling silly faces into the lens. 'See, that's us.'

Hanging from Larnie Mitchell's neck was an elegant drop-pearl necklace, almost identical with what Sue Mitchell had sketched in his notebook.

'Good mates, ay.'

'Yeah.' She smiled fondly at the memory. 'She wouldn't have done that to me.' Then she put the photo away. 'Or to Kev.'

'Kev?'

'Kevin Daines. Works down the panel shop.' Dave knew exactly who she was talking about, and he wasn't surprised to hear he was up to no good. 'He used to drive for us sometimes. Mozzie give him a cut.'

It sounded to Dave like there were way too many cooks copping a cut from this broth. Jodie and her bestie were no doubt making three parts of fuck-all for their efforts.

'So what do you think happened to Larnie?'

'I don't know.' A single glistening tear spilled out over one eyelid and ran down her chubby cheek. She pulled a tissue out of somewhere, and quickly dabbed it dry. 'All's I know is, Mozzie freaked out big time when the stash went missing, ay. He reckoned Larnie took it.' She looked plaintively into the policeman's eyes. 'He was even threatening to bash her and everything.'

'You think he had something to do with her disappearance?'

'I know he shot through straight after Larnie went missing.'

Clearly, she did think he had something to do with her disappearance, but obviously she didn't have much to support her suspicion, other than wild speculation. But what about the other name she had mentioned?

'So what's all this got to do with Tom Wilson?'

'I don't know.' Jodie Lanham shrugged again, looking like she was all out of speculation. 'Nothing I s'pose. Except for some reason he apparently reckoned Bob Proctor was responsible for Larnie taking off.'

She couldn't remember, or wasn't telling, where she'd heard that little tidbit from, and Dave didn't press her on it. He'd seen enough of

Millengarra, and a hundred other tiny country towns just like it, to know that idle gossip about who said what to whom, late at night down the local pub, wasn't much to hang anybody's hat on. Maybe the whispers on the street were right—maybe Tom Wilson did say what they claimed he did, but maybe he didn't; and even if he did, what he was saying could possibly be right, but it could be dead wrong. Either way, so far as the detective was concerned, one thing was certain—after the story Jodie Lanham had just told him, there was a very serious smell about the personable publican, Bob Proctor.

•

By the time Dave dropped Lanham off downtown it was close to nine o'clock, and his head was already spinning with a myriad of crazy thoughts and possibilities circulating through his brain. He was right about Larnie Mitchell dabbling in drugs, and obviously she'd got herself way in over her head. His hunch was spot-on, too, that she didn't just take off. If she went under her own steam, Larnie was running for good reason. From precisely who, and why, he hadn't worked out yet, but he soon would. And if she didn't go under her own steam, he'd work that out too, and he'd get whatever low bastard was responsible.

Because that was what Dave did. That was what he'd always done. He worked it out, solved the mystery, locked up the bad guys. He was Old School, a good copper, one of the best. And it didn't matter if the Special Prosecutor thought he was a crook, or Lyall Parker was too embarrassed nowadays to talk to him in public, or the baby Boys-in-Blue, fresh out of the Academy, all figured they knew better just because they had a university degree, Dave could still run rings around all of them. He didn't care how the police files read, Larnie Mitchell wasn't just some scatterbrain runaway. She was missing for a reason, and Dave was going to find out what it was, and what happened to her.

As he drove back down the main street he was thinking about Larnie's parents, how totally in the dark they both were about their own daughter, how little they knew of her life. They lived in the same small town, but they had no idea who she was hanging around with, where she was sleeping, who was threatening to bash her, or what she was up to. They didn't know about her being on the hooch, much less dealing in hard drugs. They didn't even know she and the killer cowboy were an item.

As the sign outside the Arms Hotel came into sight, up ahead on his left, Dave was thinking about the crazy, dumb things kids did, full of youthful bravado, so bullet-proof they couldn't even see the bad shit coming their way, never imagining the heartbreak it could cause to those who loved them the most. He was thinking about Denise, and how their life was gradually unravelling, day after day. And he was thinking of Janey.

Dave pulled into the carpark of the Arms. He went in through the rear entrance, found himself a quiet corner in the back bar, and did his best to dull his brain with sweet rum, and lose himself in country music on the jukebox. But the more he drank, and tried forgetting, the more his mind just kept on drifting back to what he didn't want to think about, working overtime, going over all the stuff he had been told, pawing over possibilities, dredging up memories he'd just like to forget.

He didn't remember much of driving back to the Starlight Motel that night, he just seemed to arrive there. He remembered climbing out of his car, but the next thing he knew he was back in his room. When he got there, he pulled the rum bottle out from the brown paper bag, cracked it open and poured a drink. Then he went to the closet. They were still there, sitting on the top of his open bag. *The red shoes.*

Dave didn't remember falling asleep. When he awoke, lying fully clothed on the bed in the middle of the night, a light was still on in the bathroom, but he had no idea of the time. His head was thick and unclear, his throat parched, the dull discomfort below his ribcage throbbing softly. In his chest, a vague, unsettling sense of anxiety lingered, the remnants of a melancholic dream that had woken him. *What was it about?* He had no idea, but he was relieved to now be awake.

In the semi-darkness, his eyes focused on the bag on the bed beside him, the bag with the red shoes in it. He closed his eyes and swiped one hand at it, knocking it onto the floor, out of sight. *The red shoes.* He remembered now. He remembered what it was he had been dreaming about, or maybe not what but, at least, why. He tried not to think about it, tried to drift back to sleep, but the more he tried the more he could feel the anxiety rising within him. There was something he had to know, something he had to find out.

Dave opened his eyes and swallowed, hard and dry, then rolled his feet off the bed and struggled up into a sitting position. Groggy, half-asleep, he snatched up the telephone receiver and punched in a number. As he held the phone to his ear, listening to the droning repeat of the dial tone, he began wondering what time it must be. Was it too late to be ringing? Would she be awake? He was squinting through the darkness, trying to make out his watch-face, when he heard the STD pips begin stridently beeping over the hiss and crackle of a poor connection, then a faraway, familiar voice.

'Hello.'

'Denise, it's me.'

'Dave?' She could hardly be heard through the curtain of static. 'You're breaking up a bit, love. Are you there?'

'Yeah.' The words were suddenly stuck in his throat.

'Is everything okay?'

'Do you remember the ruby slippers?'

Having got out the question, he waited, listening to the cloudy woosh on the end of the line, before her voice eventually broke through feebly.

'What?'

'The ruby slippers. Do you remember the ruby slippers?'

There was silence again, apart from the static, and this time it lasted forever. When his wife finally spoke, her voice was stretched wafer thin.

'Why are you ringing me, Dave? What are you doing this for?'

A painful lump rose in his throat. He knew how much she'd endured, how fragile they both had become. But he needed to know.

'Do you remember the ruby slippers?' He was straining his hearing, listening intently as the gravelly silence extended. 'Hello?'

'Yes, I remember.'

'Did she keep them? When she left, did she have them with her?'

There was another sad, empty silence. Then she spoke again, in a distant whisper.

'Stop this, Dave. Stop it.'

'Did she take them with her when she left home?' He could hear himself speaking insistently now, cruelly, into the phone. It wasn't what he had intended, but he had to know. 'Did she?'

'No. No, I...' The tiny voice at the other end trailed off into the noisy silence for a moment, and then came again, just as frail. 'I threw them out.' The words sounded final, and tragic, and lingered regretfully in the faint, rustling din, before she finally added, 'Are you okay?' He didn't respond—couldn't—simply holding the phone to his ear, frozen in silence. Eventually, he heard her whisper again. 'Dave?'

'Yeah.'

'Where are you?'

'I'm okay.' He felt his voice waver, and stopped, fell silent again for a moment, collecting himself. 'I'm okay,' he eventually said with more starch. 'I'm just, I'm just checking something out, that's all.'

'Dave, it's the middle of the night...' Her distant words suddenly seemed overcome by the static, disappearing into a mire of grey, crackling noise, before they eventually resurfaced again, momentarily. 'I think you should come home.'

'Yeah, I'll be home soon.'

'You're not...' The words were fading in and out unintelligibly. '... in the middle ... should come ...'

A series of indecipherable sounds struggled on hopelessly, before they eventually disappeared, replaced by the strident, repeated beep of a disengaged signal.

FOURTEEN

When Dave Hocking opened his eyes, he was looking out across King Street to the broad vacant block on the other side of the road, and the endless outback beyond. As he lay there, gathering his senses, he gradually began to focus on the soft, distant glow of the early morning, draped over the distant horizon. It had already started to thaw the chill from the cold night air. He pulled the blanket away from his chin and allowed it to fall down over his folded arms.

He was stretched out uncomfortably over a wooden slat deckchair, alongside the blue painted mock oasis and plastic palms outside the manager's office. He wondered how he got there, and where the blanket had come from. It certainly hadn't come from his room. Lying half-asleep, staring out into the distance, he gently tried to engage his brain, piece together enough of last night to make sense of where he now found himself. The brick-like mobile phone was poking into him, somewhere under the blanket. He remembered staggering into the driveway, holding the phone up over his head, into the air, hoping to somehow find a connection.

Across the road, someone was pottering around on the vacant block, bending over, reaching down into the long, scraggly grass. He watched her idly moving about, going from spot to spot, foraging, collecting something into a bunch she had held in close to her chest. What was she doing?

As he ambled onto the block, the blanket draped over his shoulders, and walked towards Carol Graham, she straightened up and shaded her eyes, looking this new apparition up and down with a whimsical smirk.

'You just can't quite get the hang of sleeping in a bed, can you?'

Dave looked down at his crumpled clothes, silently conceding she had a good point.

'Thanks for the petunias.' She held out the little bouquet of bright yellow flowers clasped in her hand. 'I'm just picking some wattle to plant in with them.'

Standing there, holding the floral bouquet in the thin morning light, she looked sweet and kind. He was gratified to think he had pleased her, perhaps even redeemed himself.

'Thanks for the blanket.'

'Gets cold enough to kill a black snake out here at night.'

Dave nodded. He still had the chill in his bones.

'It's a hard country.'

She was looking him straight in the eye, the whimsy now fading away from her face.

'All you've got to be is tough enough.'

She was tough, alright, he had already worked that out. But as he turned his head and looked out over the desolate landscape around them, stretching out to the far horizon in every direction, Dave couldn't help wondering if that was enough. What kept anyone—especially a woman like her—out here, in a place like this, all on their own?

'Don't matter how tough you are,' he eventually offered. 'You can't eat dust.'

As they stood opposite each other on the uneven earth, she silently nodded, as if carefully considering what he had said, weighing it up and dissecting it. Eventually, she looked down at her feet, bent forward, and yanked a tuft of stringy, grey grass up out of the ground.

'See that?' she said, holding the strands in her open hand. 'Know what that is?'

He looked down at it, scraggy and desiccated.

'Dead grass, by the look of it.'

'Mallee grass.' She crushed it up in her hand, grinding it between her fingers, and then let the crumbling remnants fall to the ground at her feet. 'The most nutritious grass in the world. Might look dead, but it's not. It holds its nutrients for years after it's had its last drop of rain.' She slapped her hand on one hip, dusting the last of it off. 'Even dry and brown like that, Mallee grass'll sustain hungry livestock for years.'

'Is that right?'

'Yes, it is.' As she nodded silently at him, she was staring him straight in the eye. 'There's always life somewhere, if you look hard enough.'

Dave Hocking shifted uncomfortably. He had a feeling she wasn't just talking about dried-up grass.

'I take it that was your daughter in that photograph.' She held his gaze as he stared back at her, completely silent. 'She looks exactly like you.'

Dave pulled the blanket forward on his shoulders, close up to the back of his neck.

'Yeah,' he said quietly, nodding his head. 'That's what they reckon.'

They stood opposite each other in the still morning air for several seconds, saying nothing, each just staring silently into the other's face, understanding some things and wondering about others. When Carol Graham finally spoke up, her voice was soft and sympathetic.

'You look like you could do with a bit of breakfast.'

When they got back to the motel, she settled him at a small table in corner of the dining room, where he browsed through yesterday's newspaper while she busied herself in the kitchen, whipping him up a greasy breakfast. Once he had heartily scoffed it down, he found himself pleased to have her company, as she sat alongside him at the table with a pot of hot tea and two cups, and proceeded to pour out, in chapter and verse, the story of her whole life.

Her clipped accent, he learned, came from the south-west of England, where she was born, went to school, and grew up, before her family escaped their traumatised homeland for the post-war promise of the Lucky Country. She met her husband, Bill, in Brisbane when she was just twenty, married him at age twenty-one, and moved back with him to his faraway home in the sprawling Paroo Shire soon afterwards. In those days Australia was still riding high 'on the sheep's back,' the wool clip bringing in record returns, and the west was awash with money and opportunity. People were on the move, and the hotels and accommodation houses were booming. What better business could there have been than the only motel in a two-hotel town like Millengarra, the perfect stepping stone into the big sheep and cattle stations up on the fertile flood plains of the Diamantina, and the grazing expanses of the great Channel Country?

In those days, life in the west was big, bold and adventurous. But, over the years, times had changed. The money dried up, the people stopped coming, and everything seemed to get harder for folks on the land. As Bill's parents grew older, and his younger brothers moved back into town, the responsibility of keeping the family farm afloat naturally fell to Bill. But dividing his time between the motel and the family property took a toll on her hard-working, conscientious husband. When he passed away, prematurely, it was a terrible blow to everyone, but not such a surprise.

'No kids?'

Carol Graham looked down into her cup, shaking her head.

'No,' she said softly, then took the tiniest sip of her tea, which seemed to instantly revive her. 'No,' she repeated, this time more sturdily. 'We tried, but…' Her voice trailed off again, and she sat silent for several seconds. 'Sometimes I toy with the idea of going back home to the UK, maybe settling back there.'

'Yeah? So why don't you?'

'Oh well, you know,' she was fiddling with her fingers self-consciously. 'Bill was born out here. He and I made our lives here. His whole family's here really…'

That was it. Her voice faded again, into silence.

'Yeah, but he's not.'

As soon as the words were out of his mouth, Dave regretted them. Her life was none of his business, and he shouldn't have said it. But she just shook her head sadly.

'No.'

She took another sip of her tea, set the cup down, and looked him straight in the eye.

'How long's your daughter been gone?'

He held her gaze. His life was none of her business either.

'Three years.'

'What happened?'

How should he answer that question? He had no idea. So much had happened, so many dumb, crazy things had been said. What was the answer? He didn't know. Maybe there was no answer.

'She took off.'

•

The aboriginal families in town lived in a cluster of ramshackle houses just off the Cunnamulla Road, on Millengarra's southern outskirts. When Brian Ingles pulled in there that morning, a few familiar faces stopped and stared, some nodding hello, a mixture of curiosity and caution. As he drove along the gravel road, he could see Kath Daley sitting on the front veranda of her place, peeling spuds onto a double-page of newsprint spread across her lap, watching him approach all the way to her front gate.

'Morning Kath,' Ingles said, as he closed the wire gate and ambled up the dusty pathway towards the house.

'Morning.'

The policeman leaned on the veranda rail and propped a boot up onto the first stair.

'Darby around?'

Kath shook her head. Her grandson had not come home last night, or the night before, and she had been worrying about him all morning; now she was both uneasy and relieved to hear the constable was looking for him.

'Him and the boys must be in town, I reckon.'

Brian Ingles nodded silently. He could see from the industrious way she had now returned to peeling potatoes that Kath Daley was uncomfortable with these questions.

'He's supposed to be living here under his parole conditions.'

'Yeah,' she fired back, without lifting her head. 'He is.'

'Did he sleep here last night?'

'Yeah, I'd say.' Kath looked up fleetingly, then back down into her lap. 'Probably just got up early and shot through, I reckon.'

'Is he staying off the grog?'

She looked up from her work, her lips stretched into a defiant frown.

'No grog here, Constable.' She shook her head firmly. 'Not in my house. Won't allow it.'

Kath Daley was a proud woman, doing her best to look after a broken, patched-together family, and Brian Ingles believed what she was telling him, about the grog at least. She had seen the damage it could do.

'Alright.' Brian was staring down at his dusty boot, wondering what to do next. He had no doubt Darby's nan was trying hard to keep him on the straight and narrow, and she was a good, decent woman. But she couldn't do it on her own. Darby Sands was suffering, and he was at risk. If Parole got wind he was staying out nights, playing up, they could send him back to Westbrook with the stroke of a pen. Brian felt helpless. 'When you see him, get him to drop into the station, will you? I just want to have a yack with him.'

As Brian pulled back onto the Cunnamulla Road and drove towards town, he was thinking about problems he knew were beyond his control. He was thinking about Darby Sands, an orphaned black boy, fresh out of

Westbrook, dead out of luck and flat out of prospects, stuck in a backwater town with no qualifications, no work and no hope. He was thinking about Larnie Mitchell too, the beautiful, bright young kid who all her life had been running rings around everyone in her hometown, who everyone always knew could be anything she wanted to be, except her whole life just happened to be a thousand miles from anywhere, so far from anything that mattered that one day she realised she just had to go, get out, leave behind everything and everyone she ever knew. And he was thinking about Rowdy McQuillan, the big, dopey cowboy who had never caused Brian a moment of strife, who was smart enough to get out, but then silly enough to come back again, back to find himself smothered in this tiny, stifling town for too long, with nothing to do but drink himself silly and sit around staring at the walls, going stir crazy, until one night he eventually goes mad on the piss and cuts loose, beating his best mate to death. Why? Where did the madness all come from? Was it just Millen?

He was still thinking about all those things as he turned off the Cunnamulla Road into Castle Street, heading down towards the police house. Up ahead on his right was Karen Millard's house, where the cowboy had run amok, and not much further down on his left was the house where Tom Wilson had died. In between, he could see a young woman walking up Castle Street on the side of the road, cradling a bag full of groceries and pushing a pram as she turned left to walk into Campbell Street. It was Jenny Deeds, and Brian figured she was on her way home, to the second house in from the corner of Castle. On a whim, Brian flicked on his right blinker and swung his car into Campbell Street.

Jenny Deeds had just got in through her front gate when she saw the police car pull up out front of her house. She parked her pram and set the groceries down on the first step, shading her eyes with one hand as she watched the constable walk to the fence-line.

'G'day Brian.'

'G'day Jen. How're you going?'

'Good.' She waited for him to say something more. When he didn't, she waited some more, then eventually added 'What's up?'

'I was hoping to have a quick word with you about Rowdy McQuillan.'

'What about him?'

'I heard he come round here the night of the murder.'

Jenny Deeds was a good girl, salt of the earth. She looked after her own, and kept herself to herself. The last thing she would ever want to do was drag herself and her family into anything that had nothing to do with them. But she was also straight up and down. Brian Ingles knew that, and he knew whatever she did, Jenny Deeds wouldn't lie to him.

'Come on in.'

When they settled around tea and biscuits, served up on the dining room table, she made it clear straight away to the constable her husband Mason had been best mates with Rowdy McQuillan forever, and she loved the big bloke. While she didn't condone for a minute what he'd done to poor Tom, and couldn't understand why he'd done it, neither she nor her husband wanted to say anything that might make things worse for their friend, if that was even possible.

Brian couldn't force her to speak to him, and he wouldn't have wanted to even if he could, but he carefully explained that the police just needed to know everything that happened that night, to try to see if they could find some explanation for why McQuillan had done what he did. The two of them talked around and about it, back and forth, for a while, until they eventually agreed she would speak 'off the record,' tell Brian the little she knew, with no strings attached, but she definitely wouldn't sign anything, and there was no way she or Mason would ever go to court and say anything bad against Rowdy.

It was a deal. She would tell Brian what she knew, and that would be that.

She started with what she remembered of their night at the Millengarra Arms Hotel. They had dinner downstairs with her parents, and ran into Rowdy down there, having tea with Ross and Lindy Lewis. Then she and Mason went up to the disco, where they met up with a few people, and when Rowdy eventually came up with the Lewises around half past ten, he looked pretty full. He came and sat at their table for a while, and Mason got into a shout with him, drinking rum, which Jenny didn't really like, because when Mason drank rum he went silly. But Rowdy was in a good mood and they all had a heap of fun, and she and Mason got up on the dancefloor together, and Rowdy eventually joined them. By then he was full as ten men, and Mason wasn't too far behind him, and they all danced around together like silly buggers until Ross and Lindy eventually came and carted Rowdy off with them. By then it was around closing time, and Jenny and Mason went straight home. She didn't remember seeing their old mate again until he turned up at their place.

'I was sitting out on the back veranda, having a quick ciggy before going to bed.' Jenny had a distracted, almost fearful look in her eyes as she recounted the events of that night. 'And I remember looking at my watch and thinking how late it was, and how we were both going to be stuffed in the morning. So I got up to go back inside, and that's when I seen him.' Her chin trembled, and she faltered momentarily, then took a quick sip of her tea, collected herself, and continued. 'He was coming over the back fence. I couldn't see who it was but, not at that stage.' She shook her head, remembering, and then looked the policeman straight in the eye. 'But I fair shit meself, ay.'

Brian could see the distress in her eyes and hear the fear in her voice. She took another sip of her tea, and stared blankly into her cup for several long moments before she eventually continued.

'I run inside and called out for Mase, and he come running down the hall. And by then we just seen this outline, just inside the back door at the end of the hall.' As she said it her eyes began glistening with tears, but she quickly and efficiently blinked them away. 'And Mason yelled something at him and next thing they're both wrestling around in the dark, and I didn't know what to do. So I turned on the hall light, and that's when I seen it was Rowdy, and he had nothing on—like, not a stitch—and he was struggling with Mason, like just grabbing him around the arms and that, making these weird noises, like grunting or something. And I was just yelling at him to stop, and get out, but he had hold of Mason and he wouldn't let go. And then Mase got one of his hands free and he whacked him, like just around the chest or somewhere I think, and he went down like a sack of spuds, straight over onto the floor.' She paused briefly, again shaking her head as she thought about it. 'He didn't even seem to hit him that hard. But even then he kept grabbing Mason's leg, like he was trying to bite his ankle or something, and he had this weird look on his face. Like he was crazy or something.'

'Did he say anything?'

'Nothing.' She looked back up, straight into the constable's eyes. 'Not a word. The whole time. He was just grunting and breathing real heavily, like a dog or some kind of animal. And trying to grab hold of Mason's leg. It was nuts, just insane.'

Brian Ingles was searching for words. He had heard the account of the strange things that happened at Karen Millard's house, had seen the destruction and witnessed first-hand McQuillan's odd behaviour at Tom Wilson's place but, if anything, this story made it all seem even more bizarre.

'So how did you finally get rid of him?'

'We didn't.' Jenny Deeds was wide-eyed and breathless, as if she was re-living the moment. 'We just bolted, ay. We cleared out.' The tears suddenly welled back into her eyes, and she mopped them away with a tissue. 'As soon as Mason got his leg free, we run straight out of the house and got in the car, and got out of there. We left the lights on and everything. Just got in the car and pissed off, over to Mike's place.' She sniffed, then daintily blew her nose. 'You know Mike, don't you, Mason's brother?'

'Yeah.'

Between sniffles and blows, she explained how they woke up her brother-in-law Mike, and his wife Shirley, who gave them both a stiff drink to settle their nerves as they told them everything that happened, and how Mike had eventually insisted he and Mason get back in the car and go track down Rowdy. So the boys left the girls locked safely away in the house, with all the lights on, while they drove back to Castle Street looking for him. But when they came past Tom's house, they saw Brian Ingles' police car out front with its flashing lights on, and they figured he had got to Rowdy before they did, and was no doubt running him in for being blind drunk and playing up around the neighbourhood like a two-bob watch. Rather than make matters worse, they decided to let Rowdy sleep it all off in the cells, and then front him for an explanation the next day.

'It wasn't until the morning we heard what happened. We were totally freaked out.'

He could see from the look in her eyes she had asked herself more than once what might have happened if they hadn't got out when they did.

'Did you see any incident at the pub or anywhere that might have set him off?'

'No. He was good as gold at the pub. Happy as Larry.'

Good as gold. Brian Ingles allowed the words to seep into his brain, doing his best to fathom them. As far as Jenny Deeds could see, Rowdy McQuillan was as *happy as Larry* when he left the Millengarra Arms that night. Her story of what happened next just deepened the mystery of what transpired on the night of Wilson's death. Rowdy had gone from being 'good as gold' one moment to a crazed, unstoppable killer the next, terrorizing Karen Millard and friends fifteen minutes later, and then rolling around on his old mate's floor, trying to nip at his ankles, like a rabid dog.

It didn't make sense, any of it. Then, suddenly, something occurred to him.

'Wait a minute. You mentioned when you were out on the back veranda you looked at your watch. Do you remember what time it was?'

'Absolutely,' Jenny Deeds replied resolutely. 'It was exactly seven minutes after midnight.'

●

The drive back to Cunnamulla that day was a lot quicker and more comfortable in the police four-wheel drive vehicle than the trip out had been. By the time Dave first got to the police house in Millen that morning, Ingles was already out and about but, as directed, he had left the keys to the truck on the hook in the office, and two copies of the McQuillan brief in the cabinet, so Dave left his car out the back of the station (with strict instructions to Ingles to get the windscreen replaced while he was away), loaded up the four-wheel drive, and wasted no time in hitting the road. They still had some statements to get—including from that little shit Mason Deeds—but the committal hearing wasn't due to start until Monday, and two weeks had been set aside, so there'd be plenty of time to plug any holes that came up. For now, Dave was satisfied the brief was in good enough shape for Bruce McKinley to get the committal hearing started. He already had the original statements of the Cunnamulla CIB boys, and the Brisbane forensics, and once Dave dropped him off the statements of the local witnesses, he would have plenty to keep the court busy for the first week or so.

As the truck rattled along the graded dirt road, south to Cunnamulla, Dave was thinking about Jodie Lanham, and her best friend Larnie. He was wondering about that big heap of speed stashed away in Bob Proctor's hotel, right under the nose of a dodgy ex-con like Jimmy Rawlings, how it had mysteriously gone missing, and what all that might have to do with the fact no one had seen Larnie Mitchell since. He was thinking about a skinny little rat called Kevin Daines, and another one called Mozzie Blane, who according to Jodie Lanham was openly blaming Larnie for his misfortune and making all kinds of threats to do her some serious harm. And he was wondering why Tom Wilson would be down in Bob Proctor's pub claiming the publican was responsible for Larnie going missing, on the very same night he ended up dead as a doornail. Tom Wilson, the housemate of Rowdy McQuillan, the former boyfriend of Larnie Mitchell.

There had to be a connection. As he looked down at the court briefs stacked on the seat alongside him, the word *murder* plastered all over them, Dave was getting a very bad feeling about Larnie. He had a hunch her mysterious absence had a whole lot to do with the killer, Rowdy McQuillan.

By the time he finally rolled into Cunnamulla it was just after midday. His first stop was the New Jumbuck Motor Inn, where he booked a room for the night, then he headed straight down to the Police Station. He found Bruce

McKinley in his office, surrounded by a bunch of sweaty, disinterested-looking detectives, including one big boofhead Dave thankfully hadn't laid eyes on in years.

'Good to see you, David.' Noel Atwood kept his fat arse firmly planted on his chair, stretching one arm out straight to shake hands, like he didn't want to get too close, in case he might catch something. 'Bruce tells me you've been helping us out with the brief.'

Dave knew precisely what was going through Noel Atwood's tiny brain, and he didn't really care one bit. The new Commissioner's Assistant undoubtedly knew all about the current Special Prosecutor's investigation into Dave, and he'd be absolutely paranoid about appearing too chummy with a suspect copper under a cloud for corruption, even though the two of them had known and worked with each other for the best part of thirty years.

'When did you fellas get into town?' Dave asked, as he went around the room shaking hands.

'We flew in this morning.' Atwood's voice was stiff and officious. 'We brought the defendant up with us.'

Of course. This was the new and improved, post-Fitzgerald police service, where policemen and prisoners flew to far-flung country courthouses in air-conditioned comfort. There were no dusty road trips for the high-flying Commissioner's Assistant. And that meant Rowdy McQuillan was already in town, cooling his heels in the Cunnamulla watchhouse.

'You timed your run perfectly, Dave.' Bruce McKinley got up from his desk, preparing to leave. He had a mischievous glint in his eye, and was clearly enjoying Noel Atwood's evident discomfort. 'Noel was just about to take us all over for a bite of lunch at the tavern.'

When the other detectives likewise got up from their seats, ready to roll, Dave could sense Noel Atwood's palpable horror, without even looking at him. But Dave wasn't inclined to play along with Brucey's game. Right now, he had something more pressing in mind.

'Thanks Noel, but I might have to give it a miss,' he said, dumping the brief folders down onto his old friend's desk. 'I need to check in at the motel.' He slid the folders across the desktop towards McKinley. 'I'll meet you back here in an hour or so to go through it.'

Bruce McKinley had had his fun. With a sly, cheeky wink and a nod to his mate, he followed the much-relieved-looking Atwood out of his office, the junior detectives tagging along as they all filed out of the station and ambled off to the tavern.

As soon as they were out of sight, Dave doubled back to the police watchhouse at the back of the station, pressed on the buzzer, and introduced himself through the intercom to the constable in charge. Within minutes he was sitting alone in an interview room, waiting to get his first look at the killer who had haunted his thoughts for way too long.

As he sat in the sterile little room, staring at the blank, closed door, he was feeling anxious and oddly uncertain. What was next? McQuillan was a defendant in custody, facing a currently unproven murder charge, and Dave knew full well he had no business being there, at least not without the okay of his arresting officer, Noel Atwood. But he was there. He had to be. He had no choice. There were questions spinning around inside his head, driving him crazy, and he needed answers. And the only one who could give him those answers was Rowdy McQuillan.

When the door eventually swung open and the uniformed constable ushered McQuillan into the room, closing the door behind him, Dave Hocking was almost startled by his appearance. He looked much younger than Dave had expected, palpably tentative and uncertain, almost vulnerable, nothing like the wild-eyed, blood-streaked suspect he had seen in the official police photographs. In his drab, brown, prison-issue T-shirt and stubby shorts, the once-suntanned cowboy was now pale and drawn, clearly anxious and feeling self-conscious, like an awkward, oversized schoolboy on the first day of term. He nodded courteously when the detective introduced himself, swiping his hair respectfully back from his forehead, and then compliantly pulled up a seat at the tiny table between them.

'Can I call you Rowdy?'

'Yeah, sure. No worries.'

Hocking flipped open his notebook on the desktop, clicked on his pen, and scratched out a quick note of the time and place.

'Alright Rowdy, as I said, I'm from the Brisbane CI Branch, currently stationed out at Millengarra, conducting certain inquiries I'm hoping you'll be able to assist me with.'

McQuillan was looking at him vaguely, as if trying to decipher what he had just said.

'About Tom, you mean?'

'No, I'm not here about the Wilson matter.' Dave looked him straight in the eye. 'I'm conducting a missing persons investigation into the disappearance of Larnie Mitchell.'

'Larnie?' He looked genuinely surprised. Then he blinked nervously and looked away. 'I don't know nothing about Larnie.'

There was something about the way he said it that instantly irritated Dave Hocking. Part of him wanted to just lean across the desk and give him a good slap over the ear. Once upon a time he might have, but he had got older and smarter. There were other ways to skin a cat.

'You were close to her, weren't you?'

'Not really.'

'I heard you used to be her boyfriend.'

'Who told you that?'

'You were, weren't you?'

The pale-faced cowboy was fumbling with his fingers on the desktop in front of him, obviously working out his next move. Dave could see he was on the right track. He waited silently for McQuillan's mumbled answer.

'That was a long time ago.'

His head was slumped forward over the desk, the detective staring silently at the tousled hair on the top of his head, waiting for him to look up. But he didn't. He was dodging. Dave was absolutely certain of it.

'I heard she dropped you, broke your heart.'

The proposition seemed to sting the young man, and he looked up with an angry insolence igniting his eyes. But Hocking held his gaze steadfastly as the moment of defiance quickly passed, and the cowboy eventually lowered his head back down.

'Do I have to answer these questions?'

'I would have thought you'd want to.' He was on the ropes, and Hocking meant to keep him there until he got some answers. 'Seeing as how you were her boyfriend, I would have thought you'd be interested to find out what happened to her. Maybe try and help find her.'

Dave waited momentarily, as the prisoner's big, bushy head wavered almost imperceptibly from side to side, in silence. He could sense he was about to jump his way, open up and start talking. All Dave had to do was keep the pressure on him.

'She was why you took off up north, wasn't she?'

'Maybe.'

'So why'd you come back?'

'I just did.'

'You came back chasing her, didn't you?'

McQuillan looked back up at him defiantly, shaking his head.

'No.'

'Yes, you did. Only she wasn't interested.'

'Larnie done her own thing.'

'Like selling drugs out of the Arms Hotel?'

The question jumped out of him spontaneously, in a rush of blood. He hadn't intended to play that card so early, but now it was out, and on the table, he was happy to see it had had the desired effect.

'What?'

The look on the big bloke's face said it all. He knew precisely what Detective Senior Sergeant David Hocking was referring to, because he was in it right up to his eyeballs. And now he was shocked to realise Dave Hocking was way ahead of him.

'Don't give me that shit.' Dave spat the words out at him angrily across the narrow table. 'Everyone in town knew she was peddling speed to the truckies. And she wasn't working on her own. Where'd she get them drugs from, Rowdy? Did you bring them back with you? Did you?'

As the policeman's words gradually faded into silence, McQuillan looked him in the eye and gradually shook his head. When he finally spoke, his voice was charged with a stiff, confident resilience.

'I don't have to answer none of this.'

He was right—he didn't—and Dave could see from the new determination in his eyes McQuillan wasn't going to be bullied into doing something he didn't have to. They were staring straight at each other, both unflinching, resolute, immoveable, as the detective's fury simmered just below the surface. McQuillan was just like every other grub Dave had had to deal with every day, all his working life, day in and day out, for more than thirty years. He knew his rights. All the half-smart, Boggo Road QCs had no doubt well and truly schooled him up on them. He knew he could just sit there with his big trap shut, thumbing his nose at all the dopey coppers, standing on his right to silence, saying nothing. Meanwhile, a young girl's grieving parents were condemned to struggle on with their lives, unknowing, keeping vigil, tending their pathetic shrine to their long-lost child, waiting endlessly for word that never came, waiting and wondering, not knowing if their daughter was alive or dead. And the coppers couldn't do a bloody thing about it.

Except they could. Dave could just reach out across the table, grab a handful of the cowboy's greasy hair, bang his big, boof head straight down into the desktop, and then ask him again, calmly and politely—*Did you give those drugs to Larnie Mitchell? Do you know where the hell she is?* Rowdy McQuillan might know all his legal rights, and he might even be so sure of them as to sit there in a police watchhouse staring straight into the face of a detective senior sergeant of police, telling him to get right-royally stuffed. But once his nose was broken and his head was spinning, and Dave took him by the scruff of the neck for one more quick refresher on his legal rights, he'd soon start thinking much more clearly than he had been. Dave was confident of that. McQuillan was no hardened, old-school crim, raised up through the boys' homes and reformatories, all their adult life in and out of jug. They could be hard nuts to crack, some of them, but not the likes of a big, dumb country boy like Rowdy. All Dave had to do with this country bumpkin was introduce him to the good old, tried-and-tested methods of subtle persuasion.

As they sat there, face-to-face, the temptation rose within him, teetered momentarily at the edge, and then slowly, eventually, subsided. McQuillan was not Dave Hocking's pinch. He was in custody, charged with murder, and he was about to face a court. In this day and age, questions would be raised if he had any tell-tale marks on him, anything at all, or made the slightest complaint of any kind, however unsubstantiated. It was a brave new world. These days, teaching a grub like McQuillan to behave would be suicide for any cop, particularly one sitting at the centre of corruption allegations, as Dave was. He calmed himself before he spoke again.

'You sound like you've got something to hide, Rowdy.'

'Like what?'

There was something about the snide, defiant way McQuillan shot the question back that brought another sudden flush of anger flooding into Hocking's face. He dropped his elbows down onto the desk in front of him and leaned forward, close into the prisoner's face, and belted out his accusation with gusto and disdain.

'Like the fact you blew back into town from fuck-knows-where, hoping to kiss and make up with Larnie, and next thing she's sitting on a shitload of speed stashed away in Proctor's pub.' McQuillan looked startled, and shaped his lips to say something, but not a word came out. 'Then the speed suddenly goes missing, and five minutes later so does Larnie. And your mate Tom Wilson starts running around telling anyone who'll listen that Bob Proctor's the reason Larnie's disappeared. And that's when you decide to go home one night and bash Tom Wilson's brains in.'

McQuillan was slumped forward on the desk, looking at him with a gap-mouthed, shocked expression on his face.

'What do you mean she's disappeared?'

It seemed a strange question to ask, in the scheme of things. Not one Dave was expecting, and it momentarily threw him off his stride.

'She's gone,' he barked back at the prisoner, but McQuillan was now squinting at him quizzically. 'Disappeared. Never to be seen or heard of since.' He looked to Dave like he was trying to play some silly game, pretend he hadn't heard she was missing, so Dave came back at him sternly. 'And I think you know where.'

If he did, he wasn't saying. He just sat silently opposite the detective, gazing unflinchingly into his face, a weird, almost uncomprehending expression in his eyes.

'Have you spoken to her mate Jodie?' he eventually blurted out. 'Jodie Lanham. She'll know where Larnie is.'

Dave was confused. What was McQuillan trying to peddle to him? Surely he knew if he steered the police off in Jodie Lanham's direction she'd soon spill the beans about the speed. How would that help him?

'Jodie doesn't know shit about what happened to Larnie. No one does. Except you.'

'What do you mean what happened to her?' The cowboy was staring him blankly in the face, as if he didn't know. 'Where do you reckon she is?'

The pure insolence of the prisoner infuriated Dave, and he snapped back at him without thinking.

'I reckon she's dead and fucking gone. That's where I reckon she is. Ten feet under. And I think you killed her, just like you killed Tom Wilson.'

McQuillan's face folded comically, as thick, glistening tears welled instantly in his eyes, and his chin began to tremble feebly.

'No, no I never,' he blurted out, shaking his big head emphatically, then buried his whole face into his hands, like a little kid hiding from the Bogeyman. 'No,' he repeated several times, before he finally seemed to settle down a bit, moved his calloused hands down off his face, and looked back up at the policeman. 'I might have killed Tom, but I never done nothing like that to Larne, no way.'

It sounded a whole lot like a crucial moment, one Dave had definitely not seen coming. It terrified him instantly, and he sat silent for a moment, trying to collect his thoughts. Was Rowdy McQuillan confessing to him the murder of Tom Wilson? If he was, his confession would undoubtedly be vital evidence in the prosecution of the murder charge, and Dave would suddenly be front and centre in the case. Should he keep going? Of course, he had to. But how would he explain in court how their conversation came about? He clicked his pen back on, and carefully wrote down Rowdy's words as he recalled them. *I might have killed Tom, but I never done nothing like that to Larne.*

'What do you mean, you might have killed Tom?'

McQuillan looked down at the note the detective had scrawled into his notebook, thought for a moment, and then looked him squarely in the eye.

'I can't remember nothing from that night,' he said, shaking his head sadly. 'Nothing. I might've done it, ay. I don't know.' With that, he breathed out a deep sigh and stared blankly at the desktop. 'Last I remember was getting a lift back home from the disco with Ross and Lindy. Next thing I was at the cop shop.'

Dave's hand suddenly felt frozen. He didn't write a single word, just waited to hear what the prisoner would say next.

'But I didn't do nothing to Larne, I swear.' He looked back up at Dave. 'And I didn't bring them drugs to town, neither. Nor did Larnie. If you want to know about them drugs, ask Mozzie Blane.'

Mozzie Blane. McQuillan was levelling with him, about that much at least. Mozzie Blane was in the mix. That was what Jodie Lanham had told him, and she obviously believed the drugs were Mozzie's. It was probably true.

'So where is she then? What happened to her?'

'I don't know.' Rowdy shrugged his broad shoulders, looking like he was all out of answers. 'Far as I know she shot through to Brisbane.' He paused for a moment, as though considering what, if anything further, he should say, and then leaned forward on his elbows, lowering his voice. 'She come to see me, just before she took off, told me all about how she'd been selling them drugs for Mozzie.' He stopped again, momentarily, and then continued. 'She said how someone apparently went and nicked them on her, along with all the cash they'd made from selling the shit. And that bloody Mozzie was standing over her about it, reckoned she'd pinched it herself.' Rowdy looked the detective directly in the eye and shook his head emphatically. 'But she didn't, ay.' He waited until Dave nodded his acceptance of that assurance, and then he launched straight back into his story. 'And he was threatening to bash her if she didn't square up with him. She was real scared, ay, shitting herself.' He sat upright, puffing out a deep and resolute sigh. 'So I went and fronted Mozzie and I gave him a good clip, told him to pull his head in, stay away from Larne. And then I give her some of the cash I'd saved up from working at Craigie Station and I told her to get out, go down to Brisbane, like she'd always talked about doing.' He paused again, momentarily, staring at the desktop, then looked back up at Hocking with a new sadness in his eyes.

'Millen was no good for her, ay. She had to get out.' When the policeman nodded back at him again, he added 'And then she did. And I never heard nothing from her after that. I thought she would've been in touch with Jodie but, by now. And her oldies.'

Dave clicked off his pen. McQuillan was saying he had nothing to do with Larnie Mitchell's disappearance, except that he gave her money to get out of town. Of course, he could be lying like a pig in shit, but Dave couldn't dislodge the feeling, deep down in his gut, that he wasn't. If McQuillan was just telling porky pies, trying to throw Dave off the scent, why on earth would he make the concession that he might have killed Tom Wilson? He must have known police could use that against him. Why would he say anything about the murder case? He had Moran acting for him; any lawyer would have worded him up on what not to say to the coppers, but especially a clown like Moran. So why did he say it? *I might have killed Tom, but I never done nothing to Larne.* It was weird. Dave Hocking closed up his notebook and put it away.

By the time he got back to the police station, he had a whole lot of names circling around in his head. Names like Kevin Daines and Maurice Blane, the ebullient publican Bob Proctor, and his flea-bitten, ex-junkie bar manager Jimmy Rawlings. They were all in or about this story, up to their necks, and even if the cowboy really couldn't say where Larnie went, Dave was convinced that one of them could.

While he waited at the Cunnamulla Station for Bruce McKinley to get back from the tavern, Hocking got hold of a fresh-faced young uniformed constable—a kid called Randall Raye, first year in the job, straight out of the academy—and gave him a detailed inventory of inquiries he wanted run through the police computer on a long list of names, including Larnie's. He told the enthusiastic young Constable Raye he could start wherever he wanted, so long as he got whatever there was on every person on the list—criminal history, traffic record, court appearances, antecedents, known associates, intel reports, financial records, current whereabouts, anything and everything—and then ran a detailed check on any known information about the movements and activities of each of them, immediately before and after Larnie's departure, and Tom Wilson's as well for good measure. Lastly, he got him to photocopy the sketch Sue Mitchell had drawn in his notebook of her missing drop-pearl necklace, with instructions to check it out against the records of all pawn shops between Millen and Brisbane.

Let's see what pops up. Dave had a feeling when he saw it all down on paper, a picture might start to emerge. And he wanted to make sure he knew everything there was to find out before he started doing the rounds.

As Police Constable Randall Raye was still diligently scribbling down notes of the senior sergeant's instructions, the phone on the desk in front of him buzzed abrasively. He snatched up the receiver and efficiently answered the call.

'It's for you, Senior,' Raye said eventually, holding out the receiver to the detective. 'Police Constable Ingles from Millengarra.'

Dave took the phone and held it up to his ear.

'What's up?'

'I spoke to Jenny Deeds this morning.' Brian Ingles sounded strangely anxious. 'About McQuillan.'

'Yeah, what?'

'I don't think he did it, Senior.' There was a brief, pregnant silence. 'I don't think he could have.'

FIFTEEN

Frank Vagianni was pissed off, well and truly. As he frantically stuffed another greasy load of fried eggs and bacon into his mouth and chomped on it noisily, he had one eye fixed on the Sunday paper, pinned under the corner of his plate. The bold print headline splashed across the front page said it all—*COAST COPS CHARGED WITH CORRUPTION*—and the photograph underneath it all but confirmed he must be guilty as they come. Frank couldn't believe he'd been played for a dumb chump like that.

Of course, it had come as no surprise to him when his lawyer, Eddie Moran, called to tell him the Special Prosecutor's Office had been in touch to say they'd completed their investigation and had now decided to charge Frank and the others with a corruption blue over the Waterworld robbery proceeds that supposedly went missing from the Police Exhibit Room all those years ago. It was always going to happen, from the moment the Fitzgerald Inquiry investigators first got their grubby fingers on the old file, and for Frank it was almost a relief to finally get started.

His life had been on hold, fraying at the seams, for months. As soon as the Commissioner suspended him from service, half his old mates wiped him like a dirty bum, and the other half were way too busy getting on with life to find much time for an out-of-work, out-of-luck ex-cop. Things at home had been worse than ordinary for a long time, so naturally his missus quickly got herself a gutful of him moping around the house all day, doing nothing but drinking beer and feeling sorry for himself. For the past six weeks—ever since she'd sent him off—he'd been holed up on his own in a one-bedroom flat at Broadbeach, doing nothing much but waiting for the show to start. *So bring it on.*

Moran had assured him it would all be brief and straightforward. All they had to do was front the Southport Magistrates Court for a ten-minute mention of the charges, and Eddie had already negotiated with the Special Prosecutor's Office they would not oppose bail without conditions on all charges. So they would go in, get a date for the committal hearing, and get out. And then get on with the show. No fuss, no bother, simple as that.

Even better, Frank had been told someone up in headquarters had arranged for the Special Prosecutor boys to push the first mention of the charges through on a Saturday morning, when the local magistrate usually convened court super-early, and most of the journos were still asleep in bed, recovering from their usual Friday big night out. Moran didn't buy it. According to him, there was no way anyone up-town was going to let a red-hot story like this one—*four cops charged with corruption*—fly under the radar, not in post-Fitzgerald Queensland. But Frank dismissed his scepticism as just more of his abrasive lawyer's natural contrariness. The defendants had all been quietly but confidently assured everything would be handled nice and gentlemanly, as low-key as it could possibly be, with minimum publicity, for the sake of everyone, including the big brass up at HQ, and that was good enough for them.

But it didn't quite go down that way. Despite all the assurances and agreements, someone—*no prizes to anyone for guessing who*—obviously had alerted the press about what an important pinch the SPO had made, because when the first defendant drove by the courthouse early that morning, a scrum of bleary-eyed journalists and TV cameramen was already milling eagerly around the front steps. By the time the word got through to Frank, mid-way through his pre-hearing conference at his lawyer's office, someone at the watchhouse had apparently already made arrangements with the courthouse staff to sneak the police defendants in through the side door, where they would hopefully avoid the cameras.

Once again, Eddie Moran wasn't too impressed.

'Fuck that,' he shot back dismissively when Frank outlined the plan. 'Walk in through the front door with your head held high. Like an innocent man.'

None of the defendants were too fussed with that advice. It was alright for Moran. When he walked in through the front door he was walking in there as a high-paid lawyer, not a dirty, crooked cop. For him it was all upside, publicity he couldn't buy. But for Frank and his co-defendants it was the ignominious Walk of Shame, a humiliating public acknowledgement of their spectacular and inglorious fall from grace. He'd been a copper long enough to know it didn't matter how high he held his head up, the presumption of innocence didn't count in the court of public opinion.

So Moran did his own thing, swaggering up the front stairs on his own, while Frank, his co-accused and their respective lawyers were all ushered in through the side door in a flurry of much scheming, subterfuge and planning, behind a carefully constructed cloak of secrecy, safely out of range of any prying cameras. By the time Frank caught up with his lanky lawyer, Moran was already sitting at the bar table in the main arrest court, thumbing his way idly through a wad of Justices Act Complaint Sworn, and Summonses. The public gallery was already full of eager journalists, but Frank was at least comforted by the knowledge no cameras were permitted to be used inside the courthouse. They were safe. Or so they thought.

As predicted, the proceedings were brief. The defendants took all charges as read, the prosecution confirmed bail was not opposed, and dates were duly set for a full committal hearing. When it was all done, the magistrate rose, court was adjourned, and the journalists quickly dispersed, no doubt keen to file their stories, while the defendants and their lawyers retired to the registry to sign their bail undertakings. Things were back on track. So far so good.

When Frank last saw Eddie Moran that morning, the lawyer was sauntering down the front stairs of the courthouse, puffing on a cigarette, with not a journalist in sight. But Frank and his detective buddies weren't interested in taking any chance of getting ambushed by photojournalists or TV cameramen as they left the courthouse. They were going out the same way they came in. As arranged, they dutifully followed the counter clerk in through behind the front desk, across the registry, down the corridor and back out to the side door that opened out onto the staff carpark.

Frank had taken about three steps into the open carpark when he saw the wall of video cameramen bearing down on the defendants, someone in amongst them already firing unintelligible questions at them from fifteen metres off. They were closing fast, in force, and their sudden, imminent attack produced a spontaneous panic in the group, the defendants scattering instantly and scuttling off in various directions out across the carpark, covering their faces with their hands and darting one way and the other to avoid being photographed. But Frank Vagianni held his line. He was a Detective Sergeant of Police, with fifteen years' service behind him; there was no way he was going to back down to a bunch of hairy, half-baked, pinko pencil-pushers.

As several cameras descended on him, and he was surrounded by journos barking questions in his face, he snarled angrily and held his palm up to the lenses.

'Fuck off, y'idiots. Get out of my way.'

And there he was, in all his growling glory, baring his teeth at the camera like a mad dog off the leash, up front and centre on the front page of the Sunday papers. It was enough to almost put Frank off his breakfast. He could still see the half-smart smirks on the faces of the SPO investigators, looking on as he climbed into his car and pulled out from the kerb through the feeding frenzy gathered all around him. It couldn't have gone worse. He should have done what the lawyer told him to, walked in and walked out with his head held high, asserting his innocence. At least that way his message would have been clear, whether anyone believed it or not. Now he just looked like a cheap and nasty B-grade movie gangster, on his way to the electric chair. They had played him for a chump.

Frank pushed his chair back angrily, strode purposefully into the tiny kitchen, and threw open the refrigerator door. He still had one last can of Fourex left over from last night, and it looked cold and inviting. Standing there in front of his refrigerator, holding the door open, he was thinking about that stupid photograph on the front page of the newspaper, watching the cold drops of condensation trickling down the glistening surface of the beer can. It wasn't even opening time, but what the hell? Frank needed something to take the edge off him, settle him down. He reached into the fridge.

Suddenly the phone rang in the living room. It startled him. Frank quietly closed the refrigerator door, still looking at the telephone perched on the side-table next to the TV. Who would be ringing at this hour on a Sunday morning? No one ever rang. An old mate calling to commiserate with him on the disastrous front page, perhaps? Or just some slimy journalist looking for a comment, hoping for a follow-up exclusive. As he stood there, frozen, staring at the telephone as it rang and rang and rang, wondering who was on the line, what they wanted, he could feel his heart rate quicken, a nervous flutter rising in his chest. *Fuck it*. Frank Vagianni had never hidden behind closed doors, and he wasn't about to start now. He strode back into living room and snatched up the phone.

'Hello?'

'Frank, it's me. Dave Hocking. I need to have a yarn with you.'

•

As it turned out, Dave hadn't seen the Sunday papers, and didn't even know the charges had been laid. When Frank explained it all to him, he was clearly sympathetic, and spent the next few minutes trying to console his former colleague, assuring him today's front page was tomorrow's fish and chip wrapper, and reminding him at least now he had a firm target to aim at, charges to defend, a chance to finally clear his name. Frank figured Hocking probably guessed it wasn't necessarily as clean and uncomplicated as all that, but he appreciated his friend's kind words just the same, and graciously agreed with them, as cheerfully as he could. Then they talked about the lawyer, what his preliminary thoughts about the charges were, and how Frank was finding him okay to get along with, after all.

'That's good, Frank,' Hocking said eventually. 'Actually, he's sort of what I rang to talk to you about.'

It turned out Dave Hocking was calling him from a motel out at Cunnamulla, where he was on a job, cranking up a prosecution case against some cow cocky charged with murdering his best mate. The lead investigator was that waste of space Noel Atwood, but Dave had been brought in to whip the police brief into shape for the committal. For the next ten minutes or so, Hocking carefully walked Frank through all the ins and outs of all the evidence, details of the extensive battering the deceased had taken, the fact the defendant had been dropped off at the murder scene just before midnight and police had been alerted to the crime at about twenty minutes past, so the window of opportunity was always pretty brief, not a second more than about fifteen minutes top.

'So what's this got to do with Moran?'

'He's acting for McQuillan, the defendant.'

'So?'

So, yesterday morning the young uniform constable assisting Dave had interviewed a woman by the name of Jenny Deeds, the wife of an old mate of McQuillan's, Mason Deeds. According to Jenny Deeds, McQuillan turned up at their place after the attack that night, covered in blood.

'She claims to be absolutely certain he came over their back fence at spot-on seven minutes after midnight.'

'Shit.' Frank got the message instantly. 'Seven minutes?' It sounded like the young constable had just put a dirty great torpedo straight in through the prosecution case, underneath the waterline. 'That's doesn't leave much time for your defendant to have beat his housemate's brains in.' There was nothing but an empty silence at the other end of the line, one that just confirmed they both knew exactly what had to happen next. 'Has anyone told his lawyer yet?'

'That's why I'm calling you, mate.'

Frank was confused. The police didn't need his help to disclose Jenny Deeds' statement to Eddie Moran. All they had to do was put it on a fax machine and send it to him.

'I told Atwood all about it yesterday, but he won't come into it.'

'What do you mean, he won't come into it?'

'He reckons it's all bullshit, that Deeds and his missus are lying, just trying to save their mate.'

That was always possible, or maybe the Deeds had just got the times wrong, but whatever way anybody weighed it up, the defence was entitled to know about what the couple had to say, especially when their evidence could be crucial to a charge that carried mandatory life imprisonment.

'He wants it buried. Nothing said to anybody.'

Frank wasn't surprised. It was typical Noel Atwood. The newly crowned Assistant Commissioner of Police had no doubt flown back out there to Hicktown beating his chest about how quickly and efficiently he had solved yet another heinous crime. Now he was confronted with the prospect he might have completely missed a vital piece of evidence that could show him up for the utter dunderhead he really was. The fact some junior constable stumbled on it, almost by mistake, would only make things worse. So Atwood's answer was to blithely convince himself it couldn't possibly be true, and to try to sweep it underneath the carpet where it couldn't possibly cause him an embarrassment.

'What do you want me to do?'

It was simple. Dave Hocking wanted Frank to tell his lawyer—and McQuillan's—what Jenny Deeds had told the constable about Rowdy McQuillan coming to her house that night. With the Special Prosecutor already breathing down his neck, Dave didn't need to make any further enemies up in police headquarters, so no one could be told he leaked the information to Moran. But if Frank could get it to him, without saying where it came from, it would then be up to Moran to carry out whatever investigations he saw fit. If the Deeds' story turned out to be true, he could use it to help get his client off. If not, he could just sweep it back under the carpet, where it came from.

Frank was more than happy to oblige. He didn't like Noel Atwood, and he didn't like to see anyone cheated out of a fair chance to defend themselves, even if they were guilty as sin. Besides, he figured it couldn't hurt one bit for him to take the opportunity to ingratiate himself to his new lawyer by feeding him a juicy little tidbit of anonymous information about one of his cases, especially a hidden gem like this, one that could turn out to be absolutely critical.

'There's one other thing I'm hoping you can help me with, Frank.'

With that, Dave launched into another story, about a young kid from the same town, who mysteriously went walkabout three weeks before the murder. It sounded to Frank like an odd coincidence right from the jump, and it seemed to get even stranger as Dave Hocking told the tale. Larnie Mitchell was reportedly a close mate of McQuillan, but she was also mixed up with a druggie by the name of Mozzie Blane, and the two of them were peddling speed together. That was until their stash suddenly went missing, whereupon Blane accused Larnie of pinching it, so her boyfriend stepped in and gave him a thick ear for his trouble. Next thing Blane shoots through, and then Larnie disappears, and then the cowboy's housemate winds up dead, all in the space of a few weeks.

Dave was right, it had a definite smell about it, and it was a short odds bet there was some connection between the girl's disappearance and the murder. As Frank sat there listening to the story, he was already considering the possibilities, making the connections and weighing up the options. As he did, it suddenly occurred to him how familiar it all felt, soaking up a summary of the known evidence and distilling all the information, speculation and assorted bits and pieces. Frank felt almost like a cop again, for the first time in months. It felt good.

'By the sounds of things, I'd start with this grub Blane,' he offered, as soon as Hocking finished with his outline of the facts.

'That's what I had in mind.'

'You think he might have offed her?'

There was another empty silence on the end of the line, before Hocking finally responded.

'I don't think so. We checked with his employer up in Gove. According to Nabalco's payroll people, someone by that name was pulling wages in the mines the week Larnie disappeared. And the week before that, and every week since, until a couple of months back, when his contract with the mines ran out.'

'Are you sure it was him picking up that paycheque?'

'Who knows. But that's where I need another favour.'

The young bloke Dave had running checks for him on Blane, out of the Cunnamulla uniformed branch, had come up with a recent traffic violation on the Gold Coast. The vehicle was unregistered, but when the coppers pulled him over the driver produced a current Queensland licence in Blane's name, and gave a local address, out back of Surfers Paradise.

'I need someone to eye-ball this bloke for me, make sure it's really Blane, not just some prick using his ID.'

Frank got it. Since Maurice Blane was last seen out in Millengarra, someone had been using his name, drawing wages at the bauxite mine up on the Gove Peninsula, and now racking up tickets right there in Frank's backyard on the Gold Coast. But that didn't necessarily mean that someone was really Maurice Blane. And if it wasn't, that would raise a whole new set of questions about where Blane might have got to, and just who might have got him there.

'Whoever it is, I don't want them spooked. For now, I just want to know if it's really him or not.'

•

As soon as Eddie Moran got into the Cunnamulla Airport terminal he went straight to the rental desk and picked up the keys to a hire car, along with a couple of road maps of the local area. Then he made a beeline for the centre of town. The sixteen-seat, twin-propellor King Air he had taken out of Brisbane that morning had been a little short on in-flight service, and Eddie was desperate for a decent cup of coffee before he hit the road. He wanted to eye-ball Millengarra before the committal hearing started, so he could check out the crime scene properly, and get a good feel for the general lay of the land. Even in the relatively short time Eddie had been doing this job, he had already worked out there was no substitute for going to the place where the case had had its genesis, laying eyes all over it, carrying out a meticulous inspection, touching it, feeling it, working out the stuff police photographs couldn't tell you, exactly what was what and where, how big or small, how obvious or not, how close or far everything was from every other thing, what instantly leapt out, and what could easily be missed.

'Can I help you?'

The young girl behind the counter of the Regency Milk Bar had a thin film of perspiration glistening along the line of her top lip.

'Just a coffee, thanks darling.'

'How would you like it?'

'Double shot espresso.'

A look of blank perplexity seeped onto her face as she wiped one finger absently across her sweaty lip.

'Coffee, did you say?'

'Coffee.'

'How do you have it?'

'What?'

'Black or white?'

The stranger's face stretched into a painful grimace as he exhaled a long, slow breath.

'Black.'

'Any sugars?'

'No thanks, princess. All good.'

'Sweet.' Her face instantly blossomed into a pretty, smiling picture of relief. 'No worries.'

Nearly two hours later, as Eddie rolled into the BP Roadhouse on the Cunnamulla Road, on the southern outskirts of the town of Millengarra, his takeaway cup of coffee was still three quarters full, but it had long since got cold and lost whatever limited attraction it had ever had. Pulling up gently to the petrol bowser, he lobbed the carboard container disdainfully into a passing rubbish bin.

As it turned out, he didn't have much better luck ordering coffee in the roadhouse restaurant, but at least when it came it was piping hot, and the eggs and bacon that came with it were exactly what he needed. After wolfing down his meal and mopping his plate clean, he lit a cigarette and flattened out the map of Millengarra on the tabletop. As he scanned the neatly creased, diagrammatic representation of a tiny little town, it looked almost comical, a sparse collection of straight lines, not much more than five streets square, plonked down out there, smack bang in the middle of absolutely nowhere. Eddie wondered how anyone could grow up in a place like that, live and die within the stifling confines of five straight streets. If it wasn't quite so silly it would be downright depressing.

The police station, by the look of things, was at the northern end of town, on the corner of Humeburn Road and Castle Street, the same street as the crime scene. Eddie had arranged for the local constable to open up the residence for him and wait while he inspected it, and they were due to rendezvous at the station house in just a little over fifteen minutes time, so his arrival time in town was pretty much spot on.

When he got to the police station, Constable Brian Ingles was standing in the grassy driveway, leaning on the side of a police car, looking like he wasn't planning to allow the lawyer too much leeway. After a brief, perfunctory introduction, he climbed into his car and efficiently pulled out of the driveway, as Eddie followed, onto Castle Street and then back up towards the Cunnamulla Road, not much more than half a kilometre, before he steered off into the dusty front yard of a squat little fibro house. As Eddie pulled up on the roadside opposite, he immediately recognised the scene from the police photographs. He reached across into his briefcase, pulled out the photographs and flicked through them quickly, orientating himself on precisely what was what, and then climbed out of the car.

'It's all been cleaned up of course,' Ingles offered, as he led the way towards the front door, shuffling though a set of jangling keys. 'Carpets replaced, all the broken windows re-done, full re-paint inside.' He finally selected one key, pushed it into the lock, and wrestled open the front door. 'The owners were hoping to get new tenants in, but in a town like this, of course, that's not real easy, not with this joint's history.'

Eddie understood entirely. Reportedly, Tom Wilson was born and bred in Millengarra; no doubt everybody knew him, and every local knew what happened to him in this house. The clean but slightly acrid smell of fresh paint and detergent in the stuffy little loungeroom would do little to disperse the ghosts, and the soft, quiet carpet underfoot only underscored the emptiness of the abandoned residence.

'They put a new toilet cistern in of course.' The constable lightly pushed the toilet door open as he walked past it, and Eddie looked into the freshly painted little room, now almost unrecognisable from the disastrous scene depicted in the police photographs. The officers who first came to Tom Wilson's house on the night of his murder had found the cistern smashed and lying in pieces all over the flooded floor, water flowing from the wall pipe out onto the tiles. It was at least one source of the water that had crept its way out into the hallway and down into the loungeroom at one end, and the bedrooms at the other, turning half the house into a soaking, squelchy quagmire. Now it was like new, clinically restored and rehabilitated, everything about it squeaky clean, dry, ordered and pristine.

'These two windows were bashed in,' Ingles said as he sauntered down the hallway, gesturing towards the bedrooms. 'And the flyscreens were all knocked around.'

'Outside in?'

Ingles stopped mid-stride and turned, looking back over his shoulder at the lawyer.

'Pardon?'

'The flyscreens. Were they knocked from the inside out, of from the outside in?'

At first he said nothing in reply, just stared curiously at Eddie for several long seconds.

'Outside in,' he said eventually, and then turned back and stepped into the main bedroom, pointing at the floor. 'That's where the body was when we first found it.'

As Eddie stepped in after him, he was shuffling through the pile of photographs, selecting those that showed the murder scene. The pictures showed the now-rejuvenated white walls painted red with blood, the neat, new sliding aluminium windows jagged with shards of broken glass, the flyscreens bent and ripped right out of shape. Looking at the room as it was now, in its sterile, refurbished state, then back at the grainy, gruesome photographs, each in turn, he was struck by the thought of what fury must have been unleashed there, the ferociousness of the attack that killed Tom Wilson.

'There was only one window damaged inside out.'

The mumbled observation roused Eddie from his reverie, and he turned to face the policeman, who was now leaning idly against the doorjamb, glaring at the floor. He stayed that way for a full second or so before he looked up at the lawyer and stared straight into his eyes.

'In the kitchen.'

'Yeah?' Brian Ingles obviously had something on his mind. But what? 'I don't remember seeing any photographs of broken windows in the kitchen.'

'Not the window itself, just the flyscreen.' He paused for a moment, still staring Eddie in the eye, before he spat it out. 'No damage to the gauze, just the aluminium frame. It was bent right out of shape, almost in two, from the inside out. The slider was wide open.'

Ingles motioned to him back towards the kitchen, and Eddie followed him down the short, narrow hallway to the living area.

'That one,' he said, throwing one hand in the direction of the sliding aluminium window over the kitchen bench, before he shuffled to one side and stood back, allowing the lawyer a clear view.

'Was it photographed?'

Ingles held out one hand in the direction of the lawyer, and Eddie passed the photographs over to him. He took them in both hands and shuffled through them, quickly extracting the one he was looking for.

'There,' he said, stabbing one finger at a photograph of the kitchen bench, and open sliding window over it. 'It's hard to see because of the lighting.'

Eddie followed a faint line in the photograph as Ingles ran one finger down it, then snatched the photo from him and held it close up to his face. It was unmistakeable, the edge of an aluminium flyscreen frame, bent back from the window, out into the darkness beyond. Directly below, inches from the windowsill, a line of jars and bottles on the kitchen bench appeared to have been disturbed, several lying flat down on the bench.

Eddie saw it immediately. If what the constable was saying was correct, the conclusion he was grappling with was inescapable. Either someone in the kitchen had slid back the window and pushed the flyscreen out, or someone had pulled on the flyscreen from outside the house, bending back the aluminium frame, and then reached in and opened the sliding window, just as an intruder might do if they wanted to break in. If it was the latter, that constituted evidence of a forced entry, which raised the real possibility of a third person in the house.

'Is any of this recorded anywhere else?'

Ingles just shrugged non-committally, staring blankly back at him. When he finally spoke, his message was crystal clear.

'I'm just showing you what's already in your brief, Mr Moran. Anything further you'll have to ask the investigating officers about.'

Eddie looked back at the clean, intact new window. If a would-be intruder saw that window open, even slightly, on a dark, hot, outback night, it would be a very easy exercise to simply take hold of the flyscreen, bend it back, reach in and slide the window fully open, then climb in onto the kitchen bench, inadvertently toppling those jars in the process. As the realisation struck him, he turned to gauge the constable's reaction, but Ingles just looked away.

Eddie looked back at the window, staring at it pensively, sizing it up. Then he looked straight through it, out to the where the large backyard of the residence stretched away, out past a lonely washing line, standing sentry amid sparse tufts of grass, to the tall, unpainted wooden fence that lined the rear boundary, and beyond it. He was looking at the back of a high, neon sign.

It read *Starlight Motel*.

SIXTEEN

On the morning of the first day of the committal hearing into the murder charge against Ronald Charles McQuillan, Eddie Moran was up at sparrow's fart. He hadn't slept well, even by his own shabby standards, and today there was way too much bouncing back and forth, around and about in his brain, for him to hold out any hope of further sleep. When the sun started threatening to poke its nose up over the horizon, he slipped his Walkman headphones on, grabbed a cassette tape, and got out of the motel room, wandering off into the cool, deserted, early-morning streets of Cunnamulla, hoping some good music might just help to clear the crowded space between his ears.

It didn't work. Even the sweet sounds of Mr B.B. King, squeezing and bending the bold, haunting notes of *How Blue Can You Get (Live at Farm Aid)* couldn't seem to rescue Eddie's mind from all the stuff still circulating through his head.

It had started the afternoon before, as he set out on the lonely, almost two-hour, dusty drive from Millengarra back to Cunnamulla, all the way turning over in his mind the strange experience of his inspection of the murder scene, what the police constable had shown him there, what he'd said to him, and what he clearly hadn't said. The bent-out flyscreen on the kitchen window changed everything. It was compelling, independent evidence consistent with the possibility of an intruder being in the house that night, and consistent with the crucial, alternative hypothesis sparked by the defendant's weird, disjointed ravings extracted under hypnosis by Dr Waylon Penfold.

It changed everything. And Constable Brian Ingles clearly knew it did. He also clearly knew if he didn't speak up no one else was going to, and if they didn't, an innocent man could be convicted of a murder he maybe didn't do. The more Eddie thought about what happened at the house the more he realised Ingles was convinced the police case against McQuillan was at least incompetent, if not corrupt. It was painfully evident that, for all the constable wished he could sit comfortably in the safety of the sidelines—just keeping his head down, saying nothing, doing his job—he knew he couldn't. So he spoke up, just enough to ensure the defendant's lawyer was doing the job he was being paid to do.

All the way back to Cunnamulla, Eddie was cursing himself for missing what had been right there under his nose all along. He had had the police photographs for weeks, looked attentively but briefly at them all and had seen what they depicted, and then set them aside. The photographs of the kitchen had always been of limited interest to him. All the evidence in the brief suggested this case was all about the bedroom, that the violence occurred solely in the bedroom where the body had been found. So that was where he concentrated his attention. He had pored over the pictures of Tom Wilson's body, the bed he had been sleeping on immediately prior to the attack, the bloodstains on the floor and on the walls, and the spattering down the hallway. But he had flicked past the photos of the kitchen, maybe twenty times or more, looking for other pictures to inspect, never pausing for a second look at the peripheries. Now, it suddenly struck him how crucial every single contemporaneous photograph of a crime scene really was. Every picture told a story, potentially the most honest and reliable one anyone would hear, but Eddie wasn't listening. He had all but overlooked half of the photographs. It was a dumb, rookie error, one he told himself he'd never make again.

He had not quite got around to eating anything that night. After he got back from Millengarra, he spent the evening in his motel room in Cunnamulla, going back through all the photographs. The more he looked at them—at that kitchen window, and the faint line of the flyscreen frame, traced out by the constable's forefinger, and at the other damaged windows, the defendant's wet clothing lying on the floor of the second bedroom, and the blood-stained baseball bat half-hidden in the long grass at the side of the house—the more obvious the conclusion was to him, and the more new questions came into his head, each one with an answer he could fashion as consistent with his client's innocence.

Except the damage to the toilet cistern. That one had him stumped. Now, as he properly studied the photograph of the toilet for the first time, it occurred to him the broken cistern made no sense at all, whatever way he looked at it. There were no bloodstains on the damaged remnants of the cistern, or in the toilet anywhere, not even on the door, or in the doorway, or on the hallway carpet, walls or ceiling immediately outside it. The only sign of violence was the smashed ceramic cistern. What could that mean? All the evidence suggested Wilson was attacked, and ultimately killed, in his own bedroom. In the process he spilled a lot of blood, but not a drop of it in or anywhere near the toilet. Even on the Crown case theory—even if McQuillan was the one who killed him—there was just no explanation for the violence that had caused the damage to the shattered cistern.

Eddie was still grappling with that quandary when Frank Vagianni rang to let him know an additional piece of information that instantly stirred up even more issues for Eddie to get his head around. Frank had some 'confidential information,' leaked to him by one of his connections on the other side, that the investigating officers in the McQuillan case had recently been told that, before McQuillan went to Karen Millard's house, he turned up at an old mate's place just around the corner, where he played up like an absolute pork chop. Crucially, the said mate's wife positively put the time of his arrival at their place at spot-on seven minutes after midnight. If that was right, McQuillan couldn't possibly have been at the murder scene for more than about five minutes, tops. That just wasn't enough time.

Eddie clicked his Walkman off and slid the headphones down around his neck. He couldn't disrespect the 'King of the Blues' by only listening in with half a brain, and right now the other half was full to overflowing. The prosecution case against Rowdy McQuillan was presenting only one side of the picture. There was more to it, but how much more, and where was it all leading to?

The committal hearing was due to start in several hours' time, and Eddie had to work out just which way he was going to approach it, right from the get-go. It was only a preliminary hearing, at which the police would present to the magistrate all the evidence they had to prove their charge against the defendant, so the magistrate could determine whether it was enough to constitute a *prima facie* case of guilt. If the magistrate decided a prima facie case had been established on the evidence, the defendant would be committed for a future trial before a judge and jury of his peers in the higher courts; if not, the charges would be dismissed and the defendant set free, there and then. But to find a prima facie case the magistrate didn't have to make a call about what evidence was true and what wasn't, or whether the defendant was actually guilty of the charge or not. The magistrate just had to work out whether, assuming the evidence was in fact true, and a jury believed every word of it, that jury could use that evidence to lawfully convict the defendant of the charge. It was a very low bar for the prosecution to leap and, not surprisingly, almost every committal hearing ended in the defendant being duly committed to stand trial.

Then again, the proceedings also fulfilled another vital function. They enabled the defence to cross-examine the police case for the first time, explore its strengths and weaknesses, sometimes unearth important aspects that had been missed, or perhaps even intentionally obscured. But the committal process called for subtle variations in approach, depending on the end game one was playing. Statistically, magistrates very rarely found the prosecution to have failed to make out a prima facie case, so lawyers almost invariably played the long game, cross-examining the prosecution case carefully, with one eye on a jury trial to come, discovering what they needed to know while still playing their client's cards close to their chest, shaping the evidence, setting traps they hoped to spring at trial, and keeping all their ammunition dry to fight another day.

But for a person locked up in prison for the best part of a year, on remand for a crime they didn't commit, the long game was a distinctly unappealing option. It hadn't even occurred to Eddie Moran that Rowdy McQuillan might not have actually killed Tom Wilson until his conversation in the courthouse cafeteria with the weird and wonderful Doctor Waylon Penfold. And even then, the story was so tenuous and uncertain, it was clearly one to be carefully teased out and explored without playing any cards too early.

But now things had changed considerably. The timeline had potentially shrunk back to a mere five minutes, or maybe less, and the photographs appeared to show the possible presence of an unidentified intruder in the house. With those new features present, was there still enough for a properly instructed jury to conclude it was Rowdy McQuillan, and not someone else entirely, who attacked and killed Tom Wilson that night?

Eddie wasn't sure which way to go. Should he roll the dice, ride in there with both guns blazing and just go for broke, or should he play it safe, set up all the possibilities, and then try to get some expert evidence from Penfold to back them up at a jury trial? A trial would be months away at least, but realistically the likelihood of a magistrate dismissing a murder charge at committal stage wasn't too much better than a snowball's chance in hell.

Or was it? In this case the assigned magistrate was Ranald McEniery SM, a very interesting draw. Over the years he had shown himself to be staunchly pro-prosecution—a tough sentencer who invariably preferred police evidence in any credibility contest. Eddie had never heard of McEniery ever dismissing anything, at a committal hearing or anywhere else. But recent history might have changed Ranald McEniery's attitude to police and prosecutors in general.

During the public hearings of the Fitzgerald Inquiry, investigators had got their hands on the private records of a corrupt Assistant Commissioner of Police, whose diaries detailed a procession of dinner parties he had held at his Brisbane home, where the invitation list included influential politicians, a host of colourful racing identities, and several members of the judiciary. Unfortunately for McEniery, his name figured front-and-centre in the diaries and, although no impropriety was ultimately proven, for months there was much lurid speculation in the press about the relationship between the now-discredited Assistant Commissioner and his prominent, high-ranking friends, all of whom were ultimately summonsed, and publicly put through the wringer, at the Inquiry. In the meantime, McEniery was officially stood down and, when he was eventually cleared of all wrongdoing and duly re-instated, he was promptly banished to the provinces, transferred from his cushy job in the Brisbane CBD to take up a back-handed promotion as Chief Magistrate out at Cunnamulla.

So, for now at least, Eddie figured Ranald McEniery SM was a distinctly unknown quantity. His recent run-in with the Forces of Evil might just make him more inclined to carefully sift through any chaff the coppers tried to feed him. But it was still a risk. If Eddie disclosed his hand at the committal hearing, and McEniery still committed Rowdy to stand trial, the police would have months to try to plug any holes he had managed to put in their case, and put together further evidence to derail a telegraphed defence before it even got onto first base.

Which way should he go? It was tough question, one that had been eating at him ever since he first laid eyes on the photograph of that kitchen window with the bent-out screen. It had kept him up last night, put him off his food, and now got him out of bed at an ungodly hour. But for all he found himself foisted on the horns of an excruciating dilemma, by contrast his spirited assistant Kirsten Foster—when had he rang her on the night before to talk the issue through—characteristically demonstrated a singular and unquestionable clarity of thought.

'You've got to get that poor guy the fuck out of there, Eddie.'

The way Slick put it, it sounded simple.

'What do you want me to do? Lasso the bars on his cell window?'

'Damn straight, if that's what it takes.' Eddie tried again to step her through the counterbalancing considerations, but she clearly wasn't interested. 'He's been in the slammer nearly twelve months already, for something he obviously didn't do.'

'What makes you so sure of that?'

'I'll tell you what makes me so sure.' She was the best part of a thousand kilometres away, but Eddie could see her in his mind's eye, sitting forward on the edge of her seat, poking holes in the air with one lethal-looking, painted fingernail. 'What you told me yourself. He said all that stuff to Penfold under hypnosis—stuff that could get him off—but he's never even tried to tell that shit to anyone else. No one. Not to the cops, not to the shrink, not even to his dickhead lawyer.' The phone went silent for a second or so, and when she spoke again, the venom was all gone. 'I'm telling you, Eddie, he's innocent.' Her words were strangely comforting, although he had no idea why. 'He didn't do it,' she added, almost in a whisper. 'And he doesn't even know he didn't. You've got to get him out, soon as you can.'

Eddie was still thinking about that late-night call with Slick as he ambled idly back into the driveway of the New Jumbuck Inn Motel. He wasn't surprised her preferred option was to jump in, boots and all, and try to save the cowboy from his fate. That was how she was. She cared about people— even ones she'd never met, like Rowdy—and Eddie loved her for that. But it didn't mean her call was right, not by a long shot.

The sun was well and truly up now, and Eddie hoped the kitchen might be opening soon for breakfast and a cup of coffee. As he headed in that general direction, a square-shouldered, straight-backed man in a crumpled brown sports coat and dark blue tie stepped out of one of the front units and strode purposefully into the carpark. He had the unmistakeable look of a police detective, locked and loaded for official business, and Eddie was sure he recognised his face from somewhere. As their paths crossed in the driveway, the policeman nodded courteously, if coldly, at the lawyer, and Eddie nodded back.

Now he remembered. Hocking was his name. He had given evidence at Southport in the case of Holden Waldo Winchester. And if Eddie remembered rightly, he had tried to fudge his evidence, big time. If Hocking was in town for the McQuillan case, Eddie figured there'd be fun and games at play for sure.

•

When Eddie Moran reached the Cunnamulla Courthouse that morning the front landing was lined with waiting witnesses and interested locals keen to take in what they hoped would be, at least for the first few days, the biggest show in town. Ada Morrow met him just inside the front doors and introduced him around to the few family members he was yet to meet, in the process discretely whispering in his ear a word of reassurance from Madam Marla Pavlovich that everything was going to be just fine, before he eventually managed to extract himself, and moved on to the watchhouse to see his client.

Detective Senior Sergeant David Hocking was sitting in the prosecutor's office in the Cunnamulla Police Station when he spotted the defence lawyer heading for the watchhouse. As he watched Moran stride down the pathway to the cells, he wondered if his old mate Frank Vagianni had passed the Jenny Deeds information onto him. He hoped he had, and prayed that if he did, he didn't say where it had come from. Once upon a time, Dave wouldn't even have considered the possibility of a good cop like Frank giving him up. *But in this day and age, how could you be certain?* He pushed the idea out of his head. Frank wasn't like that. He was staunch. If you couldn't trust a bloke like Frank Vagianni, who in God's name could you trust?

'He looks like some sort of half-baked druggie.' Atwood had a pained expression on his face, as if he had a piece of shit stuck on the end of his tongue. 'Do we know anything about him?'

The little group of bleary-eyed detectives circling Bruce McKinlay's desk were watching through the window as the lawyer walked towards the watchhouse.

'His name's Moran. He's a solicitor on the Gold Coast.'

'Oh fuck,' Atwood scoffed superciliously, to the obvious amusement of the sycophants surrounding him. 'Well, he's not going to give us any trouble then, is he.'

The comment met with merriment and a mild sense of confident self-congratulation. Dave Hocking wondered if the celebration wasn't just a trifle premature.

'I'll sit at the bar table with you, to assist,' Atwood magnanimously announced to his prosecutor.

The offer was obviously intended to impress upon his little band of merry men that even though Noel had scaled the lofty heights to the Commissioner's office, he was still a man of the people, ready to roll his sleeves up and do the hard yards when required. But Dave knew different. Atwood's offer wasn't about pitching in, it was about taking bows. The McQuillan murder case would be Atwood's swansong as an operational policeman, his last press-clippings for the scrapbook, and he wanted to keep an eagle eye on it from start to finish, make sure it all went through like clockwork.

'I'm not sure you'll be able to, Noel.' It gave Dave Hocking a perverse sense of satisfaction to think he might upset the Assistant Commissioner's apple cart. 'You're a witness in the hearing. You'll have to wait outside.'

Atwood scoffed again, this time with even greater gusto.

'Oh, bullshit,' he blustered, casting a disdainful smirk around his circle of supporters. 'It's just a committal. Magistrates don't worry about that sort of shit.'

'Well, I'm not so sure. I…'

'You've been spending too much time behind the desk, Dave,' Atwood interrupted, climbing to his feet. 'Leave the court stuff to us.'

The silly smirk plastered across his face made Dave want to slap him. But he didn't. Noel would keep. Having sat through Moran's histrionics in the Winchester trial, Dave was confident the lanky lawyer would do all the slapping necessary.

It didn't take too long. The first thing Bruce McKinlay did, after announcing his appearance as prosecutor, was to advise the magistrate that Assistant Commissioner Atwood would be assisting him administratively at the bar table during the proceedings. The words were no sooner out of his mouth than Dave immediately spotted, from three rows back in the public gallery, Moran's long legs sliding swiftly in under his chair, as he poised to leap up to his feet with an objection. But Mr McEniery SM beat him to it.

'Isn't he a witness in the proceedings?'

'Well…' Bruce McKinlay hesitated for less than a second. 'Yes, your Worship.'

'Then he can sit outside and wait, like all the other witnesses.'

Argument over. Eddie Moran eased back comfortably into his seat. The brief exchange had conveniently answered the burning question he had been asking himself for days about Ranald McEniery. Now he knew. The magistrate's short-lived stint on the wrong side of Right and Might had obviously left a lasting mark on him. This wasn't the old McEniery, and that couldn't be a bad thing.

Eddie glanced across to the dock, where his client was sitting obediently on the bench seat, a bored-looking constable slumped in the chair alongside him. But Rowdy didn't pick up the lawyer's glance; he was too busy looking the other way, smiling and blushing as he awkwardly waved one big hand in the direction of friends and relatives lined up in the back row. Gawking clumsily at them, red-faced, that big, silly grin on his face, Eddie hardly recognised him. This wasn't the surly, scowling prisoner he had spent so many hours conferencing with in the grimy, stifling interview rooms at Boggo Road Gaol. Here in his hometown, surrounded by people who cared about him, Rowdy McQuillan didn't look much of a killer at all.

When Eddie looked back to the other end of the bar-table, the kerfuffle around Atwood's ouster as the prosecutor's administrative assistant seemed to have settled somewhat already. As the Assistant Commissioner indignantly made his way from the courtroom, a replacement was called up from the gallery and efficiently assumed the position in the seat alongside Bruce McKinlay. It was Hocking, the senior detective from the Winchester case. He wasn't scheduled as a witness in the proceedings, and his name wasn't mentioned anywhere in the brief as having had anything to do with the case. And yet, for some reason, he'd been brought up all the way from Brisbane to somehow be part of the show.

Eddie didn't like it. The last time he dealt with Hocking, the detective was trying to hide something important—he was sure of it—and now he had showed up here, a thousand kilometres from where he should be, in a case that had nothing to do with him, but in which, for some reason, the police once again were intent on telling only part of the story. Eddie smelt a rat. Whatever it was they were up to, they weren't going to get away with it, not on Eddie's watch.

•

The first witness on the prosecution list was Wayne Peter Grantham, the now twenty-two-year-old farm labourer, and former Castle Street housemate of Tom Wilson and Rowdy McQuillan. Having read Grantham's statement half a dozen times, Eddie knew precisely why the prosecutor wanted him right at the top of the batting order. According to the statement, during the short time Grantham lived at Castle Street, he learned that Rowdy and Tom Wilson had a fractious relationship that often boiled over into physical violence, in which the cowboy, the bigger and more powerful of the two, regularly assaulted his housemate violently and without provocation. It was the perfect way to start the prosecution case, painting a picture of McQuillan as dangerous and unpredictable, capable of spontaneous and unbridled rage.

Grantham was a big, raw-boned, long-limbed boy, whose freckled face and tousled mop of ginger hair made him look like he'd stepped straight out of a *Bluey and Curley* cartoon on the back page of the Courier Mail, the country cousin sent up from central casting. He looked embarrassed as he lumbered awkwardly towards the witness box, a low murmur rumbling around the local folk jammed into the public gallery, and then he fumbled his way clumsily through the oath to tell the truth, the whole truth and nothing but the truth, like a man who really didn't want to be there. Eddie sensed his evidence was going to be a voyage of discovery for everyone.

He wasn't wrong. Once Bruce McKinlay had led the witness through the formalities of his testimony—who he was, where he lived, how he knew the deceased and the defendant, and when and how he had first gone to live at Castle Street—and finally got down to the nitty gritty of his evidence— the relationship between Tom Wilson and Rowdy McQuillan—Wayne Grantham's evidence began to stumble and stagger erratically.

'How would you describe their relationship?'

As the courtroom waited for the answer, Eddie was looking at the same line in Grantham's police statement as Bruce McKinlay was, so he knew precisely what the prosecutor was hoping his witness would reply. *They were always arguing, and sometimes Rowdy would threaten to bash Tom for no reason at all.'* That was the first sentence of the fifth paragraph of the statement, and the jump-off point for all the evidence the prosecution hoped Grantham would give about violence between his two former housemates. But the witness didn't seem to quite be on the same page as the prosecutor, and just stared back at him for several seconds with a perplexed expression on his face, before he finally responded.

'I don't think they were related, were they?'

McKinlay grimaced almost imperceptibly.

'No, I mean how did they get along?'

There was another long silence, and then the witness nodded back pensively.

'Yeah, alright, I think. Mostly.'

'What do you mean 'mostly'?'

'Most of the time, like.'

The prosecutor paused again, collecting his thoughts.

'Were there ever any fights between them?'

A silent moment followed, pregnant with anticipation, before the young labourer commenced to lazily wave his head from side to side.

'Nah,' he said eventually. 'Not really, ay.'

The prosecutor flipped one page of the witness statement over, scanned what was supposed to be coming next, and then flipped back to his place again. Eddie could sense his agony. McKinlay knew where he wanted to get his dull-witted witness to, he just wasn't sure how to get him there. But it was a crucial point, and this was evidence-in-chief, not cross-examination, so leading questions were forbidden. If McKinlay asked anything that suggested what answer he wanted, the lawyer was loaded like a coiled spring to object.

'Do you remember Cunnamulla Show Day last year?'

It was a permissibly obscure, non-leading question.

'Oh yeah. Yeah, I do.'

'Did something happen that day with Rowdy?'

'Yeah. Yeah, it did, actually, yeah.'

'Okay.' McKinlay paused and took a settling breath, looking marginally relieved. 'Tell us what happened that day.'

Grantham scratched his ginger scalp, and casually launched into his story, like a farmer leaning on a barbed-wire fence, yarning to his next-door neighbour. He told the prosecutor how he and his housemates had the day off for the Cunnamulla Show and were planning to all drive down to Cunnamulla together that day. But in the morning Rowdy 'done his nana' about some of his beer going missing from the fridge, accusing Tom and him of drinking it.

'He was in a stinking mood, ay,' he remembered with a furrowed brow. 'So I just got the hell out of there, and I've ended up going down the Show myself with some blokes I used to work with.' This was new information that wasn't anywhere in Grantham's witness statement, which made no mention of his having left the house at any stage that day. Surprises in evidence-in-chief were never a good thing, but now the witness had a head of steam up, Bruce McKinlay was disinclined to interrupt him. 'But then, when I got back to Castle Street that night, Tom and Rowdy were still there, and they'd obviously been on the drink all day.'

So far, he hadn't even got close to the point of his story, but Grantham suddenly stopped, and sat staring silently back at the prosecutor, as though his work here was done. McKinlay cautiously ventured his next question.

'Okay. So did anything happen when you got back to Castle Street?'

'Not really.' The answer drew a mild, spontaneous grimace from the prosecutor, before his witness eventually added, 'Except Rowdy was still in a foul mood about the beer, and he'd obviously bashed Tom for taking it.'

Once again, this version bore scant resemblance to anything in Wayne Grantham's police statement, which described how he had witnessed the defendant attack Tom Wilson while he was *obviously inebriated and asleep on a bean-bag in the loungeroom,* punching and kicking him into unconsciousness. But at least Grantham had got out something about violence done by the defendant to the victim, and Bruce McKinlay hoped he could build on that.

'How did you know he'd bashed Tom for taking his beer?'

'Oh, it was pretty obvious he'd copped a flogging, ay. He was out cold on the beanbag, and he had skin and bark off him everywhere.'

'But how did you know it was the defendant that did it to him?'

'Well, he was the only other one there, ay.'

That was it. The police prosecutor did his best to drag something more useful out of the witness, and made a fair fist of it in the face of repeated, vociferous objections from the other end of the bar-table, but in the wash-up, Grantham never even got close to the true gravamen of what was typed into his statement. The highest he could put it was that, on Cunnamulla Show Day, he saw the defendant at Castle Street with the deceased, who looked all busted-up, like someone, somewhere, at some time during that day, had assaulted him. He couldn't say who, or how, or when, or where.

The evidence was so vague and equivocal, it was virtually worthless to the prosecution case, and would probably not even be allowed to be led in a jury trial. It was hardly worth wasting everyone's time and effort to cross-examine it. But something in the back of Eddie's brain was telling him there was more goodness to be wrung out of Wayne Peter Grantham yet. The prosecutor had hardly settled into his seat before Eddie was up on his feet and firing off his first question.

'So, you didn't see Tom Wilson get bashed?'

'No, not actually, no.'

'Then you don't know for sure who bashed him, do you?'

'I s'pose not. No, not really.'

'See, I suggest what in fact happened was Tom Wilson spent the afternoon drinking down at the Empire Hotel that day, and he got into a fight with a couple of shearers down there in the public bar.'

'Fair enough.'

'And Rowdy McQuillan wasn't even at the hotel when it happened.'

'I wouldn't know. I was down the Cunnamulla Show all day.'

'That's exactly right, you wouldn't know.' The lanky lawyer was staring insolently at him. 'So why would you give a statement to the police saying you actually saw Rowdy McQuillan kicking and punching Tom Wilson at the house that day?'

'Did I say that?'

Moran waited a moment, letting the answer sink in.

'I don't know,' he finally said, flicking quickly through his brief. 'You tell me.' When he settled on what he was looking for, he clicked open his folder and removed several pages. 'But it's in your statement.' He held out the copy of Wayne Grantham's statement for the magistrate's clerk to collect and deliver to the witness. 'Have a look at it. Paragraph ten on the second page.' As the clerk placed the statement in front of him, the witness hunched forward and turned over to page two. 'See that? You actually describe it as a *"brutal and despicable attack on a defenceless man."*'

Grantham silently stared at the document for several seconds, then sat back in his seat, looking resigned.

'Fair enough.'

'Did you say that?'

'I don't know. Maybe, I s'pose.'

They were eyeball-to-eyeball, both saying nothing, while the courtroom waited in silence for the next question.

'Do you even know what that word *despicable* means, witness?'

Grantham sat perfectly still for a long moment, and then slowly shook his head.

'Not really, ay.'

'Then how did you come to include it your witness statement?'

'Well, the cops sort of helped me with it a bit, ay.'

'What do you mean, "helped" you?'

Grantham shrugged and shifted uncomfortably in his seat.

'Well,' he began, grimacing slightly, 'They reckoned they'd heard Tom and Rowdy didn't get on real good, and at first I said I didn't know nothing about that, but then they reckoned I did, and if I lied to them I could be in trouble myself. So anyway, I tried to remember what I could about any blues or arguments or anything they'd had with each other and that, and the only thing I really remembered was what happened on Show Day. But, like, I'd had a few that day down the Show. Like, I wasn't full or nothing, but I wasn't all that flash either, ay. And I just remembered seeing Tom wiped out on the bean-bag when I got home, so I figured Rowdy must have give it to him for drinking his grog, and then the coppers were saying, "Well, he must've kicked him and punched him and that, for him to end up all busted up like he was," and I agreed with them, ay, 'cause that's what it looked like to me. So then they just typed up the statement, and I signed it.'

It was gold, and Eddie knew it. Wayne Grantham had seen his housemate battered and bruised on Show Day, so he naturally assumed Rowdy McQuillan had done it, simply because he was the only other one there. Just like, when Wilson was found dead a few weeks later, the police automatically assumed Rowdy did that too, because they believed he was the only one there that night. But Rowdy wasn't the one who bashed Tom Wilson on Show Day, just like he maybe wasn't the one who murdered him.

When Eddie looked up at Ranald McEniery, the magistrate was furiously scribbling notes and, if Eddie wasn't entirely mistaken, he had a look approximating mild disgust spread across his face. When he eventually added just the slightest hint of a disdainful shake of his head, Eddie was certain. McEniery didn't like it, one little bit. The police had not only encouraged Grantham to leap to an unwarranted—and incorrect—assumption, they had actively assisted him embellish their case against Rowdy McQuillan.

That just left one more point for Eddie to extract.

'When you say the police did all this, Mr Grantham, what police in particular are you talking about?'

'The older guy, mainly. The one in charge.'

'Then-Detective Sergeant Noel Atwood?'

'Atwood, yeah. That's the bloke. Detective Atwood.'

When Eddie sat back down, Mr McEniery SM was staring daggers at Bruce McKinlay, who had his head well and truly down, and Detective David Hocking, who was sitting in the very seat recently vacated by none other than the said then-Detective Sergeant Noel Atwood, now Assistant Commissioner of Police.

Eddie made his mind up there and then. Slick was right; now was the right time to attack.

SEVENTEEN

Frank Vagianni slipped the folded facsimile photograph of Maurice Blane out of his back pocket and took one last look at it. He was an ugly, skinny little rat, pretty much the same as about a thousand other skinny little rats Frank had pinched over the past who-knew-how-many years, but he knew, if this guy was the one, he'd be able to I.D. him. And that was all Dave Hocking needed him to do.

Frank stepped out of the car and dragged his handkerchief across the back of his neck, mopping up the film of grimy sweat trickling down behind his collar, and peered across the road towards the daggy, shit-brown brick, two-storey walk-up opposite. The address written on the fax sheet read 'unit two'. It was a block of eight, so this bloke must be on the ground floor. *Good.* It was way too hot a day for climbing stairs. So far, Frank figured he would just walk up to the front door, knock politely, and see who opened up. From there the plan was pretty much non-existent. But what the heck, he'd wing it if he had to.

The concrete front path was bent and broken, with strands of half-dead grass growing up out of the cracks, and the front yard looked as though it hadn't seen a mower—or a drop of water, for that matter—since Frank was playing front row for the Burleigh Bears. The whole joint looked to Frank like a flea-bitten, junkie flophouse. But that was probably precisely where a piece of shit like Mozzie Blane would be holed up.

The scratched and faded white door, with the tarnished number two screwed to the front of it, looked like it would fall right over if anybody gave it half a decent shove, but Frank just knocked firmly and waited. No answer. He knocked again, this time with a tad more oomph. These druggies liked their beauty sleep, and even though it was getting on for midday, Frank figured his lordship was probably just having himself a little late lie-in.

'Come on buddy,' he mumbled to himself as he rapped again, this time even harder. 'Wakey-wakey, hands off snakey, pal.'

Still no answer. Frank put his face up to the window, shading his eyes from the outdoor glare, and peered into a tiny lounge-room inside. The place looked like a train wreck. He could see down the hallway, in through an open door into a bedroom where an unmade bed added to the overall impression that a force twelve typhoon had just blown straight through the front door. But still no sign of life. It looked like whoever was living in number two was up, out and about.

Frank made his way to the side of the unit block and stepped over a series of articles and obstacles skirting the boundary fence through to the backyard, which looked equally as shambolic as the front. From the corner of the building he could see the back door to number two, slightly ajar. Someone had either left in a hurry, or was about to. Frank immediately stepped back behind the wall, his eyes still on the door, thinking through his next move. Should he wait where he was until his lordship eventually emerged? Or should he just go knock on the back door, see what happened?

He was still kicking over the alternatives when suddenly, without warning, someone burst out of the bushes lining the side fence and bolted frantically for the back boundary. Spontaneously, without a second's thought, Frank took off after him. But the rangy young man up front had a healthy head start on him and was already halfway up the high fibro fence before Frank even got into stride. He would have been long gone by the time Frank got there, if not for one protruding nail that jagged his tatty T-shirt, leaving him desperately impaled, one leg on either side, cursing and struggling helplessly, as his pursuer, puffing hard, finally reached the fence and latched onto one dangling foot with both his hands.

'Fuck off. Leave me alone.'

The fugitive was listing badly at the brink, threatening to topple back into the yard at any minute, as Frank held on for dear life, one knee jammed against the fibro, using all his weight to try to tip the balance in his favour. Eventually he did.

As the young man came hurtling headlong down on top of him, Frank could already see he had hold of the hairy, naked foot of Maurice Blane, and when his captive hit the ground Frank grappled feverishly to try get hold of the rest of him. But Blane wasn't keen to cooperate, and was desperately flailing his arms in every direction, as the two of them rolled and wrestled hectically across the grass, the younger man wildly thrashing about and pleading pathetically.

'Don't. Let me go. Please. I never done it.'

As Frank finally got hold of one of his hands, he jammed a vice grip onto his thumb and wrenched it down and back against his forearm.

'Settle down, buddy.' The young man's body stiffened with a tortured groan. 'Fuckin' settle down.' Blane groaned again, whimpering piteously as Frank kept the pressure on. 'I'm not going to hurt you. Alright? I'm just trying to find Larnie.'

Despite his obvious pain, Mozzie Blane looked startled by the mention of the name.

'What?'

'I'm just trying to find Larnie Mitchell.'

'Larnie? What for? Who sent you?'

Good question. No one had sent him, certainly not to do what he was currently doing, trespassing on private premises, crash-tackling the occupant over his back fence, and rolling around in the garden bed with him.

'Her parents.' The lie fell out unexpectedly, but it would do for now. Frank figured he'd broken a few laws already, so what difference would one little white lie make? 'They hired me to find her.'

Ten minutes later, he was sitting on a lumpy sofa, surrounded by a wasteland of dog-eared magazines, pizza boxes and unwashed dishes, as he watched Maurice Blane squeeze the last bit of goodness from a dry, daggy teabag. He hadn't even thought to question Frank's feeble claim he was a licenced private investigator retained by the Mitchells to track down their daughter, much less ask for any form of identification, and now he was free of Frank's wristlock, he seemed more than happy to chat away openly with him, like he was some sort of long-lost friend.

'Larnie was smart, ay. Real smart.' As he settled into his seat, Blane blew a cooling breath across the surface of his tea. 'When that gear went missing, I knew it was her that done it.' He took a noisy slurp and swallowed it down. 'Then that fuckin' Rowdy rolled up, trying to heavy me. So I figured he put her up to it.'

He was looking scornfully into his cup, scowling like a jilted lover. Frank wondered what he was glaring at down there. *The drugs, the money, or the girl? Maybe all three.*

'So where do you reckon Larnie got to?'

'Don't know.' Blane didn't look up, he just shook his head slowly from side to side. 'At first I figured she'd just fucked off, down to Brisbane or somewhere, to spend some of the dough they pinched off me.' He sat silently for several seconds, still staring down into his cup, then lifted his head, and looked Frank straight in the eye. 'But then, when I heard what Rowdy done to Tommy Wilson, it got me thinking.' They sat eyeball-to-eyeball for a moment, before Mozzie slowly shook his head again. 'That was crazy shit, ay. Like he was high on something.'

'You think he knocked her?'

'I'd say so.' Blane sucked in another mouthful of tea, and quickly gulped it down. 'Cut her out of the deal permanently, I reckon. Used up the rest of that speed himself. Him and Tom maybe.'

'Tom?' Frank was surprised to hear it. There'd been no mention, so far as he knew, of any drug use by Wilson, or any speed found at the house.

'Tommy liked a taste. Him and his other mate Wayne.'

He was talking about Wilson's former housemate, Wayne Grantham. According to Blane, Wilson and Grantham had been customers of his, scoring the odd deal of speed here and there, before Mozzie's supply suddenly vanished. Frank had no reason to doubt what he was saying, but so far it sounded like, according to Mozzie, everyone in town was up to no good, except Mozzie himself.

'So why did you take off when you did?'

Blane dropped his head back down, shook it from side to side, then peered back up at him cautiously. 'Mate, there was ten G's worth of speed gone missing. All on spec.'

'On spec from who?'

'Fuck that,' Blane shot back firmly, again shaking his head and shifting nervously around in his seat. 'I'm not getting into none of that shit, ay. No way.' Whoever Mozzie Blane's supplier was, they had him shit-scared; that much was clear and certain. Frank didn't blame him. Any street-level peddler like Mozzie, who opened his mouth when he shouldn't, was destined to have a very short life span. 'That's why I shit meself when I seen you in the backyard, ay. I knew someone was going to come looking some time.'

'How did you know that?'

"Cause I got the fuckin' call, didn't I.' His voice was trembling, his eyes glistening with fear. 'And mate, they weren't fucking around, ay.'

He dropped his head again, sniffed hard, then took another slurp of his tea, trying to settle himself. Frank knew from bitter experience, now was the time to tread slowly and cautiously, or Blane might just clam up completely.

'What did you tell them?'

'I told them the fuckin' truth,' Mozzie spat back anxiously. 'That someone fuckin' flogged it all off me.'

'Larnie?'

He hesitated, sighed, and shook his head sadly, running one hand through his long, greasy hair.

'Larnie was a good chick, ay,' he mumbled disconsolately. 'It wouldn't have been her idea. No way.'

'So what did you tell them?'

He looked Frank straight in the eye, scowling defiantly.

'I told them that fucking prick Rowdy done it,' he seethed, his gaze now fixed and unwavering. 'I even told them where I figured he'd be hiding it.'

Frank could see in his eyes Maurice Blane was totally convinced Rowdy McQuillan was directly and solely responsible for all of the mountains of shit that had recently descended upon his miserable existence. He had stolen his drugs, his money, and his girl, and he was the reason why Mozzie still had to keep one eye over his shoulder. Maybe it was all true. Maybe the reason for all that had happened—even Larnie Mitchell's disappearance—was the fact that someone decided to steal Mozzie's stash.

'So where did you figure he'd be hiding it?'

'In the dunny at Castle Street.' Blane curled his lip into an insolent snarl, as if he was some sort of tough guy. 'Wayne told me. That's where him and Tom used to keep their stash, in a waterproof box, sunk in the cistern.' The sneering, pock-marked face and long yellow teeth reminded Frank of a mangy dog. 'Reckoned the cops'd never think to look there. Stupid fuckin' pricks.'

•

Dave Hocking crossed Mozzie Blane off his list. According to what Frank had found out, Blane was up on the Gove Peninsula when Larnie disappeared. And what he'd told Frank confirmed what both Jodie Lanham and Rowdy McQuillan had told Dave. Someone had snatched Mozzie's stash from under his nose, and he was convinced it was Larnie, so Rowdy McQuillan stepped in and worded him up. Dave didn't buy Mozzie's theory the cowboy was behind it all; he'd heard enough from McQuillan to convince him the big bloke had nothing to do with it. But Blane thought he did, and if he told his suppliers McQuillan was sitting on their cash and drugs, that was more than enough to buy Rowdy plenty of trouble. It might even have got Tom Wilson killed.

But that was McQuillan's problem. Dave had already seen enough at the cowboy's committal hearing to work out his lawyer was one of those uppity, half-smart, jumped-up show-ponies that made Dave want to chunder, just at the sight of him. But he was no fool, that was for sure, and now Frank Vagianni had a sniff of what was really going on with his case, and was feeding the information back to his lawyer. Whatever Dave thought of Eddie Moran, he could see he was smart enough to know what to do with it. Maybe McQuillan deserved to be saved, and maybe he didn't. But if he did, this bloke could certainly do it.

But none of that answered the question burning a hole in Dave Hocking's brain. *What the hell happened to Larnie Mitchell?* If Rowdy had nothing to do with her disappearance, and Mozzie was long gone before she shot through, where the hell did she get to? Had she just done what every half-baked yokel in town took for granted, shot through in search of the big city lights, like all the rest? Had she simply disappeared into the ether, as they all seemed to blithely accept, never to be seen or heard of again? Were her devastated parents sentenced to lie awake every night, just like Dave did, for the rest of their crumby lives, waiting and wondering?

Not on Dave Hocking's watch. He'd been a cop all his life, and if he'd learned one thing in all those years, it was that for every question there was an answer. Every mystery had a solution. All you had to do was work hard enough, for long enough, to find it. He'd put a line through two names, but there were plenty more still on the list.

The first thing Dave did that morning when he got to Cunnamulla Station was check in on PC Raye for an update on the inquiries he was supposed to be running for him on the police computer. The conscientious young constable had made a good start, but most of it was stuff Dave already knew, including three pages of prior convictions and a series of intel reports on Jimmy Rawlings, and confirmation Bob Proctor was out of town at the time of Tom Wilson's murder.

Of more interest was an entry on Kevin Daines. It showed a string of priors for low-level B & Es as a juvenile, and one as an adult for shoplifting.

So, the grease-monkey had a penchant for larceny. *Interesting.* Dave stuffed the folded page into his pocket as he pushed away from the desk and got to his feet.

'Good work, constable.' Randall Raye looked pleased with himself. 'Keep digging. And keep me posted on whatever comes up.'

Bruce McKinlay had already headed off to the courthouse, and had left word for Dave to come there as soon as he clocked in for work that morning. Court didn't start until ten, so Dave figured that, for Bruce to have set up shop at the courthouse so early that morning, there had to be some sort of last-minute crisis on foot—a statement unsigned, an exhibit gone missing, a witness who hadn't turned up. Court cases were always the same; some sort of disaster invariably blew up at some stage when least expected and, whatever it was, it had to get patched up quick smart. So, as soon as he got the message from the front desk, Dave pushed his way out through the front door, and headed off for the Magistrates Court.

When he got there, he was surprised to see Bruce McKinlay standing in the courthouse carpark, in a huddle with a couple of suits. On first impression, they all looked like lawyers, or maybe big brass of some sort from up town, but no one Dave recognised. As he walked towards them across the tarmac, Bruce McKinlay turned to face him, looking like someone had died. Whatever was up, it was obviously serious.

At that precise moment, the front door of the courthouse pushed open, and a familiar face emerged out onto the landing.

'G'day Dave.' Inspector Roger Page had a tense-looking smile on his face as he stepped forward and extended his hand. 'Good to see you, mate,' he added, as they shook hands. 'Sorry it's in these circumstances.'

What circumstances? Dave looked back at Bruce McKinlay, who was now hanging his head, gently nudging pebbles of carpark gravel around with one foot. Maybe someone had died.

'These gentlemen are from the Special Prosecutor's Office.' Page turned to the suits and introduced them as Conroy and Wade. Dave shook their hands without speaking. 'I thought it better we do this here, rather than down at the station.'

•

According to the cool, calm, collected inspector, Roger Page—the man who Dave Hocking had worked with for most of his life, who had been at his wedding, and had shared plenty with Dave through the years—all this was nothing but good news for Dave. As they sat cramped together around a small table in the centre of the only witness room in the Cunnamulla Courthouse, while Bruce McKinlay sat alone in the hallway outside, standing sentry for them, Page ran through the scenario they were facing, from start to finish.

The Special Prosecutor now had sworn statements from the two uniformed officers who helped Dave and the others execute the warrant on the premises of Peter Penisi, the small-time drug dealer who claimed police detectives had stolen four thousand dollars from him in a drug raid more than a year ago. Both uniforms had been granted indemnity from prosecution for their part in the raid, on condition they give evidence against the detectives who did the stealing. But the only person either of the two junior constables ever remembered seeing actually handle the cash was Detective Laurie Morris. They had made no mention whatsoever of seeing Dave Hocking in possession of any of it. So that was good news for Dave. Great news. And now there was some even better news.

'The Special Prosecutor subpoenaed all the bank account records.'

'Whose bank account records?' Dave interrupted.

Page looked taken aback.

'Well…' he faltered. 'All three of you. Laurie Morris, Paul Ballard and you.'

Dave stared back bitterly at his old friend. He couldn't help wondering whether the plan Roger Page had come up with—to send him out west for a couple of weeks—had less to do with keeping the Special Prosecutor investigators out of his hair, than it did with keeping Dave Hocking out of theirs. While he'd been out of town, they had ransacked his personal records, searching for anything they could possibly pin on him. And now, it seemed to Dave, while he was out here and Morris and Ballard were back there, the SPO was hoping to divide and conquer.

Conroy, a big, block-headed youngster with a distinctly superior attitude, took up where Page had left off.

'We turned up cash deposits of two thousand dollars each in Morris and Ballard's accounts, both within days of the Penisi search.'

Page edged forward anxiously over the desk.

'Which means the SPO is willing to accept you didn't take the money, Dave. See? No one's suggesting you pinched a cent of it.'

Dave Hocking couldn't disguise his contempt. Roger Page hadn't ended up where he was sitting right now by accident. He was there for a reason.

He'd been in the loop all along, to assist in the SPO probe, to get his old friend out of the way while they did it, and now to sell whatever it was they were selling.

'But you were there,' Wade chimed in, coldly. He was older than Conroy, and Dave was sure he recognised his face, but he couldn't remember where from. 'You swore out the warrant, and you were the senior officer in charge when it was executed. That means, at very least, you saw exactly what happened.'

Hocking scoffed at the investigator's cock-eyed logic. How did the fact he swore out the warrant mean he saw everything that happened when it was executed? It wouldn't be the first time a crooked copper adeptly avoided a senior officer spotting what he was up to.

'If you're willing to give evidence that both Morris and Ballard were in on the snip, but you took no part in it,' Conroy tag-teamed back in, 'we'll leave it at that. You'll just be a prosecution witness.' When Hocking scoffed again, even more loudly, the young officer was palpably annoyed, but he pushed on regardless. 'If not, we'll have no option but to charge you along with them, let the courts decide who knew what.'

It was a none-too-subtle and decidedly grubby attempt at blackmail, so far as Dave Hocking saw it. The SPO was convinced he was in on it, up to his eyeballs, but they were willing to turn a blind eye, so long as he shopped Morris and Ballard. The two uniformed constables who were there on the day had both identified Laurie Morris as pocketing the cash, but the SPO's case against Ballard was obviously a bit on the thin side. So that's where they figured Dave Hocking would come in, to save his own skin. He'd plug all the gaps for them, in return for a clean bill of health for himself. So, corrupt or not, their star prosecution witness would walk, free as a bird. But the Special Prosecutor didn't know shit about Detective Senior Sergeant Dave Hocking.

'How do you know I wasn't in on the deal?' Dave leaned back in his chair, his hands clasped behind his head, sneering cynically back at the three of them. Everything about this discussion was making his skin crawl. 'My sling might've come under the table. You could be dealing with a criminal mastermind.'

'Look, fuck you, Hocking.' Now Dave remembered where he knew this Wade from. Last time he saw him he was behind a desk, wearing a sweat-stained uniform and pushing a pencil around down at the Toowong Traffic Branch. But now, by the look of disdain in his eyes, it seemed the New

Broom had swept him into the hallowed halls of power. 'The offer's there if you want it. But only for a limited time.'

Hocking flipped his eyebrows curiously.

'You boys sound like you're selling steak knives.'

That was it. The discussion was over. Wade got to his feet and clicked open his briefcase, rummaging around, loading his papers back into it, as Roger Page slid forward in his seat one more time.

'Dave, come on,' he implored, leaning in close to his old friend. 'You know as well as I do, if you go to a joint trial with Morris and Ballard, they'll drag you straight down the shit-chute with them.'

He was right—they both knew it. This was the worst possible time for a cop to be facing a criminal charge, with the smoke of Fitzgerald still lingering, and the ears of every potential juror in Queensland still ringing with the last two years' lurid revelations about crooked coppers caught with their paws in the cookie jar. In this day and age, cops were guilty until proven innocent. But so what? What choice did Dave Hocking have? He sat forward, resigned, and sadly looked his old friend straight in the eye.

'I've worked with Morris and Ballard for ten years or more, Rodge.' They were only inches away from each other now, eyeball-to-eyeball. 'They're mates. Just like you are.' Dave sat silent for a second, then quietly added, 'You want me to start shopping my mates now?'

Roger Page looked away, down at the desktop between them, as Conroy pushed his chair back away from the desk and got to his feet.

'We fly back on Saturday afternoon,' Wade said officiously, still shuffling through his briefcase. 'We want an answer before we go.' When he found what he was looking for, he slapped it down on the desktop. 'Meanwhile, this might help you come to a decision. It's an Official Suspension from all police duties. You're out of the job until further notice.'

•

By the time Dave Hocking had packed up his gear, and was ready to load up the car and check out of his room at the New Jumbuck Inn Motel, it was getting close to eleven o'clock. That was plenty late enough, he figured, to crack his first beer. After all, he was on days off until further notice. Why shouldn't he? His stomach was churning painfully, his brain turning over and over, trying to decipher all that had happened, and all that was yet to come. Thoughts were swirling around disjointedly, going nowhere, making no sense. He swung open the fridge door and reached in for a can, pulled back the ring-top, and guzzled down several mouthfuls. As he slumped back into the armchair, he could feel the first hit of alcohol taking hold, slowing him down, settling his thoughts.

By the time he reached the outskirts of Millengarra, it was after two in the afternoon, and the last of the six-pack of cans was long gone, only the empties now rattling around on the floor. He had raked over everything a hundred times in his head by then, but he still had no idea what would come next, or what he could possibly do. He had tried repeatedly—how many times he couldn't say—to punch the number into his mobile telephone but each time he eventually just hit the disconnect button. It was no use. Even if he managed to somehow get through, what would he say? How could he tell her what had happened, what came next? He had no idea. For now, all he knew was he had to get back to Millen, drop off the police car and pick up his own, and get the hell out of there.

The nausea that had come in waves had mercifully receded now, at least for the moment. The frantic blast of cold air-conditioning had finally cooled the flush of his face, settling his breath and relaxing him. It had been a rough couple of hours. He had been racked by cruel, random thoughts: memories of the day he shot Mark Trindall dead in front of his two little kids, the awful look on their tiny, round faces as he turned to confront them, watching them screaming hysterically, their hands pressed up against their ears, tears streaming down over their cheeks. He had writhed with a throbbing pain in his side, breathless and gagging, his ears ringing and his eyes itching incessantly. But it had passed. He had settled. When he did, he was left with only a sense of fatigue, and remorse, remembering his home, his wife, and his daughter, Jane, years ago, as a little girl, the same age as the Trindall children, happy and safe.

Something about the sight of the BP truck-stop, as it loomed up ahead on the road into Millen, made Dave Hocking's brain instantly latch onto Larnie Mitchell. She was at the centre of all that had happened here, and yet she hardly seemed to rate a mention. She was everywhere but nowhere to be seen in any of it, just a long-lost girl who somehow seemed almost forgotten. The whole Cunnamulla CIB, and half of Brisbane, including the Assistant Commissioner of Police, had been sitting around a country courthouse all week trying to fit up her boyfriend for murdering his mate. The Special Prosecutor had flown two of his fanciest goons and a senior inspector of police all the way out to Bum-Fuck Nowhere to turn over yesterday's man about whether somebody pocketed some druggy's ill-gotten gains. Yet, right in the middle of it all, a vibrant young woman had just faded away, right under everyone's nose, and nobody even seemed to give a square root. Larnie Mitchell had shot through, looking for greener pastures, like all the young sheilas did. That was the way of the west.

It wasn't that simple, not by a long shot. As the truck-stop slipped past into the rear-view mirror, Dave Hocking gritted his teeth. He was thinking about a cache of amphetamines and stolen drug-money stashed away in room number eight at the Empire Hotel, about a grinning publican and his grubby bar manager, a skinny little drug dealer who liked to make threats, and a dodgy grease-monkey with a string of dishonesty convictions. And right in the middle of it all was Larnie Mitchell—better and smarter than all of them—there one day, and mysteriously gone the next.

As he swung right into Castle Street and passed Karen Millard's house on the right, then the Deeds' further down and Tom Wilson's place on the left, heading towards the police house, he knew the truth was still hidden somewhere below the surface. Whatever it was, it wasn't out yet, but it would be. Dave Hocking had unfinished business in Millengarra.

When he got to the station house, he was pleased to see his own car parked out front, and now fitted with a brand-new windscreen. At least Kevin Danes had done something of use. He was relieved, too, when he got into the house, to find Brian Ingles had obviously heard nothing about his suspension from duties. Ingles just inquired if the committal was going okay, which Dave assured him it was, and asked if everything was still on schedule for him to give evidence early next week, which Dave likewise told him it was. When he wanted to know whether Dave was feeling okay, the detective ignored him, told him he had to go book back into his motel room, and strode out the door.

Ten minutes later, when he stepped into the cool, air-conditioned front office of the Starlight Motel, Carol Graham was already standing behind the front counter, a soft, welcoming smile on her face.

'Welcome back,' she said warmly. 'I didn't expect to see you so soon.'

He was surprised how comforting it felt to see her face, hear her voice again.

'I have to check out some things back here, for the hearing.'

She nodded thoughtfully, then slipped the key to room fourteen off the board and placed it down on the counter in front of him.

'How long do you think you'll be back for?'

Dave hesitated. He had no answer to that question. Who knew how long he'd be back? The truth was Dave didn't even know why he was back. What was he looking for? How would he find it? He should be heading home to Brisbane right now, back to his wife, and back to his life. But how could he do that? What was his life now? He wasn't a cop anymore. He didn't know what he was now. The one thing he knew for sure was the SPO had made him an offer his whole future hung on, as well as his past, and he had until Saturday to give them an answer.

'Till about Saturday, I'd say.'

The words came out oddly and awkwardly, a weird quaver tickling his voice. He quickly cleared his throat, trying to regain his composure.

'You okay?'

He hesitated again, embarrassed to realise he wanted to tell her the truth— that no, he wasn't okay. He hardly knew her at all, but he still wanted to tell her he felt like his whole life had just been pulled out from under his feet, that he felt lost, betrayed and alone. He wanted her sympathy, her comfort, perhaps even her help.

'Yeah, fine,' Dave said stiffly, sliding the key from the counter. 'Just a bit tired, that's all. It's been a long drive.'

Pocketing the key, he quickly turned on his heels to leave. But before he got to the door, Carol Graham called after him.

'There was a lawyer in here on the weekend.'

'Yeah?'

'He wanted to know if I heard anything on the night of the murder.'

The detective stood still, silently processing what she had said. She had to be talking about the defence lawyer, Eddie Moran.

'And did you?'

'No. The first I knew anything had happened was when the police arrived, in the early hours.'

She had risen around four in the morning, unable to sleep. Having tiptoed in darkness through to her kitchen, she had looked out through the back window, only to see the dawn was still nowhere in sight, and the calm, moonless night was as black and as silent as any she ever recalled. She knew from bitter experience she had no chance of getting herself back to sleep, so she turned on a lamp in the loungeroom and began pottering around at the kitchen sink, filling the jug for a hot pot of tea, and rummaging around in the cupboard for a cup and saucer. While she was doing that, she noticed the lights of several cars, over the back fence, coming slowly down Castle

Street, followed by what looked like flashing police lights. She heard the cars pulling over onto the gravel in the next street, and then the sound of many men speaking and walking around. It was all coming from the old Killopp place that Tom Wilson had been renting for the past couple of years, so she figured something must have happened there during the night.

A couple of hours later two policemen came to the motel saying there had been an incident over at the Killopp house, that someone had been seriously hurt, but the perpetrator was now in police custody, and they couldn't release any further details as yet. They told Carol Graham they were now just doing the rounds of the neighbouring residences, checking to see if anyone may have seen or heard anything that night. Carol Graham told them the truth, that she had seen nothing, and heard nothing, at all.

'Was that it?'

'Yes. They just thanked me and left.'

Dave Hocking nodded pensively, looking her straight in the eye. There was obviously some reason she mentioned the lawyer, something she wanted to get off her chest.

'Is that what you told the lawyer?'

'Yes,' she said tentatively. Something in her voice told him she had more she needed to say, and he waited silently, until she eventually added, 'He wanted to see my guest register. To see if we had any guests staying that night.'

'And?'

'I told him we had a confidentiality policy.'

'And?'

'Well, that was it. He left. But after he did, I checked back through our records.'

'And?'

'And when I did, I realised we did have someone staying that night. Two men. They checked in late. Around seven the night before.'

'Under what name?'

Carol promptly reached down behind the counter, pulled open a drawer, and lifted out a large register book with both hands. She did it with such efficiency Dave figured she'd put it aside in advance, and when he saw a yellow Post-it note marking one page, he knew he was right.

She flipped it open at the marked page, and spun it around, pointing with one finger to the relevant entry. *John Baker. Brisbane.* Not much to go by.

'Did you get any kind of ID?'

'No. They paid cash in advance.' It wasn't unusual. People spending the night in motel rooms didn't always want to say who they were, or who they were spending the night with. 'But I always take a car registration number. Just in case.'

She reached into the same drawer and pulled out a duplicate cash receipt, made out to Mr J. Baker of 17 Smith Street, Brisbane, then flipped it straight over to show where she had recorded in her scrawled handwriting the registration number of J. Baker's car. It was a pretty nondescript address, and there was something about the whole *John Baker* thing that had 'dodgy' written all over it. Dave slipped a piece of notepaper out of his pocket and copied down the registration details.

'Do you know if the police spoke to these guys?'

Suddenly, Carol looked more troubled than ever.

'No,' she said breathlessly. 'That's the thing, they weren't there when the police came. Even when I first woke up, their car was already gone.'

EIGHTEEN

Dave Hocking called Frank Vagianni that afternoon. Between the rushes of static and the gravelly wall of interference on the phone line, he managed to pass on the rego number, and what little detail Carol Graham had been able to give him about her mysterious overnight guest. J. Baker probably had nothing to do with Tom Wilson's murder, but if Rowdy McQuillan's defence team was trying to work up an alternative theory that some unidentified intruder was in the house that night, they should certainly hear about the elusive Mr Baker. If anyone did break into Tom Wilson's house and did what was done there that night, they'd be anxious to hightail it out of town pronto, so the fact two strangers booked into a room just over the fence from the murder scene, a few hours before it all happened, then checked out again in a rush straight afterwards under the cover of darkness, in the wee, small hours of the morning, made them definite candidates.

In fact, the more Dave thought about it, the more it appealed as a real possibility. But it wasn't his problem. That was the lawyer's job, and maybe even Frank's as well, but it certainly wasn't Dave Hocking's. He had an entirely different mystery to solve.

When he left the Starlight Motel, the first thing Dave did was go grab more beer. He intentionally bypassed the Empire Hotel to do it, stopping in at the Arms on his way past to pick up another cold six-pack, then went straight to the all-purpose store in Connell Street, where he collected the keys to a locker out at the Millengarra Golf Course. Dave needed some time and space to relax, slow down, think everything through, and he couldn't imagine a better way of doing it than over a round of golf.

By the time he had bounced his ball all around the craggy, four-hole course and back to the shed, Dave had well and truly worked up a thirst. The sun was starting to settle, and the anxious flutter in his stomach that had left him alone while he played was now starting to tickle his innards again, ever so slightly, as he sat himself down on the slab seat out front of the shed and cracked open the first frosty can. As he tipped his head back, and felt the cold flood of beer cooling a track to his stomach, he felt his worries gradually subside.

Three beers later, Dave Hocking was still sitting there, feeling numb, all alone in a broad, endless vista, with nothing and no one in sight. He stared blankly out over the orange-tinged desert, as the last long shadows of day gradually stretched towards the faraway town. Suddenly, something intruded, disturbing his daze. A distant cloud of dust, racing across the horizon, just like the last time he sat here, and in front of the dust-cloud, the same VJ Valiant utility—Kevin Daines' VJ Valiant—the same car he saw the last time. He followed its progress, sitting there, completely still, for several long moments, as his brain tried to process what he was watching, and where it was leading him.

The moment it dawned on him, Dave dropped the beer-can and leapt to his feet.

By the time he got to the spot on the lonely stretch of dirt road where the Valiant was parked, half-on and half-off the gravelly verge, the late-afternoon light was fast fading. But he could still make out, well off in the distance, a solitary figure, stooping down, it seemed, doing something, or reaching for something, close to the ground, then standing up straight and still for a moment, as if looking towards the road, and then quickly crouching back down again, this time almost as if on all fours. Dave leaned across, flipped open the glovebox, and pulled out his service revolver. The safety was on, all chambers loaded. He pushed it into the back of his waistband and climbed out of his car. By the time he had got to his feet and swung the door shut behind him, the faraway figure was upright again, and moving.

Dave stepped off the dusty roadway and into the scrubby surrounds, striding purposefully towards the man he was looking for—the grease-monkey, Kevin Daines. As he trudged awkwardly across the uneven ground, he kept his eyes firmly fixed on his target, hundreds of metres away in the darkening distance, moving up and down and rocking from side to side. He was walking, by the look of it, straight back in Dave's direction. The detective instinctively reached back and touched the butt of his handgun, then felt for the safety; it was on. Last time he saw Kevin Daines walking around in these parts he was carrying something that looked a lot like a shovel. If he had something buried out there, he had gone to a whole lot of trouble to make sure it was out of the way, and well-hidden.

When Kevin Daines got within a hundred metres or so, he stopped in his tracks and stood still, shading his eyes with one hand, looking in Dave's direction. The policeman kept walking towards him, quickening his pace with every stride. He had got close enough now to see, in Daines' other hand, the shaft of a long-handled shovel, the metal blade hanging down in the dirt. As soon as he saw it, a dark, sickly sense of horror descended spontaneously upon him, and his heart began thumping hard in his chest. But he kept trudging forward unfalteringly, his teeth tightly clenched together now, each hand closed in a fist. Kevin Daines had buried something, or someone, out there in the dry, sandy soil—some secret he wanted no one to see. But no secret was buried so deep Detective Senior Sergeant Dave Hocking wouldn't get to see it, sooner or later. Larnie was out there—somewhere—and he was going to find her.

As Dave closed quickly on Daines, he had his eyes trained on the shovel. It wasn't an axe, but it would do just fine to chop a man down, and Dave wasn't going to take any chances. The slightest movement by Daines with that shovel, and he was ready to go for his gun. But the young man made no movement at all, just stood there perfectly still, both feet firmly glued to the ground, shading his eyes from the sun and squinting cautiously at the approaching policeman.

'G'day,' he eventually drawled, as the detective came withing earshot.

But Dave didn't stop, or say anything. His face was now flushed with a mixture of anger and anxious foreboding; he heard nothing, saw nothing. Without deviating, he strode blindly up to the young man, snatched at the shovel with one hand and, with the other, swung a wild haymaker that knocked Kevin Daines right off his feet. As he scrambled frantically onto his hands and knees, the policeman descended upon him, snatching a handful of shirt at the back of his collar and wrenching him over backwards, down onto his buttocks. As soon as he hit the ground, Dave was lifting and dragging him by the collar, backwards through the dusty scrub, over the uneven earth, back in the direction from which he had come.

'What are you doing?' the young man whined plaintively. 'Fuck, man, what are you doing to me?'

'Take me to her.'

'What?' His face was now crinkled into a comical grimace, saliva dribbling from his mouth. 'What are you talking about?'

The pathetic sound of his whimpering voice released a new, sudden surge of rage. Dave reached down and grabbed him with both hands, dragging him to his feet.

'Where'd you bury her?'

'Who?'

The grease-monkey's eyes were charged with a mixture of terror and panic, his lips shaping unspoken words, as if he was about to say more. But before he could get a lie out of his mouth, Dave spun him around and pushed him hard, back in the direction he had come from.

'Show me.'

As he stumbled awkwardly through the low tufts of foliage, Daines was snivelling and slurping, glancing intermittently over his shoulder, like a hunted beast staggering piteously on its last weary legs, waiting to be finished off.

'What are you…?'

He didn't manage to finish the question before the detective's heavy, police-issue boot struck his dusty buttocks with a forceful thud, projecting him forward in a stumbling rush.

'Show me.'

The rage in Dave Hocking's voice, and the power in his boot, put an end to all further conversation. Both resistance and reason were useless. Kevin Daines just hung his head forward, trudging on without speaking, his whole body stooped disconsolately, as his captor followed behind him, watchfully, the shovel slung over one shoulder. As their long, dancing shadows floated over the desolate landscape ahead of them, like two lost souls, it all felt eerily familiar to Hocking, a stroll through the Valley of Death. He had taken this walk before, a voyage of dreadful discovery, filled with both horror and anticipation.

They continued that way for a good five minutes or more, following the tracks Daines had left, until they eventually came to the edge of a large, clear section of sandy soil. It was almost devoid of all vegetation, like some sort of ancient, long-dried-up watering hole. The tracks stopped there, two or three metres into the clearing, circling a distinct, rough patch of freshly turned earth. Daines stopped directly in front of it, silent, his head still bowed like a penitent sinner. As Dave stood behind him, looking down at the site, a sad sense of foreboding descended upon him. Somehow, it was always like this. No matter how hard he worked to get to this moment, how much he craved and anticipated it, this moment was always the same.

With one hand he tossed the shovel onto the ground at Daines' feet. With the other, he drew his revolver, and flicked off the safety.

'Dig it up.'

Kevin Daines bent over submissively, picked up the shovel, and got straight to work. Behind him, the detective watched as he turned over sods, one after the other, waiting to see the first signs of a terrible secret revealed. It went on and on, each rhythmic stab of the shovel blade followed by the slap of the next load of sandy gravel, cast aside, as the hole got deeper and deeper. Finally, Daines dropped the shovel beside him and stepped down into the ditch, crouching almost onto all fours, dusting and scraping at something down there, before he reached in, took a hold with both hands, and heaved it out.

He lobbed a large flat tin onto the ground at Dave Hocking's feet, then turned to face him, shielding his eyes from the setting sun as he squinted from under one dusty palm. Hocking said nothing, just stared down intently at the dust-covered tin.

'What's that?'

'That's it. That's the money I stole.'

Daines clawed at the top of the tin and then pulled it open, revealing a series of fat, crinkled wads of dog-eared cash notes, a long-handled torch, and what looked like two empty plastic bags scrunched into balls and fastened with thick rubber bands. Dave was confused. What story was this grease-monkey trying to sell him?

'Stole from where?'

'From Larnie.' Now Daines looked puzzled himself. His mouth hung open quizzically as he slowly removed his hand from his forehead. 'That's what you're looking for, isn't it?'

Dave Hocking felt a sudden flush of rage flood into his face. He bared his teeth like a rabid dog as he raised the gun from his side.

'Where is she?' he growled.

The policeman's obvious intent was not lost on the young man standing in front of him, knee-deep in a make-shift gravesite.

'Who, Larnie?' he gasped desperately. 'She took off, mate. Ages ago.'

Dave Hocking had heard it too many times. He couldn't hear it again. It was no answer to anything. No one just took off to nowhere. They went somewhere; something happened to them. And Dave wanted to know what, and where, and why. He wanted answers. He needed them. He needed to know. Because, whatever else had been taken from him, he wouldn't let them take this away—the chance to find Larnie Mitchell, dead or alive, to put an end to her parents' blind agony, solve their unanswered questions, restore some order into the world. Every mystery was there to be solved, and Dave Hocking just had to solve this one, no matter what happened to him, whatever the consequences. He straightened his arm and lined up the barrel of his revolver to the face of the young man standing in front of him.

'Where is she?' he growled again, this time coldly and cruelly.

Gradually, almost curiously, Kevin Daines seemed to almost physically melt away before Dave's very eyes, disappearing down into the hole he was standing in. His face folded into a trembling, blubbering mask, muddy tears streaming over both his cheeks, snot running into his mouth, and spittle slobbering over his chin, dangling down and swinging in long, daggy strands.

'I don't know,' he was pleading, almost incoherently. 'Please. Please. I don't know.'

He was grunting loud, heavy sobs now, each one seeming to shake his whole body, as his quivering hands rose up in front of his face, and the front of his dusty jeans turned a deep blue colour, his crutch flooded with urine. Dave Hocking found himself looking down the gun-barrel at a terrified, lonely little boy weeping like a newborn baby, cowering and pleading pathetically. As he looked down at this wretched, disquieting sight, the rage drained away, and he wearily closed his eyes. As blackness descended upon him, the two Trindall children appeared there in the darkness, crying hysterically, their little hands clasped tightly over their ears. Their father Mark Trindall was there too, a vacant, empty look in his eyes, no pain and no anger, as if he was looking right through him.

Dave Hocking stuffed the gun back into his waistband and stepped resolutely into the hole. As soon as he planted his feet on the upturned earth, he thumped one open hand into Kevin Daines' chest, knocking him off his feet again, then snatched up the shovel and began stabbing it into the soil all around him, while the young man cowered and whimpered beside him. Each time he drove it into the ground, the blade sliced easily into the sandy soil, sinking deep in the earth, and with each thrust he became more anguished, puffing hard as he scraped, dug and gouged, deeper and deeper. If the body was there, he would find it. It had to be there. It couldn't be much further down. He had to hit something, soon. But the more he jammed the blade up and down, time after time, grunting with painful exertion, the hoarser and more frenzied his breathing became. He went on and on like that for minutes, spearing the shovel into the ground, yanking it back, lifting it up, and driving it back down into the earth.

Eventually, exhausted, he dropped the shovel beside him and collapsed onto his buttocks in the upturned sandpit. As he sat there, sucking deep mouthfuls of oxygen into his lungs and blowing them out in long, raspy breaths, he was looking straight into the piteous, blubbering face of Kevin Daines, still sprawled on his back, just metres away. With each desperate gasp of air, in and out, his breathing gradually began to settle, slowing down, eventually ordering itself, until he finally was able to get the words out.

'Where'd you find it?'

'At the Empire.' His voice was little more than a feeble, trembling whisper. 'I knew that's where she'd have it. '

'How did you know that?'

'I used to work there when I was younger.' As soon as he said it, his eyes filled up with tears again, and his voice reverted into a grating whine. 'There was a hidey hole under the floorboards in the staffroom. We all used to hide our weed in there.'

'What staffroom?'

The young man stopped sobbing instantly and looked back at him, mouth gaping, as if surprised to be asked.

'Room eight.'

•

Dave dropped the tin into the boot of his car, and slammed it shut. It was only a matter of time until word got out about his suspension, so he figured there was no time to waste. He needed to shake the trees as soon as he could, and see what fell out of the branches.

Kevin Daines was potentially in plenty of trouble. By acting as Larnie's driver, he'd been a party to her selling amphetamines, not to mention his theft and possession of the proceeds of drug supply. But he didn't have a clue where Larnie Mitchell was. Dave was certain of that. In those few lonely seconds, staring straight into the end of a barrel, balls-deep in a half-dug hole, miles from anywhere and anyone else, pissing his pants, Kevin Daines would have told whatever Dave wanted to know, if he knew it himself. But he didn't. He didn't have a single clue where she was. To him, Larnie Mitchell had just taken off, shot through, like everyone said, like so many young sheilas did, sooner or later, if they had any sense.

As Dave sat alone in his car on Connell Street, outside the old town hall, idly knotting a tie around his neck as he watched the front door of the Empire Hotel, he was thinking through what he had so far, and what his next move should be. It would be crucial, and he would only get one shot at it, so he had to get it just right.

By the time Brian Ingles pulled up it was getting on for half past six, and the yellow flood light out front of the town hall had already come on. It turned the constable's uniform a sickly colour of green as he stepped out of the police four-wheel drive and sauntered across the street to Dave's car.

'Did you get it?'

'Yeah.'

Ingles held out a three-page search-and-seizure warrant, which the detective took in both hands and quickly digested. It was all there, authorisation to search room eight at the Empire Hotel, 56 Connell Street, Millengarra, for any evidence relating to the suspected offences of possession and supply of a dangerous drug, and to seize all records and articles that may provide proof of the commission of those offences.

But Brian Ingles looked nervous.

'Are you sure about all this?'

Dave Hocking folded the warrant in half and shoved it into his pocket.

'Sure as there's shit in a cat.' He fastened his top button and pulled the necktie into place. 'Come on, let's go.'

When the two policemen walked in through the front door, Bob Proctor was propped on a stool at the public bar, regaling a handful of pot-bellied regulars with some evidently amusing tale, while Jimmy Rawlings was ferrying freshly poured beers from the taps and handing them over the counter. As soon as the personable publican spotted his newest arrivals, he broke off his story and greeted them warmly.

'Hello boys. You're in early. What'll youse have?'

Dave Hocking ignored the question, striding up to the publican like he intended to walk right through him.

'Why didn't you tell me she stayed at the hotel?'

The affable grin faded from Bob Proctor's face.

'What?'

'Larnie Mitchell.' Hocking was standing up close to him now, glowering into his eyes. 'She had a key to room eight of this hotel in her drawer at home.'

An uncomfortable smirk briefly started to tug at the publican's mouth, but then waned. Fumbling for something to say, he cast his eyes quickly around his startled drinking companions, and then over his shoulder at Rawlings, who simply lowered his eyes and stared down at the bar. Suddenly, the publican looked slightly panicked. He turned back to the policeman, sneering at him with a manifest effort at utter affront.

'She was staff,' he said breathlessly. 'If they need a room for the night, I let them stay over for nicks.'

'So how come you never mentioned that before?'

'What?'

'I've been drinking piss with you in this pub for days. How come you've never once mentioned that kid was staying here, at your hotel?'

For the first time Brian Ingles could ever remember, Bob Proctor looked totally flummoxed. The uncomfortable grin had now reappeared, and was fading in and out like a flattening battery as he looked back at Rawlings, who ignored him, and then around at the others, mouthing words that just wouldn't come. Eventually, he turned and faced the detective.

'What do you mean?' he mumbled lamely.

'What do I mean?' Hocking bellowed so loudly it visibly startled the young constable standing beside him. 'What the fuck do you think I mean?' Proctor was now back on his heels, pouting self-righteously, his mealy mouth still working overtime, and still saying nothing at all. 'I want to know what a part-time barmaid was doing with her own key to a room in your hotel.'

For a moment Bob Proctor looked like he might just burst into tears, but he quickly recovered his equilibrium, set his beer-glass down on the bar, and turned to Brian Ingles with a look of deep moral outrage.

'Jesus,' he exclaimed. 'What the fuck is this, Brian?'

Brian Ingles opened his mouth, clearly shocked and unsettled, but before he could get a word out, Hocking was back up in Proctor's face.

'What the fuck is it?' he barked at the publican. 'I'll show you what the fuck it is, Bob.'

He pulled the warrant out of his pocket and waved it around with a flourish.

'This is a Queensland Criminal Code warrant authorising a comprehensive search of this hotel,' he announced, so loudly no one anywhere on the premises could possibly have failed to hear it. 'Police have received reliable information from a confidential source that a young woman by the name of Larnie Mitchell was concealing and trafficking dangerous drugs on these premises.' He paused for effect, and made a point of looking straight at Jimmy Rawlings as he added, 'In collusion with others.' Rawlings held his gaze steadfastly as the detective continued his announcement.

'We have been further informed that a certain party absconded with those drugs and the proceeds of their sale from this hotel, shortly before Miss Mitchell herself disappeared in highly questionable circumstances.' He paused again, glancing disdainfully around the room. 'And, as you're no doubt well aware, she has not been seen or heard of since.'

Hocking took his time to carefully re-fold the warrant, continuing his spiel. 'So, based on that information, I have formed a reasonable suspicion, for the purposes of the provisions of the Queensland Criminal Code, that evidence of the possession and supply of dangerous drugs, and the abduction and murder of Larnie Mitchell...'—the blood visibly drained away from Bob Proctor's face as the word 'murder' fell out of the policeman's mouth—'... is on these premises.'

Dave Hocking carefully stuffed the folded warrant back into his pocket. 'I therefore now intend to search this hotel, in company with Constable Ingles here, and seize any and all evidence we may find relating to the commission of each of those offences.'

Before the publican had the chance to faint from shock, Hocking stepped up closer to him, and jabbed one finger into his face. 'In the meantime, I am directing you...,' he then swivelled suddenly and poked the same accusing finger straight at Rawlings, '...And fuckin' you...' —the craggy-faced bar manager didn't move a millimetre, just stared coldly back, as the detective turned to the rest of the room—'...and everybody else in this fuckin' fleapit, to keep the fuck right out of our way until we're done.'

With that, Dave Hocking turned on his heels and stomped off in the direction of room eight, followed somewhat sheepishly by his uniformed assistant, Constable Brian Ingles. The detective strode down the corridor and out the back door, heading for the accommodation section at the rear of the hotel. By the time Brian reached the top of the stairs, the Senior Sergeant was already inside room eight, on all fours on the floor, carefully feeling all around him for whatever loose board he could find. The constable stepped inside and closed the door behind him.

'There's nothing in that warrant about any murder charge.'

Dave Hocking didn't even turn to face him.

'I didn't say there was.' It looked like he already had hold of something on the floor. 'I just said what I suspected, that's all. I can't help it if they jump to spurious conclusions.' With that, he carefully pulled up a floorboard and peered down into the compartment it concealed.

'Eureka.'

•

On his way back to the police house, Dave Hocking stopped off at the Millengarra Arms Hotel to pick up a bottle of rum. He had a lot of thinking to do, and he figured he was going to need it, if he was going to get any sleep at all that night.

It had been a tough day, and every time his mind drifted off what he was doing, he felt that sick, anxious feeling seeping back into his stomach. With it came thoughts of the SPO's ultimatum, of what he would do, and what he had done, and not done, what he had to be sorry about, ashamed of, what he would say to Denise, and to Bruce and Jude, and to so many others. He thought about Jane, and all his mistakes, and how tired he was of the pain and anguish of life. All he could do was keep going, doing what he did best.

It had been a tough day—a very tough day—but in some ways it had also been a good day. He had learned what happened to Mozzie Blane's missing stash, and he now had a signed-up note-book statement from Kevin Daines that put Bob Proctor right at the scene of the crime. The skinny mechanic was so terrified of what might happen to him, he would give Dave whatever witness statement he wanted against the publican, and between Daines and Jodie Lanham, they could stitch Proctor up as a party to possession and drug supply in a heartbeat. To top it all off, the search of room eight had turned up a secret compartment containing a fine film of residue powder, which they had taken for testing, and Hocking knew it was pounds to peanuts the powder would turn out to be amphetamine.

But that wasn't enough for Dave Hocking, nowhere near enough. According to Jodie Lanham, the night Tom Wilson died he was down at the Empire Hotel, telling anyone who'd listen that Bob Proctor was responsible for what happened to Larnie. It was hard to say precisely what that meant, but Dave was certain of one thing—Bob Proctor had something to do with Larnie's Mitchell's disappearance. That was why the detective had purposefully put the blowtorch on him, by publicly serving the warrant on him in front of a bar full of customers. Now all he had to do was turn up the heat. If the publican was helping Larnie Mitchell peddle speed around Millengarra, there'd be plenty of locals sitting on dirty little secrets, with a whole lot to lose, and any one of them would give up Bob Proctor in two seconds flat if they had to, to save their own skin. Dave just had to find the right one, with the right information.

That was why he threw in mention of Larnie's abduction and murder when he executed the warrant, and why, after the search, he returned to the bar to again publicly announce the police had found traces of suspected amphetamine secreted in room eight and had taken samples for chemical testing. He also told all within earshot he and Ingles had dusted the whole room for fingerprints and lifted a series of latent prints for identification, and he finished with the final clanger, that charges would be laid against multiple individuals in the near future, once the identity of all perpetrators had been positively forensically confirmed.

So the trees had been shaken, well and truly. Now all he had to do was wait to see what fell out. But, in the meantime, he had to get back to the station, bag up the exhibits to be sent through to the Forensic boys back in Cunnamulla, and help Ingles fill out a full crime report. If they were going to crack open the Mitchell case, they had to start getting statements together about the drug dealing, so they could keep the heat on anyone in Millengarra with any skeleton stuffed away in their closet.

Dave was feverishly thinking about his next step as he pushed his way in through the front door of the police house. He expected to find Brian Ingles installed at his desk, behind a typewriter, tapping out an occurrence entry all about the search at the Empire Hotel. But, instead, the young constable was propped up behind the front counter, leaning forward over his elbows, staring pensively at the front door. To Dave, something didn't look right.

'What's up?'

'I've just been on the phone to Cunnamulla, Senior.' He was looking the detective straight in the eye. 'I spoke with Assistant Commissioner Atwood. He told me about you being suspended from duty.'

NINETEEN

The information Dave Hocking had rung through to Frank Vagianni from out west was potentially dynamite. Frank's lawyer, Eddie Moran, was trying to work up an alternative case theory for his cowboy client—that somebody else jumped through his window that night and did the dark deed—and Hocking's information fitted that possible scenario like a well-worn kid glove.

Two men had booked into a motel just over the fence from the crime scene, and had shot through, under cover of darkness, within hours of Tom Wilson's murder. Even better, the name they booked in under had all the hallmarks of being a dodgy. Maybe it wasn't, but there was one sure-fire way to find out. The motelier took down their rego number, so a quick, easy search of the Main Roads Department records would tell Frank precisely who owned that car, and where they lived.

This was a real opportunity; Frank could smell it. After all, he knew well enough his days in the Police Force were numbered. Even if Moran did beat the corruption charge for him, as Frank knew he would, the way things were moving up-town, Headquarters would kill him off sooner or later, whack him back in uniform, behind a desk somewhere pushing a pen, and then wear him down slowly with internal disciplinary blues, until it finally all got too hard. Frank wasn't going to give them the satisfaction. He'd go out up-front, on stress leave, then jag a discharge as medically unfit, and pick up his pension. And that's where Eddie Moran would come in. With Frank's experience as a copper, he figured he could set himself up, in no time flat, as a highly paid private investigator, making squillions out of doing the gumshoe work for insurers and big-charging lawyers. Like Eddie. All he had to do was show Moran how useful he could be to his clients, and this was the perfect opportunity to do it. A simple search of the MRD records, and Frank could serve up to Eddie the name and last-known address of his alternative culprit.

But when he got the search results back, Frank almost fell off his chair.

Shane Gillard was the older brother of a dangerous little bastard called Gary Gillard, AKA Garry Gone, a Sydney triggerman charged but acquitted of a string of underworld murders in the late seventies. Gary did a heap of time in Long Bay for a big drug importation in the early eighties, but eventually got himself out, and then promptly got himself killed in a back-street shoot-out in Bankstown. His big brother Shane was a whole lot smarter than his younger sibling—which was not saying much—and had got out early, moving to Queensland while Gary was still running amok in the old neighbourhood. Shane had set himself up on the Gold Coast, wearing white shoes and floral shirts, selling dodgy used cars initially, and trading off his little brother's lunacy to pass himself off as some sort of tough-guy. He walked and talked like a Saturday-afternoon gangster, all suntan and pearly-white teeth, impressing the hell out of all the sharpies, shifties and shonks that hung out in the back-bars of Surfers Paradise. But the truth was Shane was no hard man. He was just a big, boofhead blowhard who couldn't knock the skin off a cold rice pudding, even if his life depended on it. He was no killer. But he certainly knew one or two.

According to the MRD records, the car that scarpered from that Millengarra motel in the wee small hours after Tom Wilson's murder was registered to a Gold Coast-based business called Cash-Saver Car Rentals. Frank didn't need to check any Companies Office records to know Cash-Savers was the low-brow car rental joint Shane Gillard owned and ran on the highway at Broadbeach. For the past few years he'd been advertising everywhere, pushing out Cash-Savers' rust-bucket rentals to no-budget customers at all-time-low, bargain prices. One of those clients, it seemed, was the mysterious Mr J. Baker.

As Frank pulled off the highway onto the driveway of Cash-Saver Car Rentals, he could already see Shane Gillard and his entourage sitting around in the site shed, sucking on stubbies of beer. When Gillard first clocked him, he stiffened momentarily—no doubt a reflex reaction from years of Frank fronting him—but then he quickly relaxed and eased back comfortably into his chair. By the time Frank stepped up the front stairs into the shed, the big bodgie car-rental guy was sprawled out luxuriously, a broad, greasy grin splashed all over his face.

'G'day, Mr Vagianni,' he drawled, with obvious delight. 'Or is it just plain Frank these days?'

Gillard was casting around to his circle of sycophants, who could barely suppress their hilarity. They looked like a bunch of bushflies surrounding a plump pile of cow-shit. If Frank had a big enough swatter he could have cleaned up the lot with one swipe, but he just had to cop it. His corruption charge and suspension from duty had been on the front page of every two-bit news-rag in Queensland, so he had to expect fleas like Gillard, and his pack of laughing hyenas, would be lapping it up all the way.

'So, you learned how to read, huh Shane? When did that happen?'

'Fuck you, man.' Gillard put down his beer and did his best to give Frank the evil eye. 'You're not a cop anymore.' Frank said nothing, just stared straight back at him, with a wry, lethal smirk meant to remind Shane Gillard exactly who and what Frank Vagianni was, and what they both knew Shane was too. It did the trick. Gillard's tough-guy routine quickly melted away. 'So what do you want?'

'I'm looking for someone I think you might know.'

'Yeah? Like who?'

'John Baker.'

'Never heard of him.'

Frank stepped up close to him, planted one hairy paw on the desktop, and leaned well into the rental man's personal space.

'Well, he was getting around in your car.' He slapped a dog-eared copy of the MRD search down in front of him and pinned it with one stubby finger. ''76 Commodore. Registered to Cash-Saver Car Rentals.'

As Shane looked down at the document, and read the particulars on it, the suntan on his chubby face seemed to dial down two or three notches. If Frank was reading things right, something about this car made him decidedly nervous. Gillard slipped the paper out from under Frank's finger and took a closer inspection of it. After several silent seconds, he turned to his rat-faced employees, and motioned them all to leave.

As soon as they had cleared the office, Gillard folded the page and offered it back to Frank.

'That car was stolen from us, more than a year ago.'

'By who?'

'Don't know. Turned out to be a false name.'

'What ID did they give?'

Gillard's eye twitched, just a fraction.

'I don't think we got any.'

'Bullshit,' Frank barked straight back at him. No one—not even a big, dopey shonk like Shane Gillard—let out a renter without some ID. As he hovered over the desk, Gillard looked up at him, like he was mortally offended.

'What do you mean, bullshit?' He flustered for half a second, then switched to a different tack. 'What's this got to do with you anyway?'

Frank was scowling angrily at him now, leaning in accusingly.

'Did you report it stolen?'

'No.'

'Why not?'

'Wasn't worth the trouble. They found it out back of Toowoomba somewhere, completely burnt out. We just sold it for scrap.'

'Did you claim on insurance?'

Gillard looked like a rat in a trap. But Frank already had his answer; he could see in the big, dumb slob's face, he hadn't claimed the insurance.

'What the fuck?' Gillard pushed his chair back away from the desk, as if he was thinking of going somewhere. 'I don't have to answer your questions. You're not a cop anymore.'

'Maybe not,' Frank growled at him. 'But I've still got plenty of mates that are. And, trust me, they're going to get real excited when I tell them one of your cars was involved in a murder.'

'A murder?' The big man suddenly looked on the verge of tears. 'Leave me alone. Fuckin' murder? I don't know nothing about no murder.'

Maybe he didn't, but he sure did know something. Frank could see it all over his face. Something about that car had Shane Gillard spooked, big-time. It was time to turn up the heat.

'Listen to me, you fat, useless fuck,' he snapped at him angrily. 'A killer calling himself John Baker booked into a country motel in that car—a car you own—then went straight next door and beat some poor bastard to death with a baseball bat. Now you either tell me—right now—whatever you know about who this clown is, and exactly where, how and why you gave him your car, or I'm going to assume you were in on the hit. And if that's where we end up, buddy, sometime in the next hour or so, you're going find yourself with so many coppers so far up your fat clacker, you'll be able to dead-set smell their fuckin' aftershave, I promise you.'

'Fuck.' Shane Gillard wasn't built for this kind of drama, not like his little brother, the lunatic hitman. He slumped forward over his knees, defeated, and buried his head in his hands. 'I knew this shit would come back to bite me.'

'What shit?'

Gillard just sat there, silent, for several seconds, his carefully coiffured locks hanging down over his hands. Then, eventually, he sucked in a deep breath, blew it back out, and began mumbling woefully down at the floor.

'I never even met the bloke. One of the casuals I had on at the time done the deal. It was just a straight-forward three-day rental.' Suddenly, he sat up and swept his hair back off his forehead, looking straight at Frank, his chin trembling and eyebrows arched plaintively. 'Except the car never come back in.' He paused again, and slowly shook his big head. 'Next thing I had two bikers come in to see me, said they were old mates of me brother. They slung me five Gs in folders and told me to forget all about the car. So I did.'

He looked such a quivering mess, Frank couldn't help thinking Gillard might just be telling the truth.

'Had you seen either of these bikers before?'

'I don't think so.' He dropped his head down into his hands again, and dragged his fingers back through his long, flowing hair. 'I assumed they'd done a drug run in it or something.' Then he looked back up again, staring Frank straight in the eye with what looked like deadly earnest. 'But, dead set, I never knew nothing about any murder.'

It was probably true. Shane Gillard was a big fat obnoxious knob, who'd be in any sort of dodgy deal for a dollar, but he was no murderer, not like his little brother.

'Okay. So what about the paperwork?'

'What date was it?'

Frank wasn't surprised Gillard hadn't disposed of the paperwork. Dumb as he was, he was a certified genius compared to the kind of bone-brain bikie who went around covering tracks for a killer. Shane would have worked out quick-smart if that car had been in some sort of hanky-panky, as clearly it had, and somebody traced it back to him, that rental contract could be his only get-out-of-gaol card.

He raked through the bottom drawer of his filing cabinet and pulled out a rental contract with a photocopied driver licence paper-clipped to it. It was one of the old style, with no photograph. He studied it for a couple of seconds before Frank snatched it out of his hands.

For the second time in that very same day, Frank Vagianni nearly fell off his chair.

'Holy shit!'

•

Dave Hocking had had a rough night. All of his demons had come to disturb his fitful sleep, but finally, in the lonely, pre-dawn hours, he found himself lying awake, agonising over the ultimatum he had been served, and how he should answer it. He wouldn't have to give the Special Prosecutors Office much, he was sure of that. They had nothing on him, and they knew it. Dave Hocking had never snipped a zack in his life, and the suggestion he was somehow guilty, just because he was there, and in charge, when someone else did, was total rubbish. There was no way they could pin it on him. Surely they must know that.

Then again, in this day and age, every copper was guilty until proven innocent. No matter how skinny the case against him might be, who knew what a jury might do in such uncertain times? And regardless, even if he was charged, the slur would kill his career. He would be immediately suspended from service and forced to sit on the sidelines for a year or more while the whole ugly circus dragged through the courts. His face would be plastered all over the press as a corrupt senior sergeant of police who pocketed some grubby little druggy's filthy lucre. Even when he was ultimately acquitted, his days in the Force would be numbered. These days, just about every cop whose service dated back pre-Fitzgerald was under a cloud of suspicion. The new Commissioner was looking to clear the decks and start again with a nice clean slate. The last thing he needed was any suspect old skeletons rattling around in the closet.

But still, the SPO must know they had nothing. Surely, they would take whatever Dave was offering. One solitary line in a statement, a few paltry words, saying he saw Laurie Morris with cash in Peter Penisi's grotty dive of a flat in Kangaroo Point when they raided it, all those years ago. Even that would be enough to stitch up a deal with the SPO, enough to make all the agony go away for Dave, enough to ensure his liberty and salvage his career.

It was true, the day they raided the Penisi joint, Dave did see Laurie Morris take something out of one of the drawers, something that looked a lot like a big wad of cash. But he never saw or heard anything further about it that day. He wasn't even sure it was cash, but he believed it was at the time. He knew it was. He said nothing about it, never asked where it went to, or why, or how much it was. And Laurie Morris said nothing to him either, and Dave knew why he didn't.

Dave Hocking had been on the Force for most of his life. He'd bent plenty of rules along the way, just like the rest of them, told a few fibs here and there when he had to, to get the job done, and taken his fair share of perks. But that was it. Dave Hocking had never stolen a dollar in his life. It just wasn't his go.

Morris and Ballard knew that, just like everyone else in the job. That was why Laurie Morris never said anything to him that day, never offered him a snip, never asked the question, because he already knew the answer. And Dave said nothing either, because what Laurie Morris did was Laurie Morris's business.

Dave Hocking could tell the Special Prosecutor all that—that the others might have lifted something, but he didn't—and if he did, he would be out of the woods. He would be a prosecution witness, not a defendant. Instead of sitting in the dock, he would be in the witness box, giving evidence against his fellow coppers, blokes he had worked with, shoulder to shoulder, for years. How could he possibly do that? Who would Dave Hocking be then?

He dragged himself out of his bed that morning just after dawn, and got out of the motel as early as possible. He had too much on his mind to risk any chance of running into Carol Graham, or anybody else. The thought of conversation with anyone was all but unbearable, at least until he had thought it all through, start to finish, found some solution. So he got into his car and went for a drive.

He spent the next couple of hours, before the relative cool of the early morning eventually faded, running a one-man emu parade all around the spot where Kevin Daines had buried the tin, covering a roughly two hundred square metre circumference. He wasn't sure why he was doing it, or what he was looking for. He didn't expect to find anything else out there. But who knew? He just needed to walk, back and forth, and think. And he did. And eventually, as he did, he found it helped. He gradually began to order his frenetic thoughts, work out what his next step was.

He couldn't solve all his problems, not yet. But there was one thing he could do. To solve the mystery of Larnie Mitchell, he had to keep the pressure on anyone who had anything to do with Mozzie Blane's stash of speed under the floorboards of the Empire Hotel. And that meant keeping every one of them sweating bullets over what the fingerprint and forensic tests of room eight would turn up. To make sure they did, he spent most of the morning down at the police house, trying to talk some starch into Brian Ingles.

The young constable had developed a bad case of the jitters when he found out his Senior Sergeant was actually suspended from duty at the time they executed the search warrant on the Empire Hotel, and he was now agonising over whether he should immediately return all items seized in the search. Even after Dave showed him the Commissioner's suspension notice, and firmly made the point he had already signed on for his shift—and was therefore technically on duty—at the time it was served, and given the notice referred to suspension from all *further* duty, it didn't come into effect until his current shift had ended, Ingles looked less than convinced. So Dave followed up by reminding Ingles he had sought and obtained the warrant himself, it was directed to him as the authorised officer, and he executed it as the duly authorised officer, so it didn't matter a stuff who had assisted him. Even if someone wanted to argue Dave Hocking was not, strictly speaking, an operational police officer at the time, that didn't invalidate the warrant itself, or the subsequent search.

After a long time arguing the toss, it eventually began to sound almost arguably correct, even to Dave, and ultimately Ingles agreed to let it all ride, on the strict proviso they write up a full report of the incident in the station occurrence sheets, and Dave sign a written statement acknowledging his receipt of the notice earlier that day, his understanding of when it came into effect, the fact he didn't notify Ingles of the notice, and why. As much as it stuck in Dave's craw agreeing to dance to the tune of a half-baked, jumped-up junior constable, he needed an extra forty-eight hours or so to keep the pressure on Proctor *et al* at the Empire Hotel, so if that was what it was going to take, so be it.

As it turned out, it didn't take anywhere near that long.

When Dave Hocking pulled his car into the driveway of the Starlight Motel that afternoon, having written up all of Ingles' reports and signed up his statement, the first thing he saw was the long, scruffy figure of Jimmy Rawlings, perched on a plastic chair outside his door. He couldn't help but smile to himself. Rawlings was still on parole from an old prison term he'd all but put in the past. But they both knew if he got charged with as much as whistling in the pictures, Jimmy would go straight back inside, parole revoked. *Do not pass GO, and do not collect two hundred dollars.* When he was spruiking that warrant down at the Empire Hotel, Dave didn't doubt for a second his promise that charges would be laid 'against multiple individuals' in the near future would spook Jimmy Rawlings right out of his brain. So he wasn't in the least bit surprised to see the ex-con now on his doorstep.

'Shouldn't you be working?' the detective asked as he climbed out of his car. Rawlings rose to his feet respectfully.

'I was hoping I might have a yarn with you.'

'Well you can't.' Dave Hocking wasn't going to make it easy for a grub like Jim Rawlings. 'If you want to speak to me, you make an appointment down at the station.'

'I was hoping we could keep it a bit confidential.'

This was it; the games were about to begin. Hocking looked him up and down, as though he wasn't expecting his visit, then grunted at him, and pointed down at the plastic chair.

'Alright, sit there,' he said. 'I'll be out in a minute.' He walked to his door, put his key in the lock, and then added, as an afterthought, over his shoulder. 'And behave yourself.'

He tinkered around in his room for a minute or two, while Rawlings waited outside. It wouldn't do any harm for Rawlings to think Dave Hocking was in no hurry, that he was confident he already had plenty on him and was in no need of any extra information. So Dave was content to leave him sitting outside alone, wondering what the police had found out, what they suspected him of, what trouble he might be in, and how much he might have at stake. Eventually, after a respectable period had passed, Dave casually sauntered outside, pulled the door shut behind him, and sat down opposite his fidgety visitor.

Rawlings wasted no time in putting his case.

'I wasn't selling no drugs, Mr Hocking.'

'That's not what it looks like to me, Jimmy.'

'Mozzie and Larnie were selling it.'

'You think I don't know that already?' Hocking waited a moment, looking Rawlings straight in the eye, and then added, 'But they weren't on their own, were they.'

'They were giving Proctor a sling on the side.'

Hocking scoffed impatiently, shifting around in his seat, and shaking his head.

'I know that too, Jimmy. For fuck's sake, tell me something I don't know.' Now he settled, sitting forward on his chair, both elbows perched on his knees, staring intently into the barman's eyes. 'Where is she, Jimmy? What happened to Larnie Mitchell?'

'I never had nothing to do with that girl's disappearance. I swear.'

'So where is she then?' Hocking held his gaze, unflinching. 'You can either be all in or all out, Jimmy. It's up to you.'

Rawlings blinked uncomfortably, and looked down at his hands, fumbling idly with his fingers.

'I don't know what happened to her, Mr Hocking,' he mumbled. 'Honest, I don't.' He had something more on his mind, and Hocking waited silently for him to come up with it. Eventually, he looked back up at the policeman. 'But I might know someone who does.'

•

Three hours later, Dave Hocking was sitting in his car, within sight of the modest, weatherboard home of Darren Martin, the personable young owner-operator of the only trucking company in Millengarra, Martin's Transport. It was set back on a good half-acre block, surrounded by trucks, trailers and car bodies. Even from a distance Dave could see the young proprietor's wife inside, busying herself, chasing after kids and cooking up the evening meal. Her husband wasn't home as yet, but he soon would be. As usual, he had been drinking after work down at the Empire. But if Jimmy Rawlings' information was worth counting on, Darren Martin was due home any minute.

Dave was angry. He'd been lied to by so many people in this town, he was just about ready to give someone a good slap in the chops. The first time he met Darren Martin was when he and Ingles dropped into his office to inquire about any hitchhikers his drivers might have given a lift, east to Cunnamulla and/or points beyond, and the young business-owner had a made a big deal of directing his office girl to ensure the two policemen got full access to all the logs and any information they might need. He was so friendly and helpful, in fact, Dave was more than pleased to meet up with him socially the next day, in the company of Bob Proctor, down at the Empire. He even shared a few beers with him, Good Old Bob, and their yokel mates. They all had a good laugh and a yarn together, talking up a storm, shooting the shit about all the local gossip. The subject of *that missing sheila* had even come up, briefly, as Dave recalled it now. And yet never once did any one of them ever mention the fact Larnie Mitchell had her own room at the Empire, much less that she was peddling dope from the hotel, or that she was a sometimes drinking pal of Darren Martin.

As Martin climbed down from his truck to close the metal yard gates, Dave Hocking pulled in close behind him, and stepped out of his car.

'Dave, how're you going, mate?' Martin looked less than overjoyed to see him. 'What are you doing here?'

'I want to talk to you.'

'Yeah?' The corners of his mouth curled down into an odd, uneasy frown. 'Why's that?'

The detective stepped closer, so he could see the trucker's face in the failing light.

'I was talking to Jim Rawlings today.' There was no reaction. 'He told me about the night Larnie Mitchell went missing.'

Darren Martin said nothing for a full three seconds as he stared into the policeman's eyes, the frown gradually melting down into an almost scowl.

'Yeah?' he said eventually, then fell silent again, for several more seconds, before he finally added, 'So what's Jimmy reckon?'

'He says she was drinking in the pub with you that night.'

Martin shrugged disdainfully.

'So what?'

'Says she was trying to bum a ride on one of your trucks down to Brisbane.'

'Was she?' He shrugged again, feigning indifference. 'Maybe. I can't remember.'

His casual dismissal sent a new wave of irritation into the detective's face. Darren Martin obviously thought he was way too smart for any dopey cop. Hocking ground his back teeth, barely suppressing a rising temptation to blow his stack.

'Really? You can't remember?' He was standing up close to the younger man now, sneering into his face. 'That's strange, because Jimmy Rawlings reckons you were all over her that night, plying her full of piss, trying to chat her up.'

Darren Martin's lips stretched into a thin, contemptuous smirk.

'It's not a crime to crack onto a bit of stray stuff, is it Dave?'

Hocking stared scornfully into Martin's eyes, waiting for an incendiary wave of bitter fury to slowly subside.

'He says you left with her that night.'

The trucker held his gaze, that same insolent grin mocking and defying him, as he arched his eyebrows quizzically.

'That's what Jimmy Rawlings reckons, is it?' He shook his head, and blew out a long, disinterested sigh. 'Well, I've been working all day, Dave. It's time I was home. I'll talk to you tomorrow.'

With that, he stepped around the policeman, and did his best to walk away. But he didn't get far. Hocking snatched at his shirt-front with both hands, and wrenched him off balance, swinging him wildly around in a semi-circle, until his back slammed hard against the side of his truck.

'You'll fucking talk to me right now, you little shit.'

In that instant, Dave Hocking was completely unhinged and unshackled. His eyes were burning, his teeth grinding, with a blind, pent-up fury, fuelled by the agony, fear and frustration of the past three years. An uncontrollable rage had exploded inside him, and in that moment, he couldn't see anything, hear anything, think anything. All he knew was that, in his fierce, desperate grasp, he had hold of a liar, a cheat and a killer, a cop-hater, everything and everyone he detested and who despised him, everyone that had defied and defeated him, all that had damaged and destroyed his life.

Martin clawed at his attacker's hands, hopelessly struggling to pry himself free, then began swinging wildly with one fist, smacking hard on the policeman's temple and jaw with a series of sickeningly audible thuds. But Hocking held on, enraged and out of control, now violently wrenching him forward, then pile-driving him back into the side of the truck, where his head snapped back heavily each time with a loud, metallic *dong*, and a breathless grunt of pain and exhaustion. Somewhere behind them, all but obscured in the darkness, a woman was hovering now, hysterical, bouncing about, screaming at Hocking to stop, while Martin was calling back desperately to her, demanding she go and get help.

Eventually the two men, entwined together, tumbled onto the ground, where they rolled and wrestled around for a long time, clutching, clawing and grappling their way back and forth, all over the dusty driveway. By the time the police car eventually pulled in through the front gate, Dave Hocking was back on his feet, puffing and staggering around precariously as he swung wobbly, unwieldy kicks at the man on the ground in front of him.

As soon as Constable Brian Ingles spotted him, he sounded the siren and flicked up the high beam onto the two dishevelled combatants at the end of the driveway. Stunned by the flood of light, Dave Hocking straightened up and stumbled a few steps backwards, turning to face the police car and squinting against the glare, as Martin dragged himself gingerly onto all fours.

'Shit,' Brian Ingles mumbled to himself, disconsolately.

By the time he got Martin into the house, helped his distraught wife clean him up a little, and called for the ambulance, Brian could see a couple of concerned local residents had already drifted in through the front gate, and were gathering dangerously close to where Hocking was now casually leaning against his car, dusting himself down and wiping the blood off his hands and face. The constable went straight to the new arrivals, assuring them their help was not needed, that there had just been a bit of a dust-up—nothing serious—which was all over now, with no real harm done. They looked less than convinced when the ambulance promptly appeared, but Brian assured them it was all just precautionary, thanked them for their concern, and suggested they all head home. As the ambulance pulled up to the house, he ambled over to Dave Hocking's car.

'He's talking about pressing charges,' he said to the senior sergeant. As the words came out, Brian felt a sad, hollow ache in his chest. Hocking was already suspended, and under investigation for corruption. There was also a big question mark hanging over his search of the Empire Hotel. Now, a criminal charge of assault would be downright disastrous for him. But what choice did Brian Ingles have? 'I'll have to get a statement from you.'

'Not tonight you won't.' Hocking did one last wipe of his face, then tossed the bloodied rag into the boot of his car. 'I'll come down the station first thing tomorrow.'

Brian Ingles was okay with that. There was no rush; Dave Hocking wasn't about to abscond. He watched on sadly as the senior detective slammed the boot shut, then walked to his driver's side door.

'You alright, Senior?'

Hocking stopped and stared at him silently for several seconds.

'Couldn't be better,' he said eventually.

And with that he turned, climbed into his car, kicked over the engine, and motored off down the driveway.

•

The first thing he did, once he had showered and changed, was pour himself a stiff rum. It had been quite a while since Dave Hocking had been in such a physical stoush, and the rush of adrenalin had left his hands trembling like a leaf in a stiff summer breeze. He felt slightly nauseous, and the dull, painful ache had returned to his side, throbbing rhythmically. As he put the glass to his lips, it rattled gently on his bottom row of teeth while the first few mouthfuls went down. He slumped into a chair, exhaled slowly, and tried to relax.

Like so many others in Millengarra, Darren Martin was hiding the truth. Dave was sure of it. Whatever happened that night after Larnie Mitchell and he left the Empire together, he wasn't telling anyone about it, least of all the police. He was just like all the others, half-smart, convinced he could stay one step ahead of the pack, keep his mouth shut, and bury his sins where no one could see them. But he was wrong. He couldn't escape Dave Hocking. Dave knew what Darren Martin was hiding, what he had done to that girl. And before he left Millengarra, he was going to prove it.

He swallowed down one more mouthful of rum. As he closed his eyes, he saw see two happy, black-and-white faces, posing together in a pokey little photo booth, pouting and giggling playfully. Then suddenly, and unexpectedly, he saw Jane too—young, vital, alive. He quickly opened his eyes, poured in another deep swallow, and tried hard not to remember.

There was a brusque, urgent knock on the door of his room. He had left it slightly ajar, unwittingly, and now it drifted gradually open under the force of the knock. As it did, Carol Graham was slowly revealed in the doorway, resplendent in her slippers and dressing gown, looking stressed and indignant. Dave had a fair idea what was rustling her feathers. He raised his glass in a mock toast to her.

'And to what do I owe this rare honour?'

'I heard what you did down at the Martins' tonight.'

The thought of the after-hours bush gossip line running red-hot, telling everyone in Hicktown everything and absolutely nothing about what had happened between him and Darren Martin that night, made Dave spontaneously set his jaw angrily.

'I'm not surprised,' he seethed, as he climbed out of the chair and walked to the door. 'News travels fast in this shit-hole.'

Carol Graham looked deeply offended.

'What are you still doing here? What in God's name do you want from this town?'

He took hold of the door with one hand, tempted to slam it shut in her face. But he didn't. Instead, he snarled cruelly back at her, as tears of pure rage welled up in his eyes.

'What do I want from this town?' he growled angrily. 'I'll tell you what I want.' He moved his face closer to hers. 'I want to know why every bastard in the joint knew exactly who I was and what I was doing, five minutes after I got here. And yet Larnie Mitchell, who's lived here her whole bloody life, disappears into thin air one night, and no one's got the first fucking clue where the hell she got to. And no one gives a flying fuck, either.' He stopped momentarily to throw back a mouthful of rum as his landlady glared back at him, shocked and disturbed. 'I want to know what the fuck's going on in this shithole. I want to know what this town's hiding.'

They were face to face now, angrily confronting each other. The startled look in Carol Graham's face had hardened into an indignant, exasperated scowl, as a mounting flood of emotion suddenly and spontaneously spilled out.

'This town's not responsible for your daughter.'

His teeth were clenched tightly again, his hand gripped vice-like onto the doorhandle, as they eyeballed each other contemptuously for several seconds. When his fury eventually subsided, he spoke again, his voice quieter now, but still laced with a lethal disdain.

'The other day you asked me what happened to my daughter. You want to know the truth?' He stared at her, coldly and silently, for several seconds. 'I turfed her out. Told her to fuck off and never come back.' The odium in his eyes quickly passed, fading away to a blank kind of sadness. 'And she didn't,' he said, and then added, 'Ever.' He stared absently into the void for a moment, and then looked back into her eyes. 'So every day for the past three years I wake up wondering. Nobody deserves that.' He put the glass back to his mouth and poured in another swig. Then he gulped it down, his lip curling churlishly. 'You want to know what I'm still doing here? I'll tell you. I'm going to find that kid. I'm going to find Larnie Mitchell. Even if she's just in a hole in the ground somewhere, or down someone's bloody incinerator. I'm bringing her home, simple as that. And I don't care if I've got to kick every arse in this pissant bloody town of yours to do it.'

Against her better judgement, Carol Graham almost felt sorry for him; he was so full of rage and resentment he was like a wounded animal lashing out at anyone who tried to come near him.

'Your guilt is not this town's problem, it's your problem.'

'Yeah?' the policeman spat back at her bitterly. 'Well, fuck you too, lady.' He barked it so loudly into her face, she was physically startled. 'What about your problems? Why the fuck are you still here? Locked up in this fucking haunted house of yours, just you and your dead bloody husband?'

In a sudden burst of unbearable outrage, Carol swung one open hand at him, collecting him with her full force, flush on the cheek. But Hocking hardly flinched, he just kept going, bellowing his invective into her face.

'Cleaning rooms for customers that never come. What the fuck's that all about? My problem? Are you kidding me? What about your problems, lady?

What the fuck are you still doing here? What the fuck are you hiding from out here?'

She swung at him again, and again, and again, her vision now obscured by her rage and resentment, and the bitter, salty tears that had filled up her eyes and now ran in free-flowing rivulets down over her cheeks, as she sobbed and gasped pathetically for breath. She wanted him to stop, stop saying things she feared and was ashamed of, things she regretted and resented and couldn't bear to hear out aloud. And each time she struck him—on his face, his arms and his hands—she grunted painfully and breathlessly, desperately needing to strike out again, needing him to stop, needing to silence and erase all he was saying about her, and her life.

He was holding both his palms up now, surrendering to her attack, deflecting her blows, grasping tentatively at her flailing hands, eventually grabbing her arms, taking hold of them, gently restraining them, settling them. As they stood there, grappling in the doorway, her arms began weakening and folding as her rage gradually started to wane, and then drained slowly away, until she eventually collapsed in against him, sobbing fitfully, physically and emotionally exhausted.

Dave Hocking held her loosely in both arms, feeling sad and ashamed, as her shuddering sobs slowed and lessened, bit by bit, until they eventually faded and disappeared into a deep, slow, comfortable breath. He had been unfair and hurtful to her, for no reason but his own self-indulgent misery, and he regretted his cruelty. He held her, unmoving, trying to comfort her, hoping for her forgiveness. As they stood welded together, both breathing in synch, he felt her palms slide gently onto his back, drawing him closer to her, holding him tightly.

And there they remained, two strangers entwined in the open doorway of a deserted motel in the middle of nowhere, clinging desperately to each other like a couple of stranded castaways, seeking solace and warmth in a cold, wintery wilderness.

•

Brian Ingles had one last job to do before he left the Martin property that night. The ambulance officers had taken Darren Martin in for a couple of stitches, so his wife Rhonda was busily getting the kids fed and ready to come back into town with her, sometime in the next hour or so, when the ambos assured her Darren would be all cleaned up, stitched up, and ready to be picked up and taken back home. So, Brian had agreed to lock up the truck, which was still where Darren had left it out in the yard, just inside the gates, and then drop the keys back to his wife at the house.

It had taken a while to settle both of the Martins down, and Brian could understand why. According to Darren, Dave Hocking had just showed up, out of the blue, demanding to speak to him about something he seemed to think had happened down at the Empire Hotel, which Darren knew nothing about. When he told him he'd had a long day and would come down to the station tomorrow and answer whatever questions he had, Hocking went berserk and just started swinging. It sounded like pretty bizarre behaviour, but from what Brian had seen of him in the past few days, Hocking certainly wasn't in a good place. Brian didn't put the breathalyser on him that night, but he wouldn't have been a bit surprised if the senior sergeant had had a few drinks, and he certainly had a bee in his bonnet about the Empire. It was clear, too, he had unloaded plenty on Martin, who was left with a bad cut over one eye that, according to the ambos, would need a couple of stitches at least.

So, naturally, the Martins were all fired up, and they both wanted Hocking charged there and then. But, as Brian explained at length to them, the priority right now was to get Darren's injuries seen to, and make sure everyone was safe and sound for the night. He would come back to the house tomorrow and take a full statement from them, and then take the matter from there.

The truth was Brian hoped once he'd spoken to Hocking and got a version from him, and a bit of time had passed, maybe the heat might come out of the whole affair, and Darren Martin might not be so all-fired-up about laying a criminal complaint. In Brian's experience, things often tended to go that way out here in the bush when it came to one-on-one punch-ups. Once the dust had settled, and everyone took a deep breath and went back to their respective corners, often no one was all that interested in replaying the drama in court.

So, Brian hoped it might go that way. But he wasn't too confident it would, going by the initial reaction of Rhonda Martin in particular. Wives generally didn't think too kindly of anyone coming to their home and beating up hubby in front of the kids. Who could blame her for that?

Brian pulled the driver's door open and climbed up into the truck, then clicked on his torch and quickly located the keys, where expected, still in place in the ignition switch. As he jiggled the lock and wrestled the keys free, he was thinking about what would happen if Darren Martin insisted on pushing ahead with a criminal complaint. He would have to lay a charge—there was no way around it—and given the injury to Martin's eye, the charge had to be assault occasioning bodily harm. That meant the matter would probably go on indictment before a judge and jury, and would take an age to resolve. He could speak with Hocking about whether he would prefer to proceed by complaint and summons, rather than arrest and charge, to give him some time to resolve his suspension issues before the assault matter got to court. But whatever way he weighed it up, Brian knew it would be a very tough conversation to have with the senior sergeant, and he felt a faint, sickly wave of anxiety just at the thought of it.

He struggled with the stiff window handle, laboriously winding the pane into place, and then flashed his torchlight across at the passenger side. The other window was open too. He leaned across, still tossing over in his mind what he might say to the senior sergeant, and reached out for the opposite handle. As he did, his other hand slipped awkwardly off the edge of the passenger seat, dislodging the keys he was holding, and they rattled and jangled their way down between the seats, lodging themselves snugly alongside the heavy hand brake.

'Shit.'

Brian groped in the darkness, trying to retrieve the keys. He pushed one hand in after them, squeezing between the vinyl and metal until his fingertips brushed over one of them, whereupon it immediately escaped and tinkled further down into the void. He grunted in frustration, and cursed under his breath. Then he flicked his torch on again, training it down between the seats. There they were, tantalisingly close to his grasp. He pulled a pen from his breast pocket and, following the beam of the torchlight, poked it down into the breach, trapping the keyring against the side of the seat. Then he gently began dragging it upwards, pressed against the side of the seat.

Now, as the pen inched upwards, he could see something else attached to one of the keys. It was metallic and shiny, a dainty, silver thread, draped over the ignition key, and dangling down below it. As Brian meticulously eased the collected bundle up alongside the seat towards him, the thread sparkled and glistened in the light, intriguing and mesmerising him. He kept dragging it watchfully towards him. Then suddenly, the whole package came free of the void and he snatched it up, clinking softly in the palm of his hand.

With two fingers he carefully pinched the broken silver chain swinging down off the end of the keys, and drew it away, holding it up in the torchlight to get a good look at it. In his hand, he saw he was holding a piece of fine jewellery, a thin silver chain—a necklace—broken away from its clasp, weighed down by an elegant drop pearl pendant, swaying gracefully below it.

As Constable Ingles sat in the darkness, watching that beautiful white ball swing gently back and forth, from side to side in the torchlight, it gradually occurred to him what it was. *The drop-pearl necklace.* He had seen it before, when the grieving mother Sue Mitchell had drawn a sketch of it into the notebook of Detective Senior Sergeant Dave Hocking.

TWENTY

When Assistant Commissioner of Police Noel Peter Atwood walked to the witness box, Eddie Moran was nervously bouncing his knee under the bar-table, and absently gnawing on one ravaged fingernail. He had been awaiting this moment for days, but now he wasn't quite sure he was ready.

Atwood was crucial. The proceedings had gone well so far. Eddie was satisfied he had effectively defused Wayne Grantham's intended evidence of Rowdy's violent pre-disposition towards the deceased, and Pat Keenan, the senior forensic scientist from the Queensland Government Health Laboratory, had given some useful evidence Eddie knew he could work on. But if he was going to set up an argument that the magistrate should dismiss the charge against Rowdy McQuillan, he had to do it through Atwood.

Mr McEniery SM's brief but harrowing stint on the wrong side of the criminal justice system had evidently left him with a good dose of healthy cynicism about prosecution allegations, and Eddie knew if he had anything to say, McEniery would listen. But whatever he was going to say, he had to say it through Atwood. He was the key to it all.

'Witness, would you have a look at this document please?'

Looking all spruced-up in the freshly ironed shirt his Aunty Ada had dropped off at the watchhouse that morning, the lonesome cowboy looked on from the solid, silky-oak dock at the side of the courtroom, as Bruce McKinlay went through the motions with his arresting officer, rattling out routine questions, by rote, to each of which Atwood responded accordingly.

'Is that a statement of the evidence you are able to give in relation to this matter?'

'It is.'

'Is there anything you would like to add, alter or delete in that statement?'

'No.'

'Your Worship, I tender that statement pursuant to section 110A of the Justices Act.'

McKinlay walked the witness's statement up to the bench and handed it to the magistrate, who duly marked it as an exhibit and admitted it into the record as the evidence-in-chief of the Assistant Commissioner. There was nothing contentious about its contents, and the prosecutor didn't expect the cross-examination of Atwood would take too long at all. Moran might want to have a shot at him about Wayne Grantham's claim he had boofed up his statement about the Cunnamulla Show Day incident, but Bruce knew Atwood would just flatly deny it, so that exercise couldn't take more than about half an hour, tops. He was already thinking about what witness he could usefully call next-up.

But, that morning, Senior Sergeant Bruce McKinlay was having a little trouble concentrating. One of his oldest and very best mates in the world was in a world of pain, and Bruce didn't know quite how to deal with it. Dave Hocking hadn't answered his calls since the day he left Cunnamulla, and even his wife Denise hadn't heard a word from him. According to the constable at Millengarra, he was still checked in at the motel up there. The phone reception in Millen was pretty ordinary at the best of times, so that might explain his old mate's radio silence. But Bruce was still worried about him, and he planned to take a drive up that way on the weekend.

In the meantime, he had to get through the McQuillan murder committal, and that meant putting up with that idiot, Noel Atwood. That would have been hard enough in any event, but it was now made infinitely worse by Atwood's obvious delight with the recent suspension of Bruce's mate, Dave. Atwood and Hocking hadn't seen eye-to-eye for many a year—mainly because the Assistant Commissioner was always a big, dumb, lazy boofhead—but now Atwood seemed to be celebrating Hocking's current troubles as some sort of personal triumph.

The press was out in force, and on his way into court Bruce had even noticed a local news camera crew hanging around, for the first time since the hearing kicked off. They were obviously there for Noel Atwood. Ever since his stint as a 'whistle-blower' at the Fitzgerald Inquiry, when the press wrote him up as 'the last honest cop in Queensland', the former head of the Cunnamulla CIB—and now personal assistant to the new Commissioner of Police—had been something of a local celebrity out in those parts, and Bruce figured he'd probably tipped off a couple of journos he was due to give evidence that day.

Of course, Noel didn't know what Wayne Grantham had said about him, and Bruce wasn't about to enlighten him, quietly savouring the prospect of the obnoxious young defence solicitor giving the Assistant Commissioner a right royal rogering about it in cross-examination.

'That's the evidence in chief of this witness, Your Worship.'

McKinlay sat down and buried his head in his hands, as Eddie Moran leapt to his feet. Even as he did so, the young lawyer was still debating in his own mind how he should start. The evidence he had elicited in cross-examining the government forensic scientist Keenan had provided a good factual basis to argue more than enough reasonable doubt, but now he needed to package it all up and tie it together. The easiest option for Mr McEniery SM was simply to commit Ronald McQuillan for trial, and let a Supreme Court jury decide his guilt or innocence, six months or more down the track. But, in this case—like Slick had said—that just wasn't good enough. McQuillan was innocent, and it was Eddie Moran's job to spring him, as soon as he could. If he was going to do that, he had to charge in and throw down the gauntlet, right from the jump.

'You only charged my client with murder because you thought he was the only one in the house when it happened,' he scowled insolently from the bar-table. 'Didn't you?'

It was a clumsy, ham-fisted start, but Atwood looked ruffled nonetheless. He hadn't expected to encounter such patent discourtesy, and it took him the briefest moment to adjust and compose himself.

'He was the only one there,' he eventually replied, emphatically. 'Apart from the deceased, of course.'

'How do you know that?'

'Well,' Atwood opened, thoughtfully, sounding surprised there could possibly be any doubt about it at all. 'Because he was dropped off at the house just before it happened, and he was apprehended straight afterwards, covered in Mr Wilson's blood.'

'Are you serious, witness?'

Eddie Moran's face was screwed into a derisive, almost comical glower, which Atwood quite evidently found most objectionable. He pursed his lips in a distasteful pout, squirming uncomfortably around in his seat, before he eventually answered.

'Yes.'

Moran rolled his eyes and scoffed contemptuously.

'Seriously? Did you just say "He was dropped off just before it happened"? Is that what you just said?'

'Yes.'

'But you don't know when the murder happened, do you?'

'Yes, we do.'

'Well, when?'

'It happened just after midnight.'

'What?' The lawyer barked it out so loudly a middle-aged lady three rows back in the public gallery jumped in her seat, visibly startled. For a moment, McEniery SM peered disapprovingly down from the bench, but the young lawyer seemed unaware and pressed on, oblivious. 'How do you know that?'

'Because...' Atwood looked genuinely confused as he fumbled for words. 'Well, because that's when the defendant was dropped off at the house.'

'What?' Once again, the question was fired back so robustly McEniery SM was taken aback, turning testily on the young cross-examiner, but once again the lawyer didn't seem to notice, as he forged on regardless. 'Oh, come on, Mr Atwood,' he persisted. 'Please. Are you serious?'

Atwood was clearly dumbfounded and, for a moment, the magistrate himself seemed somewhat bewildered, and poised to impose, before Moran promptly picked up from where he had left off.

'Are you seriously telling his Worship that the reason you know the defendant was in the house when the murder occurred is because he was dropped off at the house at around midnight, and the reason you know the murder occurred around midnight is because that's when the defendant was dropped off?'

Moran was leaning forward aggressively over the lectern, staring disdainfully at the witness, who was now sitting back in the witness box, eyebrows arched, looking entirely clueless. Eventually, he straightened up, puffed out his chest, and replied.

'Yes.'

'That's how you calculate the time of the murder?' the lawyer shot back incredulously.

'Yes.'

'Are you serious?'

'Yes.'

'You can't be, surely?'

'I am.'

'You can't possibly be serious.'

'Yes, thank you Mr Moran,' the magistrate interrupted abruptly, pushing his way into the unseemly spat. 'I think you've made your point.'

Eddie Moran glared back at him, still stuck to the lectern. This time it was his turn to be ignored, as McEniery turned to the prosecutor.

'Sergeant, the witness's logic does seem a bit circuitous, doesn't it?' he said pensively. 'Does the prosecution have any more definitive evidence as to when the murder occurred?'

It was like music to Eddie's ears. The point was a simple and obvious one, but it was still a relief to see the magistrate clearly got it, and wasn't prepared to ignore it. Ranald McEniery wasn't looking for easy options.

Eddie held his breath while the prosecutor sat, temporarily frozen, at the bar-table, considering the question. McKinlay hardly got his buttocks clear of his chair as he rose to reply, perfunctorily.

'I don't believe so, your Worship.'

'So, witness,' the magistrate calmly concluded, turning back to face Atwood, 'May we proceed, then, on the basis that the precise time of the murder is currently unknown?'

As everybody in the courtroom—not least of all Eddie Moran—waited in silent suspense, Atwood tossed the question over for several long seconds. He shot a quick glance to the press gallery, then to the prosecutor—who kept his head down—and then back to the bench. Eventually, the Assistant Commissioner set his chin firmly, and held his head high.

'Yes, your Worship.'

'Yes, thank you, witness,' the magistrate replied, turning back to his notebook, and scribbling something down. 'You made proceed, Mr Moran.'

Eddie felt good. Very good. He had got to first base, just where he needed to be. Now all he had to do was lay the case out, clinically, coherently and efficiently.

'So, if you don't know precisely when the murder occurred,' he proceeded in a carefully measured tone. 'You can't be certain the deceased wasn't already dead when the defendant got home that night, can you?'

'Yes, we can,' Atwood answered emphatically.

What?! The answer was obviously dumb and untenable, and Moran just wanted to throw something at the eminent Assistant Commissioner. But instead, he resisted the temptation, drew in a deep, cleansing breath, and proceeded on evenly.

'Really? And how can you be sure of that?'

The witness aimed his answer straight at the journalists in the press gallery.

'The defendant had the deceased's blood all over him when we arrested him.'

'So what?' Moran snapped at him, irritably. The witness was grandstanding, making vacuous and opportunistic motherhood statements that didn't prove a thing, and suddenly Eddie was again struggling to contain his exasperation. 'That could have happened when he came home after the event, and innocently stumbled upon the dead body, couldn't it?'

Atwood shook his head confidently, again directing his answer straight to the press.

'His fingerprints were all over the murder weapon.'

'But you don't know when those prints got onto the weapon, do you?'

'They were imprinted into the deceased's blood.'

'So what?' he snapped again, his tone now charged with a deal more pique than it had been. 'He could have just picked that weapon up at the house, where the killer left it. Just like you police later picked it up off the front lawn.'

'His were the only fingerprints found on the bat, or anywhere in the house.'

Atwood was enjoying himself, playing up to his audience, and with every answer Eddie could see the collected journalists furiously scribbling his quotable quotes into their notebooks.

'What if the killer was wearing gloves?' the lawyer proposed. 'He wouldn't have left any prints in that case, would he?'

'Not a lot of people wear gloves out here in the bush, Mr Moran,' Atwood smugly replied, casting a knowing smirk to the public gallery. When his clever quip was met with a muted snigger rustling through his audience, he added 'You're not in Surfers Paradise now, you know.'

As the snigger erupted anew, and even more audibly, Atwood sat back comfortably, with a self-congratulatory smile splashed over his face. Eddie bit down on his ire.

'But if a professional criminal broke into that house intending to harm someone, there's every chance he would wear gloves, isn't there?'

Atwood scoffed, shaking his head dismissively.

'Nonsense,' he said to the gallery, further irritating his cross-examiner. 'There is no evidence whatsoever of any professional criminal, or anyone else, with gloves on or not, being in that house at any time that night.'

As the journalists jumped headlong into another frenzied flurry of notetaking, Moran quickly countered.

'And there's no evidence the defendant was there either, is there, not at the time of the murder?'

Atwood waited until he was sure the press had completed their note of his previous pronouncement before he smugly launched into his next.

'We don't have any witness who actually saw the defendant in the house at the time,' he said carefully, 'But it can be comfortably inferred from all of the evidence that he was indeed there at all relevant times, and that he was in fact the killer.'

'Really?' Of course, it was an impermissible and entirely inappropriate attempt to state the prosecution case, but Eddie didn't care. More important to him, it was the perfect segue into a place he wanted to get to. 'How long was he there for, precisely?'

'We don't know that.'

'Well, he'd have to have been there some considerable time, if he was the killer, wouldn't he? I mean, the evidence suggests this was a prolonged and sustained attack.'

'He had all the time he needed.'

Atwood blurted it out, emphatically, then glanced at the gallery and gave an almost imperceptible nod of his head, before turning back to Moran. Eddie could see in his eyes they both knew this was the killer point, the big problem for the prosecution in the case against Rowdy McQuillan. *Time*. Did Rowdy McQuillan have enough time in the Castle Street house to do what he was alleged to have done?

'Yeah?' the lawyer said quietly. 'How much time was that?'

'We estimate it was around fifteen minutes.'

'It'd take every bit of that to do what was done to Tom Wilson, wouldn't it?'

'It was enough time.'

Atwood knew that was all they needed; all the defendant had needed.

'It was enough time,' Eddie repeated. 'And how do you work out the defendant had that much time?'

'Ross Lewis dropped him off at the house right on midnight.' The policeman was instantly more comfortable now, systematically spieling off what he saw as the high points of the prosecution case. 'The first complaint was made to police at twenty-one minutes past. Allowing for the time spent at Karen Millard's house—and Millard and her associates' travel time by car to the station—we estimate the defendant was at the Castle Street house for at least fifteen minutes.'

Eddie had him all lined up in his sights. Now all he had to do was gently squeeze the trigger. He picked a folder up off the bar-table, placed it carefully on the lectern, and opened it up at his notes.

'But he went somewhere else before he went to Karen Millard's house, didn't he?' he said, doing his best to convey the impression he was reading from some document he had in his folder.

Atwood frowned and squinted back at the questioner, doing his best to look like he didn't know what the lawyer was talking about. But Eddie could plainly see that he did.

'Where was that?' the witness stuttered awkwardly.

Eddie's lips stretched into a wry smile as he held the Assistant Commissioner's gaze with his own.

'Weren't you told that he turned up at the home of his good friend Mason Deeds that night?'

Noel Atwood felt a sickly stab in the pit of his stomach. Dave Hocking had filed an occurrence report about the claim, said to have been made by the Millengarra housewife Jennifer Deeds, that Rowdy McQuillan came to her house on the night of the murder. It couldn't possibly be true. The times were all wrong, and they clearly didn't coincide with the other prosecution evidence. Besides, her husband had mentioned nothing about it when he spoke to the police at the time. Neither of them reported any such incident on the night of the murder, and even now—twelve months after the event— Mrs Deeds still hadn't given a formal statement about it. It sounded like no more than a lame, small-town attempt to take the heat off an old friend, so Noel had made the executive decision to ignore it.

But the cat was now obviously out of the bag. *How did the defence get hold of it?* It could have been Hocking, just out of spite for the whole suspension thing, but he wasn't the only one who could have done it. The story apparently originated with some young constable out in Millengarra, Hocking had openly discussed it with the whole murder investigation team, and now it was all written up in the investigation log. The leak could have come from anywhere, and anyone who subpoenaed the log would see it was there. So, whoever the rat in the ranks might be, Assistant

Commissioner Atwood—the last honest cop in Queensland—now had to tread very warily.

'Yes,' he mumbled shakily. 'Yes, yes, I think there may have been some mention of that.'

'And that was before the defendant went anywhere near Karen Millard's house, wasn't it?'

'I believe that's what was reported.'

'And according to Mason Deeds' wife, Mrs Jenny Deeds, the defendant turned up at their house at precisely seven minutes after midnight. Correct?'

There it was again, the elephant in the room, the prosecution's big problem—time. As the courtroom awaited his answer, the witness was silently mouthing something for several seconds, before it eventually trickled out in a feeble stammer.

'I'm … er…I'm…'

'Seven minutes.' Moran boomed the words out into the courtroom. He was now leaning over the lectern again, snarling derisively at the Assistant Commissioner. 'That means, Mr Atwood, taking into account travel time, the defendant would have had no more than five minutes in that house. Correct?'

Atwood's chin was trembling pathetically, the words still seemingly stuck in the back of his throat.

'Yes,' he eventually conceded, falteringly. 'On those times it could be, but…'

'It's not enough time,' the lawyer bellowed again, scowling obnoxiously. 'Is it, Mr Atwood? The defendant couldn't possibly have done what was done in that house in five short minutes.'

When the response finally came, it was frail and uncertain.

'We're not sure Mrs Deeds' account is reliable.'

'Well, did you interview her, or her husband?'

'Not yet.'

'Why not?'

There was another long silence, as Atwood fumbled for words.

'Well,' he mumbled eventually, 'As I said, we weren't…' He trailed off for a moment, then collected himself, and resumed with more confidence. 'The investigation is still ongoing.'

The young lawyer stood bolt upright abruptly, looking a picture of righteous indignation. But before he had the chance to go into his planned outraged conniption, the magistrate intervened.

'What?' his Worship said to the witness. 'Twelve months after the event?'

'Yes, Your Worship.'

McEniery SM looked deeply troubled.

'Well, when do you propose to interview Mr and Mrs Deeds?'

Atwood appeared to consider the question momentarily, and then stuck his chin out and boldly responded.

'That's undetermined at this stage, Your Worship.'

The magistrate stared at him silently for several seconds. Then he grunted, shook his head with obvious dissatisfaction, and scribbled something down in his notes. The reaction was unmistakeable. Eddie could see immediately he didn't need to press the point any further. McEniery got it.

'Anyway, witness, one thing's for sure,' Eddie resumed, leaning back over the lectern, now more relaxed and conversational. 'If it turns out Mrs Deeds' account is reliable—if it turns out the defendant was in fact at the Deeds' residence at seven minutes after midnight—Rowdy McQuillan couldn't possibly have committed this crime, could he?'

Atwood could feel himself being boxed in.

'Seven minutes could be…'

'Not seven,' the lawyer interrupted. 'Five. Five minutes in the Castle Street house.'

The sickly feeling in Noel Atwood's stomach made him shift uncomfortably in his seat.

'Even five minutes,' he said breathlessly. 'Five minutes could be enough.'

'Really?' Eddie knew he had the witness right where he wanted him. 'Have a look at exhibit sixteen, would you please, Mr Atwood.' When the crime scene photographs were delivered to him in the witness box, Atwood picked them up and began leafing through them. 'In particular, photograph number twelve in that exhibit, which shows the room in which the body was found.' Eddie knew the magistrate was well acquainted with what it depicted; he had taken the forensic scientist Keenan through it at length. 'What happened in that room was clearly a prolonged and sustained attack, wasn't it? There was blood all over the floor and the three adjacent walls, right up to the ceiling cornice, even across the ceiling itself.'

'Yes.'

'And that was partially because of splashing and splattering of blood, but also because various major arteries were damaged in the attack, causing extensive actual spurting of blood from the head.'

A murmur of suppressed horror filtered through the public gallery.

'Yes.'

'Such that whoever inflicted those injuries would have been virtually spray-painted with the victim's blood, wouldn't they?'

Atwood could clearly see where all this was going. McQuillan's clothes had very little blood on them, but there was a perfectly logical explanation for that.

'The defendant washed all the blood from his clothes before leaving the house. They were sopping wet when we found them.'

'"Sopping?"' The lawyer nodded pensively. 'What does that mean?'

'Wet.'

'How wet?'

'They'd been washed.'

'They were lying on the floor of the second bedroom, which was flooded in water.'

'Yes.'

'And that water appeared to be coming from the broken toilet cistern on the other side of the hallway.'

'Yes.'

'They were wet because they were lying in water on the floor.'

'They were wet because the defendant had washed all the blood off them.' When the impudent young lawyer rolled his eyes disdainfully, Atwood quickly added, 'Blood washes straight out in water.'

Pat Keenan had already given that evidence. It changed nothing. In fact, it was exactly where Eddie wanted to go.

'Where did he wash them out?'

'We don't know. In the bathroom sink probably, or in the laundry tub.'

Moran nodded again, silently processing the witness's answer.

'We've heard evidence from the Queensland Health Laboratory forensic scientist Mr Keenan that he would expect something in the order of ten millilitres of blood to have been sprayed or splattered onto the killer. Would you agree with that?'

'It sounds reasonable.'

'And Mr Keenan has also told us it would take more than twenty gallons of water to completely dissolve ten millilitres of blood.'

'There was plenty of running water in that house.'

'That's true. But Mr Atwood, I suggest to you the average house tap flows at the rate of approximately two hundred gallons per hour.'

'That may be right.'

'Here in the west, of course, the water pressure is much less. You'd be aware of that, wouldn't you?'

'Correct.'

'But even at two hundred gallons an hour, it'd take around six minutes just to get twenty gallons out of the tap, wouldn't it?'

'If you say so.'

With that, the defence lawyer suddenly gripped the lectern, and leaned forward over it, and barked at the witness abrasively.

'Well you do the math, Mr Atwood.' Startled, McEniery SM looked up from his notes, peering censoriously at the young lawyer. 'Two hundred gallons an hour,' Eddie continued. 'Twenty gallons is a tenth of that. A tenth of an hour is six minutes. That's how long it would take, isn't it? Six minutes. Absolute minimum.'

'Yes,' the witness replied indignantly. 'On those calculations, yes.'

'Six minutes,' Moran roared in response. The magistrate was still staring at him, but now his expression had changed. He nodded once, curtly, then scratched down a note in his notebook, as the lawyer expounded. 'If the defendant was at the Deeds' home at seven minutes after midnight, as Jenny Deeds says he was, he had five minutes tops in that house. That's not even enough time to get the water through the taps. He couldn't possibly have killed Tom Wilson and then washed all that blood out of his clothes in six minutes.'

Noel Atwood was staring back at the lawyer defiantly.

'The defendant killed Mr Wilson.'

Moran snatched up the forensic report and waved it around theatrically.

'The U-pipes under the sink, the bath and the shower recess were all removed and tested for the presence of human blood. Correct?'

Atwood faltered visibly, for the briefest millisecond, before he replied.

'Yes.'

'And not one of those U-pipes showed any trace of blood in them, whatsoever.'

He paused again, longer this time, contemplating the significance of his response.

'Yes.'

'Which means either an enormous quantity of water passed through the pipes—as in at least twenty gallons plus—or those clothes weren't washed in that house.'

Atwood's mouth was moving again without any words coming out, as he shifted and shuffled uncomfortably around in his seat. When he eventually spoke, his voice was frail and unconvincing.

'They could have been.'

'Not in five minutes they couldn't,' the lawyer bellowed at him, leaning forward over the lectern. 'Five minutes wouldn't even get enough water through the taps to get the job done.'

Noel Atwood looked like a rat in a trap, squirming uneasily, glancing around him, first at the prosecutor, who kept his head down and eyes averted, then at the media, all poised expectantly, ready to record his reply, and finally back at the magistrate. His Worship sat, grim and stony-faced, peering down from the bench through his eyebrows.

It was all just nonsense and mumbo-jumbo. Noel Atwood knew that. McQuillan was in the house that night, drunk and out of his mind. When they found him, he was covered in the victim's blood, his prints were all over the murder weapon, and he never made any attempt to deny he murdered Tom Wilson. He did it. Of course he did it. His bumptious young defence lawyer was just trying to kick up a whole lot of irrelevant dust and confuse everybody.

Noel just needed to stand his ground. He set his jaw and turned back to face the lawyer.

'The defendant killed Mr Wilson,' he pronounced defiantly, and then quickly added, 'He admitted as much in the record of interview'

'What?' Moran's face contorted into a quizzical grimace. 'Where?'

'At answer twenty-seven.'

'What?'

The lawyer snatched up the typed Record of Interview from his papers, huffing and puffing, feverishly slapping the pages back, searching for answer twenty-seven. Before he could find it, Ranald McEniery SM intervened.

'Sergeant McKinlay,' he said to the prosecutor, in a stern but measured tone. McKinlay got to his feet. 'We've already heard evidence in these proceedings that the defendant had a very high blood-alcohol reading when he was first detained, and he subsequently told police he could not remember, and did not know, what happened in the house.' Eddie Moran remained glued to the lectern, listening attentively, cautiously assessing, word-by-word, where his Worship was heading. 'This witness now points to the defendant's alleged statement, in his answer to question number twenty-seven in the police interview, where he says "I can't believe I killed Tom." It appears the witness seeks to rely on that statement as a confession by the defendant that he murdered Mr Wilson.'

A confession? It wasn't a confession. Eddie quickly read and re-read the question and answer. *'I can't believe I killed Tom.'* That wasn't a confession, surely. But then again, maybe, debatably. If it was—even arguably—a confession of guilt trumped everything. If Rowdy McQuillan admitted to the police he killed Tom Wilson, then his guilt or innocence was a jury question, and he had to be committed for trial, no matter how shaky the rest of evidence was.

Eddie Moran had ten toes over the sandy banks of the Rubicon, and for him there was no turning back. He had to disabuse McEniery of any notion the answer could possibly constitute a confession of guilt, and he had to do it emphatically, right up front, before the idea gained any traction at all.

'Your Worship,' he dived in stridently, desperate to get his point out. But the magistrate abruptly cut him off short.

'Just a moment please, Mr Moran.' McEniery was staring daggers at him, clearly miffed to have been so rudely interrupted. Eddie stopped in his tracks and waited, until the magistrate eventually added, irritably, 'Sit down.' The young lawyer briefly assessed the position; he figured he could take the magistrate on, have a bunfight about it, maybe get somewhere, maybe not. But it was a gamble. McEniery was behaving himself so far, so why risk getting him totally off-side? Eddie would get his chance to respond, sooner or later. He promptly slumped back into his seat, already scribbling notes of his counterattack, as McEniery sedately turned his attention back to the Assistant Commissioner.

'Witness, is that your position?'

'Yes, Your Worship. Yes, it is.'

McEniery SM turned back to Bruce McKinlay.

'Sergeant, I can indicate that I am presently not minded to accept that contention.' Eddie Moran stopped scribbling his notes and looked up, wide-eyed, from the bar-table. 'So far as I see it,' the magistrate continued, 'the alleged statement, in the context of the whole of the interview and the other evidence, is ambiguous and, at best, quite equivocal. I don't consider it to be a clear admission by the defendant that he killed the deceased. Certainly, as currently advised I would not be inclined to rely on it as such for the purpose of assessing whether a prima facie case of guilt has been established in these proceedings.'

Eddie Moran suppressed an overwhelming urge to leap up out of his chair and fist-pump the air. McEniery was not only rejecting the notion that answer twenty-seven could ever be interpreted as a confession to murder; he was laying firmly on the table the fact that he wasn't yet convinced a prima facie case of guilt had been established against Rowdy McQuillan. And Eddie knew, if McEniery wasn't convinced so far, things weren't about to get any better for the prosecution.

'Now,' McEniery SM continued, 'You may or may not wish to be heard on the point, sergeant. If you do, of course I'm happy to hear your argument, and any response Mr Moran may have. So I'm going to ask you—do you rely on that statement as a confession of guilt by the defendant?'

Bruce McKinlay was standing at the bar-table, looking down at answer twenty-seven in the Record of Interview, with a weary, undecided frown on his face. He hadn't at any stage even considered the answer could be a confession. Atwood hadn't suggested any such proposition to him, they had never discussed it, and he had never considered it. And now, as he looked down at the type-written answer, he could see precisely why. It didn't look like any sort of confession to him.

'I don't seek to rely on that statement as an admission, Your Worship.'

The magistrate nodded.

'Yes, thank you, sergeant,' he mumbled, making a note. 'Mr Moran, you may proceed.'

At the bar-table, Eddie Moran secretly breathed a sigh of relief as he slowly rose back up to his feet. Now he was certain. It was time to charge in, full tilt, all or nothing. Ranald McEniery SM wasn't convinced by the prosecution case, and even the prosecutor himself didn't like it. The stars were aligned. Rowdy McQuillan was never going to get a better chance than right now —with this prosecutor, before this magistrate—to walk out of there a free man.

He began quietly and carefully.

'Mr Atwood, I suggested to you earlier that if a professional criminal broke into that house that night, intending to commit a crime in there, he may well have been wearing gloves.' With that, Eddie paused, soaking up the silence that had suddenly descended over the room. Everyone in the courtroom— the press, the public, the magistrate, the prosecutor, even the witness—were waiting in suspense to hear a story the lawyer would tell them, waiting to be convinced, or not. 'I now want to positively put to you,' Eddie resumed, 'That someone else—someone thus far unidentified—did indeed enter the Castle Street house that night, and that unidentified person murdered Tom Wilson before Mr McQuillan even got home.'

A rustle of murmured comment and the scribbling of notes instantly arose from the gallery, as Noel Atwood scoffed loudly, shaking his head back and forth demonstratively.

'No, no,' he said, casting around the courtroom. 'No, that's definitely not right. That's rubbish. There was absolutely no evidence whatsoever of any other person having been in the house that night.'

'Wasn't there?' Moran shot back at him sceptically. 'Go back to the photographs, Mr Atwood—exhibit sixteen.'

Eddie moved through the exercise as quickly and efficiently as he could, pointing out to Atwood what Constable Ingles had pointed out to him at the house—the police photograph of the damaged flyscreen in the Castle Street kitchen, bent back, almost in two, from the inside out, the sliding window wide open, and directly below, inches from the windowsill, the line of bottles and jars up-ended, lying in disarray on the kitchen bench.

'That photograph suggests, doesn't it, Mr Atwood, that someone bent back that flyscreen from outside the house, then pulled open the sliding window, and climbed in through the window onto the bench.' The witness was staring blankly at the photograph, dumbfounded. 'Doesn't it?'

Atwood looked up at the cross-examiner. He said nothing for several seconds, and then shook his head absently.

'There was no sign of any property having been stolen from the house.'

'Well that depends on what was there in the first place, doesn't it? What if whoever broke in there was looking for drugs?'

'There was no evidence of that.'

'Really? The water cistern was smashed, wasn't it? As an experienced police officer you'd know, I suggest, illicit items, such as drugs, have often been known to be hidden in toilet cisterns.'

'We found no evidence of drugs on the premises.'

'But you did find a toilet cistern that had been cracked open, didn't you?' Moran flicked through his copies of the photographs, and held up the relevant one. 'Can you give his Worship any other explanation, or theory, as to why anyone would have smashed open that toilet cistern that night?'

Atwood looked all out of answers.

'It could be anything.'

Eddie carefully replaced the photograph and stood fully erect, placing one hand on either edge of the lectern.

'Mr Atwood,' he said, in a quiet, measured tone, 'That house backs onto the Starlight Motel in King Street, doesn't it?'

'That's right.'

'And on the morning after the murder, you had officers canvas the various residences in the area, including the Starlight Motel, to see if anyone had seen or heard anything unusual that night. Correct?'

'Yes.'

'I suggest a Mrs Graham, the proprietor of the Starlight Motel, told police she hadn't seen or heard anything out of the ordinary that night.'

'Yes, I believe that's correct.'

'But you didn't check with any of her guests at the motel that night, did you?' As the Assistant Commissioner struggled ineptly to answer, the lawyer continued. 'See, I suggest that in fact two men were booked into the Starlight that night, in room number six.' The courtroom was totally silent again, as Atwood stared back at the lawyer, open-mouthed, his chin trembling faintly, as if he was searching for something to say. Meanwhile, the lawyer continued his story. 'And the back door of room number six at the Starlight Motel is, I suggest, just a skip and a jump from the back fence of the Starlight Motel, which also happens to be the back fence of the Castle Street house. And once you're over that fence you're in the backyard of that house, and if you cross that yard you come straight to that back window into the kitchen.' By now, Eddie could have heard a pin drop. He paused, then completed his point. 'The exact same window where someone bent back that flyscreen and climbed into that house.'

Atwood sat silently for several seconds, looking slightly disorientated, then cleared his throat, collected himself, and did his best to respond.

'I don't know who was staying at the Starlight Motel that night.'

There was a rustle from the bench, and McEniery SM looked up over his glasses.

'Well,' he mumbled testily. 'It'd be a pretty relevant thing to find out, wouldn't it?'

'It could be, your Worship.'

The magistrate grunted, and went back to writing his notes.

Eddie felt good. McEniery was obviously onside. He could see it was a sloppy police case, with holes all through it, and Eddie knew he was running downhill. All he had to do was finish his story, without interruption, and get to the punchline.

'I suggest, Mr Atwood, those two men booked into that motel under a false name and left hurriedly and unexpectedly in the dead of night, very shortly after Mr Wilson was murdered.'

'I'm not aware of that.'

'I further suggest they were travelling in a car that was rented from a hire car company on the Gold Coast, again using a false identity.' The lawyer didn't wait for an answer. 'And you would be well aware, as an experienced police detective, that whenever someone rents a hire car they're required, as a matter of course, to produce a copy of their driver's licence.' Eddie was moving so fast now, unravelling his story to everyone in the courtroom, the witness had almost become an irrelevance. As Atwood stuttered feebly, trying to find a response, Eddie forged on, unrelenting. 'And I suggest that's precisely what happened in this case. The person who hired that car supplied a Queensland driver's licence, which was photocopied and kept in the hire company records.'

Moran reached down into his papers and extracted three sheets of paper, one of which he slid down the table to Bruce McKinlay, one he tendered up to the magistrate, and one he asked to be shown to the witness. When they looked at the photocopy of the licence in question, each one of them recognised the licensee's name immediately.

'Do you see that document, Mr Atwood?'

'Yes.'

'That's the Queensland driver's licence of a person with the rather distinctive name Holden Waldo Winchester, isn't it?'

'Yes.'

'Do you know who Holden Waldo Winchester is?'

'Yes.'

Everyone who'd picked up a newspaper or turned on a TV set in Queensland in the past twelve months knew who Holden Winchester was. The small-time heroin dealer, with a long history of fraud and drug offences, had been found dead in a seedy Gold Coast motel room, alongside his drug-addict girlfriend, both beaten to death in what looked to police like an intentionally messy payback-style execution, sparking speculation of a violent drug turf-war in South-East Queensland. When the unsolved investigation was openly mentioned in state parliament three months later, with claims being made of suspected infiltration by Asian drug-lords into the Queensland market, assisted by southern-based outlaw motorcycle gangs, and even mafia hit men, the trashy press outlets went into overdrive, and the public went into shock. The newspapers, radio and television press had been running sensational snippets about the so-called *Winchester execution* for months, and there had even been calls for a judicial inquiry into the whole affair. So, not surprisingly, the very mention of Winchester's infamous name in the Cunnamulla Courthouse, sent the good folk in the public gallery spiralling into a new, frantic round of rustling, murmuring and shuffling.

'Holden Waldo Winchester was murdered on the Gold Coast, several weeks before the death of Tom Wilson, I suggest.'

All the blood had drained out of the Assistant Commissioner's face.

'Yes.'

'And his wallet, in which he presumably kept his driver's licence, went missing at the same time, didn't it? Suspected stolen.'

Atwood was just nodding now, saying nothing.

'And it remains missing to this very day.'

He nodded again.

'Except, two days before Tom Wilson's murder, someone showed up at a hire car company on the Gold Coast, and handed over his driver's licence as ID.'

This time the witness didn't nod; he just sat open-mouthed, staring back at the lawyer. Moran leaned over the lectern, and asked his next question quietly.

'Did you know someone using Holden Winchester's missing licence was lurking just over the fence from Tom Wilson's house on the night he was murdered?'

Atwood's head shook, his lips wavering erratically, before he finally got the word out.

'No.'

Eddie had got out his story. Now he only had one last question.

'Had you known that, do you think you would have wanted to investigate that person, and that connection, very thoroughly, before you charged my client Mr McQuillan with this charge?'

The Assistant Commissioner looked at him vacantly for several seconds, and then nodded.

'Yes,' he said feebly. 'Yes, I think I would, yes.'

TWENTY-ONE

Brian Ingles had a sad, sinking feeling in the pit of his stomach as he pushed on intently, due north, into the harsh, late-morning sunlight. All around him, the police car was rattling and shuddering violently over the corrugated dirt surface of Station Road, the orange-tinged, dusty strip stretching out ahead of him as far as the eye could see. With each passing kilometre he felt more anxious, unsettled, as though the long, lonely road was leading him on to an ominous, inescapable conclusion.

Already, it had been a difficult day. It had started early, at Lyall and Sue Mitchell's home, where the devastated couple identified the drop-pearl necklace he retrieved from Martin's truck as the one Sue's mother had given to her, the one their only child, Larnie, had been so fond of. The constable could not reveal where he had found it. That had to remain confidential for now. But he could see in their cold, fixed eyes that they both knew, from their first, startled glimpse of those delicate, damaged links in the chain—twisted, broken, and ripped apart—where the story was ultimately leading. A look of resigned, helpless sorrow enveloped them, as they clung to each other, pale and drawn, saying nothing. Once his job was done there, Brian had hastily taken his leave, assuring the Mitchells he would let them know more as soon as possible, and then got out of their house as quickly as he could.

When Darren Martin left his home to accompany the constable back to the station, he probably thought he was just going there to make a statement about his assault complaint against Detective Dave Hocking. But when they got into the police house, Brian Ingles placed a recorder on the desk between them, turned it on, and read him his rights. The truck driver looked bemused, even guarded, but assured the constable he was more than happy to speak freely and openly about whatever he wanted to ask him about.

From there, Martin confidently answered a series of questions about Larnie Mitchell, his relationship with her, the fact he had met her occasionally at the Empire Hotel, where she had worked from time to time, and had sometimes chatted to her, briefly, strictly in that context. He knew her parents, of course, as the local newsagents, but not well. He had never socialised with Larnie outside the hotel—and, even then, only in passing—and he knew little or nothing about her. On the night before she went missing, he may have been speaking with her briefly in the public bar—he couldn't remember specifically—but it would have been nothing more than the usual, casual banter. He had absolutely no recollection of her ever having asked him about hitching a ride on one his trucks down to Brisbane. She may have raised it, possibly, in passing, but he seriously doubted she did, because that was the sort of thing he would remember. Yes, she may have left the hotel at or about the same time as he did that night, but certainly not with him. And no, he definitely didn't offer her a lift home, or anywhere. She had never been in his car, or in any of his trucks, so far as he was aware. She was just a young barmaid he occasionally saw in the hotel, and he knew absolutely nothing about where she might have gone after she left the premises that night.

Darren Martin was clearly becoming more comfortable and confident as the interview proceeded, so much so he eventually hooked one arm over the back of his chair and sprawled out casually, grinning and shrugging things off, as though he didn't have a worry in the world. But all that changed when Brian held the broken necklace up in front of him. When he did, and asked the truck driver whether he knew what it was, Martin slid forward in his seat, leaning over the desk, closely inspecting it, his eyebrows knotted together in a deep and troubled frown. At first, he genuinely appeared not to recognise it, but when the policeman told him he had found it in his truck the night before, Martin's lips instantly began quivering, as his brow began to fold into a glum and piteous demeanour. For what seemed like forever, he fumbled awkwardly with an attempt to claim the necklace was one of his wife's, but when Brian Ingles eventually informed him it had been positively identified as a family heirloom handed down to Mrs Sue Mitchell, and was known to be worn by Larnie at the time she disappeared, the floodgates veritably opened.

'I didn't hurt that girl.' Martin blurted it out, almost from nowhere. Before he said another word, he was sobbing fitfully into the constable's face; thick, glistening tears streaming down both of his cheeks. 'I didn't,' he blubbered. 'I swear it, Brian. You've got to believe me. Last time I saw Larnie Mitchell, she was alive and well.'

His story, as he now spat it out, was simple enough, but totally different to every single word he'd said so far. According to this version, Larnie fronted him in the bar that night, doing a line for him, chatting him up. She was drunk, he claimed—and maybe a little bit stoned as well—trying to get him to find her a place on one of his trucks going through to Brisbane in the next week or so. She was saying she needed to get out of Millen in a big hurry, but she didn't want anyone to know she was going, or where she was headed. So when he heard her story, Martin suggested they go for a drive somewhere, to discuss it further in private.

'What were your intentions at that point?'

Martin was blinking back guilty tears as he shook his head from side to side.

'Well, look mate,' he stammered, 'You've got to admit, she's a good-looking sort, ay. Isn't she?' When he saw no sympathy in the constable's eyes he looked down at the desk, wringing his hands, and continued muttering his story. 'And I'd had a few drinks by then. Well, what can you expect?' He looked back up, plaintively. 'She really was all over me, mate, honestly. She really was.'

'So what happened then?'

'I took her out up along Station Road.'

'And?'

'Nothing, mate, nothing.' He was looking Brian Ingles straight in the eye. 'I kissed her a couple of times. That's all. I've grabbed her once on the tit, and she's just gone off her head, started yelling and screaming, pushing me away.' The policeman stared back coldly at him, until he eventually bowed his head again, almost repentantly. 'And so then we've wrestled a bit,' he continued. 'Nothing serious, like. I was just doing my best, and she's trying to push me away. And I guess that's when she's broken her chain. I never even knew it happened.'

With that, he stopped speaking, and just sat silently, with his head lowered, looking down at the desktop, as if the story was over. But it wasn't.

'So, then what happened?'

'Nothing, mate, nothing.' He was now looking at the constable again, shaking his head emphatically. 'I never touched her. Honest.' He slid in even closer to his questioner. 'She was rotten drunk, mate, that pissed she could hardly stand up. She got out of the truck, onto the road, screaming and ranting and carrying on. And then she's just sat down, or fallen over or something—I'm not sure—but next thing she's just lying in the middle of the road. And I'm telling her to get up and get back into the truck. But she wouldn't, mate. She wouldn't. Any time I even come near her she'd start yelling and screaming again. So eventually I just thought fuck it, I can't handle this shit no more, I just can't. So, I've got back in me truck and pissed off.'

He lowered his head again, looking down at his hands, now clasped together like a soulful sinner.

'And that's it, mate. I swear. There was nothing wrong with her. I left her out there, not ten Ks out of town. She was fine.'

Maybe he was telling the truth, and maybe he wasn't. Either way, Brian Ingles felt nothing but utter revulsion for him.

'You left her there, lying on the road?'

'Yes mate,' Martin replied energetically, as though expecting absolution. 'She was absolutely fine.'

Now, hours later, as Constable Brian Ingles sadly drove the police car over the long, rutted gravel road that reached northward to the horizon, a hundred kilometres or more, all the way straight up to the vast Channel Country, he could see the truckdriver in his rear-view mirror, sitting alone behind the wire screen, his head hanging down, snivelling miserably and wallowing in self-pity.

Up ahead, half a kilometre or so, Brian could already see the spot he had been thinking about ever since he left the police house, an ominously familiar point in the long, dusty, featureless road. He had been there before, spent time there, walked around it, observing the lay of the land, measuring and photographing it. He remembered it all too well, and hoped it wasn't where this journey was leading him.

'Up here,' Martin whined from the back seat. 'Just up ahead.'

•

The lead story on the ABC radio news was nothing short of sensational. As soon as Dave Hocking heard the afternoon headline announced, he sat down on the bed, spun up the volume dial, and leaned in close to listen.

According to the national broadcaster, a court hearing into the brutal slaying of a man in the western Queensland town of Millengarra had heard evidence the death was linked to the controversial 1990 underworld execution-style killing of known Brisbane drug dealer Holden Waldo Winchester. *During a week-long committal hearing in the Cunnamulla Magistrates Court, into allegations that rural worker Ronald Charles McQuillan murdered twenty-five-year-old painting contractor Thomas William Wilson, the court was told today that two unidentified men, driving a car hired from a Gold Coast hire car company, using Holden Winchester's name and identification, less than twenty-four hours before Mr Wilson's death, were in the small outback town at the time he was murdered, and disappeared without trace straight afterwards. When the allegations were aired in court, Cunnamulla magistrate Ranald McEniery immediately adjourned the murder case against Mr McQuillan, to allow police to urgently investigate the shocking revelations, saying unless he could be satisfied, they had no substance he would dismiss the charge against the defendant. Late this morning, the Police Minister and the Commissioner of Police issued a joint statement confirming the allegations, and the charge against Mr McQuillan, are currently under urgent review by the Queensland Police Service.*

Dave Hocking sat back and smiled to himself. He hadn't heard back from Frank Vagianni since he passed the J. Baker car registration details on to him. But obviously, with a little bit of good old-fashioned policework, Frankie Box had come up trumps. He always was a first-class detective. Just like Dave, Frank knew how to get the job done. They might both be suspended and out of the job for now, out of favour with the big brass at Police Headquarters, but between the two of them they'd still managed to turn Noel Atwood's bullshit case against McQuillan on its ear.

Dave felt good about that, in some way vindicated. It was the right outcome, he was sure of that. Ever since his little chat with the cowboy at the Cunnamulla watchhouse, Dave had had serious doubts about the murder charge against him, and even more serious misgivings about Atwood's call to shelve the evidence of Jenny Deeds. From there, things had only gone in one direction for the prosecution—straight downhill—and if the afternoon news report was right, and J. Baker and his mate really were linked to the murder of Winchester, Frank Vagianni had just blown the Tom Wilson murder case wide open.

But there was one more case to solve before Detective Senior Sergeant David Hocking, temporarily suspended from all duties, said goodbye to the thriving metropolis of Millengarra. And for Dave, this was the one that really mattered.

He had not been able to raise Brian Ingles all morning, and when he drove down to the station house late around lunchtime, he found it deserted. The police car was gone from the yard, so Dave figured Ingles was out and about somewhere, doing the rounds, probably over at the Martin house taking statements from the truckie and his missus. Before he headed back to the motel, Dave left a note on the door for Ingles to call him when he wanted him to come into the station to be interviewed.

The truth was Dave had something else in mind. He was anxious to get into the young bloke's ear about all he had found out so far about Darren Martin, and the goings-on down at the Empire, and what Jimmy Rawlings had to say about the night Larnie Mitchell was last seen. Brian Ingles was about as junior as a cop could be, still wet behind the ears, but Dave could see he was good kid, keen to learn, and keen to get it right. You couldn't ask for more than that. And besides, now Dave was under suspension and probably about to cop a criminal charge for belting Darren Martin, Ingles was pretty much his only hope. Martin was the key; Dave was certain of that. If he could just convince Ingles he was right, the young constable might do the rest.

Dave clicked off the radio and sat still on the bed, staring out into the silence. The news about McQuillan had left him feeling strangely tired and depleted, his shoulders, arms and feet now slumped and heavy, all but immovable. In his mind's eye he could see that devastated look on the cowboy's big dial. *I never done nothing to Larnie. Millen was no good for her.* Larnie Mitchell didn't steal that stash off Mozzie Blane. But when it went missing it became her problem, and that made it Rowdy's as well. It was weird how people seemed to hurt the people closest to them most.

Dave fell back against the pillows, and stared up at the ceiling. It was blank and featureless, shrouded in long, grey shadows. Absently, he swiped one hand across the bedside table, feeling for his wallet, then picked it up and held it out in front of him, fumbling for a well-worn photograph. Eventually, he found it, slipped it out into his hand, and looked at her—his only child, Jane—smiling back at him, happy, healthy, and safe.

As Hocking lay there, numb and motionless, staring at the photograph, there was a sudden, heavy crunch of gravel in the driveway, and the accompanying, mechanical whir of a car engine outside. When he saw the police car cruise into the motel grounds, he hauled himself onto his feet and staggered to the door.

'Senior.' Brian Ingles nodded courteously to his superior officer, shielding his eyes against the sunlight.

'Constable.'

'I've got some news for you.'

'What's that?'

'I think we might have found her.'

As they sat together in the motel room, Brian Ingles laid it all out for the senior sergeant. He had found the drop pearl necklace in Darren Martin's truck, and Sue and Lyall Mitchell made a positive identification of it as the one Larnie had taken. In his formal interview that morning, Martin initially denied any contact with the girl after she left the Empire Hotel that night, but when Brian produced the necklace he'd located in his truck, Martin recanted, confessing he was with her that night, and took her out along the Station Road. He admitted he'd propositioned her out there, but claimed he didn't harm her. According to Martin, she got out of his truck, very drunk, and refused to get back in. So he left her out there, all alone, lying on the roadway, to find her own way home.

Dave could see, from the constable's flushed face, he was so angry and disgusted he could hardly get the words out of his mouth.

'I locked him up for sexual assault. Watchhouse bail refused. He can sort it out on Monday with the magistrate in Cunnamulla.'

Dave nodded silently. There was something Brian Ingles wasn't telling him. On a sexual assault charge, Darren Martin might spend a couple of nights in lock-up before the magistrate eventually released him on bail, but sexual assault was a long way short of murder.

'You believe him?'

Ingles nodded solemnly and silently, looking the detective senior sergeant straight in the eye. He knew it was true. Darren Martin didn't murder Larnie Mitchell.

'So where is she then?'

'Someone ran over her.' The constable looked tired, and utterly crestfallen. 'Killed her,' he added. 'Accidentally. After Martin left her lying on the road out there, someone's come along and run right over the top of her. Didn't even see her lying there till it happened.'

How the hell could Ingles know that? According to Darren Martin's story, he would have been already gone. He couldn't have told Ingles what happened to Larnie after he had left? So, who did? Or was all this just guesswork by the constable?

'Who?'

Brian Ingles was still staring the detective straight in the eye, but now with a look of steely determination. He held his gaze for several seconds, before he finally responded.

'Does it matter?'

There was something so resolute and final in the way he said it, Dave could see immediately what the constable was saying, and that his mind was all made up. He knew the answer, but he wasn't going to share it. Whoever had told him the story, Ingles had decided he was going to leave them out of it. *And why not?* If Larnie Mitchell was abandoned out there, choked down on the piss, lying on a long, straight, un-lit, gravel road in the middle of nowhere, the whole thing was just a tragedy waiting to happen. Whatever poor, unsuspecting bastard came along that road that night was every bit as much a victim as she was.

As they sat there in the shadowy room, opposite each other, staring eye-to-eye, Dave Hocking thought he had a pretty good idea who the driver was. He remembered a young black kid, sitting in the back of Brian Ingles' car, the first day they met. As Dave remembered it, the kid had just done time in Westbrook—shithole joint it was—for stealing a car and rolling it out on the Station Road. *There's not a kink in that road between here and the Gulf.* Anyone would have had a hard time rolling a car out on that road, unless they unexpectedly hit something. Or someone.

'She's buried in a shallow grave, not more than twenty metres off the Station Road.'

Ingles had obviously prised the whole, ugly story out of someone and, whoever it was, he'd decided he didn't need them in it. The way Dave saw it, that was Ingles' call. A kid like Darby Sands—*fresh out of Westbrook*—could do without getting dragged into a coroner's inquiry, or worse still a manslaughter or a dangerous driving causing death blue. He'd be straight back in Westbrook before anyone worked out anything. A good cop made the call, did what he thought was the right thing to do. But that didn't always mean it lived up to the letter of the law.

'Why are you telling me all this?'

Ingles lowered his eyes, rubbing both hands together for a moment, and then looked Dave in the eye again.

'If it wasn't for you, Larnie Mitchell would be just another unsolved missing person's file, senior. I thought you might want to help me to...' he faltered for a moment on the words, and then added, '...bring her home.'

No doubt Brian Ingles' story to the coroner would be that, after Darren Martin told him he had left her there, lying on the road, he put two and two together and figured she might have been accidentally run over, so he went looking around the area for any possible remains, and fortuitously stumbled upon the shallow grave. There'd be questions asked, of course. But it would be Ingles' job to answer them, not Dave's. All Dave had to do was help him photograph the site, dig up the body, and bring a lost girl home, so her grieving parents could give her a decent burial.

He climbed out of his chair.

'Let's do it.'

•

Ranald McEniery's dismissal of the murder charge against Rowdy McQuillan made national news. For two or three days, it put Millengarra on the map. Every news bulletin, every hour, had a new angle, with commentary about the possible connections between Tom Wilson's murder and the underworld execution of Holden Waldo Winchester. There were red-faced excuses from the Commissioner's office over the failed prosecution of McQuillan, general handwringing by state and federal politicians across the political spectrum, experts of all shapes and sizes bleating about the influence of international drug rings and southern crime gangs in regional Australia, and renewed calls for a Royal Commission into drug trafficking and organised crime. At first, out-of-town journalists converged on Cunnamulla to follow the story up, one or two of them even making the arduous, dirt-track trip out to Millengarra, unsuccessfully trying to track down the cowboy defendant. But then Millen faded out of the limelight, as quickly as it had entered.

The people of Millen had long since come to grips with the tragic tale of Tom Wilson's murder. They knew all too well that the vast, outback stretches of the Paroo Shire and beyond could be a cruel, unforgiving wasteland, where frustration, fury and booze could send a man out of his mind. They understood that implicitly. They had come to expect it.

What they weren't prepared for was the awful news about Larnie Mitchell. The prettiest girl in Millen, the smartest, the one who everyone always figured was capable of anything, who had everyone wrapped right around her finger, hadn't taken off to the Big Smoke like they all thought. She hadn't travelled to far horizons, leaving her hick town behind for the bright lights, headed for greener pastures. She didn't go to St George, or Brisbane, or Sydney. She didn't even get past the Station Road. She didn't go anywhere. She was sealed into Millen—entombed, just like the rest of them—crushed and broken, and covered in outback dust.

Dave Hocking had thought about waiting in town until her funeral was held. He wasn't sure why, but at first it had seemed important to him that he be there, to be witness to what had happened, to mourn her passing, show his respect. But as the days in Millen dragged by, mostly down at the police house, working with Ingles, compiling reports and planning the prosecution of various charges against Darren Martin, Bob Proctor, Maurice Blane and Kevin Daines, the changed mood of the town had gradually seeped through into his consciousness, enveloping him. It had brought down a sad, unspoken veil of shame, not just for what had happened, but for why, a painful guilt they all had to share. No one in Millen had intentionally killed Larnie Mitchell, but the townsfolk now seemed to be gripped by a sense they had all contributed somehow, unwittingly, in different ways. Perhaps not least of all Millen itself.

It was time Dave Hocking went home. His work in Millengarra was done, and now it felt to him like no more than a cruel intrusion that he should remain, witnessing what had been lost by the grieving town, and the pain that was yet to be suffered. As he cast around his motel room, collecting his things and dropping them onto the bed to be packed, he was thinking through his trip back to Brisbane. He would get on the road around lunchtime, drive through as far as St George, hopefully by around six o'clock, stay the night there, then get off to an early start the next day, and drive the last five or six hours to Brisbane. He wanted to be reasonably rested when he finally got home. There was a lot to be thought through, and a lot to be talked about.

He folded his Official Suspension Notice in two and stuffed it into the side of his bag. Roger Page and the SPO investigators had left town days ago, to fly back to Brisbane, taking their generous ultimatum right along with them. Dave hadn't been able to bring himself to accept the lifeline they'd offered him, to give a statement against Ballard and Morris in return for an indemnity from prosecution for himself. It just wasn't in him to give up his mates like that. No doubt, he would now be charged, along with Ballard and Morris, over the cash deposits that had showed up in their bank accounts, supposedly stolen from Peter Penisi. And they probably were. All Dave knew was he didn't steal them, and he would defend any charge that came his way. But it would be tough—he knew that—not just for him, but also Denise.

Dave reached into the closet and lifted out the plastic bag, then emptied it onto the bed. The two tiny red shoes fell out, and lay there, looking weirdly out of place alongside the policeman's collected accoutrements. *The red shoes.*

The ruby slippers. Dave felt a painful ache in his chest as he stared down at them on the bedcover, memories of Jane as a little girl flitting in and out of his head, and thoughts of Denise, all she had suffered, how she had endured, and how he had failed her. He had to get home and talk to her now, comfort her, if only he could, try to find a way to deal with the past, and how they could possibly deal with the future. He picked up one of the shoes and caressed it, looking into its sparkling red sheen. It was beautiful.

'All packed up?'

Dave Hocking turned to see Carol Graham standing framed in the open doorway. When he made no reply, she glanced down, momentarily, at the shoe in his hand, and then back up, into his eyes.

'You okay?'

Dave Hocking nodded silently. Then, as a wistful smile crept onto his face, he looked back down at the shoe.

'When Jane was about eight years old, I took her to the Police Stand at the Exhibition one year. Somehow she wandered off, got herself lost. Only for about—I don't know—an hour or so, maybe.' He looked back up at Carol, a tinge of regret glistening in his eyes. 'But she was a pretty timid kid, you know, and I think it shook her up a bit.' He shrugged off the memory, and continued. 'Anyway, after that she started getting these nightmares, about being lost and that.' Carol nodded to him, empathetically. 'It got so bad that one day Denise took her out and bought her a pair of red shoes, just like this.' He looked down at the shoe in his hand, watching it sparkle. 'She told her they were like the ruby slippers. You know, like from that old movie. And if she ever got lost again, all she had to do was put on the ruby slippers, and click her heels and say…' He faltered, trying to recollect. 'Oh, what is it?'

'There's no place like home.'

'Yeah,' He looked back up at Carol, and nodded. 'Yeah, that's it. *There's no place like home.'*

Carol Graham smiled softly back at him.

'Funny, after that, Janey never had any more nightmares.' He flipped his eyebrows at her, and shrugged again. 'I guess she figured she could get back home anytime she wanted.'

'I guess she can.'

Dave Hocking nodded silently, and looked back down at the shoe.

'Yeah. I guess she can.'

•

Frank Vagianni eventually beat the SPO charge against him for official corruption, over that unfortunate incident involving the missing Waterworld robbery proceeds. Or, more correctly, his lawyer Eddie Moran beat it for him. Moran fought the good fight for Frank all the way, even after the Union dropped him like a sack of old spuds, and he ran out of money for fees. Eddie had hung right in there, and got the job done. So Frank figured, if it wasn't for Eddie Moran, right now he'd be cracking rocks as a guest of Her Majesty. He owed Eddie big-time, and he wasn't about to forget it. Which was why he had made an early-morning appointment with him, and was now shovelling mints from Eddie's reception into his mouth to cover up last night's stale rum and cigarettes.

'I've got a brand-new job for you, pal.' The portly, former-policeman-turned-private-investigator was grinning like a Cheshire cat as they settled across the desk from each other. 'A prime, fully-paid-up, Police Union job.'

The good news was it was a high-profile, criminal defence case for a senior police detective, charged by the SPO with two others on an official corruption blue, and the Union was committed to cover all the fees for his legal defence. He was an old mate of Frank's, so naturally when Frank heard he wasn't getting along so well with the lawyers the Union had plugged him into, he convinced his old mate to sack them and bring Eddie into it. According to Frank, it was an obvious win-win for everyone, because, now Eddie was in, of course Frank would be more than happy to do all the investigation work on the job as Eddie's PI.

The bad news was, as it turned out, Eddie could be an obstinate, pig-headed prick. The moment he heard the client in question was none other than Detective Senior Sergeant David Hocking, he dug in his heels, claiming he had good reason to believe Hocking was a crooked cop, and had tried to conceal crucial evidence in the McQuillan murder case, and he wasn't interested in acting for anyone who would try to frame an innocent man on a murder he didn't commit.

Frank Vagianni had promised his old mate Dave he wouldn't tell anyone he was the secret source that had helped the defence in the Rowdy McQuillan case. But, by the same token, he wasn't about to let a big, fat Police Union pay-day float idly by, just because Eddie Moran wanted to be a stubborn, intractable knob. So they argued the toss, up and down, around and about, until Frank was eventually convinced a sweet, juicy opportunity was about to fly straight out the window. Luckily for him, he was saved by the jingle of keys at the front door, and the click of stilettos stepping across the tiled floor to the doorway to Eddie's office.

'Slick, help me here, will you?' he pleaded, as Slick poked her head inquisitively into the room, loaded up with the morning mail. 'This is crazy shit.'

It took her all of two minutes, on the briefest of briefings by Frank, to digest the issue at hand, sum it up, and deliver Eddie her considered opinion.

'What the fuck do you care what he tried to conceal or didn't?'

Eddie thought the guy was a crook. *So what?* He worked for crooks every day. What made this guy so different? The fact he almost put one over on Eddie Moran? *So what?* It was a paying job, and a good one. Of course he would do it.

As Eddie sat back in his chair, looking miffed, hating the fact he knew she was right, Slick studiously ignored him, slapping the bundle of morning mail on the desk, and sifting through it industriously.

'So, speaking of Rowdy McQuillan, look what I just picked up from our PO box.'

She slipped a coloured post card out of the bundle and held it up for Eddie to see. It was an early morning view of the Eiffel Tower, taken from the Jardins du Trocadero, into the thin, Parisian sunlight.

'It's addressed to Mr E.C . Moran,' she began, reading from the back of the card. 'And it says *Dear Mr Moran…*'

'Wait a minute.' Eddie's brow was knitted into a quizzical frown. 'If it's addressed to me, how come you're reading it?'

'Yeah, right,' she said dismissively, then continued. 'Anyway, it says *Dear Mr Moran, I'm living in London now, labouring on a building site. It's good work, but pretty cold sometimes. I went down to France two weeks ago, and I went to see the Eiffel Tower in Paris. This is a picture of it. It's real big, and beautiful, just like Larnie always said it would be.*'

Her voice trembled slightly as she said the last words, and faltered momentarily, blinking away glistening tears. Eddie puffed out a frustrated sigh, reached forward across the desk, and snatched up the postcard, turning it around to read it.

'Thanks again for all you done for me. Rowdy.' He lobbed the card onto the pile of mail on the desktop. 'Another satisfied customer. Account paid. Job done. Move on.'

Slick slipped a tissue out of her purse as she shot him a poisonous look.

'Creep.'

'Yeah, I love you too, baby.'

As she daintily dabbed one eye dry, Eddie climbed to his feet.

'I'm going down for a coffee. You want one?'

'Sure, why not?'

'Frank?'

'They do a hot chocolate down there?'

'Sure. Don't ask me why, but yeah, they do.'

'Sweet. You've got me.'

ABOUT THE AUTHOR

Chris Nyst was born in Blackall, Western Queensland, and raised in Brisbane, where he obtained a Law degree from the University of Queensland, before commencing practice as a solicitor on Queensland's Gold Coast. As a lawyer, he has been involved in some of Australia's most high profile and sensational court cases, and is recognised as one of Australia's most experienced criminal defence advocates. He turned his hand to fiction writing in 1999, producing a series of bestselling legal thrillers. His first two novels, *Cop This* and *Gone*, received excellent reviews, and his third, *Crook as Rookwood*, won the coveted Ned Kelly Award for Crime Fiction. In 2003, Chris wrote and co-produced the highly acclaimed Australian film *Gettin' Square*, which was nominated for a record number of Australian film industry awards, and won him the 2003 Lexus IF Award for Best Screenplay. His 2008 film *Crooked Business*, which he wrote and directed, was voted Best International Film at the 2009 New York Independent Film Festival.

The father of four adult children, Chris lives with his wife, Julie, on the Gold Coast, where he conducts his legal practice.

www.ingramcontent.com/pod-product-compliance
Lightning Source LLC
Chambersburg PA
CBHW020842020726
47497CB00005B/1215